THE

END

OF

INTERLUDES

THE
END
OF
INTERLUDES

katherine turner

Copyright © 2023 by Katherine Turner
www.kturnerwrites.com

First edition: September 2023

Editing by Kayli Baker
Cover design by Murphy Rae
Print formatting by Shanna Hammerbacher
E-book formatting by Jo Harrison

Library of Congress Control Number: 2023903410
Library of Congress Cataloging-in-Publication Data available upon request.

ISBN 978-1-955735-13-1 (ebook)
ISBN 978-1-955735-12-4 (paperback)

Josha Publishing, LLC
Independent Publisher
www.joshapublishing.com
Haymarket, VA

Printed in the United States of America

NOTES FOR THE READER

Content

This novel contains references to and some description of self-harm and sexual violence in various settings. While not intended to be unnecessarily graphic, the content may be triggering for some.

Music

Music plays a role in this novel. For an enhanced reading experience if you enjoy listening to music, refer to the playlist on page 329 for a recommended soundtrack while reading.

ONE

Kate pouted with her hands clasped tightly together in front her and waited for me to give my verdict. Would I or would I not go to a party with her? On the one hand, I hadn't been outside since the day before, and some fresh air sounded nice; I'd meant to but then was so engrossed in my work that hours flew past unnoticed. But on the other hand, I still had homework to do. And my roommate had plenty of friends she could ask, but she usually wanted me to go with her for some reason I had yet to figure out.

"Please, Nina?" she begged, bouncing on her toes. "We're only in college once."

I snorted. "Unless we fail our classes."

"You're not going to fail—you always do your homework and study. But you have to unwind, too."

I rolled my eyes, laughing. "This has nothing to do with me, and you know it."

"Please?"

Trying to stifle another laugh, I looked at her pleading face for a moment. "Okay, okay. But only for a few hours. And only because my ass is numb."

She squealed and flung herself into my arms, which almost knocked me off my chair. "You're the best, Nina."

Shaking my head as she pulled away to check her makeup, I set my notebook on top of my open textbook and stretched. She would probably end up ditching me before the night was over; more often than not, she ended up leaving with Mark, her almost-boyfriend. They hung out a lot and slept together, and they appeared to be head over heels for each other, but they both shied away from calling it anything more than casual.

"Where are we going?" I asked, peering into my wallet-sized closet, trying to decide what to wear.

She rubbed her lips together after applying her favorite red lip stain and some lip gloss using her reflection in the mirror over my dresser. "Parker's house."

I watched her fluff her shiny blonde hair while I searched my memory for what Parker's house was; there were a lot of buildings on campus with peoples' names. "What's that?"

"You remember Parker. He's the tall guy with Mark sometimes— the one with long hair."

"The one who's always wearing a bun?"

"Yeah, him."

"I thought he was Mark's roommate. He has a house here?"

"Yeah, he is. And it's his parents' house. Apparently they're rich and have like a mansion or something over in the Woodlands area, and they're out of town for a while, so Parker's having a party there tonight. Like everyone will be there."

I rolled my eyes again and yawned. "Only a few hours, Kate. And where is the Woodlands?"

"Other side of town."

"Like north side?" I asked. Our campus was on the south side of the city.

"I dunno. The other side." Kate shrugged, then added, "Too far to walk, so we're getting an Uber."

I groaned. "If we have to Uber, you can't ditch me tonight." I did not want to get into an Uber at night alone. And if it really was too far to walk, I wouldn't have a choice.

"I won't," she said, but she always said she wouldn't, so that didn't mean anything.

With a sigh, I scanned the contents of my closet again. We were going to someone's house—a *rich* someone's house. What the hell was a not-rich someone supposed to wear to a party like that? I glanced at Kate, but she came from a rich family, too, and was always dressed in designer clothes. I came from a decidedly *not* rich family—we weren't poor, but we weren't much better off—and I didn't have anything as nice as her pajamas in my closet except something she'd given me. Not that I really cared most of the time, but I didn't want to stick out here. I didn't mind going to parties with Kate sometimes, but not often and only if I could just kind of sit in the background and watch people. If I stuck out too much, it would garner a lot of attention. And I wasn't the kind of person who should be the center of attention. I was more the kind of person who made everyone else a little uncomfortable if I was.

Kate walked up next to me, peering into my closet with me. "Hm... you can wear one of my dresses."

I tried to hide my snort. "No, thank you."

While we wore the same size, and her clothes were definitely nicer than mine, I would never wear dresses as short as hers were; I liked more of my legs covered. Instead, I opted for what I was most comfortable in: jeans and the nicest sweater I had, a cream-colored cashmere v-neck Kate had given me. She'd said it contrasted nicely with my tanned skin and dark, curly hair. And *this* I actually agreed with.

Kate's description of the house as a mansion wasn't entirely accurate, but it was still the nicest house I'd ever seen in person. It also wasn't on the north side of town; it was on the west side of town, and while it wasn't exactly close to campus, it was definitely walkable. It was part of a strip of old, large residential homes just outside the historic district of the city, only a few blocks from shops and restaurants and bars and clubs in charming brick buildings. The historic district was my favorite part of the city, and I walked in sometimes just to wander around and admire the architecture when I had the time. I'd grown up in a fairly small town and the vibe reminded me of home.

As much as I felt at home in the historic district, however, I felt out of place in Parker's house, even though it was filled with college kids from both colleges in the city. This wasn't the normal college kid crowd, though; as I scanned the living room, they almost all looked like they came from wealthy families. *Ugh. I should have said no tonight.* As soon as we'd gotten our drinks and migrated to the far side of the living room, Mark had appeared, and Kate had wandered off with him just as I'd known she would. I'd wait a while, but if she didn't come back, I'd go ahead and leave.

Two drinks later, I'd rebuffed four horny guys who thought they could talk their way into my pants and texted Kate. I was ready to go. These rich kids were worse than the normal crowd, like they thought their money would get me to sleep with them. I rolled my eyes just thinking about it while waiting for Kate to respond. As I waited, another guy walked over and handed me a Solo cup filled with the same beer I'd already been drinking. I grabbed the cup, wishing it was something stronger to get me through this crap, and, without a word, stood and headed for the front door. My phone buzzed with a text from Kate that she was probably going to stay with Mark for the night, and I sighed in relief; that meant I could leave. I downed the remaining contents of the cup as I walked out the front door.

"Fuck," I bit out under my breath.

I looked around, but no trash or recycling cans appeared out of nowhere. However, it was apparent many people had mistaken the front yard for a dumping ground; I spied several Solo cups upside down over the branches of a rose bush, among other plants.

"Lazy assholes," I muttered as I walked over and began snatching up cups, sliding them inside one another.

Ten minutes later, I had three tall stacks of Solo cups I'd collected off the plants and the ground in the front yard. The smell of beer rose from the soil, and I felt the need to apologize to the plants.

"Sorry that some humans are dumb-asses," I said. "Lazy, self-absorbed, assholes who don't give a shit that we aren't the only ones on this planet."

I heard a chuckle behind me and jumped, nearly tripping over my own feet. I'd thought I was alone. Turning, I found four guys standing behind me on the massive front porch. Flames consumed my face and I groaned. Two of the guys fit right in with the crowd inside with their perfectly-styled hair, clean-shaven faces, khakis and polos. The third guy also wore a polo but had on jeans, and his head was shaved. The last guy seemed out of place with the others. While they were all tall compared to my short frame and looked like they were a few years older than me, this one was a little shorter and a little broader than the others. If the other three looked like they came from the right side of the tracks, this guy looked like he came from the *wrong* side; he had short, reddish-brown hair, chocolate brown eyes, and a full beard that was at least three or four inches long. His hands, at the ends of arms covered in tattoos, were tucked into his dark jeans, and he wore a black t-shirt that said in white letters "Music Literacy Matters." I squinted and stepped closer, reading what was below, laughing as I read it again. If you knew how to read music, it said "I like to eat. I like puppies." But if you didn't, it said "I like to eat puppies."

There was a resonant rumble and the funny shirt moved as the guy chuckled—the same chuckle I'd heard before.

"Did you piss someone off and get trash duty?" preppy guy one asked.

I squared my shoulders. "I'm just someone who gives a shit about the environment. Beer can kill plants, you know. And they didn't do anything to deserve it. And these cups are plastic—they shouldn't be all over the ground. You think the plants can breathe with this shit all over them? You think that rosebush over there can bloom with cups covering its branches? But I bet that thought never crossed your self-absorbed mind, did it?"

The one who'd asked the question threw up his hands in a faux defensive gesture, his mocking laughter joining that of his friends. Mr. Wrong-Side-Of-The-Tracks, though, was just watching me, his mouth pulled up on one side and his head cocked, his eyes somewhat narrowed.

I rolled my eyes and climbed the steps with the three towers of cups. "Excuse me," I said. They parted and I headed inside, dumping the cups in a trash can when I couldn't find one for recycling. I fully expected the guys to all be gone when I walked back outside, so I stopped short in surprise when I walked out the door to find Mr. Wrong-Side-Of-The-Tracks still there.

He looked over as I headed toward the stairs. Our eyes connected and I felt a weird, warm, tingly sensation in my chest. It was unsettling, so I looked away.

"So, you like music?" he asked, walking down the stairs next to me.

"What makes you think that?" I snapped. He hadn't really done anything, but I was still irritated with him and his friends and all the drunk college kids hurting plants that hadn't done anything wrong.

"Not many people get my shirt," he replied. "But you laughed."

I glanced over at his chest and felt some of my aggravation lift as I scanned his shirt again. "It's funny," I replied with a shrug.

"It is," he agreed. "To people who like music."

"Why are you following me?" I asked, suddenly nervous as we approached the sidewalk in front of Parker's house. It was twilight outside and I had no idea who this guy was. While I didn't get a danger vibe from talking to him, he looked unlike any other college student I'd met.

"I'm not," he laughed. "I was hoping you'd come back out, but I was already leaving, remember?"

"What happened to your friends?"

We'd reached the sidewalk and he pointed to the left. "We're heading to Nina's."

My eyebrows lowered and my feet stopped. "What?"

"Nina's," he replied, stopping, too. "It's a bar in town. They've got live music tonight."

"Oh," I replied quietly. I hadn't known there was a bar with my name. I laughed, then felt compelled to explain. "I was confused for a minute. My name's Nina."

He reached out a hand. "Myles, with a 'y.' Nice to meet you, Nina."

I shook his hand, my heart stuttering while we touched, and then we both turned to the left. I had to walk through town to get back to campus.

"Where are you heading?" he asked.

"MU," I said, using the abbreviation everyone used for my school.

He nodded. "I'm at Paddenton," he said, giving the name of the other university in the city.

"Studying music?" I asked, feeling a little more comfortable knowing he was a student, too.

"Yeah. And education. I'm going to teach music in middle school."

I almost stopped walking and turned to stare at him. "You're going to be a teacher?"

"A music teacher," he clarified.

"Really?" I asked again, my eyes scanning over his beard and tattooed arms a second time.

His face hardened. "You shouldn't be so judgmental, you know," he said.

My face leapt into flames, and I stared at the ground as we walked in an uncomfortable silence. He was right, and I couldn't believe that I, of all people, was the one judging him, after being on the receiving end of judgment for not having a lot of money growing up. I stopped walking, holding out a hand and touching his forearm so he'd stop, too. I tried to ignore the shocks that ran through my hand, up my arm, and spread through my body before I removed my hand. He held my gaze, but I could tell he was wary.

"You're right," I said. "I *was* being judgmental. And I'm sorry."

His eyes bored into mine for a long moment, then he turned to keep walking, and I quickly fell into step next to him again. I wanted to ease the tension between us and scrambled for something to say. I'd never done small talk well.

"What year are you?" I asked eventually.

"I'm in my last year of grad school," he replied. "You?"

"Junior."

"Hm. I'd have guessed you were older," he mused.

I let out a short laugh. "That's what everyone always says. My roommate says it's because I'm boring."

"Boring?" he repeated, like he thought he'd heard wrong.

"Yeah, because I study a lot. My education is really important to me. I don't have the same... advantages, I guess you could say, as a lot of other kids. My family couldn't afford college, so I worked my ass off to get scholarships, and I continue working my ass off so I can keep them. It matters to me how well I do, not whether or not I get wasted or whose party I go to."

In the silence that followed, I mentally berated myself. What the hell was I thinking? Why was I saying these things, let alone to a complete stranger? I never should have had three drinks—apparently, I didn't have a filter anymore.

"How'd you end up at *this* one, then?"

"My roommate. She and Parker's roommate are kind of a thing. But she never likes to go to these things alone, so I go with her sometimes."

"And you left without her?"

I laughed. "No. *She* ditched *me*. She almost always does. She just doesn't want to show up alone, so drags me out with her, but she disappears once we arrive. What about you? That party doesn't look like something that would be your scene."

He tipped his head down the sidewalk where I could barely make out the backs of his friends; we were walking more slowly than they were. "We're all roommates, and Jackson, the one in the middle up there, is Parker's brother. He wanted to check in and make sure Parker wasn't doing anything stupid tonight before we went to Nina's."

I nodded; that made sense.

"What are you majoring in?" he asked.

I shrugged. "I don't know yet—I keep changing my mind. It's going to take me five years to get my undergrad."

"What are you interested in?"

"Nature," I replied without hesitation. "I love being outside and plants and animals and insects. When I was little, I wanted to be a trail guide for a national forest or a park ranger or something like that."

"What about biology or forestry for a major?"

I shrugged again. "I don't know. It's not very practical, either. My parents have worked hard for a long time, and I feel like I should do something that pays better so I can take care of them as they get older, something in finance or accounting or computers or something."

He gave a nod. "I took a bunch of finance classes for similar reasons, and I've got a friend who's now working in commodities trading and he's teaching me. I figure I can do that on the side or something for extra cash since teaching doesn't pay that well."

"That's a good idea. I would, but I'm terrible with math. It's so hard for me."

We talked the rest of the way into town, conversation easy and natural over the next thirty minutes or so. It was the most I'd enjoyed a conversation with another college student since I'd arrived on campus the previous August, and I paused when we reached the corner where he was going to turn left; I needed to continue straight to get back to my dorm.

Myles' eyes flitted over my face, then he tipped his head to the side. "Wanna join us?"

I laughed. "I doubt your friends would like that after I yelled at them earlier."

He shrugged, his eyes still holding mine. "I don't give a shit if they do or not. *I'd* like you to come."

Should I go? I wanted to—it was the first time I'd actually *wanted* to go do something—but was it a good idea?

"I don't really even know you," I said. "I don't know if I should be going to obscure bars with strangers."

He raised his eyebrows and looked like he was trying not to laugh. "My name is Myles Edwards. You know that I'm going to be a middle school teacher, that I have three roommates and I attend Paddenton, that I'm in grad school, that I have a thing for funny music shirts, that I like hiking, music, kids, and tattoos. What else do you need to know so I won't feel like a stranger?"

I narrowed my eyes and crossed my arms over my chest. "If you were driving down a highway and running late for your best friend's wedding and you saw a turtle about to cross the road, what would you do?"

He snorted. "That's what you want to know?"

"Yes."

"What kind of turtle?"

"Let's say it's a snapping turtle."

"Well, I'd pull over. Then I'd take off my suit jacket—if I'm on the way to a wedding, surely I'm wearing a suit—and grab some microfiber towels from the back of my car."

"You keep microfiber towels in the back of your car?"

"You don't?" he laughed.

"Why would I?"

"Why *wouldn't* you? They're absorbent and versatile. You spill your drink—microfiber towel soaks it up quickly. You have a big smear on your windshield? Microfiber towel will clean it off without scratching the glass, and you don't need anything but a little water. Have to change a tire? Microfiber towel can help keep your hands clean. *And*, when you're done, you can wash it, so you're not adding to a landfill."

"Okay, so you'd grab some microfiber towels," I said, laughing at this ridiculous conversation but also loving that he pointed out the environmental friendliness of keeping reusable towels in a car. "What next?"

"Well, I'd wrap them around my hands to protect myself, and then I'd pick up the turtle and walk it across the road so it could get where it was headed without getting hit, making sure to hold it out far in front of me so when it likely pees, it won't end up all over my fancy suit pants and fancy shoes."

I eyed him.

He winked.

I laughed.

"Okay," I said. "You pass. We can go to the bar."

"Whoa, whoa, whoa," he said, holding his hands up, his eyes glittering with good humor. "I'm not sure I should be going out with strange women."

I bit my bottom lip and he grinned. "Fair enough. What do you want to know?"

"Favorite instrument?" he asked, setting off toward the bar before I could respond.

I walked next to him. "To play or listen to?"

"Hm. Both."

"Piano to play—it's the only instrument I know how to play. And I'm okay at it. But my favorite to listen to would be a tie between piano and the oboe, especially in a minor key."

He closed his eyes for a split second and bent his knees a little, like he was melting into the pavement, as he groaned. "Please tell me you don't have a boyfriend, let alone a serious one," he said, fixing his eyes on me as our steps slowed.

I snickered. "Why?"

"Because that could make it complicated to marry you one day."

I bit my cheeks.

"Not impossible, of course, but it would just be a big mess no one really wants to deal with. At least there would only be one mess since I don't have a girlfriend. But you'd have to break his poor little heart."

A giggle slipped out. "His poor little heart? That's a little condescending, don't you think?"

"I mean, of course—I don't like the guy."

"How can you dislike someone you don't even know?"

"Easy—he's dating the woman I'm going to marry."

I was now laughing, and Myles let out a chuckle.

"How do you know I'm not going to marry my boyfriend?"

"Because he won't have an oboe play for the wedding, of course."

"And you would?"

"Absolutely. Oboes are one of the sexiest instruments on the planet. They're so undervalued and often overlooked, but that reedy, plaintive sound?" He shivered.

"Let me guess, next you're gonna tell me you play the oboe?"

"I mean… yes. I play a lot of instruments, though. I just don't play most of them particularly well. The only one I play really well is piano."

"Too bad you don't play the oboe well," I teased, giggling.

"Don't tell me your boyfriend does?"

"What boyfriend?" I replied, tittering from trying so hard not to laugh.

"Aha! So you *don't* have one!" he exclaimed as we neared the entrance to Nina's. "Right?"

I tried to pull in my grin as I looked at him and shook my head. "No, I don't."

"Well, that certainly simplifies things." The smile he'd had for the last while pulled wider into a grin, and then he opened the door to the bar. "After you, Nina."

TWO

Seven years later

I was jotting notes about the demo I was receiving via video conference on my computer, my eyes shooting to my second screen every few minutes, when I heard the ping indicating the arrival of another email. When it rained, it certainly poured... like a damn hurricane. I glanced down at my phone as it vibrated on my desk with a reminder for dinner that evening. I rolled my eyes and pulled my attention back to the screen. Dinners with my boyfriend, Landon, who was a financial consultant, and his coworkers were about my least favorite thing to do, but it was important to him. And the one tonight was a big formal corporate affair where they typically talked about the state of the business as the fiscal year came to a close, but I knew they also had a big announcement since Landon had worked on the project.

The demo was over, and I glanced down at my notes, firing off a series of questions and raising some concerns I had, discussing the timeline for remediation with the technical lead on the call, then hung up, jotting a few additional notes from our conversation. With a sigh, I turned to the emails. I didn't have long before lunch, which I couldn't skip this time, then I had to be really efficient all afternoon if I didn't want to be late for dinner. The story of my life—I was always a few seconds from being late for the next thing. It was a miracle I ever got any sleep. I'd only taken a sporadic day off since my first day at my firm five years earlier as a project manager for the business side of the in-house development of their primary software application.

There was something validating about being so important and needed, but there were days I wished I could take a break or hand the baton to someone else for just a while. It had been a breakneck speed since day one, and it was starting to wear me down. Landon assured me I'd get used to it—he was twelve years older than me and worked as much as I did. It was part of why our relationship worked so well. We both worked a lot and had no desire to step back in our careers, we were comfortable enough going long periods without seeing each other since Landon traveled three weeks out of every month, and neither of us was interested in having kids. For all intents and purposes, it was a match made in heaven. And because I got paid very well and had almost no expenses—Landon was loaded, owned the condo we shared, and insisted on paying for just about everything—I invested almost every dollar I made. I'd be set for life financially in a few years' time thanks to Landon's keen financial eye. I'd chosen this career path so I could afford to take care of my parents, but they'd both passed away four years ago, so now I was saving for my own retirement, I supposed, even if I couldn't imagine not working until the day I died. I'd probably end up leaving everything to a charity focused on natural conservation.

"Knock, knock," a female voice called, along with a knock on my office door. "Lunch in ten?"

"Yup, I'm coming," I replied without turning.

Every other Friday, several of my coworkers and I grabbed lunch at a restaurant down the street. I'd have preferred to get another item or two knocked off my to-do list, but participating socially made work relationships easier to navigate, even if I didn't feel like I really had anything in common with my peers.

Exactly ten minutes later, I was walking out of my office with my purse, responding to a text message from Landon reminding me of his company's big event that night. I'd never once in the years we'd known each other forgotten something we had planned—I was too organized for that—but he always sent me reminders anyway. While it was unnecessary, I figured it shouldn't bother me if it made him feel better to send them.

"Have you met the new CTO?" Jess asked, taking a bite of her salad.

I shook my head and there were murmurs of "no" from the other women.

"He looks likes a young Brad Pitt, I kid you not," she said.

"No way!" Candace chimed in.

"Mm-hm," Jess said. "He's a total misogynistic pig, but he's hot. His personality almost ruins his looks... almost, but not quite."

"You think everyone's hot," someone else said, and laughter rippled around the table.

Jess shrugged. "Guess that's the benefit of not being tied down like you guys."

"I'd trade your freedom for this pregnancy hell any day," Megan, who was six months pregnant, said with a groan. "Being pregnant sucks. *Sucks.*"

Two little lines stared up at me. It wasn't possible, and yet there it was—I was pregnant. What the hell was I gonna' do?

"When do you go on maternity leave?" Candace asked, pulling me from my long-ago memory. I took a sip of water to clear my thoughts and tried to focus on the conversation rather than the past that had no place in my life anymore.

"Ugh, not until I go into labor. The maternity leave policy here sucks almost as bad as being pregnant does."

"And that's why I'm not having kids until I find somewhere else to work," Candace said.

"Smart," Megan replied. "What about you guys?" she asked, looking at the rest of us.

I walked in the doors of the medical building, my eyes darting over my shoulder. Even in a city where no one knew me, I felt paranoid and numb and confused and scared. I wished Myles were there with me before remembering how much worse it would be if he were.

I shook my head, pushing away the rest of the memory that had been loosened—one of many that I didn't want.

"No kids for me—I don't even have a steady boyfriend," Jess laughed. "What about you, Nina? You've snagged the catch of the century with Landon—rich *and* cute *and* he's out of your hair—when are you guys getting hitched and popping out the cutest babies of the year?"

"No kids for us," I replied

Megan reached over and laid a hand on my arm. "I'm so sorry."

I shook my head again. "No, don't be. We don't want kids, that's all. Being parents isn't for us." I shoved a bite of salad in my mouth to preclude having to say anything else. I hated salad after eating them for nearly every meal for years. But it's what everyone expected me to eat, so it's what I ate almost every meal. Ugh.

"But you guys are getting married, right? I mean, you've been dating for forever—when's he going to pop the question?"

I shrugged, chewing slower than necessary so I wouldn't have to answer. I wasn't sure he *ever* would. Landon wasn't the affectionate or romantic type, and he gave the impression of being utterly content with how things were—there was no reason for him to change the status quo, and Landon didn't do anything without a logical reason.

"I'm friends with Nick's wife," Candace said. "I'll see if she can find anything out or get Nick to give Landon a nudge."

Nick was the closest thing to a friend that Landon had from what I could tell—they worked closely together and talked every day. Nick was a partner at Landon's firm, Lorman Investments, and was responsible for Landon leading the project that was the reason for the event later that night—the project that was going to lead to Landon moving from junior to full partner.

But, even if it came from Nick, giving Landon a nudge was completely pointless—he wouldn't propose unless he could see a benefit to doing so. Besides, I wasn't worried about making any big changes. Of course, if he asked, I'd say yes, but I wasn't in a hurry to get married, either. These women wouldn't believe me if I said that, though—if they did, they'd treat me differently—and it wasn't likely to change what Candace was going to do regardless, so I didn't share any of it.

"Oh, did I tell you guys I got a new car?" asked Rebecca, Candace's sister and the only woman present who didn't work at the company. "You'll never guess what I got."

"Wait, didn't you just get a new car a few months ago?"

Rebecca waved her hand dismissively. "Yeah, but I didn't like it. The leather felt cheap, and the software was just blah. It was making me crazy."

"So what did you get? I love my little BMW M5."

"Too small," Rebecca fired back. "I got the Mercedes AMG G63."

"Whoa! Isn't that car like two hundred thousand dollars?"

"Basically," Rebecca laughed. "Hubby got it for me."

I had to fight to keep smiling, as opposed to rolling my eyes like I wanted to, as I listened to the other women in the group talking, and my teeth nearly bit through my tongue. Not only was it such a waste of money to spend that much on a car, but it was one of the worst cars for the environment. The gas mileage was atrocious. But this crowd didn't care about the environment—one was even married to a politician who didn't believe in global warming.

"Who wants to go shopping this weekend?" someone else suggested, and conversation immediately shifted to who was free and where they were going. I glanced at my phone and unlocked the screen so I could read the emails I'd missed since we left, looking up occasionally and smiling and nodding as expected. About twenty more minutes before I'd be back in the solitude of my office.

At least I only had to do these twice a month.

"Nina?" George asked, pushing the door to my office open slowly. "Do you have a minute?"

I moved my lips into a smile and spun my chair toward the door after glancing at the clock. Ten more minutes. "Of course, George. How are Courtney and the baby doing?"

George was one of my new testers and was doing the majority of the work for this next release. It wasn't a large one, so it was a good way for him to get some practice and demonstrate his capability. He was eager to prove himself as one of the youngest employees in our department, especially after an extended unexpected absence. He had a newborn at home and had gotten a week off per company policy, but then a week after his return, his wife had hemorrhaged, and he'd stayed home for almost two weeks to take care of her and the baby. He'd been worried about getting fired since he'd been with us for less than six months, but I was only relieved his family was okay.

He smiled, his eyes brightening. "They're great. Courtney is really tired, of course, but otherwise she's feeling pretty good. And Joshua is wonderful." He pulled his phone from his pocket and showed me his lock screen, which was a picture of him with a baby sleeping on his chest, his wife next to him. The baby's chubby cheek was smushed against him, mouth open.

"Beautiful," I murmured, meaning it. The memory of when I'd changed my mind about having kids tried determinedly to make its way to the surface, but I shoved it back down again. "What can I do for you? I have a hard stop at five thirty today."

He pocketed his phone. "I'm having some issues with testing the new publishing functionality, and I think I figured out why. Can you pull up the test one environment? I'll show you."

THREE

"Hi, darling," Landon called as I walked into the lobby of the nicest hotel in the city after checking my coat.

I smiled, my eyes scanning him in his formal wear, which wasn't all that different from his everyday wear, with the exception that he wore a bow tie tonight. He looked handsome, as always.

"You look lovely," he said, kissing my cheek in greeting then resting his hand between my shoulder blades as he walked us toward the ballroom where the event was being held.

"Thank you. How was your flight?" He'd just gotten back from spending three weeks in Milan advising a client who resided there most of the year.

"Long. It's always long from Milan. At least when I fly out next week, it's just a few states over."

I grimaced in sympathy. "It always takes you a few days to recover from those long flights."

"No kidding. It seems to be getting harder, too. Like I needed a reminder that I'm forty."

"Well, at least you don't look it," I said, smiling. And for the most part it was true, especially since he'd started dying his hair the year before.

"Thanks, darling." He glanced down at me, his eyes lingering on my cleavage. "I like your dress tonight." His hand slid down and rested just shy of inappropriately low on my backside.

I had to fight the urge to roll my eyes and laugh. He was so predictable. He was always particularly horny the night he got back from a long trip, and sometimes the next morning as well. It was the only time he really took the time to notice what I was wearing and how it fit my body. Otherwise, he only noticed if he thought it wasn't appropriate for some reason—not that anything like that happened anymore. It had earlier in our relationship because he wasn't a fan of how casually I tended to dress, but now I rarely ran around home in sweats or went out in jeans and a sweater.

He squeezed my hip and leaned down. "I missed you," he whispered, straightening back up.

I looked up and smiled, then someone was calling his name. We'd arrived at the ballroom and it was time to mingle.

Three and a half hours later, all the old white men who ran the company, including Landon this time, had informed everyone about how much money they'd made that year and announced a merger with another financial consulting firm—that was the project Landon had been working on for the last year and why he was able to join the company's leaders up front. He was going to be one of them now, as well as the young, charismatic leader of the company they'd merged with. It seemed an unlikely match, but maybe that was the reason they'd done it; the other company would get the experience Landon's company had, and Landon's company would get the young, fresh approach for consulting to the younger generations from the other company.

I stood and clapped along with everyone else before sitting to smile and nod with the other women at my table—wives of some of the other men up front—waiting for Landon to return so I could finally leave. He'd be there for another few hours at least, but I'd be able to get back to the office and get some work done. Or maybe I'd just bring my laptop home; I had a headache from the speakers in the room.

At long last, Landon approached the table smiling broadly, as he did at these occasions, despite the circles under his eyes betraying how tired he was. I stood and gave his arm a squeeze. "Congratulations, honey."

"Thank you," he replied. "You're leaving?"

I sighed. "Yeah, I have tons of work to get done, and I'm getting a headache."

"Take some Advil and maybe just bring your laptop home tonight."

"I was thinking the same thing, actually."

"I'd walk you out, but I'm needed for a private meeting." He continued to smile and leaned forward, kissing my cheek. "I'll be home in a few hours or so. I'll try not to wake you if you're in bed."

What he meant was that he would definitely wake me up, apologize, and say he just missed me so badly he couldn't wait another minute to have me. At least it wouldn't take long—it never did.

It wasn't that I hated sex or anything—I'd just never really enjoyed it and would rather go without. And it wasn't a matter of who, because Landon certainly wasn't my first. Which was another reason we fit well together—between his travel and his preoccupation with work when he was home, sex wasn't something expected of me very often.

I took my leave of the women around me, and by the time I was walking away, Landon had already disappeared into the crowd. As soon as I made it outside the ballroom doors, I let the smile I'd been holding on my face for hours fade away and rubbed at my cheeks. They were sore. When I reached the coat check, I stepped in the line and sighed, feeling the ever-present tiredness trying to take over. As always, I ignored it and instead mentally sifted through my work to-do list to pull out the tasks I'd try to tackle before going to bed. I was so absorbed in my mental organizing that it took me a minute to realize someone was standing near me, staring at me. When I did, I startled, then gaped back, my jaw hanging slack. He looked almost the same as the last time I'd seen him.

"*Myles*?"

He huffed out a breath, his mouth pulling into that breathtaking grin I remembered. "Nina. It *is* you."

Before I thought to do something to stop him, he'd pulled me into a hug. And then, before I thought to stop *myself*, I was hugging him back. Squeezing him for dear life, it felt—much like he was doing to me. When he stepped us sideways out of line, I realized my eyes were closed, my face pressed into his chest. I breathed deeply and a torrent of emotion moved through me rapid-fire at feeling and smelling him again. Excitement, attraction, happiness, longing, safety... then terror and shame. I pushed away from him abruptly, blinking rapidly. Why the hell was I tearing up? I hadn't cried in over six years.

Not even when my parents died.

But then again, Myles had always brought out the parts of me no one else was ever privy to. That had been the problem back then—at least part of it.

My eyes scanned over him deliberately, taking in the changes since the last time I saw him. He'd always been attractive, and nothing had changed. He looked much the same as he always had, except he had a few rogue gray hairs. Not many, but a few. Would have been too many for Landon, but Myles didn't appear to mind them. And I actually liked them.

I startled from my inspection at a loud throat clear, and my eyes darted to Myles' face. He was still grinning, his eyes glassy. Good lord, his grin still made my stomach flutter, even after all these years. There was a way I reacted to him that I'd never reacted to another person, before or after meeting him. All of a sudden, I felt like a nervous college student again, my mind drawing a blank when I tried to find something to say.

"It's been a long time," I said.

He nodded slowly. "Six years and seven months tomorrow."

Oh my god. He's been counting?

"Goodnight, Nina," someone called.

I searched for the voice, abruptly remembering where I was. Raising a hand, I responded, then looked back to Myles, my eyes now rushing around me nervously. These people all knew Landon, and most of them knew me, too. This might get awkward.

"I.. I was just leaving," I said. "I just need to get my coat."

"I was, too. These types of affairs aren't my thing."

"Wait—you were at the Lorman event?"

"Remember I told you about my friend in finance?" He tilted his head toward the ballroom. "My friend is Marcus."

Marcus was the CEO of the company that was merging with Landon's company, Lorman—the young, charismatic leader who'd spoken earlier. "Holy shit. What a small world," I muttered.

He tipped his head toward the ballroom again. "What's your connection? You don't work for Lorman, do you?"

I froze. For some reason I couldn't explain, I didn't want to tell him about Landon. "Um..." I swallowed. "No. I work for PLMT. I'm a project manager, business side, for software development."

"I guess you decided to go the financial security route." He cleared his throat, looking around. "Since we're both leaving... wanna grab a drink and catch up?"

He scanned my face, earnest and hopeful. I tried to make myself tell him no because being around him was a terrible idea, but I'd never been able to speak anything but the way I felt to him, no matter what I tried to force my tongue to do.

"Sure. Coffee?"

"You drink coffee this late?" he asked as I stepped back into line. He walked along with me.

"I drink coffee if I'm awake," I laughed. "With my hours, it's a requirement. I'd never make it through the day if I didn't. Besides, this isn't late for me. But if you don't, we can get a drink instead. But only one—I have to get back to work tonight."

He looked sad as he took in my response, but I was probably just reading too much into things. Luckily, I was distracted from worrying about it by reaching the coat check counter. Myles already had his coat, so once I had mine, we headed outside and down the street to find a bar that wasn't too crowded.

Once we were settled into a tiny booth in a cozy, crowded bar, with drinks ordered, I looked up at Myles and just took in the feeling of being out with him again. We'd sat in a similar booth in Nina's, talking until the bar closed... how many times? More than either of us should have, but we'd done it anyway. It felt both familiar and strange to be out again with him now.

"So, you were at the hotel to celebrate Marcus' merger. Did you come into town for that? Where do you live now?"

He nodded, his gaze intense on me. "Yes, I was supporting Marcus. No, I didn't come into town for that. I live here—well, technically in Bathlin, but it's barely outside the city limits. What about you? Why were you there and where do you live now?"

My heart picked up speed and I decided to ignore his first question. I still felt a strong aversion to telling him about Landon. "I live here, not too far from where we are actually. West on Marvin a few blocks, then north on Sixteenth for three-quarters of a mile."

He squinted. "Morgantown area, right?"

I tipped my chin down; that was the neighborhood. "Yeah, that's right."

He sat back, his brows drawing in a little. "Ritzy area," he said.

The waiter arrived with our drinks—bourbon for both of us—saving me from having to figure out how to respond to his observation. He was right; Morgantown was the richest, most exclusive neighborhood in the city.

I took my first sip of bourbon, and it was like silky caramel on my tongue. Bourbon had been my drink of choice ever since Myles introduced me to it, though I rarely had it anymore; Landon thought it was odd and was determined I preferred wine. "This is *good*," I said, raising my eyebrows.

He rolled some around on his tongue for several seconds, then swallowed. "It is," he agreed. "Much better than that shit we used to drink."

I laughed. "I can't believe at one point I thought that was good. But to be fair, it was so much better than that cheap beer at all the parties."

"Oh, Christ yes," he chuckled.

He looked around, and when he looked back, our gazes locked. Time seemed to slow, and everything around us just kind of faded away. My respiration rate increased as I remembered another time much like this one, though many years earlier.

"Tell me everything I don't already know about you," Myles said, leaning across the small table so our faces were less than a foot apart.

I laughed. "Everything?"

He nodded, his mouth doing that pulling in thing that I'd figured out meant he was trying not to laugh. "I'm not gonna go around kissing strange women."

I giggled, and the crowd and noise receded until it felt like it was just the two of us. "You think you're going to kiss me?"

"Of course not," he said.

My brows fell in.

"I know I will."

"Oh, really?" I asked, feeling my cheeks leap into flame.

"I mean, obviously. If I'm going to marry you one day, I'm sure as hell gonna kiss you." He leaned forward, more serious and intense. "And it's going to be the kind of kiss we feel on our lips for days."

I lifted my hand and touched my fingertips to my lips... I could already feel it and it hadn't even happened yet.

My fingers pushed delicately into my lower lip, which was now tingling, remembering the night he'd told me he was going to kiss me... remembering the kiss later that night that turned my world upside down and left me thinking about it not for days, but for years.

"I told you," Myles said with a smirk.

I glanced away as heat moved up my neck and engulfed my face, but I couldn't help but smile. He had. And he'd been right. He'd been right about a lot of things about us.

His smirk shifted into a soft smile, his eyes looking faraway before returning and dropping to my mouth. When they returned to mine, they burned with intensity. It felt like we were back in that night before everything changed, picking up where we'd left off. I even felt almost desperate to kiss him again; I'd never been kissed by anyone the way I'd been kissed by him. It was a kiss that communicated thoughts and feelings and desires, telling a story, shifting and changing as emotions did. He kissed like the music he liked to listen to. Deep and raw and gritty. Emotional and sexy and longing.

I swallowed.

His tongue darted out to moisten his lips.

My breath stuttered.

"You two ready for another round?" the server asked, checking in as they passed by.

We said yes at the same time, then laughed, releasing some of the tension. I sat back, letting my seat support me as I dragged air into my neglected lungs and relaxed a bit. It was a relief he appeared to be as nervous as I was.

Myles watched me in contemplation. Then he pulled in the corners of his mouth to keep from smiling. "Please tell me you don't have a boyfriend, let alone a serious one," he said with a wink.

It was meant to be a joke, repeating the same words he'd said to me the night I met him seven years earlier, but this time it wasn't funny because I did. And I didn't want to tell him that, especially after I'd nearly kissed him. I laughed to cover my discomfort. "You haven't changed a bit," I said, in lieu of answering his question.

He stared into his glass for a second before looking back up. "*You* have."

I let out an awkward half-laugh, my heart hammering. "In a good way, I hope."

"I don't know yet," he said.

"Well, what has changed?"

"Your hair, for starters. I almost didn't recognize you."

I reached back and touched my hair. It had been straightened and twisted into a bun. It was the same way I wore it nearly every day. And when I didn't, it was still straightened and pulled back in some way. It became apparent early on that curly hair was unprofessional based on the looks I received at work and from Landon, so I forced the curl out every morning.

"Your skin. It's much paler now."

I touched under my neck and could feel the heat spreading as I flushed. It was true—I used to be tan because I spent so much time outside, but I never did anymore.

"Well, I spend a lot of time in my office."

He tipped his head in acknowledgement.

"Is that all?"

"You want to know the rest?"

I don't know. "Yes?"

He studied me. "You know what hasn't changed a bit?"

"What?"

"The way your cheeks look like they're stained with cherries when you blush."

My blush spread and I grinned.

"Or that gorgeous smile." He grinned back at me.

My heart beat seven times without a breath moving in or out before I could break eye contact. I looked down at my bourbon and lifted the glass, taking a hefty swallow and finishing the glass as my heart raced. I felt exposed, like I'd been stripped down, except this was more vulnerable than nudity—it was my soul that felt bare.

Why the hell had I agreed to this? I needed to leave. *Right away*. I looked back up to tell him so.

"What do you do? Are you teaching?" I asked instead. *Damn it*. Why did he have that effect on me?

He leaned forward, resting his forearms on the table, his eyes lighting up. "Yeah. I'm teaching music at George Washington Middle. My first year there. I haven't taught for a few years because I've been moving around helping to start up music programs at underprivileged schools that didn't have one. GW was the last one, but I missed teaching, so I'm going to do that again for a while."

"That's amazing," I said, reaching across and resting my hands over his. "This is what you wanted to do and you're doing it."

He nodded. "I love it. There's nothing like seeing what music can do for a child. These kids, they live in poverty. They don't have anything. Many of them only have one parent, some don't even have consistent housing. Some are abused, many are neglected, others are hungry. You can see the despair in their eyes. But music, it gives them something to enjoy about life, you know? It helps them find hope again. It's not just about music for them. It changes how they do in all their classes, which will change their entire future."

"You're making a real difference in those children's lives, Myles. That's incredible."

completely different things. I swallowed, looking down to take in his abdomen, the hair running down from his belly button to disappear under the waistband of his shorts.

I swallowed and forced my eyes to return to his. Without breaking eye contact, he grabbed the hem of my shirt and lifted.

"What are you doing?" I giggled, unresisting.

"It's not fair if I'm the only one shirtless and being ogled," he said.

I rolled my eyes as my shirt cleared my arms. "Ogled, right."

He wasn't wrong.

My cheeks were hot from being called out, but the embarrassment faded as I watched his eyes roam over my body in much the same way mine had over his. I'd never felt sexy in a sweaty sports bra before, but I did with Myles looking at me the way he was.

I closed my eyes, yet I could feel his gaze on me, my breath puffing out as if I'd just finished the scramble. When I opened them a moment later, his eyes were on my face, just watching me. I licked my lips, then caught my bottom one between my teeth, not wanting to smile the way my mouth was trying to right then. His fingers slid into the waistband of my shorts and yanked, pulling me into him, and then his hands moved between pressing my back to keep me flush against him and touching my face and skating over my shoulders and cradling the side of my neck, and all the while he was kissing me. Fast and slow and soft and hard. My lips were swelling with blood and becoming more sensitive.

He broke off and trapped me between him and the railing, an arm on each side of me. Breathing hard and sweaty, our noses bumped as our bodies shifted to draw in breath. My knees felt weak from the kiss, and I leaned back against the railing while he fiddled with his shorts pocket. As quick as lightning, Myles had an arm around my back, and I was compressed against his chest.

"Jesus Christ, Nina, don't do that. You could fall." His chest heaved in a different way, his breathing had changed, and he still held me against him. He pressed a long kiss against my forehead near the hairline, and I closed my eyes. "That scared the shit out of me." He rested the side of his face on the top of my head, his chest

moving up and down under me. After a moment, he kissed my forehead again, then let his arms slide down to circle my waist. When I opened my eyes, he was looking over the top of my head at the valley spread out before us.

"Where's Marksburg?" he asked.

I stepped out of his arms as I replied, "Northeast."

He squinted, still studying the valley that lay to the west of us.

I snorted and grabbed his hips, turning him around. Lifting an arm, I pointed toward the northeast. "That way, Mr. Directionally-Challenged."

"Another name?" he asked with mock incredulity.

I smirked and lifted an eyebrow, shrugging. I'd called him Mr. Wrong-Side-Of-The-Tracks, Mr. Not-As-Fit-As-You-Think-You-Are, Mr. Music-Nerd, and now Mr. Directionally-Challenged. What he didn't know was that he was also Mr. You've-Stolen-Nina's-Heart.

"Maybe if you knew what direction you were facing..."

"You know, not everyone is a walking compass," he laughed. "Do you always know which way you're facing?"

"Pretty much. I don't get disoriented easily. My dad used to test me by having me navigate us home or to the doctor or the grocery store or wherever by using cardinal directions rather than left and right."

"You can navigate places just using like north, south, that kind of thing?"

"Yup."

"How do you get from your dorm to my apartment?"

I closed my eyes to see the path then fired off the instructions using cardinal directions and street names. When I finished, I opened my eyes and looked up. His eyes were dark again.

"That's fucking hot," he said.

"I thought I was a nerd," I said, biting my cheeks. "A nature nerd. And a walking compass."

"You are. And it's hot."

I started to laugh, but his lips on mine cut me off. I couldn't focus, though, because there was a sound in the background, like a door shutting, followed by a chime. But there were no doors or chimes on the observation tower. Distracted, I strained my ears and heard another muted thumping sound.

My eyes flew open, my heart pounding, the sounds of Landon having arrived home pulling me from my dream. I rested a hand on my chest to calm my labored breath, closing my eyes again. I wanted to go back to my dream about hiking with Myles, about kissing him—a dream that was real because it had happened. In real life, moments after we had begun to kiss again, other people showed up and we'd scrambled to get our shirts back on, laughing at getting caught making out. And when we'd stood by the railing admiring the view one last time, we'd held hands, his thumb moving over my hand in a way I could feel reverberate throughout my body.

I'd been so distracted by seeing Myles earlier that I'd come straight home, forgetting entirely to go to the office to get my laptop first, and felt too tired and emotional and confused to go back out. Instead, I'd cleaned off my makeup and gotten ready for bed. For a long time, I'd laid there, staring at the ceiling and replaying every second since I'd looked over to find Myles standing next to me, studying me, his smell—cloves with a hint of pepper and vanilla—still filling my nostrils. I must have dozed off while thinking about that buzz in my lips when we'd almost kissed and ended up dreaming about him.

Landon's footsteps neared the bedroom, and a stab of guilt tore through my chest. Landon had been out of town for three weeks, but I was lying in our bed thinking about another man... after dreaming about kissing that other man. What would Landon think if he knew that? If he knew that even now, when I could hear him close by, I wanted to go back to sleep and keep dreaming about that other man? I wasn't sure—he was so unemotional and calm and controlled all the time, but there were moments I'd heard him snap on a call before, his voice booming throughout the entire apartment and vibrating the walls. I could feel his rage when that happened from the next room and instinctively knew to just keep my distance from him until he calmed down. He'd never turned his anger on me before, but would he if he knew?

I took a deep breath and focused on banishing thoughts of Myles to the same place where I kept everything else that had happened all those years ago locked up. None of it had any place in my life anymore. I was a different person, with a different life, and a different future. I was now Nina, project manager and girlfriend to Landon Jones, successful financial consultant.

How boring. You used to be so much more.

Maybe, but that was before, and nothing could ever be the same after.

A dim light penetrated into the bedroom from the closet as Landon moved around getting ready for bed. I listened to him putting his clothes away, then pulling out his pajamas, and lastly brushing his teeth. I knew there was nearly a one hundred percent chance he wanted to have sex and tried to psych myself up for it.

It didn't work.

All I could think about was the way Myles' mouth had tasted.

The way Myles' sweaty body had felt against mine.

They way he'd growled when I'd grabbed his ass seconds before we'd been interrupted by other hikers.

The way that had made me want to have sex for the first time with the man I'd met only a few months before.

We never did end up sleeping together before everything happened, but he was still the only man out of everyone who'd come after that had made me feel that kind of desire. The bed dipped under Landon's weight, sending that guilt stabbing sharply through my chest again, and I held my breath. Maybe this time he would just go to sleep. *Please just go to sleep tonight, Landon.*

"Nina?" His voice was soft and he rested his hand over my belly.

I shifted a little, like I might in my sleep.

"Darling?" He gave my shoulder a light shake, then kissed down my neck. His hand shifted across to my hip, sliding up under my shirt, and I tried not to cringe. "Nina, darling, are you awake?"

I couldn't keep pretending to be asleep, as much as I wanted to. "You're home," I said, my voice soft.

He leaned over and kissed me. I tried to summon something—*anything*—like desire or passion for Landon, but it just wasn't there—it never really had been. "I missed you, darling," he said, already pulling my pants down over my hips.

"I missed you, too," I replied.

And I tried to—I really did. But I didn't really feel that, either. It was more like we co-existed one week a month. There were occasional moments when he said something that made me genuinely smile, or when he kissed my cheek and I thought it might be because he really wanted to, or when he looked at me with something close to affection and I thought that maybe I really did matter to him. But most of the time, it was more like I was convenient for him. And I'd been okay with that—it was convenient for me, too. I'd thought once that maybe I could love him in time, and I did sometimes enjoy being around him, and maybe that was actually what love was like. I wouldn't know. I just knew it wasn't anything like what I felt for Myles, and now that those feelings were stirred up, I felt dissatisfied with this transactional relationship Landon and I had.

I let him spread my legs and turned to stare at the wall like I usually did. I'd never been much of an active participant, but Landon didn't seem to mind or even really notice. What I got out of sex wasn't top of mind for him. What mattered to him was only that I did it when he wanted me to. Which I supposed was okay since I didn't get anything out of it, really, anyway. If it were up to me, I'd never have sex again.

But I was in a relationship, so it *wasn't* up to me. It was up to *him*.

FIVE

If this headache didn't go away, it was going to be the most unproductive day of my career. I'd barely slept in days, and my head had been pounding for just as long. Thinking clearly was nearly impossible—in fact, thinking at all about anything other than the past had become hopeless. I'd sent emails to the wrong people, mixed up instructions, missed a dinner with Landon, and even forgotten to rinse conditioner out of my hair before getting out of the shower. At this point, Landon wasn't the only one giving me strange looks. I needed to get my shit together before being in a funk ended up with serious consequences.

It was all Myles' fault. If he'd never approached me after the merger announcement, none of this would have happened. I'd still be living my carefully organized, purposefully predictable life. While it was busy and tiring, it was what I was used to and what I wanted.

I sighed and typed up an email to let my coworkers know I'd be out of the office for a day. My computer would still come home with me, but I was going to take time off for the first time in over a year and see if I could get some sleep and shake off whatever was happening to me. As soon as the email was out the door, I closed up my laptop and left the office, stopping on the way home for some extra strength headache medicine. I got a little of everything on the shelf. I typically only used Advil, but I was going to try them all until something worked.

Less than an hour later, I walked through the door into the condo and halted; I could hear Landon's voice firing off financial statistics. This was just another example of not thinking clearly; I'd forgotten that he was home that morning getting packed to hop on a plane for his next three weeks out of town. He'd be in Denver this time. If I'd remembered, I would have suffered through at my desk until he'd left for the airport.

While I was debating whether or not to slip back out and find a café or something for the next while until I'd have the condo to myself, Landon walked past the front hall. I froze and he passed, still talking, but then backed up and looked toward me with a lowered brow. Then he was talking again and walked away. No walking back out the door now.

Nice job, Nina. There you go not moving again.

My heart stopped at my own words to myself, and I gave a sharp headshake to try to rid myself of them, which only made my headache feel worse.

I'd just finished getting myself set up to work from the dining table for the rest of the day when Landon walked in, phone in hand, and kissed the top of my head.

"I wasn't expecting to see you back before I left. Everything alright?"

I turned and smiled. "Fine. I just have a headache."

"You've had a headache since the merger announcement, haven't you? Have you taken some Advil?"

"Yeah, I have. I think I'm just tired. This is a busy time of year and there's a lot going on, and now Matthew wants me to take over for Megan's project while she's out on maternity leave."

"You'll figure it out, darling. You always do," Landon said, squeezing my shoulder and kissing the top of my head again. "I have to get to the airport."

He bent and gave me a quick kiss on the lips. But instead of straightening up, he kissed me again. His hand slid from my shoulder toward my breast.

"Don't move," I heard in my ear. *"If you do, I'll hurt you."* I squeezed my eyes closed as sickening tension flooded my body. My hand shot up and stopped the descent of Landon's. It wasn't his voice in my ear, but it didn't matter.

"You'll be late, Landon."

"You're right," he said, giving me another peck, then straightening. "It'll have to wait. I'll see you in a few weeks, darling."

"Have a nice trip."

As soon as he was gone a few minutes later, I stole into our bedroom and pulled off my work clothes. They felt more like a uniform, and it always gave me a sense of freedom to get out of them and into something more comfortable. Before fresh clothes, however, was a shower.

Even with a cavernous bathroom and the fan on, the room was soon filled with steam, and the enormous mirror behind the sink was fogged up by the time I stepped out, my head pounding. With a towel wrapped around me, I tapped out more medicine and tossed it back with a glass of water. Unwrapping my towel, I used it to wipe the fog off the mirror, and for the first time in years, I stood there to look at myself naked, but the steam in the room quickly fogged the mirror again.

In the closet was a full-length mirror, and I stood in front of that now, no more than a foot away, looking at my body. While I could see the changes Myles had pointed out and more, that wasn't why I was standing there. My fingertips traced over the small scars in my forehead that were normally hidden behind makeup, the larger horizontal scar that ran over my right breast, followed by the one in the crook of my neck on the left side. The one on my neck was easy to miss because of where it was, and because it was thinner. The one over my breast was wider and more noticeable, though there was no one to notice it except me. Landon rarely saw me naked except in the dark, and when he did, he was focused on other things. I wasn't sure he'd ever even noticed. There was only one person other than myself who would know what the scars were from.

My fingers continued to trace over the scars, and my eyes fell to take in the rest of my body. For the first time, I noticed my hip bones were protruding and I could see the outlines of my ribs. I'd never been heavy, but I was downright skinny now. My collarbones stuck out, and no matter how I turned, I couldn't find even a hint of the muscular definition I used to have anywhere on my body. It was all gone after years of sitting behind a desk and doing nothing else.

For a minute, I didn't recognize the woman looking back at me in the mirror. Not only was she thin, but as Myles had pointed out—she was pale. I'd never seen her so pale before. The only places that weren't pale were the dark circles under my eyes, so much more visible now that the makeup was washed off. My fingers moved under my eyes over the dark skin as I took in the strange woman's resting expression, the corners of her mouth and eyes pulled down. She looked so unhappy.

A wave of pain rose out of nowhere, compressing my lungs as it came, and then I was crying, my arms wrapped around myself as I tried to stem the flow. But I couldn't. Now that I'd begun, the first tears to fall in over six years, I couldn't hold it in. I crumpled to the floor and laid there, curled in a ball, my tears soaking the carpet.

When I eventually peeled myself off the closet floor, shadows were lengthening from the lowering late afternoon sun. My burning eyes were still moist, and as hard as I tried, I couldn't make the tears fully dry up. Everything hurt, and I felt this profound, intense desire to talk to Myles. To fall apart in his arms. I wouldn't even need to say anything for him to understand. But if I wanted to, I'd be able to say anything, I knew, and it would help. It would be like a compress on this raw wound inside me. It had been like that before, and I was certain it would be that way now.

That was the problem, though—it was a wound I needed healed that came open when he was in my life, and he'd be the only one who could soothe it. This was why I'd turned my back on him now six years, seven months, and six days ago. And it was why I needed to ignore this urge to find him again. Why I needed to forget I'd seen him a week ago, and in time, I knew from experience, I would. I just had to hold on long enough for that to happen. At least Landon would be gone for a few weeks so he wouldn't see me like this. He'd be confused and have no idea what to do; he'd never seen me emotional about anything before, let alone crying, bent into a ball for hours on end. But someone else had.

I ended up never being able to even look at my closed laptop for the rest of the day. I curled up on the sofa, snuggled with a pillow, and watched musicals on Netflix the way I'd done the last time I was like this, and eventually fell asleep that way. My dreams were vivid and unwanted, but for the first time in the last week, none of them were nightmares, and I woke a little refreshed; eleven hours of uninterrupted sleep would do that.

It was Saturday, and while I usually spent the day in the office, I decided to stay home again. While my emails loaded, I shuffled around the kitchen, looking first in the fridge, then the pantry, unsure what I was even looking for. I didn't want anything—I hadn't all week. I'd barely eaten or had anything to drink in days, even water.

I slammed the fridge door closed in frustration and, scrubbing my hands over my face, decided to just sit down and get to work.

It was hours later when I caught a glimpse of the clock and yawned, stretching. I hadn't moved the entire time and my body was stiff. The dining chairs were even less comfortable than the chair in my office. But I felt a little more normal after getting in a few hours of focused work. Maybe I'd just needed to have one good cry after so many years of nothing, and now I'd be able to get back to the way things were.

SIX

Landon had been gone for a week and half, and things were finally settled back into how they'd been before Myles appeared unexpectedly. It almost felt like that evening was something I'd dreamed up. I was focused and productive at work and only found my mind wandering into the past on occasion. Soon, I was sure, it wouldn't wander at all anymore. Things were definitely looking up.

As I always did, I turned on the small television screen mounted in the bathroom to listen to the news while I readied myself for work this Wednesday morning. There was the usual news of foreign conflicts and tragedy, reports of financial activity in the markets and predictions from analysts, updates about what the Supreme Court would be deliberating on, and so on. Next, however, was something new. I stared at the screen, turning off my hair dryer and setting it on the counter in front of me.

The reporter's words were flowing in, but I was having trouble digesting them, my eyes stuck on the image behind her.

I knew that alley between buildings.

"So, for this article type, we need to be able to utilize the same functionality as the other article types, with the exception that these will not be available to our front-end users, but only viewable by our back-end users. Additionally, we need…"

"*Additionally, we need a description if you expect us—*"

"Nina? What are the additional requirements? I think we might have lost connection."

I stared at the screen, hearing the voice from six and a half years ago in my head at the same time I heard my tech lead's voice over the conference call. It was like slow motion, the words all sinking in from both times, my body split between two different periods, and I remained silent, feeling a little confused. What had I been talking about?

"Okay, while we wait for Nina to get reconnected, we can take a look at our backlog…"

Jacob's voice faded and the voice from long ago grew stronger.

"Look, kid, it sounds more like you're embarrassed you got caught by your boyfriend, here." His eyes scanned me. "And with clothes like that…" He trailed off, letting his meaning sink in. I squeezed my knees together tighter and tried to pull down the material to cover more of my legs, then sank further into Myles's jacket that I'd had on since we left the hospital. I'd only worn Kate's dress because I knew I was going to be seeing Myles, and I wanted to see how he'd react to seeing me in something other than hiking clothes or jeans. Myles was arguing with the man, but I couldn't focus on his words, and then he was coaxing me to open the jacket and show the stranger the bandages covering my knife wounds, but the top of the dress was as risqué as it was short and I didn't want to.

My body shuddered and I disconnected from my call. I fired off an email that I was having some connectivity issues before heading to the nearest lactation room for nursing mothers. It was to be used for new moms who needed to pump during the workday, but I needed some privacy. Besides, I knew there weren't any new moms on my floor. I locked the door behind me, then leaned my forehead against it.

Focus, Nina. You can't zone out like that during calls. You can't zone out like that at all. Get your shit together before someone notices. You have too many balls in the air—if you keep it up, they're all going to come falling down, and you'll end up fired and Landon will leave you out of embarrassment.

I banged my forehead against the door a few times, and as I did, I imagined banging it harder and harder until the bones in my forehead began to crush. I imagined them splintering under the skin. Flattening, then caving inward. I wouldn't stop; I'd keep slamming my head against the door until there was nothing above my neck but a bloody stump. A bloody stump without thoughts or memories or headaches. I'd be dead, sure, but at least I'd be in peace because, without a head, I wouldn't be able to feel anything, either.

I swallowed, mortified by my own thoughts and glad no one could see them. I'd be committed for something like that. And maybe I should be—where the hell did something like that come from?

Get. A. Fucking. Grip. Nina.

I gave a definitive single head nod, inhaled to the bottom of my lungs, clenched my jaw together, made my lips curl up into a smile, and headed back to my office, arriving just as my desk phone rang.

I made it home without spacing out at work again, but I immediately turned on the news, which I didn't normally do at night. I sat, switching channels, until the next morning, hearing the same information regurgitated over and over about the near homicide in that alley I'd been in before. The young woman had escaped with her life, but barely.

She was a sophomore at MU and had been walking home from Nina's. *I was on my way there.* A man had appeared behind her and shoved her into the dark alleyway with a hand over her mouth and a knife at her throat. *The metal was so cold against my skin, and he smelled like stale cigarette smoke and cheap liquor.* He'd told her not to move or scream or she'd get hurt, but if she cooperated, he might let her live. *I nodded in understanding.* Then he'd raped her, leaving her with cuts where the knife had been held against her that required stitches but weren't life-threatening. *Thirty-four stitches to breast, neck, and forehead.* But he'd shoved her away from him when he was done, and she'd hit her head on the corner of the dumpster—that was what nearly killed her.

I sent out a message that I was sick and would be working from home the rest of the week, but really I barely worked. All I could do was hunt down news channels and websites about this case. I read and listened to the same reports over and over and over. This was the first time something like this was in the news from there, but how many times had it happened before this young woman nearly died? How many women were dismissed when they reported it because they weren't near death like this one? Or because they'd had a drink or two? Or because they hadn't tried to fight back against an attacker with a fucking knife?

By Friday, I had barely slept and had a bruise on my forehead. I had to stop banging my head against things. To do that, though, I needed to talk to someone about this case. The question was who? I had lots of connections, but no real friends. Except Myles.

Myles? No, Myles is not my friend. We barely know each other. And he's part of this whole problem. Except that, in our short shared history, he knew me better than anyone else in my life ever had.

"No," I said aloud, gritting my teeth. "If I need to talk to someone, I'll talk to my boyfriend. I'll call Landon."

I stared at my phone, my finger hovering over the button to call him. I'd never once called him while he was away... How would he react? He always initiated contact, and that was usually just a sporadic text message. It was early, especially in Colorado. I would probably catch him while he was eating and watching the news. I pushed the button, and the line rang.

"Nina?" he answered on the third ring. "Is everything okay?"

I swallowed and my eyes welled up with tears I didn't want. "Yeah," I said as brightly as I could. "Everything's fine, don't worry. I just wanted to talk to you about something if you had a moment."

There was a pause, and I knew he was checking the time and his calendar. "I have about ten minutes."

I took a deliberate, slow breath in. I'd only ever tossed around ideas about solving a problem I'd run into at work or talked about the financial news with him before. "Did you see that news report of the woman who was nearly killed in Marksburg?"

"Yes. She hit her head on a dumpster or something."

I nodded even though he couldn't see me. "That's right. It was in Marksburg. That's where I went to college."

"Okay," he said.

I sighed. "I've been there. I mean, the place in the photo on the news. I know that alley, Landon."

"Okay," he said again, then waited for me to elaborate.

"I know it," I said again. I wanted him to ask me why, or if something had happened, or anything, really.

"Okay," he said a third time.

"I mean..." I huffed out a breath, trying to figure out how to tell him what happened, especially when he seemed so disinterested. I chickened out. "I've walked past there before. What if that had been me, you know?"

"It wasn't, Nina. It was this other girl."

"But it could have been."

"No, it couldn't. You're smarter than that. You'd never be stupid enough to walk somewhere like that at night by yourself, let alone dressed like that."

My mouth opened, but I had no words.

"Put it out of your mind, darling. Things like that don't happen to people like us. Maybe take a few days from the news—I'm sure this will fizzle out soon once there's something more interesting to report. I have to go. I'll see you next week."

"See you next week," I echoed mechanically before the call disconnected.

But all I could hear was Landon's words on repeat. *"You're smarter than that. You'd never be stupid enough to walk somewhere like that at night by yourself, let alone dressed like that. Things like that don't happen to people like us."*

I was filled with a sudden molten rage mixed with shame. Why did clothes matter? And maybe walking alone at night *was* stupid, but why did that justify what happened? It was only stupid because it was dangerous, and it shouldn't have been. And why did any of that excuse the bastard who'd raped and nearly killed her anyway? I felt the urge to violently beat my head against the wall again, but managed to keep myself from doing so, remembering the already dark bruise that was hard enough to cover with makeup. I couldn't keep doing things like that.

But I had to do *something*. I paced for several minutes, then decided I had to leave. I had to get out of the condo before I suffocated.

SEVEN

The next thing I knew, I was dressed in jeans and a sweater under my winter coat, waiting outside a middle school in one of the roughest neighborhoods in the city. In every way, it was the opposite of the neighborhood I lived in, but while I felt nervous something would happen to me, I also felt more like I belonged there than I did in the one where I lived.

What the hell was I doing there, though? I had been on autopilot for the last few hours and was only just becoming aware again as I looked around me. I'd barely noticed pacing around after my call with Landon. Once I decided I had to leave, I had no idea where I was going. Not when I walked to the metro station after hours of aimless wandering. Not when I got off the metro and started walking. Not until I'd arrived was I conscious of where I'd been headed the whole time. Did it make me a stalker to show up outside someone's work when they weren't expecting me? When it was someone I had no contact with? I didn't want to be a stalker, but I had to get this stuff out, and it hadn't worked when I tried with Landon. There was only one person I knew could handle what I was feeling, and that was Myles. Maybe then I'd be able to get back to my life again. Which I had to do. I didn't know who this person was who kept tearing up—like I was now—and who intentionally banged her head until she was dizzy and couldn't finish a train of thought during meetings and who would stare into space for sometimes hours. I was desperate to get rid of this person I was becoming… desperate enough to go to the one person I knew I should stay away from.

I took and released a deep breath, trying to calm the rising nausea in my stomach, and watched the puff of white cloud from my breath. It was bitter cold outside as we arrived into mid-January. It made the tears that fell onto my cheekbones feel like lava. I lifted a gloved finger and swiped them away, then sniffled loudly, trying to get control over myself as I heard a bell in the distance. Moments later, the perimeter of the school was flooded with students. I was near the entrance to the designated faculty lot and watched for Myles, but I didn't see him. When the trickle of students and teachers slowed, I decided to go inside and look for him. I was freezing and was afraid for a moment that he hadn't been teaching that day and I'd been there for nothing. There was exactly one hybrid vehicle in the lot, however—an SUV—and I had a hunch it was his.

In the office, I was directed dispassionately toward Myles' classroom after walking through a metal detector and getting a nametag. When I approached the door to the classroom, a tall, skinny kid walked out, his pants and shoes with holes and only a worn sweatshirt under his even more worn backpack. In one hand, he carried an enormous black case by the handle—a cello, I guessed—and the shininess of the case looked out of place with the faded and tattered appearance of the kid. It made my heart ache.

"Later, Mr. E," he called with his other hand lifted.

"Later, Dwayne," Myles' voice rang out. "See you Monday. Practice if you want that trip!"

"Yeah, yeah, whatever, dude," Dwayne called back, but he was smiling.

I watched him briefly, then stepped across the hall into the classroom. From just inside the doorway, I looked around and took everything in. The back of the classroom had several rows of desks—the type with the chair attached to them—arranged very close to one another, and in front of that were several rows of chairs in a semicircle with music stands. On the other side of the chairs was a podium, to the left of which was a piano, and to the right were several music stands without chairs. And, lastly, at the very front was a chalkboard that Myles was clearing with an eraser. I stood and just watched him as the chalk lines on the board disappeared, his tattooed arm showing below his rolled shirt sleeves, swiping back and forth to clear them. When he reached the other end of the board, he set the eraser down in the tray and struck his hands together to clear off the chalk dust, then turned, stopping in his tracks when he looked toward the doorway.

Neither of us moved or spoke, but something was definitely being communicated between us—I just wasn't sure what it was. For my part, I was screaming for him to make it all go away. His face took on a sadness I'd seen in the past before the moisture in my eyes blurred him entirely.

I jumped when a knock sounded immediately behind me.

"Have a good weekend, Myles," a man's voice called.

Myles raised a hand, looking past me. "You, too, Greg."

He cleared his throat, and I wrapped my arms around myself, looking down.

"I just need another minute to pack up," he said after a beat.

My nod was small, and I shifted my weight. I was suddenly embarrassed that I'd shown up at his school the way I had. And I hadn't even said a word to him yet. What kind of crazy person did shit like that? This one, apparently. I heaved a sigh. It was too late now—I was already there.

I was still in the same spot when he walked over a minute later with a messenger bag in his hand. He stopped in front of me, and I stared at our feet pointing toward one another, our toes inches apart. I looked up and my tears spilled over. Myles dropped his messenger bag and wrapped his arms around me. I buried my face in the curve of his neck and fell apart like I used to, my whole body shaking as I huddled into him. I wasn't even sure what I was crying about in that moment, but I couldn't stop.

"I wondered how you were holding up with the news," Myles said, breaking the silence that had followed us until we were on the road in the vehicle I'd thought was his. I didn't even know where we were going—I didn't ask. I also didn't care.

I turned away and looked out the window. "I didn't cry for years. Not once since the day after the last time I saw you years ago. Both of my parents died, and I didn't shed a single tear, Myles. Not one."

His hand joined both of mine on my lap. He gave them a light squeeze.

"But since I saw you at the Lorman event, it's like... I can't *stop* crying."

There was a long silence after I spoke, then Myles looked over at me as we came to a stop at a red light. "Did you ever see a therapist?"

I stared at him, everything hurting even more after that question.

"*I* did," he continued. "For *years*, Nina. I had to."

I shook my head and looked down. I remembered him urging me to see someone in those last weeks before I walked away from him.

Another silence thickened between us until we pulled into the driveway of a single-family home in the suburbs.

"I assumed you didn't want to be at your place since you came looking for me at the school," he said by way of explanation.

"This is your house?"

"Yeah, it is. And my parents are right down the street," he said, pointing east.

I smiled; he'd wanted to take care of his parents and be close to them wherever he ended up, and he'd done it.

His house was spacious, but not too large, still small enough to feel cozy. Nothing like the cavernous space I lived in. It felt warm and inviting, and as soon as I walked in, I didn't want to leave. It was an extension of how I felt in Myles' arms, and I let out a sigh of relief. From what, I wasn't sure, but it felt like just walking inside had relieved *something*. He gave me a quick tour of the house, lingering in the rooms he'd converted for music. One was for recording, one for playing with different instruments in stands all around the room. He talked to me about how he'd gotten back into composing over the last few years, then showed me his piano, his "splurge instrument" he said. It was beautiful, all sleek curves. It looked like it belonged in a jazz bar in a bygone era. My fingers lightly whispered over it as I walked past. It had been years since I'd touched a piano.

"Would you like to play?" Myles asked.

Flashes of playing side by side with him on the beat up old upright piano he'd been given for free—crammed into his tiny, shared apartment in college—filled my mind, and I couldn't help smiling. But that was a long time ago.

"I haven't played in years, Myles. I probably can't even read music anymore," I said, my voice soft.

He walked over to a shelf and pulled something out from a messy stack after digging around for a minute, placing it on the music rack. "It's like riding a bike, Nina. Give it a shot while I get changed."

I watched him walk out of the room, then turned to the beautiful instrument in front of me and the music he'd placed on the stand. "To A Wild Rose" by Edward MacDowell. In an instant, I was flooded with memories of practicing this piece with him. My hands trembled as I sat down and placed them over the keys. I scanned the first page, then played the first notes, clumsily, but by the time I reached the end, my fingers remembered what to do, and I restarted the song, playing with my eyes closed this time. On my third time through, somewhere around halfway, I felt Myles lower onto the bench next to me and scooted over to give him more space for his large frame. Our hips and thighs smushed tightly together, the music took on even more richness with the addition of the harmony he played. We ran through another time from start to finish together, and by the end, I felt light and elated. Like I was floating above the Earth and was filled with sunshine, as if I'd experienced some transcendent event no one else had. It was the same feeling I'd always had when we played a duet together. It was exhilarating and addictive.

My eyelids blinked open, and I turned toward Myles. His face was close—so very close—his eyes already resting on me. His mouth pulled into an easy, relaxed grin. Mine followed.

"You've still got it," he said.

"So do you," I replied.

He laughed. "I better if I'm going to teach it. Wanna play another?"

"Yes, please."

He walked over to his shelf and replaced the music we'd just finished on top of the messy stack, then sat back down without bringing anything with him.

"I think you forgot something," I snickered.

He just raised his eyebrows and smiled. I understood a second later when he played the first few notes to "My Immortal" by Evanescence. I closed my eyes again, and again my fingers found the keys of their own accord. We played through this piece so many times I lost count, my cheeks damp. It was one of the most hauntingly beautiful pieces of music I'd ever played. Eventually, my fingers were cramping from using them in a way they were no longer used to, and I brought them down to rest on my lap.

"Thank you," I said, looking down at my hands. "I think I needed that."

"Everyone needs music in their life," he replied. "It helps us with feeling and processing emotions and stimulates just about every part of our brains."

My head bobbed slowly. "I'm sorry about earlier. I didn't mean to show up like I did, let alone break down on you. I mean, really, you barely even know me, and that was a bit presumptuous of me."

"I know you, Nina. The stuff that matters, anyway."

"Regardless... I'm sorry. And thank you for just... rolling with it, I guess."

"When have I not?" he said with a smirk.

I smiled but didn't say anything. He was right. Whether I was texting him last minute to meet me somewhere after Kate had ditched me at a party or calling him in the middle of the night for reassurance about a big exam that had me nervous or I was yelling at strangers for littering when we were walking somewhere. He always just... rolled with it.

"Would you like something to drink?" he asked, standing.

"Sure."

"Make yourself at home. I'll be right back."

He disappeared from the room, and I rose from the bench, feeling as relaxed as I might if I'd just had a session in a sauna. Glancing toward the windows, I was shocked to see it was dark outside already. Hours had passed without notice. Tension crept back in as I thought about all the work that would be piling up and about the fact that I was at a man's house after dark while Landon was halfway across the country. I figured I should probably check my phone in case he'd tried to reach me for some reason. When I glanced at my screen, though, he hadn't. And he probably wouldn't, I knew. Either way, I knew I should go home. I remained standing as the battle between my heart and my logic played out, and then Myles walked into the room.

For the first time since he'd changed, I took in what he was wearing; low-slung gray sweatpants and a black t-shirt that said "Being a music teacher is as easy as riding a bike, except that the bike is on fire, you're on fire, everything's on fire."

I let out a small giggle.

He looked down, grinning. "My students at the last place I taught got me this for teacher appreciation day. It's pretty accurate."

"I can only imagine."

He tipped his head toward his living room. "Let's go sit. I ordered pizza."

I closed my eyes and groaned, laughing. Just the mention of pizza made my mouth water; I was famished. My eyes roved over the bourbon bottle tucked under his arm, one hand with two empty rocks glasses and the other with two tall glasses of water balanced, and I almost reached out for one of them—I was also really thirsty. I followed him into his living room and watched as he cleared off stacks of sheet music from his coffee table.

"Some things certainly haven't changed since college, huh?" I mused, taking in the mess.

He snorted but didn't say anything. When he was done clearing, I sat in the middle of one side of the sofa. He moved all the drinks closer to where I was, then turned and headed toward the wall. I gulped down the entire glass of water, trying to look anywhere but at Myles' backside while he fiddled with something. Suddenly the air filled with music.

"The Dovelyn Trio. I saw them perform live last year, and you wouldn't believe it, Nina. They're incredible. Piano, violin, and... drumroll please... oboe," he said with a smirk. "Their covers of 'The Sound of Silence' and 'Numb' are going to blow your mind."

He sat as he finished speaking, right next to me, our hips and thighs and arms touching, and poured us each a glass of bourbon. When he noticed my water glass was empty, he got up and refilled it, sitting back down where he was before. We didn't talk, instead lounging on his sofa and sipping bourbon as we listened to The Dovelyn Trio, at times with tears streaming down our cheeks. It was almost an irritation when the doorbell rang with our pizza.

Until I smelled it.

My stomach was grumbling, and I was afraid I'd start drooling. He brought it in with a few cloth napkins and set the box down on the table. No plates. Just like we used to do it.

"Pepperoni and black olives," he said, flipping the lid open with a grin. "I hope your taste in pizza hasn't changed."

I tore into a piece and moaned. It was *so good*.

He laughed. "I'll take that as a no."

"Nope." I licked sauce from my thumb for emphasis. "And this? The. Best. Ever."

"Better than Valenti's, I think."

I nodded in agreement. "Definitely. Although Valenti's will always have a place in my heart considering we practically lived off it for a while."

He chuckled. "Our old bodies couldn't handle a diet of pizza and bourbon anymore."

"Old? Speak for yourself," I laughed.

"You're not that much younger than me, you know," he said, draping an arm around my shoulder after cleaning his hands on a napkin.

I took a final bite of my pizza and cleaned my hands off, then topped off our bourbons. Pulling my knees up, I leaned back, resting my head against the crook of his shoulder. With a sip of bourbon rolling around on my tongue, I closed my eyes, focusing on the sounds of piano and violin and oboe surrounding us. The notes gently caressed me, and everything that had felt so raw before now felt softened.

"You smell the same," I murmured sometime later, not sure Myles could even hear me above the music. My body was warm and buzzed from proximity with his body as well as the bourbon. I felt tipsy and everything was soft and beautiful, especially since he'd extinguished all the lights except a small lamp when he'd gotten up to put away the pizza and fill our water glasses. "Spicy and sweet. And now a little caramelly from the bourbon."

His chest rose and fell heavily, and I felt his lips press into my forehead near my hairline, just above where I'd been hitting it all week. Landon kissed me there sometimes, but it was different. Landon gave me a peck, then moved away, his mind already elsewhere. But Myles lingered, keeping his lips pressed into me so long the skin felt cold when he pulled away, and then he remained so close I could feel his breath where his lips had been. It felt like he *wanted* to do it. With Landon, it felt like an afterthought, a responsibility he'd nearly forgotten.

It felt good for someone to do something because they wanted to.

It felt good that that someone was Myles.

I yawned, snuggling into Myles' neck, my hand holding my bourbon glass resting on his chest.

"Do you want to go home?" he asked, his voice low and rumbling his chest under me as his fingers pulled out my ponytail holder, then began combing through my hair.

My body broke into goosebumps from the sensation—home was a place I never wanted to go to again. I wanted to stay right where I was forever. Feel the way I did right then forever, that soft, pleasant haze, where nothing hurt, and I didn't have to be any certain way. There were no expectations, even from myself, and no judgment, either.

"No," I replied. "Do you want me to?"

His reply was quiet and issued directly from his chest. "No."

EIGHT

I woke in the morning with less of a headache than I would have expected considering how much bourbon I'd had to drink the night before, but then again, Myles had made sure I kept hydrated, and I remembered vaguely that he'd given me some sort of over-the-counter painkiller at one point. We'd listened to his Dovelyn Trio record a few times, sitting mostly in silence together on the sofa, sipping bourbon, until... I wasn't even sure when. I couldn't remember how the evening ended. I remembered listening, and smelling Myles, and feeling so relaxed... then waking up. I wasn't sure what happened between.

It felt strange to be waking with light breaking in through the blinds rather than well before sunrise, though not as strange as waking in a bed I'd only seen briefly during a house tour. I could smell Myles on the sheets, but he wasn't there. Who knew if he had been the night before or not. It had been ages since I'd woken up unsure of what or who I'd done the night before, and I felt a little sick. I couldn't become that person again.

I lifted the blankets and looked under, dreading what I might find. I was wearing a t-shirt that didn't belong to me and my panties.

The same t-shirt Myles was wearing the night we met.

My eyes burned and I pulled the blankets down as I remembered that night long ago. The night it had all begun. After all the good he'd brought into my world, I could never regret meeting Myles. But if I'd never gone to that party, or started spending time at Nina's, or tried to impress him with that revealing dress... so much of my life would have been different. I wouldn't have been working the office job I was or living in the stuck-up neighborhood I lived in or dating a man who—

Oh, shit. Landon. Please, please, please, don't let me have slept with Myles last night when I have a boyfriend. Christ, Nina, you know better than to drink that much.

Shaking, I climbed out of bed and found my clothes folded haphazardly on the other side of a nightstand. Grabbing them, I crept into the en suite bathroom, closing the door behind me, and took a quick shower, then used Myles' toothbrush to brush my teeth. Feeling fresher and a bit more presentable, even if my hair was wet and I had no way to straighten it, I took a measured breath in and left the bedroom to hunt for Myles.

I found him in the living room, intensely focused on several sheets of paper spread out before him, tapping his pencil and rocking his head from side to side in time, then pausing and marking the paper or erasing something, then starting over. He was writing a piece of music, and I stood in the doorway for a long while just watching him, slipping back and forth in time to other moments I'd watched him composing. He looked up, his eyes toward the ceiling, thinking about something, then back down before he startled and his eyes darted toward me.

I smiled.

He smiled bigger.

I looked down as my face heated, my hair falling in front of me.

"Good morning," he said, rising and walking over.

He grasped my arms and kissed that same spot where my forehead faded into my hairline. I leaned into the kiss for several seconds, then remembered I had a boyfriend and leaned back. He studied my face, still partially hidden by my hair, and I looked down at the floor again, crossing my arms over my chest.

"I have a question," I said, my voice hesitant.

"And hopefully I have an answer," he said with a trace of laughter as his hands fell from my arms and he walked back toward the sofa.

My heart beat into my throat. It was a question I'd had to ask of someone more than once in my life, but I'd never felt as nervous about asking as I did right then when Myles was the one I had to query. I lifted a hand and slid it under my damp hair to hang over the back of my neck and turned to look out the window at the bright sunshine sparkling off the frost covering the grass in his front yard. It was beautiful.

"What's up, Nina?" Myles asked.

I glanced at him, then back toward the front yard. "Did we... I mean, last night..."

"Are you asking if we slept together?"

My face flamed. "Yeah."

The only sound was of his footsteps nearing me. When I looked down, I could see his bare feet in front of mine. When he didn't speak, I couldn't help but turn up to look at him, getting trapped in his gaze. He stood so close I could feel his breath, and I shivered lightly. His eyes were serious. Intense. He almost looked angry, but not quite... I'd seen this look in his eyes before, a handful of times, years ago, and I swallowed, knowing that whatever he was about to say was something he felt strongly about. And if it was anything like when we were younger, it was probably also going to knock me on my ass.

"You were drunk, Nina. Drunk enough you can't even remember if we did or not. Besides the fact that I would never take advantage of you in that state, that much alcohol dulls the senses. When we do sleep together, neither of us will be drunk, because that's going to be something we want to feel every second of."

Every thought fled my mind and all I had was feeling. The feeling of a magnetic field pulling us together. The feeling of desire and anticipation I hadn't felt in over six years deep in my belly, heavy between my legs. My heart was beating so hard it restricted my airway and my breath struggled to move in and out. I could taste Myles' breath as he exhaled, his body and his mouth growing closer.

In the moment I realized if he touched me, I'd sleep with him right then, right there, because it was all I could think about, he leaned back, letting out a harsh breath. He lifted an arm and ran his hand over his hair, turning to face the other side of the room. And in the space that created, I knew I'd been within seconds of sleeping with a man who wasn't my boyfriend.

"I need to go home," I said, looking around for my coat and my purse. I'd known that going to see him would be a bad idea, but I hadn't realized how bad an idea. I needed to leave while I still had some willpower.

"Why are you here, Nina?" Myles asked without turning around.

"You drove me here, Myles."

"No—why did you come to the school?"

I sucked in a breath. He turned.

"Explain it to me. A few weeks ago, we run into each other and go for drinks and have what I thought was a great time. Without warning, you run out on me and make it clear you don't want to stay in contact, then you show up at my school yesterday, in tears, a mess. You come home with me and then tell me you don't want to go home. You slept in my bed for fuck's sake, and then, as suddenly as you showed up, you're trying to leave again. Why? Why did you come find me in the first place?"

I slid down the doorframe until my ass hit the floor, hugging my knees to my chest. My cheeks were already damp again. He sat down on the other side of the doorframe, our shoulders touching.

"Talk to me, Nina."

It felt like something inside me was tearing open. My eyes could no longer focus on anything and stared through the floor in front of me. "I feel like I'm losing my mind, Myles," I said softly. "I can't focus at work. I lose large chunks of time. I keep crying." I swallowed, and when I spoke next, my voice was even quieter. "I've been hurting myself."

I heard his swallow and felt the tension in his body, felt his gaze burning into me. I turned, resting my cheek on my knees and facing him. He watched intently as I swiped my hair back, holding it away from my face. I saw the instant he registered the bruising on my forehead because he looked like someone was torturing him.

"Oh, Nina," he whispered, reaching out and skating his fingers over my skin.

I blinked, sending tears skidding down my cheeks, then turned to replace my chin on my knees and stare through the floor in front of me. "I don't know what's wrong with me. I've been fine for years, but ever since I saw you, it's like I can't handle life anymore. And I thought I was getting things under control again, then I saw the news and…" I shrugged. "I just snapped, I guess. Before I knew what I was doing, I was there to see you. I guess I hoped talking to you might help. I think I have to talk to someone, because feelings I don't want are just exploding out of me right now. I'm so fucking angry and upset and frustrated and devastated and about a million other things I don't even understand. And I don't know what to do with it all. You know?"

I could see him nod out of the corner of my eye. "I do, to some extent. That's how I felt back then. I blamed myself for a long time for what happened. I kept thinking about how if I had insisted on picking you up that night, or if I'd walked to meet you partway, or if I'd agreed to go to the party with you guys to begin with, or if I'd never waited for you outside Parker's house the night we met, your life would have been so much better. If I'd never been a part of it, things would have been so different for you. I had nightmares about that night, about what I interrupted. I still do sometimes. I was so angry with myself that I hadn't come outside ten minutes earlier to look for you, or just decided to wait outside for you once you were on your way. And it was bad enough, but after you walked away from me, it was worse, because I was sure you felt the same way and couldn't forgive me for not protecting you and that that's why you were gone. I didn't blame you—that's why I only tried to call you once after you left."

"It wasn't your fault, Myles. I never once blamed you."

"Then why'd you turn your back on me, Nina? It destroyed me when you walked away from me. *Destroyed* me."

A sob rose in my throat. "Because I felt too much with you. And I needed a break from feeling. I couldn't feel so much with…" I broke off, not sure I could tell him what I'd done back then… also not sure how I couldn't.

"With what?" he asked, his voice watery.

My mouth turned down and I cried hard into my knees for several minutes before Myles' arm wrapped across my back, and he pulled me into his side. I shook my head.

"What, Nina?" he asked gently, his fingers twisting the ends of my hair.

"I was pregnant," I whispered.

"Oh my god," he breathed out.

"I got an abortion."

"Oh, Nina."

"I didn't tell anyone—no one. But I don't know if I did the right thing, Myles," I cried. "I kept thinking I hated it because it was a reminder of what happened, and that he would ruin my life in another way if I didn't do something about it. But not a day has gone by since I did it that I haven't felt guilty, like maybe I made the wrong decision. But I also *don't* think I made the wrong decision. I don't know. I'm a horrible person."

He kissed the crown of my head. "You are not a horrible person, Nina. You were violently raped. There's no guidebook for that, let alone for finding out you're pregnant afterward. Whether you decided to keep the baby, have the baby and put it up for adoption, or have an abortion, there was no right or wrong decision."

I cried until there was nothing left to come out—years' worth of tears came pouring out of me—and Myles held me through all of it. It felt good to get my secret off my chest, to share the burden of knowing what I did with someone else.

"Okay," Myles said, dusting his hands together to get off the crumbs from the cold pizza we'd just had with a cup of coffee as our breakfast. "We need some fresh air."

"I should work, actually," I said, eying the last two bites of pizza crust before deciding I was done and setting it down.

"It's Saturday."

"I know. I usually work every day. And I'm already behind because I haven't been able to focus and took off early yesterday."

When I looked up, Myles was studying me, his brows hunched together. He reached over and grabbed my unfinished crust, turning and dropping it in the trash. "I'm not going to tell you what to do, Nina, but you need to take some time off. It's not healthy to work that much to begin with. And right now, all your issues with focus? Your body is trying to tell you something. It's trying to tell you that you need a break. If you don't listen, it's just going to get worse—it's not going to go away."

I returned his stare, digesting his words. Logically, I knew he was right. I also had responsibilities, and if I didn't do something about that soon, I was going to start letting a lot of people down. But when I thought about work, I felt nauseous. "Okay," I said with a small nod. "But I don't have clothes."

"We can go by your place first."

My heart skipped at the thought of him being inside the space I shared with Landon. "No," I rushed out, looking away. "I don't own any," I clarified. "What I'm wearing is as close to hiking clothes as it gets." When I glanced up, he was staring at me in bewilderment.

"You studied forestry."

"I know."

"Your dream was to be a trail guide."

"I know," I said again, more forcefully.

"You dragged my ass out hiking with you every chance you got, for fuck's sake, Nina. You said you didn't feel like you if you didn't hit the trails often enough. How the hell do you not own anything to hike in?"

I inhaled a measured breath, trying to find words to explain why I struggled to go until I stopped trying altogether. It was so many different reasons, but they all came back to that one night in a dark alley.

"I..." My eyes examined the ceiling. "I haven't been on a trail since it happened. At first, I tried, but I couldn't. I kept freaking out about being out there alone. I freaked out about being *anywhere* alone. At some point, I just stopped trying. I put that part of me behind me. I needed to be someone different. I don't know how to explain it, but I couldn't be me anymore because this thing had happened and changed me, and I needed to create someone new. I became a different person in a lot of ways, Myles. There's a lot I did trying to make sense of what happened that..." I huffed out a breath. "I'm not the same person you knew back then. I've done things... You'd never look at me the same way."

"Tell me," he said, stepping closer to me. We were both leaning against his counter facing each other, now about a foot apart.

I gave a quick headshake. I couldn't do it.

"Nina, listen to me. Things happen in our lives—sometimes things that are done to us and sometimes things that we are doing ourselves. Sometimes those are things we aren't proud of, but they don't change who we are fundamentally. And I know who you really are. I'm not sure *you* do right now, but *I* do. I always have. I want you to tell me, not because I think I deserve to know or something like that, but so you can look in my eyes and see that nothing changes."

I stared into his eyes and even opened my mouth, but the words were caught up somewhere in my chest. He leaned forward and touched his lips tenderly to my bruised forehead. "I'm here when you're ready," he said against my skin. "In the meantime... are you coming with me?"

I glanced toward his front door where I knew my cell phone sat on a table, thinking about how many missed messages from work I was likely to have, then looked back at the man standing in front of me, waiting patiently for my response.

I took a deep breath and my lips lifted at the corners. "Where are we going?"

NINE

The trail was relatively easy, only a few hundred feet in elevation over two miles, but it was significantly more than I was used to nowadays, and I was already slowing us down before we'd even reached a mile; it was going to be a long four-mile roundtrip hike.

"I think I'd like a rematch on who can hike faster... maybe today," Myles said, chuckling, when I paused for what felt like the thousandth time.

I rolled my eyes. "You're hilarious."

"You certainly *used* to think so," he replied. "Though, then again, you also thought *you* were hilarious."

"That's because I was." I set off again and Myles adopted a more moderate pace, thank god. I would never have asked him to, but I was grateful he did. "Shit, I'm out of shape," I muttered. At least the clothes and hiking books we'd picked up were comfortable—it would have been a nightmare if they weren't.

"We can go back to the trailhead and take a flatter trail," he offered, not joking this time.

"No."

I *wanted* to do this one if it killed me. I *wanted* the challenge, to remind my body of what it was once capable of. Even so, it did feel like I might die—everything hurt already. My abs, my hamstrings, my quads, my glutes, my calves. Even my lungs. The cold air felt like inhaling needles when I grew short of breath.

"I can't believe I was once that girl who could jog a trail like this and barely break a sweat," I mused out loud a little tearily. I sniffled and widened my eyes, hoping they'd dry out.

"You still are, Nina. You're still the same woman who hiked every chance she got and could never get lost. You're the same woman who told me the types of trees we passed and pointed out edible shrubs. You're the same woman who kicked my ass on the trail and made sure I knew it. The woman who spent hours playing duets with me because I wanted to practice, and the woman who encouraged me to start composing. The woman who cried when she stepped on a snail shell on the sidewalk, and the woman who insisted on taking a spider from my room outside instead of killing it. You're the same woman with a sharp tongue and sense of humor who wasn't afraid to speak up about things she believed in, no matter what anyone else thought. Those qualities will always be a part of who you are, Nina."

I sighed. "I don't know, Myles. I don't even recognize the woman in the mirror anymore. I was standing there the other day when I got out of the shower and didn't know who the hell was looking back at me. I don't know this woman who doesn't do anything but work and sleep, but I also don't know the woman who did anything else. I think I've just lost the parts of me that made me *me*," I finished, my voice cracking.

"They're still there, Nina. I know it. Look around you—tell me what you see?"

My eyes flitted around before returning to the path. "A hiking trail in the middle of winter."

Myles reached out and stopped me, stepping in front of me to face me with his hands on my arms. For a moment, the only thing passing between us was the white cloud from our mingled breath.

"Close your eyes," he said.

I closed them, and immediately my heart rate sped up. My eyes shot open, and I looked over my shoulder. No one was behind me.

Myles pulled off his gloves and shoved them in his pockets. Then he pulled off mine, tucking them alongside his. He grasped my hands in his. "Do you trust me?"

I nodded. I couldn't explain it, but I did—I always had, and that hadn't changed.

"Okay," he said, his voice still soft, jostling our hands lightly. "I'm right here. You're safe. No one will hurt you, because I'm right here with you and I'd never let that happen. Are you here with me, Nina?"

I nodded again, pulling a hand out of his briefly to swipe the tears gathering below my lower eyelids. "I'm here with you, Myles."

"Close your eyes, then."

I closed them again, and this time when the fear rose up, I squeezed his hands. He squeezed back.

"What do you hear?" he asked, repeating what I'd once asked him when I was teaching him some survival skills I knew. The first thing to learn was how to tune into your senses so you could be aware of what was around you. It was something that at one point had come naturally to me.

I listened intently. At first, all I heard was a light buzzing in my ears, the pounding of my heart, the raggedness of my breath. But as the minutes ticked by, my heart calmed to a steady beat, my breath evened out, the buzzing in my ears receded. Tension began leaving my body, and as it passed, my sense of hearing improved.

"I hear the breeze rattling some leaves still clinging to a branch somewhere close by. I can hear a small animal... a squirrel, I think. I can hear it's claws on the bark of a tree. And a little further away, maybe a deer crunching through the snow. I can also hear the crackle of ice breaking apart as it melts. And I can hear *you*—I can hear your breathing, steady and slow."

"Good, Nina," he said, his voice husky and soothing. "And what can you smell?"

I took another moment and concentrated on what my nose could detect in the air. "I smell leaf rot and mold or mildew, I think. I can smell sassafras bark, and I can definitely smell a cedar somewhere nearby. There's a dead animal, too—not close, but I can smell it." I inhaled again through my nose. "And I can smell you. Your skin and your shampoo."

He squeezed my hands. "Okay. And what can you feel?"

"I feel the cold air, but there's like a buffer of warmth from our bodies between me and that air. Thin, but I can feel it. I can feel the silkiness of my new long johns against my skin, and that lofty softness of my thick socks. I can feel the ground beneath my feet and the trees on either side of me. I can feel the warmth of your hands, and I can feel your gaze on my face right now. I can feel that you're focused on me. I can feel that you care about me."

"Good, Nina," he said again after I heard him swallow. "Very good." He shifted to slide his fingers between mine, holding them up between us, and squeezed. "Okay. Now open your eyes and tell me again what you see."

I blinked as my eyes refocused and I looked around. I knew nothing had changed, but it looked vastly different. "I can see the dark streaks through the lighter bark on that oak tree there where the meltwater is making its way down to the ground, and scratches from a buck on the one next to it. I can see that there are maples and rhododendrons and some white pine and cedars around us. There's pristine snow, broken by water drops, and rabbit and deer and squirrel tracks, and bits of dead shrub branches. I can see white, fluffy clouds in an electric, robin's-egg blue sky. God, it's the bluest sky I've ever seen, I think."

I admired the sky for a while, distracted by the beauty I'd been missing earlier. My eyes drifted down over the treetops until they came to rest locked with Myles'. As always, there was so much emotion there, his heart so easy to read. It felt like coming home after a long trip. "I see you, Myles. I see the softness at the corners of your eyes and around your mouth that you get when you're listening attentively. I see... *you.*"

He lifted a hand and cupped my face, his thumb running along my cheek. His palm felt warm against my cold skin, and I shivered. We stood like that for a while, just looking into each other's eyes. It felt so intimate I almost looked away a few times, but I didn't. And the longer we stood that way, the more connected to him and myself I felt.

"You taught me to do that a long time ago, Nina," he said, his voice deep and crackly. He cleared his throat and continued. "The first and most important survival skill is to be aware of everything around you, to be able to use your senses to their full potential, right? Those are skills for all kinds of survival, Nina—not just for staying alive in the woods. Using your senses will help you stay alive in your life."

I gave another nod, teary again, but this time because I was grateful, and I felt hope in my chest again. "Thank you," I whispered, barely a sound slipping between my lips.

His mouth softened, and his hand drifted from my cheek. Slowly, reluctantly, we separated our clasped hands, put our gloves back on, and continued our hike.

"Mmmm," Myles groaned dramatically, chewing, then swallowed. "I still make the best damn peanut butter sandwiches."

I chuckled. "Yup," I agreed. He did, although he preferred peanut butter and jelly, while my favorite was peanut butter, banana, and honey. And he'd made both for us to have for lunch on the trail. "Mine is better than yours," I said, my voice a little muffled from the peanut butter.

"No way," he said, pointing at his sandwich. "Hands down, you can't beat strawberry preserves."

"With bananas and honey, you can," I countered.

"I'm sorry, I can't understand you," he said, his mouth pulling in as he tried not to laugh. "So whatever you're saying must not be true."

I snorted and bumped him with my shoulder. "It's the peanut butter," I said.

"I'm sorry, did you say something?" He laughed.

I laughed, too. "You know, you used to call me obnoxious, but I think you're the obnoxious one."

"Oh, you're absolutely right that I'm the most amazing one of the two of us."

It took me a minute to finish my last bite around my laughter, then I took a swig of water, swishing it around in my mouth before swallowing to clear some of the peanut butter. I glanced askance at him.

"So amazing you have food in that scruff on your face."

"Hey, it's not scruff," he said as I reached out and swiped a jammy strawberry from his beard. "I was wondering where that went," he added, grabbing my hand and sucking the strawberry from my fingers.

The skin on my face went from nearly uncomfortably cold to hot in an instant, and I averted my eyes. I felt what Myles had done throughout my whole body. My mind flashed back to the hike I'd dreamed about, and I tried to force the memory away. I shouldn't have been thinking about that day at all, but especially not while I was out on a hike with him again.

"Nina," he said, his voice deepening again, his hand on my face. I closed my eyes for a second. When I opened them, he was watching me intently. His eyes were bright and earnest. "In all seriousness. I don't have a girlfriend." His thumb stroked my jaw. "Tell me you don't have a boyfriend."

I looked away and pulled back, tearing up again. I wished I could tell him that I didn't, as unfair as that was to Landon.

"At least tell me it isn't serious," he said a minute later.

My breathing stalled. "I don't know."

"How do you not know?"

"It's... complicated."

"How long have you been dating him?" he asked. His voice was thin and strained.

I couldn't look at him; I knew I'd see hurt and couldn't stomach knowing I was the cause. "Three and a half years."

"Jesus," he muttered. "Fuck." He put away the rest of his food, wiped his hands together, then leaned forward with his elbows on his knees, his hands clasped, staring into the distance at the small valley we had a clear view of from the log we were sitting on at the hike's summit.

My appetite disappeared as well, and I packed up my food and stood. My ass was numb and stiff from sitting on the log for so long. "Ready?" I asked quietly.

He tipped his chin down and stood without saying anything.

We hiked for a long time before anyone spoke, the ease between us replaced by an uncomfortable tension. Myles was the one to break it.

"You've been dating this guy for over three years, but you don't know if it's serious, and you're here with *me* right now—you even spent the night in my house last night. I mean... is he hurting you? Is he abusive?"

"No," I replied. "He's not abusive. He's just... he's not... I mean..." I was struggling to come up with a way to describe Landon and our relationship, but I couldn't. "This isn't stuff I can talk to him about. I tried. It's not that he's—"

"Nina," Myles interrupted. "Please. If he's not hurting you, I don't want to talk about your boyfriend." He sighed heavily. "I'm not sure if I can do the strictly friends thing or not, honestly, but I'll try. You can't talk to me about your boyfriend, though. I can't..." His body shuddered. "I can't do that. I want you to tell me if he ever hurts you, but otherwise..."

"I understand. I'm sorry, Myles."

We hiked another twenty or thirty feet before he responded. "Me, too, Nina."

"Are you sure you shouldn't go home?" Myles asked after we'd been in the car for a while. He glanced over before returning his attention to the road.

"No," I said in a quiet voice. "I know I should. I should have gone home much earlier, actually. Hell, I shouldn't have even gone to your school," I added in a murmur.

"But you did." He sighed. "And you haven't even talked to your boyfriend since you did, either."

"We don't have that kind of relationship," I replied, staring at my hands as they squeezed together in my lap. I'd heard the thinly veiled disgust when he said "boyfriend."

"The kind where you talk to each other?"

"I mean..." I shrugged. It sounded bad the way Myles put it, but it was also fairly accurate. "His job is demanding. So is mine. And he travels for work a lot, too—he's out of town for weeks at a time."

Myles ran a hand over his face, muttering something unintelligible, pulling into his driveway and shifting into park. I could feel his gaze on me, but didn't look up. I was embarrassed about how he saw my relationship with Landon, embarrassed that I had a boyfriend to begin with. As strange as it was, it felt like dating Landon was somehow wronging Myles, as if I were cheating on him. Myles' fingers tapped on the steering wheel, then he shifted in his seat to face me, his fingers lifting my chin until I was looking at him.

"You deserve better."

"He's not a bad guy, Myles," I said in a barely audible voice, defending Landon.

"You still deserve better, Nina."

I lowered my eyes, unable to keep eye contact, and he sighed again, withdrawing his hand.

"Are you staying or going?" he asked, resuming the tapping on the steering wheel. "If you want to go, I'll drive you home."

"I'll go home," I said, despite the fact that everything in me longed to stay.

"That's what you want?"

"No," I whispered. "But it's what I *should* do."

"Maybe," he responded after several seconds had crawled past. "But it's not what *I* want, either." He pushed a button on the dash and the car turned off. "Come on—let's go figure out what we're making for dinner."

After scouring his pantry and fridge, we decided on baked chicken and broccoli with potato wedges. One pan meals were Myles' favorite if he was in the kitchen. After sliding the pan into the oven and setting a timer, he turned to me, mischief in his eyes. We were facing each other, me leaning back against the kitchen island with my arms crossed, him doing the same against the counter next to the oven.

"So, being in a middle school, I'm learning a lot. You wouldn't believe the things these kids teach me."

"Really?"

He laughed. "Yeah, totally serious about that."

"Like what?"

"Like, did you know that by the time you turn twelve, knock-knock jokes are no longer funny?"

I giggled.

"It's fact," Myles said, holding up his hands. "One day it makes them laugh, and then the next, they just roll their eyes. I test it often."

I burst out laughing. "You don't."

"Of course I do," he said, chuckling. "I'm studious, too, remember? I have to test my hypothesis. I need plenty of samples."

"Oh my god, those poor kids."

"The *kids*? I'm the one standing there laughing alone."

I looked at him and snorted, trying not to laugh again.

"I also learned a new game. It's a bit sadistic—right up your alley."

I giggled.

He reached out and grabbed my hands, uncrossing my arms. "Hold your hands out flat, palms down between us."

I did as he instructed, then he held his hands out flat, palms up, so our hands were suspended between us, barely touching. I steadfastly ignored the speeding of my heart and tingling shooting up my arms.

"Okay," he said after sucking in a sharp breath. "So, the game is called slaps. I'm going to try to slap your hand. You need to move it before I do, but you can't move until I make an actual attempt. If you do, I get a free slap and we reset. If I try to slap you and miss, we switch and *you* get to try to smack *me*."

I laughed. "You've never played slaps before?"

He squinted at me. "Of course I have. I learned this game months ago."

"You seriously never played before that?"

He shook his head.

"I played this all the time when I was kid. I'm going to destroy you," I giggled. "You're going down, Mr. E."

He hmphed. "We'll see about that. Ready?"

I focused my attention on his hands. "Ready." The second the word was off my lips, he'd smacked my hand. "Shit," I laughed. "I wasn't ready."

"But you said you were!"

"I know. I was ready to play, but I wasn't ready for you to be that damn fast."

"Middle schoolers *really* like this game," he said with a chuckle. "I've had a lot of practice."

I shook out my arms and blew out a slow breath, centering myself, then replaced my hands over his. "Okay. This time I mean it. Ready."

He moved and I jerked my hand back, except that his movement had been tiny—a flinch to fake me out. *Damn it.* Already wincing, I held my hand out and he smacked it, grinning shamelessly.

"That's two," he said.

"Oh my god, Myles—you're keeping count?"

"Naturally. I need to know exactly how bad I kick your ass in this game."

I groaned and reset. "Ready."

Smack.

"Three."

I bit my cheeks and reset. "Ready."

Smack.

"Damn it, you're fast!" I laughed, shaking my hand out.

"I told you," he said, smirking. "Four."

"That's obnoxious—stop counting!" I narrowed my eyes, trying not to laugh. I shimmied a little with my eyes closed, opened them, and reset. "Ready."

Smack.

"Don't do it," I said, shaking my hand again. I saw his mouth shift. "Don't," I repeated.

"Five," he said, the corners of his mouth pulled in as he over-emphasized the word.

I walked over to the cabinet I'd seen him pull a glass out of that morning and grabbed one out. Once it was filled with water, I took a few sips, then set it on the counter and reset, my eyes boring into his.

"Ready."

His hand, still lightning fast, flipped, but this time I was faster, and he smacked air.

"Ha-ha!" I shouted.

He was smiling now, his eyes dark and intense as he tilted his head down. His hands were already set on top. I slipped mine underneath.

"Ready?" I asked.

"Always," he replied.

I stared into his eyes, letting the seconds tick past. That had always been my strategy: distraction. Either by letting time pass or by carrying on a conversation. But my body was buzzing and my heart doing somersaults in my chest—I couldn't think clearly enough for conversation right then. Then, in the middle of an in-breath, I flipped my hand over and smacked the top of his. He jerked it back, but he was too slow. We reset. Apparently, I'd just needed to warm up and jog my muscle memory because, slap after slap, I was getting him.

"Hey, Myles," I said casually, resetting after another slap I'd won. "That makes six. And correct me if I'm wrong—you're the teacher, here—but I'm fairly sure that's more than five."

His body shook as he tried, unsuccessfully, to hold in his laughter. "And you told me *I'm* obnoxious."

I shrugged. "It's okay if you want to call it quits now while some of your dignity is still intact."

"Woman," he growled out in warning.

I smirked and quirked an eyebrow.

"You're going down," he said in a voice that made my breath stutter.

"Good luck," I replied airily. I flipped my hand, quick, nailing my target again. "That's seven, Myles."

By the time I reached ten, I was laughing so hard I couldn't get reset again as Myles shook out his hands, the backs of which were now a nice, robust crimson. He was glaring at me, his mouth pulled in tight as he tried desperately not to laugh with me, which just made me laugh even harder.

The next thing I knew, Myles was there, the space between us having disappeared, his hands grasping my head as he held our faces together. The light laughter disappeared, and I couldn't breathe. I could feel Myles' chest heaving against mine. If I shifted just the tiniest distance, our lips would be touching like our foreheads and noses and bodies now were. I knew I couldn't kiss Myles because I had a boyfriend, so I didn't shift, but I didn't pull away, either. And I didn't know what I'd do if Myles was the one to shift. I wanted to think I wouldn't kiss him back, but I wasn't sure that was true because I wanted to kiss him more than I wanted to breathe right then.

Myles pressed our faces together more firmly before releasing me and stepping back. "Jesus, Nina," he muttered, running a hand over his hair, his eyes raking over me.

I should have been running for the door after that—I'd come too close to doing something I shouldn't—but all I could do was hold Myles' intense, heated gaze, feeling it run throughout my body.

I blushed and bit my lip.

He smirked.

I grinned.

TEN

Myles dropped me off outside Landon's condo on Sunday evening after a weekend full of more laughter, talking, music, and, of course, crying. We vacillated between comfortable and relaxed with one another and thick tension when it felt we were in college and navigating a new relationship all over again. All in all, it was the most amazing weekend I'd had since the last one I'd spent with him when we were in college, and I dreaded the return to real life. Stepping out of his car, I could feel a heaviness weigh me down, and my customary frown took over. By the time I stepped into the entryway of Landon's condo, I felt a bit nauseous. I wanted to run back out the door and into Myles' car.

But I didn't. Instead, I changed into pajamas, made a pot of coffee, and booted up my laptop.

Many hours later, my eyes burned, I felt nearly drunk from exhaustion, and the sun would be rising soon, but I was mostly caught up from playing hooky. Mostly—it would be an exceedingly long day or two to get there the rest of the way, but I was closer than I'd expected I would be at this point.

I stood, stretched, and put on another pot of coffee to brew while I hopped in the shower. As the water beat down on my back, I thought about what Myles had said about knowing me. Collectively, I'd known him only a tiny fraction of the time I'd known Landon, and yet there was no question I knew him better than I knew Landon, and that he both knew *and* understood me in ways Landon didn't. And likely never would because he didn't seem to care or even want to.

Maybe I'm being unfair. Maybe he would care to and it's just that I've never given him a chance or tried. It's not like I know that much more about him than he knows about me.

But it wasn't Landon I wanted to know more about—it was Myles. It wasn't Landon I wanted to bare my soul to—it was Myles. Every feeling I'd had for him before I walked away from him was still there as strong as ever. Maybe even stronger. I'd been so sure they were gone, but evidently they'd just been hidden. And they no longer were. Which apparently meant no other feelings were hidden anymore, either.

When I got out of the shower, I stood for a minute, looking at my long, dripping hair. I'd discovered at Myles' house, where I'd had no brush or hair dryer, that when left alone, my hair was the curliest it had ever been. Myles had called it beautiful. When I'd known him before, that's what I'd thought, too.

I pulled a section over my shoulder and scrunched it up in my palm, squeezing out the excess water. When I released it, it was beginning to coil and fell inches higher on my body than the rest of my hair. The idea of straightening it—of forcing it to be something it wasn't—felt like an analogy for my life after a weekend immersed in all the things that used to define who I was and wanted to be.

But this was the life I lived now, like it or not. It was too late to be something different... to be some*one* different. So, I pulled out my hair dryer and my brush and got to work creating sleek, smooth hair I'd pull back into a bun. With hair done and clothes on, I poured coffee into a travel mug, took some Advil for the headache that had returned, and packed up my bag. With a last glance around, I headed out the door.

When I approached my office building, my phone vibrated—an email about something that could wait until I'd reached my office in five minutes, I was sure, but I pulled it out to look anyway. To my surprise, it was a text message from Myles.

Good morning, sunshine. Remember
your survival skills and have a good day.
If my students allow me to live through
the telling of another knock-knock joke I
found this morning, maybe we should
have dinner. You know, to celebrate that
I survived their death stares.

I giggled, shaking my head and grinning as I stepped onto the elevator. I looked up from my phone screen just long enough to push the button for my floor. I loved that he'd called me sunshine, the nickname he'd given me the week after I'd met him. I'd given an impromptu and heated lecture to a group of college kids who'd tossed some wrappers and Styrofoam cups toward a garbage can without waiting long enough to see it all miss entirely and hit the ground. Myles had called me "a veritable bucket of sunshine" and it had stuck.

Hm. Not sure they will. What's the joke?

Knock, knock.

Who's there?

Britney Spears.

Britney Spears who?

Knock, knock.

Who's there?

Britney Spears.
Britney Spears who?

Oops, I did it again.

I burst out laughing outside my office door, then clapped my hand over my mouth. Not that there were that many people in the office that early, but still.

> Myles. They're going to destroy you.
> There won't be anything left. That has
> got to be the absolute worst knock-
> knock joke on the planet.

Did you laugh?

> Yes, but not because it was funny.
> Because it was so bad.

Well, the kids will laugh, too, then. Since
we both know you have a juvenile sense
of humor.

> Says the 32-year-old man telling knock-
> knock jokes. And bad ones, at that.

That's why I'm Mr. E, the cool music
teacher. That and because I've picked up
on their slang and make sure to use it at
every opportunity so I fit in.

I groaned, then giggled as I plopped into my desk chair, dropping my bag unceremoniously onto the floor, forgotten.

> God, no. Don't do that.

Why not? They low-key love me, cuz I'm
savage, not sussy.

> Oh my god, Myles. Just NO. Please tell
> me you don't talk like that in class.

Not ALL the time, obviously... So are we
on for dinner? I'll look snatched.

I don't know... because I have no idea
what the words you just said mean.

Come to dinner and you'll find out. ;)

FINE. You pick a place and let me know
where to go. I have to get to work now.
Thanks for the laugh.

:) You're welcome.

And no slang at dinner.

No promises.

My cheeks ached as I reluctantly closed my phone screen. It was going to be a very long day waiting until I could meet Myles for dinner, but this was the best mood I'd ever been in to start my workday, in spite of running extraordinarily low on sleep.

Maybe I should start every day with a conversation with Myles.

I was yawning as I stepped in the front doors of the tapas bar I was meeting Myles at for dinner. Concern flickered in his eyes as he grinned at me, stepping forward and kissing my cheek as he held my shoulders. My entire body relaxed, and I felt even sleepier. With my eyes closed, I sighed into the contact.

"You look tired," he said, his face still close. Even so, it was hard to hear him; the restaurant was *busy*.

I yawned again, then laughed. "I am. That's what happens when you don't sleep."

"You didn't sleep at all?"

"I had a lot of work to get caught up on after spending the weekend with you."

"That seems crazy."

"That's just my job," I shrugged. "I haven't taken a weekend off like that since I started it a few years ago, and this is why. I stayed up all night to get caught up. And I'm still not there, but I'm closer."

"Jeez, Nina," he said. "If I'd known, I never would have suggested dinner. We can do this another time. You should go home and sleep."

My mouth pulled into a soft smile. "You're thoughtful, but I have more work to do before bed anyway. Besides, I could have said no, but I didn't want to."

Once we were seated and had ordered drinks—bourbon, of course—and our selection of tapas to share, conversation resumed.

"So, it looks like you survived unscathed despite your ill-advised decision to tell that joke to a room full of middle schoolers."

He chuckled. "Barely. Eighth-graders are a tough crowd."

"How'd you manage it?"

"Well, they weren't impressed and told me I'd never get a girl if I didn't improve my game. So I told them they were wrong, that my game was just fine, because I was having dinner with the smartest and prettiest girl in the city."

I snorted, almost spitting out my bourbon as the waiter arrived with our food. I waited until he walked away before speaking. "You didn't."

"Of course I did. Only they didn't believe me."

I quirked an eyebrow.

"They insisted I bring proof to class on Wednesday. I have to bring a picture of us together."

"Myles, your credibility is going to be shot."

"Are you kidding me? Sunshine, I'm about to be the envy of the school. Rather than Mr. E, they're going to call me Mr. Savage."

I slammed my hand to my mouth to keep the contents in. *Maybe I should just give up trying to eat and drink for the evening.*

Myles' eyes sparkled as he laughed, too. "I'm kidding about them calling me Mr. Savage. I suggested it and called for a vote by show of hands, but everyone's arms must have been sore from gym because not one went up."

He shrugged.

I giggled.

He told me more about his day, and I learned a lot about how his classes were structured and how they related to the extracurriculars he was in charge of. As usual when he talked about something he was passionate about, he was lively, animated, and I could have sat there for hours longer, just listening and watching. It was enthralling and his excitement for life was infectious.

After the bill was paid and he'd wrapped an arm around me for a picture of us taken with his phone, he helped me into my jacket, but we lingered just outside the entrance. We needed to go separate ways, me to get home, and him to get back to the school where he'd left his car.

"Since I spent the whole evening talking about myself... should we do this again so I can hear more about how you spend your days?"

"Oh, my life is boring. I'd much rather hear about you."

"Told you I was savage."

I bit my cheeks.

"Is that a yes for dinner, then?"

"When?"

"Thursday, for starters."

I blushed, smiling. "Okay."

"Your pick this time."

"Alright. Though I'm not sure I can top this place. The only restaurants I've been to are expensive, but the food kinda sucks, honestly."

"You just need to look a little harder. This city is full of great restaurants."

"Why don't you just send me a list to choose from and I'll pick one of those?"

He looked appalled. "If I did that, how would I wow you the next time *I* pick?"

"Okay, okay, I'll pick on my own."

We both sighed at the same time and our eyes locked as we laughed, shuffling our feet and shifting our weight. Neither of us wanted to leave. The whole evening had been so natural and fun, and now—in the brisk air, streetlights and storefronts illuminated and creating a romantic haze along the street—it felt like I was in a different world. Living the life I might have had if that one night hadn't happened.

I yawned again, out of nowhere.

Myles smiled, even with his brows falling in. "You need to go. If I asked you to please go home and skip working to sleep... would you?"

"Probably not." I yawned again and my eyelids drooped after this one. I felt like I might fall over. "Well... maybe."

He stepped forward and grasped my arms, his eyes searching mine. "Please, Nina? For me?"

I studied his face, the worry clouding his eyes. "Okay. I will. For you."

"Promise?"

I yawned again and laughed lightly. "I promise. I might not even make it to my bed before I fall over asleep."

"Can I go with you, then? Make sure you get home safely without falling asleep walking or in the cab?" His hands smoothed up and down my arms as he spoke.

The thought of Myles at the door to Landon's condo made me quail. "No, I don't think that's a good idea. I'll be fine."

His face hardened. "Why? Is *he* there in your apartment? Right now?"

"N-no," I replied, a little surprised by his question as well as his demeanor. "He's out of town right now." I paused. "I thought you didn't want to talk about... him." I'd almost said "my boyfriend," but the words stuck in my throat.

Myles lifted a hand and pulled it down his face. "I don't. I just don't like thinking about you going home to him."

"You don't know him. You don't even know who 'he' is."

"It doesn't matter who it is, Nina. I don't like him, and I don't like you with him." He looked away and sighed. "I'm struggling a bit with this... friendship... between us," he said, his voice quiet and serious. "That's not *your* problem—it's *mine*—but the bottom line is that this is really hard for me. Maybe the hardest damn thing I've done in my life."

"It is for me, too," I replied softly. I wanted him to know he wasn't alone.

He tugged me into his arms, folding me into his chest, our cheeks connected. "Then leave him, Nina," he whispered into my ear. "For the love of god, leave him." He touched his lips to my cheek just in front of my ear, lingering for several breaths. "Leave him and take a chance on *us*—a chance on *me*—instead."

My eyes swam, and between Myles' emotion and my own emotion and exhaustion, I couldn't organize my thoughts and I felt sick. "I need to think, Myles," I whispered back. "I need sleep first. I'm so tired, I can't think straight."

He kissed my cheekbone. "Okay, Nina."

He kissed my cheekbone again, then the top of my forehead. He took half a step back, then rushed forward, taking my face in his hands and pressing his lips to mine. *Hard.* By the time it registered what was happening, he'd stepped back and was running a hand through his hair. My fingers rested against my lips, which continued to tingle as if he were still kissing me, and I stared at him, my heart pounding, my body hot, and my mind racing.

"I..." he began, then swallowed. "I'll go now. Goodnight, Nina."

I watched him rush away in the opposite direction, speechless. In a daze, I caught a cab home and got ready for bed, then stared at the messages from Myles on my phone from a few minutes after he'd rushed off.

Let me know you made it home safely.

I'm sorry if I made things complicated for you, but I'm NOT sorry I kissed you. I've been wanting to since the last time I kissed you years ago.

Unless you really didn't want me to. I don't think that's the case or I wouldn't

have done it—I never want to make you
do something you don't want to. Then I'd
be sorry I kissed you. But only then.

I'll try not to do it again. But unless you
tell me you don't want me to, I can't
promise I won't.

My phone screen went dark while I was still staring at his message. I couldn't sort out all the ways it made me feel. I was excited, aroused, happy. I felt a tremendous amount of shame and fear—of what exactly, I had no idea. And when I thought of Landon, I was filled with guilt—choking on it.

Technically, nothing between Myles and me had crossed a line—at least not physically—until he'd kissed me. And while I hadn't kissed him back because it was over before I registered what was happening, I knew if it had lasted any longer, I very well might have.

I didn't.

But I might have.

Because I wanted to.

There was no doubt about that.

What I wasn't certain about, however, was: should I tell Landon? Or leave him?

ELEVEN

Waking the next morning was strange. I was relatively well-rested and came to consciousness with a smile on my face. After reaching over to turn off my alarm, I rolled onto my back and closed my eyes, trying to return to my dreams. They were already slipping away; I only knew they had involved Myles and that they were good dreams. Happy ones. I sighed, still smiling, and rose out of bed. When my eyes landed on a picture of Landon and me on a table, my smile disappeared. I'd forgotten my dilemma until right then.

I showered quickly, then turned on the news while I was brewing a pot of coffee to get some highlights before heading into the office. As I half listened to the news, I checked my bag for work and opened up emails on my phone.

"... in Marksburg a week after the story broke..."

My hand with my phone floated downward, and I turned up the volume on the television.

"...many want to know what this woman was doing in an alley alone at night."

"Well, Jeff, in the latest statement, remember, she states she was *passing* the alley, but she wasn't already in it."

"And that's another thing—how can we trust what happened when the alleged victim's story has changed important details during the course of the investigation?"

"Obviously *something* happened—the girl was in the hospital for over a week, but the question is why."

"For hitting her head. But she admits she'd been drinking, so she could have done that herself, which brings in the question of a revenge accusation. And if she didn't, the question is why was she wearing so little clothing in the middle of winter?"

My phone clattered to the floor, startling me out of my stupor. My hands and armpits were sweating profusely, my heart racing. I felt like I was looking through a tunnel... I felt like I had that night. My eyes shot back over my shoulder, then I thought I heard something in the next room and whimpered, jumping. Was someone in the condo?

"Hello?" I called, my voice trembling as violently as my body was. "Is someone there?"

There was no response—in fact, I could hear nothing over the television, which had moved onto the next news story. *Get a grip, Nina. There's an alarm system here—no one can get in without you knowing about it. You're hearing things.* But I didn't *feel* like I was hearing things. I felt like I was in mortal danger, and I didn't know what to do.

Snatching up my phone from the floor, I clicked "call" without thinking. The line rang and rang, then a voicemail picked up. I hung up, then dialed again, tears now streaming down my face as my eyes rushed around in constant vigilance.

"Hello? Nina?" Myles' voice was scratchy with sleep.

"Myles!" I said, wiping my eyes with the heel of my hand.

"Nina? What's wrong?" His voice was more alert now, tense with worry.

"I don't know, Myles. I think there's someone here, but I don't know how there could be, but I'm so scared right now and I didn't know what else to do so I called you but then you didn't answer and I—"

"Shh, I'm here now. I need you to slow down—I'm having a hard time understanding you."

"Please, Myles," I begged, without knowing what for.

"What's going on, Nina? Where are you?"

"I'm at home. I think there might be someone here, Myles."

"Are you safe right now?"

I heard sounds in the background coming from my phone as I scanned around me. "I don't know. I'm kind of between the living room and the kitchen."

"Where did you hear someone?"

"From everywhere—all around me."

"Nina, I need you to tell me exactly what's going on."

"I was watching the news and making coffee and they started talking about that woman in Marksburg and then I heard someone and I got scared. It's just like that night, Myles, right before he grabbed me. It's the same thing."

Myles sighed heavily over the line. "Nina," he said, his voice low and soothing. "Breathe, alright? Slow, full breaths."

I complied the best I could when I was still freaked out.

"You're safe right now."

"No, I'm not, Myles, I can feel it, I'm—"

"Nina! Listen to me, okay? It's because of the news. It's not happening again, alright? Your building—it probably has some sort of security, right?"

"Yeah, it does. And so does the condo."

"Okay, good. Can you go to the control panel and make sure everything is set?"

I walked, checking over my shoulder repeatedly, to the entryway where the closest control panel for the alarm system was on the wall. "It's set and nothing has been tripped."

"See? You're safe, Nina. No one's there."

I nodded as I listened to his reassurances, forgetting he couldn't see me, and trying to make myself believe them. Little by little, the panic was beginning to fade. As it did, embarrassment set in. "I'm sorry, Myles. I just woke you up because I was so stupidly freaking out—"

"It's not stupid, Nina. It's called a panic attack. The news set it off."

"How do you know that?"

"Because I used to have them a lot, too."

"Why is this happening?" I mumbled to myself, beginning to pace. "I've been fine for years. Years! I haven't had something like this happen in so long. Why now?"

"Do you have a therapist, Nina?"

"Why do you keep asking me about therapy?"

"Because this isn't something you should be trying to deal with alone."

"How would *you* know about that? It didn't happen to *you*," I bit out. My pacing picked up in speed.

"No, it didn't. I only interrupted it. And what I saw happening to you before I was able to stop it? What I knew already happened because I hadn't prevented it? What happened to you when I startled that guy? That was all enough that I was in therapy for years."

I swallowed, feeling a stab of guilt for yelling at him, the only person who had any understanding of what I was going through. "This isn't stuff I can talk about with anyone, Myles."

"You're talking about it with *me* right now, Nina."

"That's different. Because you already know what happened—I don't have to say that stuff. And I trust you."

"You'll build up trust over time with a therapist, too."

"I'll think about it. I just feel pathetic for needing one. Shouldn't I be over it by now? If I didn't need one before, how the hell do I need one now? I just need to get focused again on other things and stay away from the news for a while."

"Staying away from the news for a while might not be a bad idea, but, Nina, if you bury it all again, it's just going to keep coming back. It's not pathetic to need help, either. What happened to you was horrible. It would be crazy to *not* need some help afterward."

"It's this news," I said a minute later, thinking about what I'd heard. "Have you seen it? It's bullshit and it makes me want to throw the television out the window. She was fucking raped, Myles, and nearly *died*, and they're talking about what she was wearing and whether or not she was drinking and the fact that some of her memory was hazy. Of course it was! She was terrified!"

"I know, Nina," Myles said in his soothing voice.

"I'm sorry I'm yelling," I practically screamed. "It just makes me so fucking angry!"

"I know," he said again. "None of those things matter, you're right. They're intimating that she was asking for it, but no one asks to be raped."

"No, they don't! So why are they trying to make it look like it's *her* fault that some guy assaulted her?"

"I don't know, Nina. Our world isn't perfect. There are people out there who hurt other people, like that guy. There are people who judge anyone who's different than them, people who think they're better than everyone else. People who abuse their kids or their spouses. There's a lack of compassion for other people. People are afraid of things they don't understand. Maybe it makes them feel better or safer to do that. I don't know. All we can do is live what we believe in and hope it makes a difference in the lives of the people we meet."

I sighed, some of my anger dissipating. "That sounds familiar." But where had I heard it before?

"It should—*you're* the one who said it. You told me that years ago."

"Back when I was delusionally optimistic and thought I could actually make a real difference—when I was young and stupid. And didn't understand how the real world works."

"No. The real world is what you make it, Nina. That's in your control."

I balked. "No, it's not! How can you actually believe something like that after what happened to me? To that woman? I mean, you teach underprivileged kids, Myles! Kids that come from some of the worst living situations in our country. They can't just make things better than they are."

There was silence before Myles responded, and I waited impatiently. I was aggravated and anxious because I'd never felt so disconnected during a conversation with him before, but we might as well have been on different planets right then. That realization was simultaneously frustrating and depressing. I felt more alone than I had before I'd run into Myles after the Lorman event.

"Do you remember why I wanted to teach music to underprivileged kids specifically? Do you remember me explaining that to you the night we met while we were sitting in that tiny booth in Nina's?"

"Yes. You said because it would give them something good to grasp onto. Music was an outlet for you growing up in poverty, and in some ways you said it saved your life. You wanted to give that to other kids who were struggling."

"Right. Because having that something changes the way you see the future. You realize there are possibilities when you thought you had none. No matter what, the only thing guaranteed not to happen is what we tell ourselves can't be done. So, changing what you tell yourself changes your reality. Just seeing an opportunity or having hope when you didn't before is changing your reality. Two people can look at an instrument, and one sees something they don't know how to play, while the other sees something they can learn how to play. Which one do you think is going to be happier in life? Go further? Be more fulfilled, regardless of what else is happening in their lives?"

My eyes scanned the wall absently as Myles' words sank in. I understood what he meant, and at one point I'd wholeheartedly believed in it—it shaped my entire worldview, just as it still did his. But I was struggling to see how it could apply to something like what I'd been through.

"Are you gonna be alright if I get off the phone?" he asked gently after a nearly ten-minute-long silence. "I need to get ready for work."

"Yeah. I'll be fine. I'm sorry I called and woke you up."

"I'm not, Nina. I'm glad. You needed help and you asked for it as opposed to keeping it to yourself. That's a big deal. And I'm glad you trusted me enough for *me* to be that person for you."

TWELVE

The rest of that week saw a number of urgent conversations much like that first one early Tuesday morning. I couldn't stop thinking about the woman from Marksburg, so I also couldn't stay off the news. The result was waking terrified in the middle of the night and flying into sudden rages, and Myles was on the receiving end of all of it. No matter what, though, he was calm and reassuring, helping me to find a more balanced state by the time we hung up, just as he had the first time.

Even so, by Thursday, I felt my sanity was rapidly deteriorating. My mood was all over the place, I couldn't really focus on work at all, and the only thing I could think about was either the woman from Marksburg or seeing Myles again.

I was hopeful that having dinner with him Thursday evening would help me to recalibrate myself so I wouldn't feel so helpless and out of control. Before, when it had happened, Myles was the only way I felt safe and normal. The problem had been that he also kept me from being able to turn off everything I felt, and I'd needed to be able to do that. I refused to think about needing that to happen a second time, though; I couldn't contemplate a life without him in it again. I wouldn't have managed the last few days without him.

Despite the emotional rollercoaster of the week, I was breathless and excited as I rushed toward the restaurant. As soon as I turned a corner and saw Myles standing outside, my mouth stretched into a broad grin. I saw him first, scanning the sidewalk in the other direction, and watched when he turned to continue scanning the side I was approaching from. He looked relaxed, but then his features lit up, an answering grin stretched across his face, and his eyes brightened.

With one smile from him, the heaviness from the week vanished and my concerns over losing my mind melted away. Everything was right now. Everything again made sense. I knew that everything would be okay, somehow, because Myles was there. Just looking into his eyes, seeing his excitement to see me, was enough to make the ground feel solid and stable again. How the hell he did that, I didn't know. And right then, I didn't care.

He met me two storefronts down, wrapping me in his arms without any hesitation, so tightly my toes barely touched the ground. I hugged him back with equal fervor, inhaling his spicy, sweet smell and relaxing into the embrace. God, it was good to see him. As we pulled apart, he placed a lingering kiss to the corner of my mouth—not exactly my lips, but not exactly my cheek, either.

I blushed. It felt like there was helium in my chest as Myles slipped an arm around my lower back and we made our way into the restaurant.

We'd finished eating, the time having flown by as Myles regaled me with more of his adventures as a middle school music teacher. My cheeks and sides ached, and I dreaded having to leave. Instead, we ordered another drink to postpone the inevitable.

"I had a great time again tonight," he said when we left at last. We were meandering down the street toward my condo, which was walking distance this time.

"So did I." I looked up at him and grinned.

"How about my place tomorrow? I can pick you up from your office whenever you're done. And I found this nature conservancy about three hours from here that is apparently renowned for its winter wildlife. They have a lodge and cabins, so we could spend the whole weekend there. I checked and they have availability. We could leave Saturday morning. Or after dinner tomorrow if you wanted. Or even before. I can pick you up as early as three thirty or four, depending on traffic. What do you think?"

I bit my lip. I'd have to pull another all-nighter on Sunday to get caught up from not working all weekend, but it would be worth it. "That sounds amazing."

"How early can you leave tomorrow?"

I tucked my hand into my purse. "Let me check my calendar to see if I have any meetings in the afternoon." Pulling my arm from his, I typed in my password and clicked to open my calendar application.

My feet stopped.

My heart stopped.

My breath stopped.

I was vaguely aware that Myles stopped next to me, but my eyes were locked on my phone's screen and the reminder that this—what I was doing right then—wasn't my real life. My real life returned the next day on a plane from Denver, and I was meeting him for dinner.

"I can't," I whispered.

Myles' face crumpled.

"I'm sorry," I added. "Landon comes home tomorrow."

His features now hardened. "Fuck h—wait—did you say Landon?"

I moved my head very slightly in the affirmative.

"And you were at the Lorman merger announcement," his words rushed out, his eyes scanning the ground before jerking back up to mine. "Your boyfriend is Landon Jones?"

"Yes," I breathed out.

"The rich asshole whose father's company just merged with Marcus'?"

"He's not an asshole," I defended Landon.

"You're seriously dating that guy?" He was incredulous. "He *is* an asshole, Nina. How the hell are you with someone like that?"

"He's a nice guy, Myles. Being rich doesn't automatically make someone an asshole."

"You're right—being rich isn't what makes him an asshole. The way he looks down on people who *aren't* rich makes him an asshole. The way he helps the mega-rich get richer and avoid paying their share of taxes instead of helping someone it would make a difference for makes him an asshole. The way he talks about women as if they're not as smart as men and their only real purpose is to keep men happy makes him an asshole. He's a misogynist, for fuck's sake, Nina! And you're not his only girlfriend, I'm telling you that right now. He's a despicable person."

Fire burned in my chest. I knew that in some ways, nearly everything Myles said was true, but I didn't want it to be, so I ignored it just like I'd been doing for years. There was no way I would have given that much of my life to someone like that.

"That's not true," I gritted out. "He's never told me I wasn't smart or treated me like I was stupid. I've never seen him look down on someone—"

"Because you've only seen him around other people like him!"

Myles' words gave me pause; that was true. "And there's no way he has other girlfriends, Myles. He wouldn't do that. And I live in his condo for god's sake. When he's not traveling for work, this is where he spends his nights."

Unlike me.

That realization hit me hard in the gut, leaving me winded. I'd been living in this alternate version of reality with Myles when I had a boyfriend, and he was coming home the next day. If anyone was unfaithful, it was me—not Landon.

"I'm the one who isn't faithful, apparently," I added quietly.

"That's because you shouldn't be with him, Nina. You told me yourself that you can't talk to him about this stuff, that you guys don't really talk at all. I don't give a shit how nice a person is or isn't, that's no kind of relationship, and I'm sure that's not all. Not with a guy like him."

"Stop badmouthing him, Myles. You don't even know him."

"You're wrong, Nina. I *do* know him. I've known him for two years, ever since he began courting Marcus for this merger. He comes to poker night at Marcus' whenever he's in town. At least he did before the merger. I doubt he'll ever show up again once it's legally finalized. Because that's the kind of person he is."

The blood drained from my face at the thought of Myles and Landon knowing each other… at the thought they might see each other again, and now Myles knew I was dating him.

He stepped up so we were only a foot apart, his eyes intense, almost wild. "Leave him, Nina. He's not right for you."

It started small, then my head was shaking widely. I couldn't do that to Landon. I owed him giving our relationship more effort—especially after this thing, whatever it was, with Myles. If he could forgive me, because I knew now I had to tell him—I had to tell him and prove that Myles was wrong about him, and that *I* wasn't.

"Nina—"

"No, Myles. I can't. This—*us*—what's been happening between us this past week? I never should have let this happen. It's my fault, and I need to do the right thing now. I've been with Landon for years—"

"And you're obviously unhappy, Nina."

"That's *my* fault, Myles, not Landon's. And I owe it to him to try and give him a real chance."

"You don't owe him anything!" He cradled my face, his breath puffing out in quick bursts and his eyes glassy. "Please, Nina. Don't do this." He kissed my forehead. "Please don't do this."

My own tears spilled over as Myles' mouth pressed against mine, just as hard as the last kiss a few days earlier, but this time he didn't move away. Squeezing my eyes closed and digging for the willpower to do the opposite of what I wanted, I stepped back out of his kiss and his touch.

"I'm sorry. I have to."

And then I turned and rushed away.

THIRTEEN

I spent the night crying and staring at the ceiling, cycling through doubt followed by conviction about doing the right thing regarding Myles and Landon over and over and over. My chest hurt like it was being ripped apart and I couldn't make it stop. This was why I'd turned my back on Myles years earlier—so I could make the feelings stop.

This is the right thing. For Landon, and for me. When Myles is around, I lose all my control over my emotions and memories and forget who I am now. I'm doing the right thing.

But my pep talk changed nothing; I didn't want to be working. I didn't want to be doing *anything.* I didn't even feel like existing. Despite everything I was telling myself, I felt like shit for how things had ended with Myles the night before. I felt like shit for just turning my back on him and walking away from him. Again. I felt like shit because I was too much of a coward to read his text messages or listen to the voicemails from him.

I was a mess. A complete, total, and utter mess who had zero ability to concentrate.

And to make things worse, I needed to somehow pull myself together because Landon would be home later that evening, and I was supposed to meet him for dinner straight from the office. Instead, I was already home, and I hadn't even showered. All I'd done was pull my hair back and put on makeup to hide the bruising on my forehead because of having a few video calls scheduled.

For what felt like the fiftieth time, but was likely about the sixth or seventh, I tried to go through my new tester's test results. We'd had a software release into our pre-production environment, the last environment we tested in before pushing the updates into production, and I needed to provide test results by five, which was in twenty minutes. What I normally did was test the riskiest and most important parts of the application myself, then spot check my tester's results, the number of items determined by the tester's experience. But I'd accomplished nothing all day and now I was out of time. But at five was when they made the decision if they were pushing the code into production over the weekend or not, so I had to provide either sign-off or defects.

I spent the next fifteen minutes clicking around aimlessly in the application and didn't see any issues. With a glance at the clock, I sent an email providing my sign-off on the test results and giving the business side's approval for the code release.

As soon as the email was sent, I logged off, just as I heard the door close and Landon's footsteps in the hall accompanied by the sound of his luggage wheeling across the floor. *Fuck.* I scrubbed my hands over my face and closed the lid to my laptop.

"Oh, hi, darling," Landon said. "I thought you were at the office."

I turned and forced myself to smile. "I stayed home today."

His eyes flicked over me. "Are you feeling unwell?"

I shook my head. "Not exactly. I just had a bad headache this morning, then got busy and never made it in."

"Ah," he said, walking again. "Take some Advil." He gave me a quick peck on my cheek. "Our reservation's for six thirty—you'll be ready?"

I opened my mouth to tell him of course I would, but then stopped. I kept thinking that we didn't really know each other, but I'd never really tried that hard, either. *I should give him a chance.* He appeared to be rather disinterested most of the time, but so was I. And he was a nice enough man. It wasn't fair to him if I didn't give him a real chance. That was the whole reason I'd turned my back on Myles the night before.

"Actually, maybe we could order in tonight?"

"Are you sure you're feeling okay?" he called over his shoulder as he continued toward our bedroom.

"I just... I don't really feel up to going out, Landon. I'd rather stay in if that's alright with you."

He emerged from our bedroom a few minutes later, still wearing the suit he'd traveled home in. He wouldn't change, I knew, until he was ready to go to sleep. "I'll order something if that's what you really want, darling," he said, looking at his phone as he walked past.

"It is."

I headed into the bedroom to get freshened up, but decided to put on my pajamas instead. I knew Landon didn't understand lounging in anything other than what you'd wear to the office, but that wasn't really me. I'd done it for years, because I knew that's what he preferred, but it wasn't what *I* preferred. And I was going to make an effort to be more real with him.

His eyes passed over me when I joined him in the living room. "Going to bed already? I thought we were ordering in."

"We are," I replied, sitting down on the sofa. We rarely sat in the living room together, and when we did, we were usually on opposite sides. I intentionally sat down right next to him. I wanted that closeness I'd had with Myles. "I'm just more comfortable like this."

He gave a short nod of acknowledgement, his focus on his phone where he was now typing something, his fingers moving in a furious pace over his screen. A moment later, he set his phone down on the coffee table and lifted a glass of whiskey, taking a long pull from the glass. I reached out and grabbed the wine glass he'd set down for me and did the same. Landon was determined I preferred wine, but what I wanted was bourbon. Bourbon and to lose time listening to and playing music.

With Myles.

"Did you know I used to play the piano?" I blurted out.

He turned to me, his eyebrows raised. "You did?"

"Yeah. I wasn't bad, either. I mean, I wasn't going to get into Julliard or something, but I could hold my own."

"Hm."

"Did you play any instruments?"

He shook his head, but didn't say anything. Lifting his glass, he took another sip of whiskey.

"Did you always want to go into finance?" I asked after another moment of silence.

"Of course," he said. "It's what my father did. I knew from when I was young I was going to do the same thing and work in his company. One day, I want to run it."

"But was there anything else you wanted to do? Anything else you liked?"

"Not really."

I wracked my brain, trying to think of something he might have liked, but all he did was work. And play golf. "What about golf?"

"Sure. You know I like golf."

"But years ago, did you ever think about... I don't know... maybe becoming a professional golfer or something? Did the thought ever cross your mind, even if you knew it wasn't going to happen?"

He shook his head again, his brows drawing in. "What's gotten into you?"

I stopped myself from rolling my eyes and took a measured breath instead. Just because I wanted it to be easy, didn't mean it would be. But that didn't mean the relationship wasn't worth it. "When I went to college, I wanted to be a trail guide."

"A what?"

"Trail guide. Kind of like a forest ranger, you know? You guide people along trails, telling them about the history and the environment around you as you hike. I loved being outdoors and plants and insects and all that stuff."

Landon drew back, then laughed. "You almost fooled me, darling," he said, taking a sip of whiskey and reaching for his phone.

I reached out and rested my hand over his to stop him from getting engrossed in whatever message was waiting for him. "I'm serious, Landon. I used to spend every moment I could outside. I took a survival course the summer before college, and I can navigate with a compass and a topographical map. In fact, in the right weather conditions, I can do it without the compass. I know what plants along the major trail systems in the east coast you can eat and which ones are poisonous, and how to treat different ailments with what can be found along the trail."

He stared at me, looking like he was unsure if he should get up or laugh, and I was beginning to doubt whether or not I should have shared that with him. I didn't want to be laughed at. I just wanted him to know there was more to me than working my job and making sure we had reliable housekeepers and couriers and dry cleaning pickup and delivery and spreading my legs when he was horny. I had been fine with that being all I seemed to be to him for years now, but out of the blue, I wasn't anymore.

"Don't you have anything like that?" I asked through my growing embarrassment. "Anything you once loved and gave up because you had to make a trade off?"

His face sobered. "Have you been drinking?"

I huffed out a frustrated breath. "No, Landon. I just realized we don't really know that much about each other. We've been together for over three years, and I don't even know what kind of music you like to listen to."

"I don't listen to music," he replied. "It's too distracting. I can't think."

"See? That—I didn't even know that about you. Now I do. And don't you want to know what kind of music I like to listen to?"

He shrugged. "I don't see that it matters, but if you really want to tell me, you can."

"Everything," I replied, my voice forceful. "I like all kinds of music. What matters to me is that it makes me feel something, and I've encountered music of every type that makes me feel."

"Feel what?"

My eyes stared out the floor-to-ceiling window with an unobstructed view of the nighttime cityscape as I tried to find words to describe what I meant. "It's not a specific thing. It can make me feel happy or sad or wistful or nostalgic or angry, even, but it just needs to make me feel *something*."

It was clear by the way his face was drawn in that he didn't understand what I meant. He set his empty glass down on the coffee table and I got up and refilled it. He wouldn't ask me to directly, but I knew it was what he expected. He'd told me once very seriously when we were early in our relationship that he really liked when I noticed his needs that way, and I'd understood it was something he was looking for in a girlfriend. While I was up, I downed what was left in my wine glass and refilled that, too. When I sat back down, I handed him his full whiskey glass.

"Thank you, darling," he said.

"What do you think about that, Landon?" I asked after several minutes when he reached for the television remote.

He rubbed his temple. It meant he was getting annoyed. "About what, Nina?"

"About what I told you about what I like to listen to."

"Honestly, Nina," he snapped. "What does it matter? I've never even heard you listen to music."

"That's because I haven't in years."

"Okay."

"Don't you want to know why?"

"It doesn't matter to me whether—"

"Because I've been afraid to feel anything," I interrupted. My heart pounded in my chest. That was the most real thing I'd ever said to him. And only the second time I'd ever confessed out loud that I was afraid of feeling things. I had no idea how he was going to react.

He contemplated me for a minute before he responded. "Nina. It's been a long day. I have to fly back out on Sunday, I was going to tell you at dinner that I won't be home this week, and this merger is creating a lot of extra work for me. My biggest client has legal trouble that's going to hit the news any minute, and his assets might not be protected from the government right now because of decisions *I* made in order to triple his return this year. I don't really have time for chitchatting right now. Is it really that important to tell me about how you used to like music?"

My teeth ached as I clenched my jaw to keep it from trembling. I'd never been so openly dismissed before, let alone when I was trying so hard to connect. But I didn't want to start crying; it was bad enough Landon would be able to see the tears in my eyes.

"It's important to *me*, Landon," I said in a low voice.

"Are you *crying*, Nina?"

The unbridled shock in his voice sent me over the edge and I was practically sobbing. I pushed to my feet and turned, heading out of the living room.

"Nina," he called out. "Darling, I didn't mean to upset you. Don't cry."

I kept walking and didn't respond. He wouldn't follow me. I knew he wouldn't. I was sure he was genuinely bewildered by my behavior. I almost felt bad for him. But I felt too sorry for myself to feel sorry for him, too.

I was still awake, my tears dried up, when he came in for bed a few hours later. I stiffened when I heard him come through the door, then in the closet getting changed. I listened to him brushing his teeth and scooted to the very edge of my side of the bed. Not that there was any reason for him to be close to me when he laid down—it was a king size bed.

But he didn't stay on his side of the bed. I could smell the whiskey on his breath through the mintiness of his toothpaste, and it made my stomach turn. He'd had more to drink than normal, which meant he was going to be hornier than usual. His hand grasped my hip.

"Darling," he crooned, giving me a shake. "Are you awake?"

"Yes," I said, my voice as rigid as my body.

He kissed the back of my shoulder and moved his body—his erection—against my back. I couldn't scoot away because I was already on the very edge of the mattress.

"I'm sorry about earlier," he said, kissing my shoulder again. "I didn't mean to upset you. I'm just stressed out about this account." His hand inched up under my pajama shirt. "Will you forgive me, darling?"

I swallowed. I wanted to tell him no. But he was trying. He was making an effort. It wasn't what I wanted, but it was a step in the right direction.

"Yes," I forced out. "I forgive you. But I have a headache, Landon."

"Do you want some Advil?" he asked.

"I already took some."

With an arm wrapped around my middle, he scooted us backward and pushed me to my belly.

"Landon—"

"Hush, darling."

"Landon," I said a bit more forcefully as he hooked one hand into my pants and panties, the other hand on my back, pressing me into the mattress. "Stop."

He stopped. "Are you still mad at me, Nina? I apologized."

"No, it's just—"

"Okay, good." His hand continued pulling at my pants.

"Landon! I'm not mad at you, but I don't want to have sex right now."

"Darling, I've been gone for three weeks," he said, leaving my pants and panties bunched at my ankles, not even bothering to pull them all the way off. "I missed you." He kissed the back of my head. "I won't take long."

This was part of our arrangement together and had been from the beginning; I didn't refuse sex. Ever. It wasn't something we ever talked about, but rather an unspoken expectation that I'd understood early on, just like the expectation that I'd keep his whiskey full and make him breakfast and take care of dry cleaning and other things around the apartment. I'd disrupted a lot in our relationship by what I'd done earlier, and he was establishing that some things wouldn't change. He'd accepted my outburst earlier, and now he expected me to accept this. I bit into my tongue, not sure how to tell him no again.

Or if it would even matter if I did.

By the time he was done and rolled off me, my tongue was bleeding.

Landon kept his distance for the rest of the weekend before he flew out again after he found me throwing up in the toilet the next morning, afraid of catching whatever I had. I didn't tell him he couldn't catch what I had because shame and self-loathing weren't contagious. In fact, I didn't say more than a handful of words to him the rest of the weekend.

Luckily, due to the code release for my application, no work could be done in it over the weekend. I had other work to do, but all of it could wait, so I spent the weekend in bed, letting Landon think I had the flu or something. I couldn't stop thinking about letting Landon fuck me because he was horny and pushy about it. I hadn't wanted him to even touch me. I'd even tried to tell him that—the first time I'd ever told him so explicitly that I didn't want to have sex—but it hadn't mattered.

He would have stopped if I'd continued to refuse, though. He wouldn't have forced me to have sex. I didn't think. But I wasn't sure, either, because as much as I wanted to, I'd never refused when he got pushy because, like the night before, I'd never felt I really had a choice.

FOURTEEN

I hung up from a call with my tech team—our daily stand-up call—on Monday morning to see that, in the fifteen minutes I'd been occupied, my inbox had exploded with urgent messages. What the hell was going on?

I clicked on the first one, and by the end of the first sentence, I felt sick. There must have been a critical error in the code that was pushed to my application over the weekend because there was a sudden, serious malfunction. Before I'd even reached the end of the email explaining what the issue was, my desk phone was ringing.

This was bad.

Really bad.

The next several hours flew by so fast my head spun. I could barely keep up with the pace of calls and emails and people in and out of my office. I'd neglected to do any type of regression testing myself prior to signing off on the release, and this time there was a bug in the code, and it wasn't for something minor like changing the font of a random heading somewhere. This one deleted two weeks' worth of client data. *Every* client's data. We tried rolling back the release and thereby only losing a morning's worth of data, but the missing data was permanently gone. The firm was in damage control, trying to placate our clients and determine exactly how much the data loss was going to cost them.

At three, I was called into my boss' office. When I walked in, exhausted and not knowing what to expect, her boss, Roger, was already sitting across from her desk. I closed the door behind me and stood, unsure what to do with myself. I'd never screwed up like this before. I'd never really screwed up at all with this company.

"Nina, sit down," Natalie, my boss, said.

I sat in the chair a few feet from Roger.

"Our best estimate right now is that this is going to cost us about thirty-five million dollars, and there are thousands of professionals who will need to work around the clock to get us caught back up before quarterly filings are due. This kind of mistake should never have happened and it's unacceptable."

I nodded, looking down at my lap. "I understand. And you're right—this never should have happened."

"While this ultimately comes back on you, Nina, because this is *your* application, and you are going to be available around the clock to help in any capacity you can until we've made up for the lost data, we understand you are not directly responsible for what happened. We cannot, however, afford to keep employees who underperform and cut corners. It is apparent that George must not have properly executed the test scripts, and you will fire him when you leave this office because of it."

I gaped. George was enthusiastic and smart, and I knew he hadn't half-assed testing for me. In fact, he'd shown more initiative and promise than any other tester I'd trained in my time with the company.

"Natalie, this is not George's fault. It's mine."

"I'm aware of your part in what happened, Nina, and—"

"I can't fire him," I interrupted. "He did the testing he was asked to do."

"If he'd followed the test scripts, he would have found this bug."

I took a deep breath, clasping my hands so tightly together my knuckles were white. "There wasn't a section in the test scripts for regression testing. That's not George's fault—it's mine. I didn't add that section in when I prepped the scripts for him because I was intending to do the regression testing myself."

Natalie stared at me for a minute, then glanced to Roger. He hadn't spoken yet and he still didn't, but it was obvious they were communicating something with short nods and headshakes.

"It doesn't matter," Natalie said. "Someone has to go for this, and George is the obvious choice since he's the tester. We've already communicated that he was going to be separated from the firm immediately. We can replace him easily enough. And once all this settles, we'll figure out how you'll be disciplined for your role in this."

"You can't fire George," I said, leaning forward, raising my voice. "He didn't do anything wrong! And he's got a family—a new baby—you can't do this to him!"

"I'm *not* going to fire him—you are," she retorted. "Because if you don't, then you're the one who's going to be packing up your desk today. It's him or you, Nina."

"Fine," I said through clenched teeth as I shoved to my feet. I was as angry as I was upset, but I tried to keep it in check. "I'll pack up my things and be gone in ten minutes."

"Nina—don't be stupid!" Natalie called as I rushed from her office, but I didn't even slow; there was no way I could let someone else get fired for *my* mistake. I had no idea what I was going to do, but I'd never be able to live with myself if I stayed and George was fired.

When I reached my desk, I laughed bitterly as I looked around for personal items to toss into my bag. There were none except a single framed photograph of Landon and me at some charity event he attended on behalf of his company. There had been a professional photographer there to photograph all the guests, and it was the first photo I had of us together, so I'd framed it and put it on my desk. But looking at it now, all I could think about was his hand holding me to the mattress while he fucked me after I'd said "no" a few nights earlier.

I left it there.

My fingers itched to call Myles as I sat in the back of the cab heading home. I wanted to tell him what happened while snuggled into his chest, the Dovelyn Trio playing in the background. I wanted to be held and allowed to cry. But I'd ignored every text message he'd sent me since I'd walked away from him, let every call go to voicemail and then not listened to any of them.

He'd probably just tell me to go to therapy, anyway.

I thumped my forehead against the doorframe of the back seat and winced. My forehead was still really sore, though the bruising was now fading. The only good news was that Landon wouldn't be home for a month. Maybe I could find another job in that time. But how the hell was I going to get another job when I couldn't even focus on the one I had? To the point I'd made a critical mistake.

Maybe Myles was right.

Maybe I really did need therapy.

When I walked through the door into the condo, I stopped short and just stood there, staring at the walls and furniture as if seeing it all for the first time. And in a way, I supposed I was; I was seeing them as a newly unemployed person. I'd be spending a lot more time within those walls now, and that thought made me realize how cold and impersonal the space was. Everything was tastefully—professionally—decorated, but it felt more like an enormous hotel suite than a home.

Let alone *my* home.

There was practically no sign I even lived there, nothing personal except my clothes in my designated closet and my toiletries. Nothing I'd picked out or even provided input on, with the exception of the two framed photographs of us that I'd given Landon for Christmas one year. The same photograph that I'd left in my office—one in the entryway and one in our bedroom. I had an urge to flip them down, but I didn't.

What would happen if I did something to leave my mark? If I bought a different throw for the sofa or a piece of art for the wall? What if I bought a plant or a stereo? Or a piano? What would Landon do? What would he think?

He probably wouldn't like it—he liked things to be predictable and was averse to change without a logical reason for it. None of those changes would qualify as logical. But would he get angry? Or would he accept it? Or would he pressure the changes away like he'd done with *me*? My stomach turned at the memory.

But you didn't fight back, either. Not the other night, not seven years ago, and not any of the many times between.

I clenched my jaw against my unwanted thoughts so hard my teeth ached. Turning, I opened the door and walked back out—I didn't want to be there. Instead, I went to a coffee shop and sat, my fingers picking at the cardboard cuff since I'd rushed out without my reusable mug. I felt like I was living in a dream—a nightmare, I supposed—and had been since I'd seen Myles a little over a month earlier. And in this dream, it was like being stuck in a giant whirlpool, gradually circling at first, then picking up speed, descending toward certain destruction with no way to escape. How the hell had things gotten so bad so quickly? How had six years of careful planning and execution of a life with certainty and predictability and freedom from feeling and thinking about things I didn't want to fallen apart so easily? Had it always been a mirage instead of the life I depended on for my sanity? I'd worked so hard for it, and now it was all dissolving in what felt like an instant.

And what kind of life had I built, anyway? One in which I didn't matter to anyone? If I was hit by a car while crossing the street after I walked out of this café... who would really care? Every relationship I had was carefully crafted to be safe or one Landon would approve of so it would reflect positively on him. The women I lunched with periodically would never notice my absence. They wouldn't even invite me again since I'd been fired, I knew. The women I talked to at events with Landon were the wives or girlfriends of his colleagues, and we never spoke outside those events.

What about Landon? I'd never actually seen him upset about anything before. The only time I'd ever seen any kind of heightened emotion was when something was going exceptionally well or exceptionally bad at work, and his irritation with me the other night. Would he truly be upset if I died? Would he cry? Would he even care? I tried to picture it, but I couldn't. There'd be no sadly going through my belongings for him—he'd just pay someone to come gather everything and throw it away. He wouldn't even donate my belongings so someone less fortunate could make use of my clothes and jewelry because it would be easier to just toss it all into a dumpster.

There was no one in my life who cared about me enough they'd mourn if something happened to me. That was the life I'd built, I realized. A life free of any real feeling; I wouldn't myself be much more upset than I would for a stranger for most of those people. I thought I'd probably cry if something happened to Landon now that I was crying again, but I wasn't positive about that, either. I hadn't allowed myself to feel any more for the people part of my life than they felt for me. With one exception.

Myles.

The thought of *him* dying stole the breath from my lungs and my eyes flooded with tears. I would be gutted—destroyed—despite having turned my back on him. I had more feelings for that one man who wasn't a part of my life for years than I did for all the people who *had* been combined. He stirred up *all* my feelings, and I wasn't sure I could recover if something happened to him.

And I knew it would be the same for him if *I* died. I knew he'd mourn me, that he'd miss me, that he would be stricken with grief. If I lived with *him*, probably every item of mine would hold a memory or some significance, and he might never be able to go through everything because of the pain he'd feel.

This all seemed backward to me, but the idea of changing it was one that stirred up a serious aversion. *I'd rather just... go away. Be hit by that hypothetical car while crossing the street.* I sighed. Myles was onto something—the way I felt couldn't be normal. Looking around, I was sure most of those people weren't sitting there, sipping their coffee, thinking they'd rather die than deal with the mess their life had become. Not that it would matter, as I'd just realized, except to Myles. So, for him, I'd do something to make sure my morbid thoughts didn't progress into something more concrete. Because I'd already been the source of too much pain in his life—I didn't want to cause him anymore.

Pulling my phone out, I typed into the search bar for a local therapist.

FIFTEEN

"Nice to meet you, Nina. I'm Leslie. Please, have a seat and get comfortable. Then I'd like you to tell me a little about why you're here today."

I sat on the edge of the sofa opposite of Leslie and clasped my hands between my knees. I'd found someone faster than I'd expected, so I was sitting there in my first therapy appointment only two days after losing my job. Looking at the floor, I replied, "I wrote it down on the intake form."

"I know," she said warmly. "But I'd like to hear it directly from you. Why are you seeking therapy?"

I rubbed my hands together, my fingers twisting almost painfully as I did so. "I'm struggling with some things. And I don't know what to do. Someone..." I swallowed and forced myself to breathe. "Someone suggested I go to therapy. And I decided to give it a try."

"Okay. What kinds of things are you struggling with?"

"Life," I said with a huff, glancing briefly at her before my eyes continued all around the office, not really seeing anything. "Seriously. Everything is hard all of a sudden. I can't focus on anything, really. Well, except... I keep crying, like really easily. I didn't cry at all for years. At all. But now it seems like everything makes me cry. And I was just fired. On Monday. That was because I can't focus and I made a really big mistake."

"Okay," she said kindly when I fell silent. "Anything else?"

I eyed her, trying to decide if I wanted to share any more right then.

"This is a no-judgment zone, Nina. Nothing you say is going to be judged in *any* way. I give you my word."

"I hurt myself sometimes," I whispered, wringing my hands violently now. "Sometimes I think about dying. I don't mean that I'm planning ways to kill myself or anything, but I think about what it would be like to die. That it would be a nice break from everything, that no one would even care, you know?"

When I glanced at her, she was nodding gently. "Yeah."

I felt like she really meant that "yeah" and I began to cry. "See? This is what I mean," I blubbered. "Why am I crying right now?"

She handed over a box of tissues and didn't say anything. I blew my nose, then felt compelled to keep talking.

"And I get angry sometimes, too. Out of the blue. I get so angry I want to hit something or throw something and I yell."

"What kinds of things make you angry in that way?"

"Like this news coverage of the college student who was raped in Marksburg."

"What about that makes you angry?"

"All of it!" I exploded, my chest filling with that same anger I'd just been talking about. "Why did something like that have to happen to her? Why is the media making it sound like she deserved it? She didn't deserve that! I don't care what she was doing—no one deserves to be raped! They say she was stupid for walking alone at night, that she was intoxicated because she'd had a few drinks, that she was embarrassed she'd knocked herself out and been found and made up the rest. Who makes up a story like that?"

I shoved up to my feet, unable to sit still any longer. "No one, that's who. What she did—telling people what was done to her— wasn't easy. No one realizes how much courage you have to have to tell someone about something like that because there are people out there who aren't going to believe you, people who are going to blame you. Why were you there? Why were you dressed that way? Why didn't you fight harder? None of that matters! Why don't they understand that? It doesn't matter! He had a fucking knife—who's going to fight someone with a *knife*?"

I fell abruptly back to the sofa and cried into my hands for a while. When the tears began to slow, I peeked out over my fingertips. "It makes me so angry," I said. "And I feel helpless. I want to help her. I want to tell everyone to leave her alone. I want to tell her that it doesn't matter what they're saying about her, that it wasn't her fault."

Leslie studied me, then I blew my nose again. When I was finished, she spoke for the first time in a while.

"You want to tell *her* that... or you want to tell yourself?"

As the fourth person entered the waiting area and sat down, avoiding the tight smile I offered them, I wondered what the protocol actually was when you were in the waiting room for therapy. I'd been there every weekday for the last two weeks, but I wasn't sure. There was sometimes a man who muttered to himself but didn't seem to notice anyone else, and there was a younger woman who liked to strike up conversation about dogs or politics or kids, but everyone else looked really uncomfortable, like they wanted to hide themselves.

I was definitely more in the last group—the people who wanted to hide. To disappear into the cushions. At first, I'd felt like my presence was a neon sign announcing to the world that I was such a failure as a human being that I couldn't figure out how to cope with life—something that comes naturally to us—without someone to help me. I didn't feel as strongly about that as I had before, but I was definitely still in camp embarrassed. It made it awkward when other people walked in because I wasn't sure if I should smile or not, say hello or not. And I didn't want anyone to think I was judging *them*.

"Nina?"

I looked up, Leslie calling my name pulling me from my thoughts. I smiled, my eyes flitting around to see nearly every other set of eyes on me. I used to think they were judging me, but now I realized they were probably thinking the same thing I was, just trying to figure out the protocol for something like this. There wasn't a set of rules on the wall to tell us, and there was a negative stigma associated with therapy. But the more I saw Leslie, the more I believed the stigma was actually bullshit like Myles had once told me.

"How are you doing today?" Leslie asked, just as she had at the beginning of every session so far.

"I'm okay," I replied, the same reply I gave every time she asked that question.

"Do you have anywhere particular you'd like to start?"

I shook my head. My thoughts were really scattered. They usually were by the time I walked in the door. Sometimes they were all day.

"Okay. Well, yesterday, you mentioned at the end of our session when I asked about your current relationship with your parents that they both died a few years ago."

I felt nauseous, my eyes already flooding. "They did. Faulty furnace. They died of carbon monoxide poisoning in their sleep." I let out a slow breath, trying to stem the flow of tears. Tears I didn't have when it actually happened.

"How was your relationship before that?"

I shrugged, my face heating in shame as I stared at my hands clasped in my lap. I didn't want to talk about my relationship with my parents before they died. "It wasn't great," I said in a thin voice. Then I smiled up at her. Why the hell was I doing that?

"And why wasn't it great?" she asked kindly. "Was it always that way?"

"I mean..." My throat was closing up, and I tried another slow exhale. I was already crying but trying to avoid sobbing like I did nearly every day. "When I was growing up, I had a great relationship with my parents. Of course we argued sometimes and all that, but they trusted me, and I trusted them. I knew I could go to them about anything. And they respected me and encouraged me to follow my interests, whatever they may be. We weren't poor, exactly, but we weren't middle class, either—far from it. Both of my parents worked really hard to make ends meet and couldn't afford to do much more than that, but they tried. I wanted to go to college, and they both wanted me to be able to go to college, but that wasn't something they could afford. I understood that, and that it was my responsibility to get myself in the door somewhere if I was going to go, so I worked really hard in school so I could get scholarships."

I accepted the tissues Leslie held toward me and blew my nose and dried my face. Not that it really mattered, because I was still crying.

"That's a lot of pressure for a kid," Leslie observed after a moment.

My eyes darted up, her words allowing me to fully feel it for the first time. "Yes. Exactly. I mean, it wasn't their fault, but I definitely felt a lot of pressure. I didn't blame them, though. It was because I wanted to go to college, and it wasn't their job to make that happen, really. It was mine."

"You were a child, Nina. It shouldn't have been your responsibility."

I nodded absently, remembering the night I got my acceptance letter telling me I'd earned enough academic scholarships to pay for my entire education. My parents were so proud of me, but they'd been upset, too, for exactly the same thing Leslie had just said. They felt they'd failed me in some way because they couldn't afford to put me through college, and I'd had to work so hard to get scholarships. I never thought of it that way, though—I was grateful they'd raised me to be so driven and conscientious so I *could* find a way to do it myself.

"They felt that way, too," I said.

"It also wasn't their fault," she added. "It shouldn't have been your responsibility *and* it wasn't their fault that it was. Both of those can be true at the same time."

I mulled over her words. I'd always felt that believing it shouldn't have been my responsibility would mean blaming my parents, and I could never blame them.

"So, what happened after that? If your relationship was good before you went to college, what happened?"

I sighed. "I don't know. After my third year—it took me five to get my undergrad—something changed. I went home that summer, and they were different toward me. They were... smothering me. They wanted to know where I was all the time. They told me I couldn't drink, as if I wasn't already twenty-one. Then they told me I couldn't come home if I'd been drinking. My dad was waking me up in the mornings when I just wanted to sleep and telling me I needed to leave the house for a while. My mom was up my ass about getting a job for the rest of the summer—I'd spent part of it in Marksburg—but I just wanted to take a break. I'd been working so hard for so long and I just wanted a break. But a break wasn't okay with them.

"I left early to go back to college and stayed with a friend because my parents and I were fighting nonstop. They didn't want me to go back early, but I didn't understand that because they obviously didn't want me home, either. It was like they'd become different people. And once I was back in Marksburg, they were still smothering me. They were calling me every day and wouldn't leave me alone. They'd trusted me and allowed me to be independent my whole life, really, and definitely the first three years I was there, but suddenly they didn't anymore, and that pissed me off. Then, when I finally declared a major, they were disappointed in that, too. I chose it so I could make enough money to take care of them, but they didn't seem to understand or care. So I just stopped talking to them unless I absolutely had to because every conversation led to a fight and just made it more obvious that they didn't love me anymore. I didn't go home again after that. I didn't even see them again until I graduated. I still don't understand why they even came. I'd told them not to, and they didn't approve of me or anything I did anymore. But they did come."

I sniffled and looked up at the blurry outline of Leslie. "That was the last time I saw them alive."

Leslie's brow was furrowed, her mouth turned down into a slight frown. When she didn't say anything, I felt compelled to keep talking.

"So, to answer your question, I don't know what happened. Something changed, but I don't know what. And it destroyed me to lose my parents like that. Then they died and any hope of fixing things between us died with them." I looked up at her. "If you can make sense of it, please tell me. It eats me up not understanding why they stopped loving me."

"I don't think they did," she said. "I think *you* stopped loving you."

I stared at her, my jaw trembling. I knew she was right about at least part of that. I'd hated myself for a long time. "I did."

"The change... if I remember correctly without checking my notes, that was the summer you were raped?"

My chin lowered. "I just needed them to be there for me, and instead it was like they weren't my parents anymore."

"Did you tell them what happened?"

My head moved sharply side to side. "God, no. I didn't tell anyone. Except the nurse at the hospital and the police."

"No one else knew what happened?"

"I mean, Myles did. Because he was there. But no one else."

"Why didn't you tell your parents?"

My eyes searched the wall blankly. "I couldn't," I whispered. "I couldn't see their faces knowing I'd gotten myself into that kind of situation. The disappointment that I'd been so stupid and then had just let the guy do those things to me. I couldn't bear for them to think the same thing the police did... that I was just a drunk slut with regret for getting caught by my boyfriend."

"That's what the police said?"

"More or less. They didn't use the word 'slut' but... yeah. The fact that I had thirty-four stitches from the guy's knife didn't seem to matter to them. They'd already formed their opinion of me before they knew, and it never changed."

"And you thought your parents would think the same thing?"

"I mean... I don't know. Now, I don't think so. But then? Yeah, I did. And I thought they wouldn't love me anymore, but then they didn't love me anymore anyway."

Leslie let several breaths pass before speaking again. "Have you considered that maybe your parents always loved you as much as they had? That maybe it wasn't *them* who were different when you came back, but *you*? You were reeling from a severe trauma—your body and your will had been violated, your life had been threatened—and you were trying to keep it all to yourself. You told me a few days ago that you drank heavily for about a year and a half after it happened. Maybe it wasn't that your parents were being ultra-strict, but that they were worried about you because you were intoxicated all the time. They didn't know what happened, but you came home a different person, and maybe they were just trying to help you the best way they knew how considering they had no idea what was going on. I don't think they ever stopped loving you, Nina. I think they were loving you the best they could when you were pushing them away."

My world tilted on its axis as Leslie's words sank in. For six and a half years, I'd believed my parents had stopped loving me, but now I wasn't so sure. What Leslie said made sense—I wasn't myself back then. I hadn't been myself since the rape happened. And I definitely hated myself afterward. I hated myself for being so stupidly independent and for not fighting back. The second the knife had touched my skin, I'd become compliant. *How does someone not fight back when another person is hurting them?*

"I want to give you some homework for today, and we'll talk about it tomorrow," Leslie interrupted my thoughts.

"Okay."

She scribbled on a notepad, then pulled off the top sheet and passed it to me. "I want you to spend some time on these sites reading about trauma responses. Start with how those responses manifest during the initial trauma. Focus on the physiological ways our brains and bodies react when they sense danger. I want you to see if you can identify your response. And be sure to read the explanations of the responses—the why behind each."

SIXTEEN

Dear Myles,

Do you remember back in college when one of us would call the other and ask to get together to play music or meet up for a live performance or to go hiking? Remember I'd see you and you'd tell me you were supposed to be doing something else, like homework or studying, but you weren't because spending time with me was what you really wanted to be doing instead? (I loved that, by the way; I always felt so special and valued by you, especially when you said things like that.) Well, I'm supposed to be journaling right now, according to my new therapist, but I'm writing you a letter instead because talking to you is what I really want to be doing right now.

I wish I could call you... or, better yet, see you, though I'd settle for just hearing your voice. I know I can't, however. I know I really hurt you. Again. And it really wouldn't be fair of me to ask you to forgive me again. Not that I ever really asked you to before; you just did it anyway. I should have apologized and asked for your forgiveness, though. Maybe you'll accept this as my apology for all of it.

If I could talk to you right now, I'd tell you that I took your advice and I started therapy. My therapist's name is Leslie and I really like her. You were right that I'd grow to trust her. It seems to have happened quickly, but it was like that with you, too. I guess that's a good sign? I was also seeing her every day for a couple of weeks, so we have spent a lot of time together.

I don't even know where to start, honestly. So much has changed already in the last month. Leslie introduced me to this concept called self-care. The name is pretty self-explanatory, but the concept was foreign to me, as I'm sure you could guess. But I'm starting to get used to it. I downloaded a music app on my phone so I could start listening to music again. I listen to a little of everything like I used to, but I spend the most time listening to Evanescence and The Dovelyn Trio. Sometimes I listen to "Bring Me to Life" by Evanescence on repeat and wonder if you can sense that I'm thinking about you. Because I am when I listen to that song. Anything I listen to makes me think about you, honestly, but especially that song. If things were different, I'd suggest we learn to play it together. I'd love to play it with you. I'd maybe even subject you to my out-of-tune voice again to sing it to you. (I imagine you just groaned remembering the last time I tried to sing for you.)

I've also started spending time outside again. I still have panic attacks sometimes, like the one I had on the phone with you, because I'm out there all alone, but I'm doing it anyway, which is a big difference for me. I go almost every day to walk the trails at Midtown Park, in the morning around nine and again around four in the afternoon. I'm proud of myself. I'm embarrassed of that because it's such a simple thing, but it's not easy for me, so I am. And Leslie tells me to let go of the embarrassment because it's something I should be proud of. I'm working on it. And I was always a good student, so I'm sure I'll get there.

Speaking of students, I was looking at knock-knock jokes the other day while thinking about you, and I found one for you to share with your classes if you're brave enough. It'll be as popular as your Britney Spears joke.

Knock, knock.

Who's there?

Weevil.

Weevil who?

Weevil, weevil rock you.

And here's another one, just for you.

Knock, knock.

Who's there?

Wicked.

Wicked who?

Wicked make beautiful music together.

I can picture your face when you hear something funny, the way your eyes crinkle at the corners when you laugh, the way the right side of your mouth pulls up slightly higher than the left. I imagine that's how you look right now. I'm smiling, because I love it when you're happy.

I want you to be, you know—happy, that is. I hope you are when you're reading this. More than anyone else I've ever known, you deserve it. And maybe it will help you if I finally answer those questions I've never let you ask. That's something I can now do, I think.

After I was raped (I'm trying, per Leslie's insistence, to call it that rather than just "that night" the way I usually think about it and refer to it), I didn't know how to process. This awful thing had happened, and you and the nurse at the hospital believed me. But you know the police did not at first. And even once they did, they questioned my character and my intelligence. I know you remember, because you were nearly arrested for punching the officer who told you that you didn't want to get involved with a girl like me. You called him an asshole and insisted I ignore him. And I tried. But I couldn't.

Their words infected me like a venomous snake strike—a sharp, painful bite followed by rapid spread of the poison. I internalized them and began to blame myself for not fighting back, and those feelings were feelings I couldn't handle. The problem was that, when

I was around you, everything was fresh and raw and right on the surface. And that was okay while I was right there with you because you could soothe those feelings, but then when we were apart, I couldn't cope. Eventually, I'd begin to bury it all again, and then I'd see you and be back where I'd begun. After a while, I couldn't do that cycle anymore.

I couldn't handle all the feelings, and I couldn't handle the hell I put you through every time I broke down. Because I could see what watching me fall apart was doing to you, and it was just getting worse instead of better. So I shut you out, then turned to alcohol to cope. When you called me about six months after I'd cut you out of my life, I wanted to answer. I wanted to tell you I was sorry and ask you to forgive me and to help me.

However, I was too ashamed of what I needed help with to even contemplate telling you. It would have completely destroyed you in a new way. Because I wasn't just drinking... I was drinking heavily. And I was sleeping with every guy who tried. The second they touched me, I complied with whatever they wanted. Sometimes I was so drunk, I couldn't remember any of it, had to ask the guy the next morning. The thing was, though, I didn't want to have sex with any of them. Not one. I didn't want to have sex at all. But I couldn't say no once they touched me. Or got me alone. Or in some other way made me feel pressured or like they wouldn't back off if I said no.

I can tell you all of this now because I had an epiphany, I guess, because of therapy. Leslie had me research trauma responses. It turns out what I did when the guy raped me was freezing. It's a common response and it's not my fault. It also turns out that we tend to respond to anything that triggers our bodies to feel like we're experiencing that trauma again in the same way. I couldn't say no, even though I desperately wanted to, because my body thought I'd be in danger if I did. You've been in therapy and probably already know all these things, but this is all new to me. I'm still trying to process it all and undo the narrative I've believed for so long—that I'd just become a drunk slut.

I know this hurts you to know, but I'm hoping it also brings you some peace to finally understand what happened with me back then. And I was doing the same thing more recently. After I saw you at the

Lorman event, I was suddenly feeling things again, so I walked away from drinks with you to make it stop. And then I sought you out at your school because walking away from drinks hadn't worked, and I knew you could help me with those feelings that were refusing to go dormant again—feelings I wasn't able to handle on my own. But like before, it was good when I was with you, but then I was falling apart away from you. That's part of why I walked away from you the last time.

The other part is Landon. I did, and still do, feel a sense of responsibility toward him, like I owe him a chance, and I couldn't keep doing what we were doing to him, especially with you pushing me to break up with him. I had justified the time we were spending together, my feelings, the way we touched each other, and even you kissing me as much as you did on my face because we did those things before and called ourselves friends. But we weren't really just friends back then, Myles—we were something more, no matter what we were calling it. And that means we were something more last month, while I had a boyfriend. I understand that you couldn't accept being different toward me than you were, but that meant we couldn't see each other at all.

I've wanted to see you and hear your voice a thousand times in the last month, but I know I can't. And even if I tried, I'm not sure you'd forgive me again, anyway. And that hurts. It's hard. But there's something to be grateful for in there, too. I haven't seen or talked to you in a month, and I'm still feeling everything, but this time I'm okay. I'm not getting drunk every night or sleeping around. I *did* lose my job, but I think it ended up being a good thing, anyway, because I now have the time to focus on myself and therapy. And I'm actually figuring it out, Myles. I think, for the first time since it happened, that I will actually be okay. At least one day, but I'm on that path now. I'm making changes, and I'm not going to hide my feelings or who I am anymore—not from anyone. Easier said than done, I'm sure, but I'm not going to give up. I don't know what that means for my future, but I'll figure it out.

Thank you, Myles. Thank you for seeing me for who I really am, always. Thank you for reminding ME of who I am. Thank you for giving me many of the best memories in my life. Thank you for caring about me and for teaching me how to feel again. Thank you for everything.

XO,
Nina

P.S. Please listen to "Bring Me to Life" again; it's my song for you. It explains better than I can what you've done for me.

SEVENTEEN

I stepped out of the cab after paying my fare and hesitated outside the middle school where Myles taught. Should I go in or wait outside? I hadn't been sure he'd get the letter I wrote if I mailed it to the school for him, and I didn't actually know his home address to send it there, though I was sure I could navigate myself there again. I'd written the letter for him, and I wanted him to have it, but I felt like I was going to be sick. How was he going to react to me showing up out of the blue again?

With a deep breath, I fussed with my hair, hoping it looked okay and not too wild after all the running around I had done that morning. My eyes fell again over my dark jeans, ankle boots, and cream-colored sweater under my gray, knee-length, wool coat and dark burgundy scarf. I was only delivering a letter but was still concerned about how I looked. I supposed I just wanted Myles to know that I was doing better than the last time I'd seen him so he wouldn't worry. Rolling my lips under and pressing them together, I took one more deep breath and headed toward the front doors.

Again, I was directed to Myles' classroom, even after I offered to leave the letter in the office for him. This time, the staff was more interested in me than they had been the first time I'd dropped by, and I wondered why briefly before my nerves took over. It felt the hallway was becoming narrower as I approached his room, and I had to force myself to breathe more evenly.

You can do this, Nina. You're just going to wait until his class lets out, then give him the letter. Then you're going to turn around and go to Midtown Park like you do every afternoon.

I stopped outside his classroom, which was still full of students and had the door open, standing where I could watch. They were playing a piece of classical music that I couldn't quite place, wrong notes here and there, which made me smile as I watched the students who'd gotten the note wrong startle a bit before continuing. I remembered what that was like from my own childhood.

Myles was in the front of the room, accompanying the class on the piano. He primarily used head movements to conduct the class, occasionally raising a hand quickly and seamlessly from the piano to gesture. I'd never seen him with a group of students this way. The closest I'd ever seen him to conducting were the head gestures he used for me when I was first learning to play duets with him in college.

He was so warm and encouraging, even behind the piano. It was no wonder his kids loved him. They came to the end of the piece and Myles stood, clapping.

"Great job, everyone! That's the best pass we've had yet."

"Carla screwed up her part and that messed me up, too," someone called out.

"No, I didn't!" a girl shouted back.

"Everyone messes up sometimes, I've told you guys that. Did you hear the mistakes I made? There were three of them," Myles said.

"The first note was one of them," another student said. "You hit an extra key or something."

Myles nodded and raised a finger. "Correct, that was one. I wasn't paying attention and my pinky played a C and D simultaneously. What's another mistake I made?"

"It sounded like on the second page you played an entirely wrong note, like it didn't work at all."

"Very good, Serena. I played a C instead of a C sharp. It's only a... what's that called?"

"Half-step," a student near the back called out.

"Half-step, that's right. It's only a half-step, but it makes a big difference in the sound. What about the third mistake? Did anyone catch that one? It was a bit trickier."

There was silence as Myles looked from student to student, waiting. After a while, he said, "Dwayne?"

The kid I'd seen before shrugged.

"Ruby?"

A girl in the front row shifted, then squeaked out, "It sounded like you rushed a few notes right before our last crescendo at the end."

Myles broke into a wide grin. "That's exactly right! I took too long to signal the clarinets, extending my rest another half-measure, and rather than skipping the notes in that half-measure, I sped through them." He paused, looking around the room. "I've been playing piano longer than any of you have been alive, believe it or not—"

"We believe it cuz you're old!" a kid near the middle of the room shouted, setting off a wave of giggles and snickers.

Myles snorted. "—but I still make mistakes. Because everyone makes mistakes. The question is... anyone? Just call it out."

"Are you learning from your mistakes," Dwayne finished in a monotone, rolling his eyes.

"That's right, are you learning from your mistakes."

"So, does this mean we get our phones now since you said if we got through it better than the last time then we could have them at the end of class?"

Myles snorted again and, grinning, looked up toward the clock on the wall just over the classroom door. His eyes passed over me to the clock, then jerked back down, his smile fading.

"Mr. E?" the same kid who'd asked the question called. "We get our phones?"

Myles looked toward the kid, then his eyes returned immediately to me. "Y-yes, Jeremy. You guys can have your phones for the rest of class *after* you clean and put away your instruments. I'll be right back."

There was an immediate rise in volume in the room.

"I'll be just outside the door watching," Myles added. "So behave."

He strode toward the doorway, and my heart pounded furiously against my chest as he neared. I was so nervous my eyes were watery. He stepped into the hallway, and I stepped back to allow more space between us as he quickly and quietly pulled the door closed.

"What do you want, Nina?" he asked. His voice was quiet and wary, his brow furrowed.

I glanced down, then back up. "I don't want anything, Myles. I swear. I just have something to give you."

"I don't want anything from you."

His words felt like a knife. But I'd known this might happen. I'd hurt him... a lot. And more than once. "I know. It's just a letter I wrote to you. I would have mailed it, but I didn't know your address and I was afraid if I sent it here, you wouldn't get it."

He scrubbed his hand down his face, then back up and through his hair, leaving it in disarray. "Just tell me whatever it is you want to say, then go. And please don't come back." His gaze fell to the floor between us after he glanced in the door of the classroom. "I can't do this again."

"I know. I'm not asking you to. I know I hurt you and I'm sorry. Everything I want to say is in here." I held the letter out to him. "And I promise you won't see me again."

He accepted the letter from me, then his other hand shot out and grabbed mine as it was falling back to my side. I sucked in a sharp breath at the contact, at the way it made me feel all the way to the soles of my feet. It was a feeling I'd never have again but would also never forget. A feeling I only had with Myles.

His eyes found mine, my hand still in his. "I miss you, Nina," he said, his voice husky with emotion.

I gave him a small smile. "I miss you, too, Myles. I always will."

He gave a nod, then dropped my hand and walked back into the classroom, my letter in his hand. I watched through the window in the door as he made his way to the front of the room, and even as far away as I was, I could see that his hand was trembling as he pushed the letter into the messenger bag on his desk. He glanced my way once, then focused his attention back on his classroom.

I didn't give in to the tears that wanted to fall until I was sitting on my favorite bench in Midtown Park. I walked the trails there, sometimes for hours, but I always stopped at this bench because it had the best view in my opinion. It was the only bench that wasn't near an expansive grassy area; instead, it faced dense trees and brush. There were rabbits and squirrels and birds to watch, and I knew there would be even more creatures as the weather continued to warm. Sometimes I spent an hour or more just watching them going about their day, mostly impervious to the presence of the humans passing along the trail.

"I gave him the letter," I said to them, pretending they could hear me and knew what I was talking about. "I was scared, but I did it. And it feels good that I did, though I realized on my way here that the last time I'll ever see him is now in the past." My voice broke and the tears that had been leisurely trickling out now came like a flood as I wept soundlessly. "And *that* doesn't feel so great."

EIGHTEEN

It was time for Landon to come home, and I was sure he wasn't going to be thrilled about this under-revision version of me he was going to find. I hadn't even told him about my job yet. Leslie told me to take things one step at a time and to just be honest. And to be prepared if he didn't respond well at first, because that was a possibility. I was still anxious, though, not to mention a little distracted by what had happened with Myles the day before.

To ease the news, I wore a cocktail dress I knew he liked on me and straightened my hair, twisting it back into a bun the way he liked, rather than leaving it down and curly and dressing in jeans and a sweater like I had been doing for the last two weeks. I had his whiskey and a glass ready and was waiting when I got the message from him that he was swinging by his office from the airport and would meet me at the restaurant for dinner. I'd been hoping to talk him into staying home again, but decided this was probably better anyway—it was what he preferred, and what was normal for us. With all the changes I was about to spring on him, having some things remain the same could only be helpful. I really wanted to make this work; we'd already given more than three years of our lives to each other. I owed him a real effort.

I don't have to even try with Myles; it's just natural with him.

I shook my head to clear my mind of Myles, something I found myself doing often, because he was always there waiting in my next thought for me. Tonight was about strengthening the relationship I already had, not pining for the one I never really did.

"You look lovely, darling," Landon said, standing from the restaurant table where he was already seated when I approached, then giving me a quick peck on the cheek.

"Thank you," I said, giving him a smile and taking my seat. "How was your flight?"

"Short, thank god. I'm getting sick of all this flying."

"Maybe you can work on more local accounts?" I suggested. While I had no overt desire to have him around more, maybe we'd be closer if he was.

"No, there's no one else my clients would trust with their assets. I'm actually planning to change things up a bit." He paused as the waiter approached the table and read us the specials. "I'll have the ribeye, medium rare, and a glass of your Macallan Double Cask Single Malt. She'll have the Cobb salad, and a glass of Chateau Pichon-Longueville Baron twenty sixteen."

"The Chateau Pichon-Longueville is only available by the bottle."

"A bottle then."

"Very good, sir."

"Actually," I interjected. "I'll have your salmon special, medium, and a glass of your Blood Oath bourbon."

"Yes, ma'am," the waiter said, then turned and scuttled away. I avoided looking at Landon for a moment. I'd never liked that he ordered for me, but that was the first time I'd ever spoken up about it. With determination, I looked up and smiled. "You were saying you were going to change things up a bit?"

His eyes narrowed slightly, but then he spoke. "Yes. As opposed to coming home for a week every three weeks, I can cut down significantly on my flight time if I just go straight from client to client. So I'll be in Milan, then fly straight to Denver, then LA, then New York, then home. Three weeks each."

I stared at him. I'd been thinking some more time might bring us closer together, but if I'd just heard him correctly, he was saying he was going to be gone more often. "So, you'd be gone for *twelve weeks* at a time, Landon?"

"Yes. It makes much more sense than what I've been doing."

I stared at him. "I mean, maybe for Lorman, but... you live here, Landon, but you'll only be here for what? Nine weeks? Ten weeks maybe? Out of the *entire year*?"

"Closer to ten, but yes."

We paused the conversation while the waiter set down our drinks.

"But, Landon... what about *us*?" I asked as the waiter withdrew.

"Nina, do the math. It's not that different than it is now, except that I'll spend less time on a plane."

"Yes, it *is* different, Landon—you'll be gone for three months at a time. How are we supposed to have any kind of relationship like that?"

He took a long swallow of his whiskey. "Nina. Nothing about our relationship will change. Is that really what you're worried about, darling? You can stay in my condo, of course, like you do now. There's no need for anything to be any different than it is. It'll just be a few more weeks between seeing each other. And when I do come home, I'll be here a bit longer than I am now."

"Landon—" I started, but stopped abruptly. I wasn't even sure what to say. "I...I was actually hoping we could start spending more time together."

"I'm sorry, darling. The change has already been made. I'll be home for this week, then the new travel plan kicks in. Cheer up—it means fewer boring functions I'll be dragging you to. I know you don't care for them."

"That's not the point," I bit out, then took a sip of my bourbon.

The flavor on my tongue made me close my eyes, and instantly I conjured Myles next to me, The Dovelyn Trio in the background. Myles was the one who'd introduced me to bourbon at Nina's the night I met him. I'd never been able to drink it without thinking about him. So now I was thinking about him while sitting across the table from Landon, who was more worried about the messages on his phone than he was about the fact I was upset with his news. He was completely unbothered by the prospect of not seeing me for months at a time.

The thing was... I wasn't bothered, either. Not really. I wanted *him* to be bothered, and in some ways *I* was, but mostly I felt relief. But how could we maintain a relationship that way? And I'd promised myself I'd make an effort to become more invested in this relationship with him.

"What if I traveled with you?" I asked.

His eyes darted up, then back down. "Just a second, darling."

Hearing him call me "darling" this time aggravated me. When someone was your darling, you cared about them and took care of them. You made them feel loved. And in some respects he took care of me—I lived in his condo and he paid for just about everything. I didn't truly want for anything, many would say. Though while I had my job, I wouldn't have anyway because I'd made really good money. Regardless, I felt starved in some way. I wanted to feel *wanted* the way I did around Myles. I wanted Landon's eyes to light up when he looked at me. I wanted him to hug me when he hadn't seen me for a while, and I wanted him to tell me he missed me aside from when he was waking me up for sex in the middle of the night. I wanted him to make me laugh and do things like find a nature conservancy to visit because he knew I'd like it.

I wanted him to be more like Myles.

I wasn't sure *exactly* how Myles felt about me, but I knew he cared about me, and I knew he felt stronger about me than Landon did. At least it seemed that way. And I knew I sure as hell felt very differently about Myles than I did about Landon, or any other man I'd ever known.

"What did you say?" he asked, taking a sip of his whiskey.

"I said... what if I traveled with you?"

"You're not serious?"

"I am, actually."

"What about your job?"

My gaze fell. "I... I don't actually work there anymore."

"What? When did that happen?"

"A few weeks ago. I wanted to tell you about it in person."

"Jeez, Nina. What happened?"

"I screwed something up. Something big, and they were going to fire my new tester for it. I took his place."

"Why the hell would you do something like that?" he practically shouted.

I jerked backward, a little taken aback by the vehemence in Landon's voice. "It wasn't his fault, Landon. It was *mine*. I couldn't let him take the fall for me. I mean, what kind of person would do something like that?"

"A smart one, Nina. Now you've been fired. Do you have any idea how hard it's going to be for you to find another job? You'll be blacklisted at any respectable company. Jesus, Nina—and you know the CEO is one of my clients. How do you think this is going to make *me* look?"

"That's what you're worried about? Not about wrongfully ruining an innocent person's life?"

"It's what *you* should have been worried about! Reputation is everything in this industry!" He rubbed at his temples and downed the rest of his scotch, flagging down the waiter and ordering another. "This is why I didn't want you to work to begin with," he muttered.

"Excuse me?" The flame of anger that had begun roared to life in my chest. I felt like I was breathing fire.

"Women make emotional decisions—not logical ones—and I knew at some point it would bite me in the ass if I let you keep working. I thought you were different from other women and were smarter than that, that you were more like me, but apparently I was wrong. And now you've created a mess I'm bound to hear about on Monday morning when I meet with Carter."

"You think this is because I'm a *woman*?" My hand was shaking, and I wasn't sure the glass I was clutching would last much longer without being crushed. Myles had been right about this at least. "This is because I have a heart, Landon, and a conscience, and integrity. I fucked up, and I took responsibility for that fuck up."

"Keep your voice down, Nina," Landon hissed, his eyes flitting around us.

Sure enough, there were other diners now staring because I'd been growing in volume. But I was too angry to care. I stood up and leaned over, my hands on the table.

"I'm sorry, Landon, but I'm a *woman*—apparently, I don't know how to control my emotional displays, so I can't keep my voice down. I'm sorry I'm a *woman* and I care about ruining people's lives. I'm sorry you *allowing* me to work has become an embarrassment for you."

"Nina—"

I turned and left the restaurant, tuning out anything that came after my name. I was furious; I wasn't even sure how I was walking. I couldn't believe the things he'd just said to me. I stepped out of the restaurant, and the blast of cold late-February air helped take the edge off my anger. I decided to walk for a while to calm down before getting a cab. Right then, for the first time since I'd moved in with Landon, I wished I had my own apartment to go to. I didn't want to be in the same building as him, let alone the same living space. As I walked, my attention drifted to my surroundings, and I looked into the windows of the shops and restaurants and clubs I passed until I reached one that had live music: a pianist, a cellist, a saxophonist, and a singer.

It was warm inside, and I pulled off my coat, hanging it over my arm as I took in the space, looking for somewhere to sit. I spied an empty, two-person table near the bathrooms and made my way there. When the server came over, I ordered bourbon and water and adjusted my chair so I could watch the musicians as they were performing.

They were good—*really* good.

Pulling out my phone, I stared at it. I wanted to text Myles and tell him about this place and the band—I knew he'd love them. But how could I do that when I'd just told him the day before that he'd never hear from me again? When he had so obviously not wanted anything to do with me anymore? But on the other hand, how could I sit there and listen to a band I knew he'd adore without telling him about it?

Before I could change my mind, I typed in a message and hit send.

> I'm at Bar Vivian on 23rd and there's a band here you'd love. The Sultry Sound. Piano, cello, sax, and vocalist. They're incredible. Look them up.

I held onto my phone for an hour in case he responded, as unlikely as it was.

He didn't.

I couldn't blame him. I'd disappeared on him with zero warning three times now. It was apparent after what happened at dinner that Myles had been right, and I should have trusted my desire to be with him. I never should have pushed him away, and I wished right then more than ever before that I hadn't. But I had, and it was too late—I couldn't take it back. No more than I could undo anything else from my past.

With a sigh, I dropped my phone back into my purse and closed my eyes, focusing on the sounds filling the air around me. I'd always liked music since I was little, but my appreciation for it—for *good* music like this, music that could move you to feel things you couldn't feel otherwise—was all thanks to Myles. In the few months we'd known each other before a stranger with a knife and a hard-on changed the course of my life forever, he'd made a profound impact on how I experienced the world. He'd taught me that music was everywhere, that it was a part of us, really. He'd introduced me to music that could make me cry just by listening to it, music that made me feel transcendent. He'd enriched my life in ways I couldn't explain—not even to him.

The tears dripping listlessly down my cheeks from under my eyelids left warm tracks. I was sad I'd pushed Myles away so stupidly when I had a chance to have him in my life again, but grateful I'd known him and could now appreciate this beautiful music. A small sob rose up my throat, but I was smiling.

NINETEEN

"Where have you been?" Landon asked as soon as I walked in the door a little past midnight. I'd stayed at Bar Vivian until the band was packing up.

I eyed him. "Why do you care, Landon?"

"Nina, I was worried about you."

"So worried that you texted and called me *once each*," I snapped, heading toward our bedroom. I had no intention of sleeping in there tonight, but I needed to get my pajamas. Landon followed me into the closet.

"Look, Nina. I don't do this kind of stuff. I don't do drama or over the top expressions of... anything, really. It's not who I am. But that doesn't mean I don't care. And it doesn't mean I wasn't worried about you."

I turned with my pajamas in my hands, guilt stabbing through my chest. He *did* sound troubled. And his forehead was definitely furrowed. Maybe I shouldn't have snapped at him. I sighed. "I was at Bar Vivian. There was a live band there tonight."

"Were you with someone?"

"No. I was there by myself. I was walking past and saw the band and decided to go in. They were really good, so I stayed until they were done playing."

His brow wrinkled like he was trying to work something out. "You like live music, then?"

"I do. A lot, actually."

"Okay. I'll remember that."

I paused, then headed past him toward the bathroom. He reached out an arm to stop me and kissed my forehead. For the first time that I could remember, he lingered for a second or two as if he wanted to be there.

"I'm sorry I upset you at dinner," he said quietly. "The news caught me off-guard and I said some things I shouldn't have. I'm sorry, Nina."

"I'm sorry, too, Landon," I replied, feeling suddenly remorseful. I'd acted without thinking, just as I had done to Myles. "I shouldn't have stormed out the way I did and then ignored you this evening. I didn't mean to worry you. I just didn't think you really cared."

"Why would you think that?"

"*Do* you really care?"

"What kind of question is that?"

"I mean... You've never once told me you loved me. Not once. We've been together for over three years, Landon. You don't seem to care about being gone for three weeks at a time—you don't call me while you're gone, or even text me more than once or twice, if that— and now you don't seem to be bothered by that timeframe increasing to twelve weeks... I just don't understand how you can care if that doesn't bother you at least a little bit."

I waited a second, but when he didn't say anything, I went into the bathroom and changed and brushed my teeth. When I came out, he was sitting on the side of the bed in his pajamas, looking blankly toward the floor. He raised his head, studying me, his brow still creased.

"What's going on with you, Nina?" he asked, sounding weary. "You've been acting strange for a while now."

"Honestly, Landon," I said with another sigh, "I don't think you want to know. Not really."

"I do, Nina. I don't like that I keep making you mad. I don't really understand why, and I don't like it. I need more information so I can figure out the best course of action."

I searched his face, trying to determine if he could handle it if I bared my past. I wasn't sure if he could or not. But I *was* sure I couldn't handle hiding parts of myself anymore. Every therapy session peeled off a little more of my shame and self-blame for what happened, and as that lifted, I felt more of the real me coming out, and, like I'd told Myles in my letter to him, I didn't want to keep myself hidden anymore.

"Do you remember that news story recently about the young woman who was raped in Marksburg?"

"Yes."

"Do you remember me calling you and telling you it could have been me?"

"Yes, which is ridiculous because—"

"It *was* me, Landon."

"What?"

"Not that woman in the news, but seven years ago. I wasn't in the news, but I was the woman who was... in that same alley."

He stared at me in silence for an uncomfortably long time. "You're saying you were raped, Nina?"

I nodded, breathing with deliberate slowness to keep the tears at bay. "I was twenty-one. Near the end of my third year of college. My roommate ditched me at a party, and I was on my way to meet up with my sort-of boyfriend at a piano bar less than a block from that alley."

"Some boyfriend who'd allow you to walk alone in the middle of the night in a place like that."

"It wasn't a bad area," I said defensively. "And it wasn't Myles' fault. He didn't want me to walk alone, but I was really independent."

"Independent or not, he never should have let you do something like that, Nina."

"He didn't *let* me," I bit out. "He had no control over what I did or didn't do—it wasn't his decision. And he saved me. He got there and stopped the guy from doing anything worse to me."

He eyed me contemplatively. "Okay. So you were raped seven years ago. What does that have to do with now?"

"Are you fucking serious right now?" I shouted.

He rubbed his temple. "Nina, stop with the yelling. I'm trying, here. If there's something I'm missing, please tell me."

"Since it happened, you are only the second person I've ever told what happened, Landon. Think about that. I've been burying this for years, and now there are reminders everywhere. Triggers is what my therapist called—"

"*Therapist?*"

"Yes. I started seeing a therapist a month ago. Two days after I got fired."

"And what did you do to get fired? You never told me."

"I was struggling, Landon. You didn't notice, but I was. I couldn't think about anything except what happened. And I missed a bug in the last release because of that. A big one."

"How big?"

"It's costing them thirty-five million to fix it."

"Jesus Christ, Nina." He shook his head and swallowed. "This is a lot to take in. It's like you're a completely different person."

For some reason, his words hurt, even knowing they were true for him. "This is me, Landon. The real me. I haven't been me since before I met you, but I am now. Or I'm getting there, anyway. And I want you to know the real me."

"I don't... I need some time to think about all this, Nina. This is... so much I never wanted to deal with. We agreed on simple, no drama, no kids. This isn't simple anymore, and there's a lot of drama lately. At least tell me you still don't want kids?"

"I honestly don't know anymore, Landon. Before that happened to me, I *did* want kids one day. And now that I'm dealing with it all at last... who knows? I may decide I want them again after all. I don't know yet." Not that I could imagine Landon as a father. He was never even home.

"Christ, Nina. I'm going to bed."

He twisted to his right and turned the bedside lamp off. I stood there in the dark, not really sure whether to stay or go, whether I was upset by his reaction or reassured. Whether I wanted him to decide to put in the work for our relationship or I wanted him to say this wasn't what he wanted anymore and release me from this feeling of obligation to make things work.

"Are you coming to bed, Nina?"

I sighed heavily. "Yeah." I made my way around the bed and climbed in opposite him.

I woke the next morning to Landon's hand sliding over my hip, his lips against my shoulder. I shuddered and slid out of reach, sitting up and heading into the bathroom. I was tired, my sleep restless and interrupted often by unsettling dreams, but I couldn't lay back down while he was there or he'd take that as a sign that I was willing to have sex.

I wasn't.

So, instead, I padded to the kitchen in my pajamas and put on a pot of coffee. After a while, I heard Landon turn on the television in the living room, and the sound of the Saturday morning news filled the air. I preferred my new morning routine of sipping my coffee with some moving music caressing me as I woke. After a couple of weeks of that, the news sounded harsh and jarring. I poured him a cup of coffee and carried it to him in the living room.

"Thank you, darling," he said, his eyes still on the screen. He was already showered and dressed in a suit, like always, his jacket carefully folded over the back of the sofa. "Would you mind getting me some toast?" he asked.

"And eggs?"

"Yes, thank you."

I'd known he was going to ask and hadn't even bothered to carry my mug out of the kitchen. While his eggs cooked—two, sunny-side up—and his bread toasted, I fished my phone out of my purse, thinking about making waffles together with Myles my second morning at his house the month before.

I wasn't sure what I was looking for on my phone. Since I'd been fired, my phone sat silent and notification free, aside from junk emails. Every so-called friend had been a coworker and stopped talking to me as soon as I walked out the door. Landon rarely called or texted, even when he was out of town. And Myles... I didn't want to think about Myles anymore. He was a part of my past for good now, as much as I might have wanted that to be different.

My phone was still notification free, as I'd expected, but now I was thinking about Myles, even as I was making breakfast for Landon.

The next few days passed much the way they always did with Landon; he spent most of the day every day in the office, then we went out for dinner on the nights he had no work events. He acted like nothing had changed, when so much had. And I could see the slight narrowing in his eyes when I did something differently, like wearing jeans and sweater around the condo or letting my hair go curly or ordering for myself at dinner or talking about things like therapy and nature and music. There was only one major exception to the way things normally were.

I refused to have sex.

Every night he tried, and I told him to stop because I didn't want to have sex. And every night, surprisingly, he let it go. Though not without a sigh or an aggravated huff. I'd felt some sexual attraction to Landon in the beginning of our relationship, but it had disappeared after the first time we had sex. Not once had I actually wanted to since then, and sometimes I felt more aversion to it than others. But I'd always done it anyway, giving in to Landon's desires and his pushiness when I said no. Being more firm—and willing to continue to say "no"—was different for me. Just as Landon accepting my "no" was different for him.

On Wednesday night after I'd rebuffed him again when he got back from a work-related outing, I lay there awake, staring at the ceiling. I was giving this relationship between us effort to see if we could make it through the changes I was experiencing; I was being more forthcoming about the things that really mattered to me and was trying to truly be myself with Landon. It wasn't natural with him, and it was apparent that he didn't appreciate it—at least not yet—but I was trying. But I knew we couldn't have a relationship if I couldn't get over my aversion to having sex.

There'd be nothing to get over if this was Myles. I actually want sex when I'm around him.

Maybe that was the problem—Myles. I turned and made out Landon's darkened form next to me in bed. He was trying to adapt to the changes I was bringing into our relationship. Change wasn't easy for him, and he had liked the way things were—what was happening was a lot for him. And it was obvious he was making an effort. But, despite having walked away from him, Myles was still coming between us. Maybe if I told Landon everything, it would help. I knew I should anyway; keeping what I'd done a secret from him was bothering me more every day.

The next morning, I rose first, yawning. I hadn't slept much the night before as I tried to figure out how to tell Landon about Myles. Shuffling into the kitchen, I made a large pot of coffee and sipped at it while I waited to hear Landon stirring for the day. As soon as I did, I started on his breakfast so it would be ready for him by the time he emerged, dressed and ready for the day.

As he sat on the sofa, I brought out his plate of food and his coffee and set it down on the coffee table in front of him. When he reached for the remote to turn on the news like he did every morning, I placed my hand over his.

"I need to talk to you about something this morning."

He was quiet for a minute, his eyes narrowing. "Okay. What is it?"

I sat on the other side of the sofa and let out a sigh. "I did something while you were away the last time."

"You did a lot of things," he said under his breath.

A streak of irritation flashed through me. That comment had been unnecessary. But, I reminded myself, I had no right to be irritated when I was going to tell him I'd basically had an affair. "Yes, but there's something else I haven't told you about."

"Honestly, darling, does it really matter?"

My face burned. "Yes, it does. I don't want to keep this from you anymore, Landon." My eyes flickered to his and away again. He looked terribly annoyed. "I don't want to have secrets between us. I just haven't known how to tell you."

I could see him lift a hand and rub at his temple, and the ankle he had crossed over a knee was now bouncing. "Oh for god's sake, Nina, don't be so dramatic. If it matters to you that much, just tell me so I can watch the news. You know I have to know what's going on to make the right decisions for my clients' portfolios."

I clenched my jaw. I was trying to do the right thing, and I was trying to make our relationship work, and he was just so damn indifferent. It was like he didn't care at all. Well, we were about to find out if he cared about his girlfriend with another man.

"I had an affair, Landon."

"That's what you're worried about?" He waved the hand that had been rubbing his temple dismissively and reached for the remote. "Is that all?"

"You don't care?" I shouted, incredulous.

"Nina. We spend weeks at a time apart. As long as you're discreet about it, and it's not happening when I'm home, I don't care about you getting your needs met elsewhere."

I gaped at him as he flipped on the news, trying to process what I'd just heard. "Are you telling me you don't care if I have sex with other men, Landon?"

He turned to me, his eyes now slits. "I didn't say I wanted to talk about it, Nina."

"For the record," I said, my voice shaking. I was furious and upset and confused all at once and was having trouble organizing my thoughts. The only thing I could think about for some reason was that I wanted him to know what I had and hadn't done. "I haven't had sex with anyone but you as long as we've been dating. But I ran into an old friend—more like boyfriend, but not exactly—and we spent a lot of time together, and feelings we used to have for each other came back. We only kissed twice, that's it. But I do... have feelings for him."

He muted the news and regarded me for a moment. For some reason, what I'd just told him bothered him more than when he thought I meant sex.

"Who's the friend?"

I looked down at my hands and remained silent.

"Where were you spending time together, Nina?"

"We had drinks once and went out for dinner twice."

"Going out like that isn't discreet."

"And I also spent the weekend at Myles' house the weekend before you were home the last time."

"His name is Myles? The same Myles you were dating when you were raped?"

I sucked in a breath. I hadn't meant to say his name. My hands clasped together so tightly they hurt. "We've never actually dated, but yes."

He was quiet for a minute, and when I looked up, he was scrutinizing me. I hoped he wasn't putting two and two together. "Does he like music like you do?"

I nodded.

Landon's hand ran over his jaw as it clenched. "You can't see him again, Nina."

I nodded again.

"Do you understand? You are not to talk to him anymore. Sex is one thing, but this is different. You're not allowed to have contact with him again. Ever. Are we clear?"

I felt like when I was a teenager and got in trouble with my parents, but I nodded a third time anyway; it was my fault for what I'd done. "Yes, Landon."

"Good." He sat back, rubbing his temple, unmuting the television to watch the news.

Things were unusually tense the rest of the week, although I wasn't sure if it was just me or if there really was extra tension between us because not much else changed. Like before, it was *almost* as if the conversation had never happened. While I'd first been convinced he put two and two together and knew that my Myles was the same one he played poker with at Marcus', I was beginning to think I'd been wrong, which was a huge relief. It was bad enough that Myles knew about Landon; it could be disastrous if Landon knew it was the same Myles, too.

We went out to dinner on Landon's last night home, and I was relieved I was going to have a break from his presence in the condo.

It felt like all my progress from therapy had come to a screeching halt while he was there; I was on edge every moment he was home. After dinner, though, Landon surprised me by suggesting we go out somewhere with live music before going home. His suggestion meant a lot to me—I knew he wouldn't enjoy himself—and I felt that stab of guilt again that I'd been thinking how relieved I was that he was about to leave.

In the back of the cab on the way home, he rested a hand on my thigh. "Did you do this kind of thing with Myles?"

My heart skipped. "No," I breathed out. "I mean, yes, but a long time ago. Not recently."

"So you enjoyed that, darling?"

I forced myself to smile. "Yeah, I really did. They were talented."

He bobbed his head up and down, his hand rubbing my thigh. I didn't like it and placed my hand over his, pressing down to stop him from moving.

His phone started ringing just then, and he spent the rest of the ride on a call. His voice, talking about financial measures, faded into the background and my mind wandered. Myles would have liked the band. If I'd been with him rather than Landon, we'd have still been there soaking it in. Then we'd have talked about all the reasons we enjoyed them, Myles slipping into musical jargon like he often did when he was excited about a piece of music or a band.

I glanced at my phone screen despite knowing I had no messages from him, and that I wouldn't. I couldn't be in contact with him, anyway. I'd agreed not to because Landon had demanded it. But I was still confused about him not being upset by the idea of me having sex with other men as long as I was *discreet*. Was that his problem with what happened with Myles? That I hadn't been *discreet* enough? Or was it that I had feelings toward Myles, and Landon actually felt some jealousy because he cared about me?

The better question is why the hell am I even with a guy who, after all this time, I still don't know if he really cares about me or not?

TWENTY

After we got home from the bar with live music, Landon and I changed into pajamas, brushed our teeth, and climbed into bed. When I leaned over to turn off my bedside lamp, Landon's body pushed heavily against my back, his erection hard against my ass, his hand sliding under my shirt to my breast.

"I don't want to have sex, Landon," I said, like I had every night since he'd been home.

Unlike the previous eight nights, he didn't sigh or hmph and then move away, though. Instead, he hooked his hands into my pants.

"Landon," I said more firmly, trying to push hard enough to roll him away from me. "I said I don't want to."

He slowed with pulling my pants down but didn't stop. "I miss you, darling. It's been a long time. And it's my last night home." He forcefully yanked my pants down between my knees, which I'd clamped together. "I've done all the things you've wanted. I've listened to you talk about whatever mundane thing comes into your head, and I even took you out to listen to music tonight. I didn't enjoy that—I did it for *you*, Nina."

"But, Landon—"

"I even forgave your affair, darling," he said, sounding like his jaw was clenched. His hands grabbed my hips tightly, and he'd pushed himself inside me by the time he was done speaking.

I was dry and it hurt. *A lot.* I scrunched my eyes closed, my jaw tight as the tears rolled out. When he kissed my shoulder, I thought I might vomit. But I didn't, and before long, he grunted and was finished and rolled off me, promptly falling asleep.

I was still in the same position, staring at the wall with my thighs clenched tightly together the next morning when he woke, and I listened to him shower and get dressed. Then he walked to my side of the bed and rested a hand on my back, bending and kissing my cheek.

"I'll see you in a few months, darling."

I didn't reply. He didn't seem to notice and a few minutes later was gone, on the way to the airport. I didn't get up for several more hours. I felt as paralyzed physically as I did mentally. There were so many confusing emotions from the night before, and I just wanted it to have been a bad dream.

I was positively disheveled for my next therapy session. I had barely moved out of bed after Landon left except to rip off the pajamas I'd been wearing and make my way to the sofa, where I'd spent the rest of the day and night and the next morning. After that, I'd gone to therapy in the same clothes I'd been wearing since the day before, my hair in a frizzy, tangly bun on the top of my head. I hadn't wanted to go near the bedroom even to shower or change into fresh clothes.

Leslie's smile faltered when she saw me, and I followed her into her office. We sat and she waited for me to say something, which was how we always opened our sessions now, but five minutes passed in silence. My mind was completely, utterly blank.

"Nina," Leslie broke the silence.

I looked up at her from where I'd been staring through the floor.

"Can you tell me what's happened?"

What *had* happened? I didn't really understand it myself. Or why I was the way I was. "I don't know."

"So, when I saw you last, we talked about your fight with Landon in the restaurant and about your talk with him afterward. How did the week go with all the changes? Were you able to stay true to being yourself the way you wanted?"

I stared at her, her words digesting on a delay. "It was mostly like nothing had changed and I hadn't told him anything, except little flashes of irritation here and there. And he took me out for live music one night."

"Okay, that's a big deal. That's a big change for him, from what I understand."

"Yeah. It is."

"So that's good."

"Yeah," I replied distractedly.

"Did you guys talk about that at all? Did it change things between you?"

I hmphed, then laughed, even though none of it was funny. "Oh, yeah, it changed things alright," I bit out, exploding with anger. "He spent all week being unusually respectful of me not wanting to have sex. He'd stop trying as soon as I said no. No pushiness. He's never done that before. But after that?" I laughed again, then scrubbed my hands over my face. It was wet; I hadn't realized I'd begun to cry. "I said no. Three times."

Leslie's brow furrowed. When I didn't continue, she asked, "What happened then?"

I looked at her and she became blurry as my tears backed up before spilling over. "Each time, he countered with something. He missed me, it was his last night home. He'd done what I wanted him to, he'd taken me out to do something he hated because I liked it. He'd forgiven me for Myles." I wrung my hands in my lap, watching the skin turn white as I did. "I didn't say no a fourth time. Not that he gave me enough time to."

My stomach lurched, and I buried my face in my hands. I was angry and disgusted, at Landon and myself. At Landon for being so pushy and not respecting me the first time I said no. At myself for not violently fighting him off me. Very urgently, I wanted to shower again, to scrub anything of Landon that might be left off my body, out of my mind. I felt dirty and disgusting. And after a while, I managed to tell Leslie all of that, too.

She listened, a murmur here or there assuring me she was listening and understood and wasn't judging me. She gave me all the space I needed to get everything out as I was figuring it out. When I was done, I was worn out. Exhausted. It had been two and a half hours of feeling everything that had been turned off since Landon didn't accept my "no."

I woke on Tuesday with a headache and feeling drained from how much crying I'd done the day before, but I also felt somewhat rested and clear-headed. I followed my new routine that I'd neglected while Landon had been home and drank coffee while listening to Evanescence and The Dovelyn Trio, then headed over to Midtown Park. I walked and spent time on the bench watching my wildlife friends, then decided to get lunch at a café before returning to spend the afternoon at the park.

As I walked the trails in the afternoon, a sense of clarity descended. My shoulders relaxed, and I could breathe more easily. I was miserable, and I knew that. What I'd just realized, however, was that I had the ability to do something about it. I'd been operating under this sense of obligation toward Landon, but why? Where had it come from? I suspected it was because life with him was familiar. It was how things had been for years, and it meant things were predictable. I knew what to expect and when, and I found that predictability comforting. I'd always liked having a plan and being organized, but it had become more severe after the rape. And clinging to predictability for a sense of control was keeping me in a relationship I could finally see wasn't healthy. It didn't truly involve love—at least not any kind of love I wanted in my life. I wanted love with passion, with heart. I wanted to be loved by someone who wanted to do things for me and show me how they felt and was excited to see me, and I wanted to want to do those things for someone else. I would never have that with Landon.

I also needed to have people in my life who respected me. Landon didn't. He'd demonstrated his misogynistic mentality and had never respected my desires surrounding sex. He didn't respect that I valued different things than he did or care enough to know about them. He would never love me the way I wanted to be loved, and I would never love him that way, either. Staying was just going to create misery, and it was a setback emotionally when I was around him.

I waited until late that evening when I was more likely to catch him when he could talk, then called him.

"Nina?" he answered. I couldn't tell from his tone if he was irritated or not, but I was glad he hadn't called me "darling." I wasn't sure I'd ever even be able to even think the word without disgust.

"Hi, Landon. Do you have a few minutes?"

"Yes, I have a few minutes."

My stomach fluttered. "I don't think this is working."

"What isn't working, darling?"

I gritted my teeth. "Us, Landon."

There was silence.

"I'm going to move out. Get my own place."

"You don't need to do that, Nina."

"Yes, I do," I said firmly. "I can't keep living here when we aren't together."

"But we are."

"No, that's what I'm saying, Landon. Our relationship isn't working, not just living together."

"What's not working, Nina? I've accepted everything you've told me, I've forgiven you for the affair. I took you out for music and I'll do it again when I'm home next. That's what you want, right?"

"It's not that. It's... us. We're not compatible. We don't like or value the same things, Landon. I don't want you to take me out when you hate doing it. But you hate everything I like."

"I don't hate it, I just don't care for it."

"That's not the point."

"Are you leaving me for Myles?"

My heart skipped. He actually sounded angry. *Really* angry. I was glad he wasn't home. "No, Landon. Myles has nothing to do with this. I'm doing this because it's what's best for me."

There was another long silence. "I'm still getting used to these changes in you, Nina. And my new travel schedule just went into effect. I wish you'd give it a little more time."

"The schedule doesn't help, but it's not about that. We can't have a relationship when we barely see each other during the year." There was a sudden flash of him talking about taking care of needs while we were apart.

"We barely see each other now and it's been fine."

"Has it? How many other women have helped to make it 'fine,' Landon?"

"What are you talking about, Nina?"

"I think you called it taking care of needs. You have women who take care of your needs when you're away from me, don't you? Since I can't?"

"Nina... what do you expect when I'm on the road for weeks at a time? It's just sex. Nothing like what you were doing with Myles."

I felt a stab of guilt; Landon *was* jealous. But none of that mattered, because I wasn't staying with Landon. I just wanted to know if he'd been sleeping around when he was traveling, and now I had my answer.

"It doesn't matter. I need to do this, Landon. I'm sorry. I'm going to start looking for my own place tomorrow."

I heard him let out a long breath. "You don't have to rush, Nina. You're welcome to stay as long as you like."

"Thank you, Landon. I appreciate it." And I did. Part of me had expected him to tell me to go ahead and be gone by the next day or something. I was already prepared to have to find a hotel to live out of for a while. "I mean that."

"I'm getting a call from Preston," he said, referring to one of Lorman's partners.

"Of course—go. I'll keep you updated on when I'm leaving. Bye, Landon."

"Goodbye, darling."

I exhaled slowly. My hands were trembling and my heart was pitter-pattering in my chest. I'd really had no idea what to expect, but I should have known he'd accept it fairly easily, that it wouldn't be that big of a deal to him. I'd thought for a moment, when I realized he was jealous about Myles, that he might fight for me. And a small part of me wished he *had* tried harder to keep me; I wouldn't have stayed, but I wanted to know that I'd actually meant something to him. If I had, maybe I wouldn't have felt so... gross... about how pushy he was about sex.

Maybe.

But maybe not. However much he may or may not have cared about me, he shouldn't have kept pushing. He should have stopped. I never should have had to keep telling him no to begin with. And he never should have continued to ignore me. But it wasn't something that would ever happen again because I'd officially broken up with him—we were no longer dating. And there was no way he'd expect me to have sex with him when we weren't dating. Not that there would even be an opportunity; surely I'd have a new place before he was home next in a few months.

TWENTY-ONE

There was a buoyancy in my steps in the following days I hadn't had in years. With each day that passed, I felt more conviction about my decision to leave Landon. If only I could figure out where to live. I liked the idea of being close to Leslie—I could walk to my appointments right now—but that was the only draw to staying in the city. Looking outside city limits, though, I had no idea where to go. I didn't know what I was going to do with myself. After weeks of finding listings all over the place and not being able to pick even a county to look into, I decided to take a step back and instead figure out what I wanted to do. In theory, that would lead me to where to live.

But what to do with myself? When I was young, I'd wanted to be a trail guide. And while I still felt the same excitement when I thought about it, I also felt a trepidation I wasn't sure would ever go away. I no longer had the same level of comfort being alone where I could encounter strangers, let alone somewhere remote like a mountain trail. What were my options?

A quick internet search provided me with a number of careers to investigate: arborist, horticulturalist, silviculturist, and forest manager were at the top of my list. After a few hours of additional research, I'd whittled them down to two: silviculturist and forest manager. And, luckily, they both had the same educational requirements, so I didn't have to decide now. Rather, I could focus on finding a school, which I did fairly quickly; there weren't a lot of schools that offered graduate programs in forestry. Luckily, I'd already taken enough undergraduate courses by the time I declared a business major that I ended up only needing one more course for my bachelor's degree in forestry and I had taken it.

Within a month of leaving Landon, I had submitted applications to four universities that had graduate forestry programs and also signed up to take four online courses to get a certificate in Forest Carbon Science and Management. I was considering also getting one in Urban Forestry when that one was over. The certificate program took only eight weeks; I'd have enough time to do both before starting classes in the fall if I was accepted into one of the graduate programs I applied to.

To celebrate having taken steps in a new direction—one that felt better aligned with who I was—I decided to go out that evening. Most of my outings were to Midtown Park, and I usually spent the evenings in, listening to music and working on various assignments or research for therapy. Most recently, I'd been learning to cross stitch, my homework from Leslie to find a new hobby I enjoyed. Tonight, though, was cause for celebration, and I did a search to see if I could find anywhere with live music. As I scrolled through the options that popped up in the search results, I stopped when I saw Bar Vivian. The Sultry Sound was playing again. It was a sign, I decided—that's where I'd go.

When I arrived, Bar Vivian was already full, and I didn't see any empty tables. There were a few tables with only some of the chairs taken, but I didn't walk over and ask to join anyone. I didn't want the pressure of being social with a stranger; I was ready to just relax and take in the music to replenish me from the excitement and anxiety of the last few days. I found an empty space where I could stand without intruding on anyone else's space after ordering a bourbon and was simply grateful there was a post I could lean against.

The band was as good as I remembered them being and I closed my eyes after a while, my back against the post reassuring me no one would come up behind me unexpectedly, and let the music wash over and through me. Again, I had an urge to share the experience with Myles and considered texting him. It was a Friday, and he usually didn't have school-related activities after the end of the school day on Fridays. He was maybe out somewhere already, but maybe he was home. He could still listen to the band regardless—they should be playing for another few hours. I pulled out my phone, unlocked it, then stared at my text conversation with him. The last message was the one I'd sent the last time I was there. I closed the conversation and put my phone away, realizing I had to pee.

I wove through people to the bar and told the bartender I'd be back for my drink. She nodded and set it behind the counter for me before turning to get the next drink order. After using the bathroom, I went ahead and ordered another, sipping the rest of my first drink as I waited. The band took a break, and the air filled with the sounds of animated conversation. It made me smile, remembering that sound from spending hours in Nina's with Myles. With my new drink in tow, I made my way through tables back toward the stage area, scanning for any tables that may have opened up.

"It's Nina! I see Nina!"

I startled, turning my head around to find the source of the muffled shout, even knowing it couldn't be for me; no one I knew would be in a place like Bar Vivian. Besides, the voice sounded like it was coming from a kid rather than an adult.

"Look, Mr. E—that's her! It's your girlfriend!"

My stomach flopped over, and my heart stuttered, my steps faltering. I wasn't sure what to do. I'd promised Myles he'd never see me again, but there was no doubt he was there to my right somewhere. I decided to go with pretending I didn't hear them and took another step, but then someone jumped in front of me. It was Dwayne, the same kid I'd seen that first time I went to the middle school.

"You're Nina, right? Mr. E's girlfriend?"

My face flamed. "Yes, I'm Nina, Mr. E's *friend*. And you are Dwayne, right?"

The boy's face lit up. "That's me. What's up?"

I smiled with a faint laugh. "Well, I'm here to watch the band. What are *you* doing here?"

He slid his hands into his pockets and cocked his head back like he was trying to look cool. "Same. Mr. E promised me and Tommy if we practiced enough he'd bring us out to hear a band that played our instruments." He half turned, pointing behind him.

My eyes followed his hand and then I saw Myles. My breath hitched. I'd thought I'd never see him again, but there he was, in a white pinstriped button up, the top few buttons undone, and his sleeves rolled up. God, he looked good. And he was watching us intently, but I couldn't read his expression because it was guarded.

"Come on, you can sit with us. We have an extra chair. And we have some food, too, if you're hungry."

"Oh, I—"

"I told Mr. E I'd come get you," he cut me off before I could decline.

I looked back toward Myles, but he was focused on the other student sitting at the table. I wasn't sure if Dwayne had told Myles he was coming to get me after Myles told him no, or if Myles had asked him to. I didn't want to go over there if Myles didn't want me there, but I definitely didn't want to turn my back and walk away if he did. Because I absolutely wanted to be there with him if that was what he wanted, too. I decided to risk it and followed Dwayne over.

"Told you it was her, Mr. E," Dwayne said, sitting down in the empty chair next to Myles.

"Hi, Nina," Myles said, his voice even, his eyes searching my face before locking with mine.

"Hi, Myles," I said. Shit—my voice was wobbling.

"Sit down," Dwayne said. "You said you were here to watch. We have the best table."

I hesitated, looking for some sign from Myles. He didn't give me one. "Thank you," I said, turning to Dwayne. "I appreciate that, but I just came over to say hello. I was actually leaving."

"Your glass is full, Nina," Myles said, just as I was turning to walk away. "And there's nowhere else to sit."

I searched his eyes, and he tipped his head toward the empty chair. In return, I gave him a small smile. "Okay. I'll sit for a few minutes."

"Nina, this is Tommy," Dwayne said. "He seems a little sussy, but he's alright."

It took everything I had not to burst out laughing. When I glanced over at Myles, I could see he was having the same struggle.

"That's Miss Covington to you guys," Myles said.

"*You* call her Nina," Dwayne said, eating a tortilla chip with what looked like spinach dip on it.

"That's because I can. You boys can call her Miss Covington."

I gave a small shrug to Myles—it didn't matter to me if the kids called me Nina. Miss Covington felt weird anyway.

"If Miss Covington is more respectful..." Dwayne said with a sly look. I was already getting the impression he was the mouthier of the two kids. "...then *you* should call her Miss Covington, too."

He'd caught me by surprise, and I burst out laughing. Myles narrowed his eyes at me, but I could see him pulling in the corners of his mouth. I quirked an eyebrow and lifted a shoulder.

"He's got a point, Myles."

"That's Mr. E to you, Miss Covington," Myles replied.

I laughed.

Myles grinned.

I blushed.

"So, Nina—" Dwayne said.

"Miss Covington," Myles interrupted him.

Dwayne rolled his eyes. "Miss Covington, Mr. E told us you're faster than anyone at slaps."

"Yeah," Tommy chimed in. "Is it true?"

I chuckled. "I'm faster than Myles—Mr. E."

Dwayne and Tommy both stuck their hands out toward me at the same time.

"Me first," Tommy said.

"No way," Dwayne replied. "I met her first."

"Dude, that's because you cheated and went after her when I won rock paper scissors."

"Fine, whatever, dude," Dwayne shot back.

I looked to Myles; slapping him to play this game was one thing. Slapping a couple of eleven or twelve-year-olds was something else entirely. I was worried about hurting them.

"They can handle it," Myles said in response to my raised eyebrows.

"Okay," I said, turning to Tommy. "But I'll start on top." That way, I could gauge how hard the kids were slapping first.

We got set up and Tommy immediately flipped a hand and slapped mine—hard. I glanced over at Myles and he was grinning. After resetting, Tommy flipped his hand right off the bat again, but this time my hand was out of the way faster than he slapped and he got air.

"Dude," he said in surprise, resetting with his hands on top this time.

I flipped my hand and slapped his, softer than he'd slapped mine.

"Shit," he muttered, then his eyes bounced between Myles, who'd dropped his chin and was eying him sternly, and me. "I mean shoot," he said, not at all convincing.

After I'd slapped his left hand three times and his right hand twice, it was apparently Dwayne's turn.

"You're slow," Dwayne said to Tommy. "Watch how a savage does it."

I snorted, trying not to laugh, and that distraction meant Dwayne got my hand on the first round.

"I'm just warming up, Nina."

"Miss Covington," Myles corrected.

Dwayne rolled his eyes. "Miss Covington."

I reset and he flipped his hand faster than I expected. He missed me, but it was close. Five slaps later, Dwayne was out.

"Damn," he said, shaking his hands out, grinning.

"Dwayne," Myles said in a warning tone.

"Sorry, Mr. E."

"Your turn, Mr. E," Tommy said.

I watched Myles' face for a sign whether to agree or not, but then the band was playing again. "Maybe later," I said.

The band was still playing an hour later when Myles motioned to the boys and they grabbed their coats from their chairs. As they were getting them on, Myles stepped close to me and bent over so I could hear him over the music.

"I have to take them home," he said.

"Okay."

"Are you staying for a while?"

I scrutinized his face before answering, and some of his guardedness slipped. He was hopeful.

"Yes," I replied. My original plan had been to stay until the band stopped playing anyway.

He gave a short nod. "Okay. I'll come back, then."

My heart fluttered in my chest, and I smiled. He stared back at me for a beat, then gave me an answering smile before turning and heading toward the exit with the boys.

TWENTY-TWO

It was a beautiful spring morning as I arrived at Midtown Park on Saturday, a week after seeing Myles with his students at Bar Vivian. I'd stayed until the band stopped playing and the bar was closing, but Myles had never come back like he said he would. I'd cried that night, as well as the next day; I'd been so hopeful when he'd invited me to sit with them and then said he was coming back. Without my knowledge, my heart had counted on being able to forge some sort of relationship with him again after that hopeful start, but then he'd never come back. And he hadn't called or texted, either. He'd changed his mind, and while I could understand, it had hurt.

But that hurt was dulled this morning as I listened to the birds chirping while making my way along the trails. There were rabbits and squirrels out enjoying the sunshine and warmth, and I even saw a few deer. The plants looked fuzzy with all their new neon-green growth, and some of the earliest flowers of the year were blooming along the ground. It was the kind of day that made you believe in endless possibilities for the future. By the time I sat on my favorite bench, I was grinning widely, filled with a sense of vitality and optimism. With my eyes closed and my ears listening attentively, I painted a lively picture in my mind of the comings and goings of the animals around me, as well as people walking or jogging past.

In the middle of my meditation, footsteps slowed, before stopping entirely, very close to me. Then someone's weight settled next to me on the bench.

My eyes flew open, and I turned. The pounding of my heart accelerated when I realized who was there.

"Myles!" I rushed out on an exhale, my hand over my chest.

"I didn't mean to scare you," he said. "I was trying not to disturb you."

I studied him, attempting to normalize my breath. "It's okay."

His eyes remained trained straight ahead on the patch of wildness in front of us, and I turned that way, too. We sat in silence for a long time... for so long that squirrels were getting brave and scooting out to check around our feet for nuts or other bits of food.

"I'm sorry I didn't come back to Bar Vivian last week," he said.

"It's fine."

"I was going to, but no one was home at Dwayne's house, and I couldn't just leave him there by himself, so I hung out with him until his older sister came home a few hours later."

"Really, it's okay, Myles. That's where you should have been. And you don't owe me any kind of explanation."

He rubbed his cheek with his hand, then ran it through his hair. "I could have texted you to tell you, though. And I thought about it, but when I opened my phone, I saw all my unanswered messages to you and I got pissed off again, so I didn't."

"I'm sorry," I said softly.

He reached out a hand and grabbed mine. My breath caught, then he let go as suddenly as he'd touched me and ran a hand through his hair again. "You don't need to apologize again, Nina. You already did. And I understand what happened—I read your letter. That's how I knew where to find you this morning. It's just that it hurt a lot. And I don't want to go through that again." He sighed, looking away from me toward his left along the trail.

My heart was in my throat, restricting my airflow. My whole body buzzed, and I didn't know what to say or what to do. So, I did nothing but sit there in silence until Myles turned to face me for the first time since I'd realized he was there. Our gazes locked for a long time. So many words welled up within me as we looked at one another, but they all got stuck before they made it out.

"You look really good, Nina," he said, swallowing, his eyes breaking away to roam over me. "You look happier. I'm glad."

His tone didn't match his words; it was filled with sadness.

"I am," I replied. "Therapy is helping me a lot."

"I'm glad you started seeing someone."

"Me, too," I agreed. "Thank you for pushing me in the right direction." I went to swallow, but my mouth was bone dry. "Not just with that, though. With Landon."

"Don't talk to me about Landon," he said, his voice sharp.

My heart was pounding. I looked at him, but he was staring straight ahead, his jaw tight. "But, he and I—"

"Nina," he cut me off harshly, working his jaw. His voice held a warning.

"It's just we—"

"Nina!" he interrupted again. "I mean it. Whatever it is won't matter and it won't change anything. Not a single word about him. Or else I can't do this."

I opened my mouth but didn't know what to say. I wanted to tell him I'd broken up with Landon, but I was afraid if I so much as said Landon's name again that Myles would get up and walk away. I couldn't believe he was there with me and didn't want to do anything to jeopardize that for as long as it lasted. He'd said it wouldn't matter anyway. "Okay," I said instead. "I just—" I stopped abruptly and cocked my head. "Do you hear that?" I asked, leaning forward. It sounded like a faint meow.

Myles shook his head. "I don't hear anything."

I strained, closing my eyes. There was definitely a meow coming from somewhere. I waited, focused, until I heard it again. My eyes popped open, and I pointed ahead of me and just to the right, standing. "There's a cat meowing over there."

Myles stood, too, and followed me as I headed in the direction I'd heard the meow coming from. After several pauses to listen and reset what direction we were heading, Myles and I were somewhat far into the wilderness area I liked to watch from the bench, staring up at a tiny bundle of dirty fur, clinging for dear life to a tree branch.

"Oh, sweetie," I cooed with my arms raised up the trunk. I was over a foot shy of reaching the branch. "It's okay. You can come down."

It meowed loudly, not moving.

"I won't hurt you, sweetie. I promise."

When the kitten still didn't move, I glanced at the trunk of the tree, trying to assess if it was big enough to hold my weight if I climbed it. Probably not. And the kitten would probably run from the motion, anyway.

"Let me try," Myles said, his voice husky and soft as he stepped toward the tree trunk. He reached up his hands, moving slowly. As he neared the kitten, it drew back in fear. Myles froze.

"It's okay, sweetie," I cooed again. "He's just going to help you get down, okay? Let him help you, sweetie."

Myles moved again, even slower, as I continued to talk to the kitten as soothingly as I could. Just as Myles reached it, it turned and clawed its way up to the next branch juncture, which was outside of Myles' reach.

"Damn it," he whispered.

I eyed the tree again. I couldn't leave the kitten there, so I had to figure out a way to get it down. I stepped forward and reached for the first branch I saw to start climbing.

"Nina," Myles said brusquely. I turned and he gave one sharp shake of his head. "Don't do that."

"I can't leave it there, Myles. And I don't know if I could find it again if we left to get a ladder or something—it could run off. I have to."

"That tree isn't going to hold your weight, Nina—even *I* know that. You'll both get hurt. Please don't."

I turned back to the tree and looked up at the kitten as it let out another meow. "I have to, Myles," I said. "Look at it. It's so scared. I can't leave it here like this. I have to get it down somehow."

"I know, but not like that." His eyes darted around before returning to me. "Come here," he said, squatting down. "Get on my shoulders."

I hesitated. It wasn't that I'd never been on his shoulders before, because I had—when we were in college and I told him he couldn't squat with my weight and he'd had me climb onto his shoulders so he could prove me wrong, which he had. It was that I wasn't sure whether or not he could still do something like that, and that my belly was doing somersaults at the thought of that much physical contact.

I walked around behind him and climbed over his shoulders. With a firm grip on my thighs, he stood, slow and steady.

"Jesus Christ, you're strong, Myles," I laughed mutedly. I had expected him to wobble or something. My whole body buzzed.

His hands smoothed up and down my thighs a few times as he chuckled, and I nearly passed out. "I still work out some."

"That's an understatement."

He chuckled again. "But that doesn't mean I can hold you up there for an hour, so let's get that kitten down."

He stepped carefully up to the tree, his hands again firmly grasping my thighs to anchor my lower body in place, and I began talking to the kitten again, my hands gradually nearing it. I was very close to it this time and could see its tiny body shaking. My heart ached to see it so terrified and alone. As I neared it, it reared back like it had with Myles, but it didn't run. When I was close enough to touch it, I paused and waited, letting it decide to lower its head and sniff my fingers.

"That's it, sweetie," I crooned. "I'm not gonna hurt you."

When it was finished inspecting my fingers, it didn't climb into my hands, but it didn't try to get away either. I wrapped both hands slowly around it after stroking its filthy fur a few times, then lifted it from the tree branch. The tiny thing was filled with renewed terror and tried to wriggle away, its claws tearing into my hands.

"Shh, it's alright, sweetie," I continued to coo as I brought it closer to me, ignoring the gashes I was receiving.

Once I'd reached my chest, the kitten clung to my shirt. I was glad I'd worn a sweatshirt—the material was more protective of my skin than a sweater would have been, and I had a large pocket in the front the kitten might feel safer in. For now, though, it was clinging tightly to my chest.

"Okay," I said in the same voice. "We're ready to get down, Myles."

Without a word, he squatted down smoothly, then bent forward. I could feel his back straining and knew my weight on the back of his neck must have been painful, but he was trying to set my feet directly on the ground so I wouldn't have to hop off with the kitten in my arms. Sure enough, when he stood after I'd stepped away, his hand rubbed at the back of his neck.

"Are you alright?" I asked, glancing up at him from my study of the tiny mess of fur in my arms.

He smiled warmly, his eyes lit up. "I'm fine." Then he bent over and considered the kitten. "You think it's okay?"

"I don't know for sure," I whispered, trying not to scare the tiny creature. "But I think so. I didn't see any cuts or anything. She probably just needs a bath and some love."

"She? You can sex a cat?"

"Mm-hm," I said, still using a soft voice. "I can sex a lot of animals."

"That's really cool," Myles said quietly.

I stood, talking to the kitten, running my hand over her gently, and she released her claws before burrowing under my chin. She smelled awful, like a cross between a dead animal and fresh feces, but I didn't try to move her away.

"Is that a good idea, Nina?" Myles asked as we headed back toward the trail. "She's gotta be covered in bugs and bacteria. Maybe she shouldn't be so close to your face?"

"It's okay for a few minutes," I responded. "She feels safe right now. I'll move her in a little bit. She needs this right now. Isn't that right, sweetie?" I directed toward the kitten.

When we broke through back to the trail, Myles asked, "So what's next? What are you going to do with her?"

"Well," I sighed, "I'm sure there's a shelter around here somewhere. I'll take her there so she can be adopted, I guess. I'd keep her, but I can't." I looked down, drawing my head back, trying to see her. "Okay, sweetie, let's move you." My neck was feeling *very* itchy. The mostly relaxed kitten dug her claws into my neck when I tried to move her, and I sucked in a sharp breath. "Ow!"

I tried for another moment to peel the small creature from me without success; all I accomplished was shredding the skin on my neck and upper chest.

"Let me try," Myles said in a low, soothing voice. "Come on, little one, you're hurting Nina and she just wants to help you." As he spoke, his fingers crept around the kitten and peeled her off me. "Oh, Nina," he said. "Your neck."

"It's okay. She wasn't trying to hurt me. She's just scared."

I accepted the kitten back from Myles and showed her my sweatshirt pocket. Rather than climbing in, though, she snuggled her face into the crook of my elbow. With her resettled, we began walking again.

"Would you mind looking up a shelter for me?" I asked. My hands were occupied.

"On it," Myles replied, already on his phone. A few minutes later, he said, "I'm sorry, Nina. I can't find any around here that are no-kill."

My heart dropped. I wished all shelters were no-kill shelters. "That's okay."

"Alright. I think we should go to the one in Bathlin, then. It's a little further out, but it's the largest, so hopefully it's not as full."

I glanced at him. He'd said "we"—had he done that on purpose? Probably not. We walked in silence together along the main trail to the south end of the park until we reached the corner where the city basically began again. Myles pointed to his left when I moved toward the right in the direction of a street where it would be easier to find a cab.

"Wrong way, Nina—I'm parked a few blocks this direction."

I paused. "Are you sure? I can get a cab back to my car and drive there myself."

"I know," he said. "I'm sure."

My heart fluttered in my chest, and I fell into step beside him, my hand smoothing over the kitten in my arms. When we reached his SUV parked on the street, an unexpected wave of emotion crashed over me, and I teared up.

"Are you okay?" he asked, his eyebrows dipping toward the center, his mouth pressing into a thin line.

My exhale was slow and controlled. "Yeah, I'm fine." I turned away and opened my eyes wide so they'd dry. For some reason, getting into his car hurt inside my chest. But I pushed through it and climbed in.

Myles reached over and helped me pull my seatbelt across without disturbing the kitten, and then we were off, the inside of the car filled with hauntingly beautiful notes from The Dovelyn Trio. After a couple of miles, the kitten lifted her head, sleepily blinking before resting her chin on my forearm, which was now vibrating with her purr.

"She likes the music," I said, running a finger along her nose. "She's purring and seems more relaxed."

We came to a stop at a red light and Myles looked down at her, reaching a finger to rub between her eyes. She pushed into his finger and purred harder. Myles' face softened and he smiled at her.

"Treble," he said, his voice low and rumbly. "That should be her name... Because she's a little bundle of trouble who likes music."

My sides shook as I laughed, trying not to startle the kitten. "That's terrible and I love it. What do you think, Treble? You like that name?" She continued rubbing against Myles' finger, and I grinned up at him. "I think that's a yes."

We drove the rest of the way in silence aside from The Dovelyn Trio in the background, and by the time we pulled into the parking lot of the shelter, I was smitten with the heap of dirty fur in my lap. I abhorred the thought of leaving her at the shelter, but I knew there was no way I could take her home with me while I lived in Landon's condo. He had an aversion to animals in general, and he *hated* cats.

When I got out of the car, Treble buried her face into the crook of my elbow again, trying to burrow between my arm and my side. I petted her and spoke to her as soothingly as I could, but it was like she could sense where we were going and got more agitated with each step. It felt like something was clawing my chest apart; I wanted to turn around and leave with her and felt guilty that I couldn't.

"It's okay, Nina," Myles murmured, rubbing my shoulder briefly. "You saved her. She wouldn't have survived long where she was."

I nodded; he was right. Once inside, I explained to the woman at the front desk that we'd found Treble in the woods in Midtown Park, that she was in a tree by herself, meowing.

"Poor thing," the woman—Phoebe, according to her nametag—said, leaning over the counter to get a good look at Treble. "Did you already see if you knew anyone who could adopt her?" she asked.

"I don't know anyone who could," I replied. "And I would in a heartbeat myself if I could, but I can't. That's why we're here."

"Are you sure? We're overflowing right now—we always are with cats, and so are all the other shelters around here because there are so many strays in Midtown. If they're not adopted within a week, we have to put them down to make space for more."

I felt sick. "A week? Just a week? That's all they get to find a family?" I tightened my arms protectively around Treble as my eyes filled. "She's wild and missing patches of fur—no one is going to adopt her in a week."

Phoebe sighed. "Probably not. I'm sorry. I wish things were different—I really do. And if I could take them all home with me, I would, but I already have too many animals I've adopted from here to save them." She paused. "We'll clean her up and get her shots and maybe she'll luck out and someone will want to take her home. We do get a lot of visitors here. We just have even more animals."

I swallowed, still holding tight to Treble, a few of my tears slipping over my lower eyelids. I didn't want to give her to Phoebe. But I didn't have a choice. I started to lift her away from my body, then Myles, who'd been listening in silence, reached out a hand and gently pushed my arm and Treble back into my body.

"I'll take her, Nina," he said, his hand resting on her back. "She can live with me."

I stared at him, hope and wonder replacing my anguish. "Really? You don't mind?"

"Really," he said, looking down at Treble. "She's growing on me." He used a hand to turn me around, calling back to Phoebe, "Thank you."

I was a sniffling mess by the time I sat back down in the front passenger seat of Myles' car. Between the upset from nearly giving up Treble to almost certain death, knowing how many innocent animals were losing their lives every week, and Myles' kindness, not to mention just being around him again, I was an emotional wreck.

"I'm sorry," I said tearily as he reached across to help with my seatbelt. "This is just a whole lot right now."

He rested a hand over mine on Treble's back. "I know, Nina. It's okay. You can cry all you need."

And I did, all the way to the local pet store, where the process of picking out everything Myles would need for Treble brought some excitement to the forefront. Not only was it fun to pick out toys and bedding and such for a kitten, but it was endearing to watch Myles taking it all so seriously, reading descriptions and touching things to compare them to make sure he was "getting the best for little Treble." I had a flash of him picking out baby things and could easily see him as a dad... a wonderful dad. It made my heart ache and I wanted desperately to wrap my arms around him and burrow into the crook of his neck like the kitten had been doing to me earlier.

After the pet store, Myles drove to the other side of the shopping center and parked in the lot by the grocery store.

"I'll be right back," he said, jumping out, leaving the music on.

I petted Treble and closed my eyes, listening to The Dovelyn Trio as she purred, until Myles returned a few minutes later. He put a small bag in the back seat and then we were off again.

"I should have asked earlier," he said when we pulled onto his street. "Are you able to help me get her settled? I can drive you back home now if you aren't."

"I have nothing going on today," I whispered, not wanting to wake Treble, who'd dozed off in my arms.

He let out a loud rush of breath. "Okay."

TWENTY-THREE

One of the first tasks to tackle once all the new kitten supplies had been ferried inside Myles' house was to give the new kitty a bath, an activity I wasn't looking forward to. In my experience, cats did *not* like getting wet. And I was already scratched up all to hell.

Between the two of us, however, Myles and I managed to get Treble cleaned up without too many more scratches, and none were as significant as the ones I'd already sustained. It was after Treble was clean and trembling in a towel on my lap in Myles' living room that I discovered the purpose for the grocery store stop after the pet store.

"Hair dryer," Myles said, holding it up with one hand while plugging it in with the other. "So we can dry her. Poor thing is freezing."

I almost teared up. "That was so thoughtful, Myles."

He shrugged. "I know *I* wouldn't like sitting there all wet like that."

Smiling, I said, "Use low speed, medium heat, and turn it on over there, then walk over to us slowly so the sound doesn't startle her."

Treble wasn't a fan of the hair dryer at first—likely because it *was* loud—but after a minute or two, she began to enjoy it. Before long, she was clean, dry, and fluffy, and we could see that she was a beautiful tortoiseshell pattern. She definitely looked more like a kitten than the wild animal she had previously resembled. Then Myles got her litter box, food, and water set up and we showed them to her. She didn't use the litter box, but sat down to happily eat.

"While she's eating, let's get *you* cleaned up," Myles said.

"I glanced down at my soaked, filthy sweatshirt. The dirty water from Treble's bath penetrated through the tank top and bra I wore underneath. "It's okay—I'll clean up when I go home."

"Even if you need to leave soon or want to wait for clothes, we should go ahead and clean out all those scratches so they don't get infected." He tipped his head toward his bedroom. "Come on."

After a short hesitation because my stomach was doing somersaults, I followed him through the bedroom and into the bathroom. Every few minutes, it hit me like it did right then that I was there with him after I'd thought we'd never see each other again. I had another urge to tell him I'd broken up with Landon, but couldn't get the words past my fear of what he'd do if I mentioned anything to do with him again.

"Let's see," he said as he pulled out peroxide, antibiotic cream, Band-Aids, gauze, tape, and more.

I pulled off my sweatshirt, wincing as it rubbed against my neck, and set it on the floor.

"Jesus, Nina," Myles muttered.

I turned and looked into the mirror and sucked in a breath. I had dried blood and long welts all over my neck and chest, and there were spots of dried blood showing through my tan-colored tank top over my belly. My wrists and the backs of my hands hadn't fared much better, though there was a lot less dried blood since it had been washed off while we bathed Treble.

"It's not as bad as it looks," I assured him, though it definitely looked gruesome.

"Hang on," he said, walking into his bedroom. He reappeared after a moment with sweatpants and a t-shirt. "You should put something clean on over those, and it would probably be easiest to wash them out in the shower since there are so many. Let me know when you're done and I'll disinfect them and get them bandaged up, okay?"

I nodded, and he turned and left, pulling the door closed behind him. I showered quickly, in a constant state of wincing because the soap burned like hell in the deeper scratches, but I knew it was necessary if I didn't want to end up with an infection. Once I was done, I pulled on his sweatpants and decided immediately that I was keeping them. But I realized when I pulled on the t-shirt that the neck didn't stretch enough to expose many of the scratches, so I took it off and pulled my tank top back on, careful not to touch any of the raw spots and tucking the bottom up under my breasts so it wasn't covering the cuts on my abdomen.

I found Myles in the kitchen, sitting on the floor next to the food and water dishes, Treble in his lap, rubbing her head aggressively against his hand and purring loudly. I smiled, watching them. Myles was talking to her, but it was so low I couldn't understand the words; all I could hear was a rich rumble.

"She likes you," I observed aloud.

He looked up, his face softened and his eyes warm, and smiled. "I like her, too. She's sweet." His eyes traveled down, and the smile faded. "Nina," he breathed out. "You've got to be hurting right now."

I glanced down at myself. "Yeah, a bit. But it's okay—it was worth it to get her out of there."

"And you put that dirty shirt back on—I brought you a clean shirt."

"I know, and I'll put it on when we're done, but we wouldn't be able to get to everything with it on."

Myles tried to lift Treble off his lap, but she wrapped her paws around his arm. "Well," he said with a chuckle as he rose, "I guess she's coming to help."

In the bathroom, Treble climbed up Myles' shirt and sat on his shoulder while he was inspecting my neck, then decided she wanted to explore and jumped down and wandered off. With brows low, Myles methodically tended to my wounds. First, he used cotton swabs to clean every scratch with peroxide, then very gently patted them dry with clean gauze. Next, he scrubbed his hands clean again and used a fingertip to tenderly spread antibiotic ointment the length of every scratch.

Every time he touched my raw skin, it burned, but it was nearly eclipsed by the buzzing in my body from his proximity to me, by the way his breath felt every time he exhaled. He worked silently, in complete and utter concentration, and I was happy for the silence; I wasn't sure I'd have been able to carry on a conversation with how I felt. After he'd bandaged the deeper cuts and inspected everything one final time to make sure he was satisfied, he straightened and sighed.

"I'm sorry. I was trying really hard not to hurt you, but I know it hurt a lot anyway."

"It's okay," I replied. "There was nothing you could do about it. And it wasn't too bad."

He swallowed, his eyes resting on me. I blushed and turned away, then he gave me privacy to change into the clean shirt he'd given me.

"Do you want to go home? Or eat lunch first?" Myles asked when I made my way back to the kitchen a few minutes later. He was avoiding eye contact with me, and I wished he would just look at me so I could see what he wanted me to do. But since I couldn't see, I decided to reply with what *I* wanted.

"I'd really like to have lunch with you, if you honestly don't mind."

Finally, he looked up at me. He was smiling. "I'd like that, too." He rummaged around in the fridge and his cabinets, making a face as he did. "So, your choices are tomato soup, lentil soup, peanut butter sandwich, grilled cheese or cereal. Or I can order pizza." He ran a hand over his hair. "Not a lot of options, I know—I need to go grocery shopping. I usually do that Saturday mornings. And I wasn't expecting company."

"It's plenty. I'm happy with any of those. And I don't mind making lunch for us, if you tell me what you'd like."

He shook his head. "No, you're my guest, Nina, I'll make it. How about soup and grilled cheese?"

"Sounds wonderful."

He got the soup into a pot and pulled out some bread and was spreading it with butter the next time someone spoke.

"The boys got a kick out of meeting you," he said. "They were really impressed with your speed in slaps. Now the whole class wants to meet you and see if they can beat you."

I laughed and could hear Myles chuckle.

"I told them we'd see. If you wanted, I could have you come in near the end of the year or something."

A thrill ran through me. That meant he was intending for us to stay in contact beyond today. "Sure. I mean, just thinking about it makes me nervous, but I'll do it."

"Why are you nervous? They're eighth-graders."

I sighed, trying to figure it out. "I know, but it's a lot of pressure to live up to a reputation of any kind. And I don't want to do or say something wrong and get you in trouble or embarrass you or something."

"Nina, you can say anything you want and it'll be fine, I promise. These kids are more mature than you think—they don't really have a choice, unfortunately, but they are. And you could *never* embarrass me, I don't care what you were doing."

"Really?" I asked, trying to think of something to test that assertion.

"I know what you're doing right now," Myles laughed.

"What if I told them about kicking your ass on the Kelm's Peak hike?"

I watched his back shake with his laughter as he tended to our lunch on the stove. "Nope. Won't embarrass me."

"What if I dug out pictures of you dressed up as Beethoven for Halloween?"

His laughter deepened. "I didn't even know you yet when I did that—you don't have pictures of that."

"Ah, but I do—I stole one from you when you showed me."

He chuckled. "Of course you did. But no, won't embarrass me. Remember, I tell my kids knock-knock jokes. Besides, I dressed up as MC Hammer in the fall and that costume was way worse."

"No—you wore parachute pants? To *school*?"

"Hell yeah I did. I told them if we could get through the first half of the level one instructional by Halloween, I'd wear any music-related costume they chose. Not much motivates kids more than thinking they're going to embarrass their teacher. MC Hammer was what they picked."

"Oh my god, Myles, that's amazing. Do you have any pictures?"

"Yeah, remind me and I'll show you after I'm done over here."

"Okay, so I need to think outside the box for this one... what if I serenaded you?" I almost couldn't get the words out before I burst out laughing. I couldn't sing on key to save my life, which Myles had affirmed the one time I sang for him.

"I think that would embarrass *you* way more than me," Myles laughed. "I'm telling you, there's nothing you can do to embarrass me, Nina."

"Hm. I'll find something."

He turned and winked, smirking. "Good luck."

Throughout lunch, we talked mostly about Treble and the plan for her; she needed to go to a vet to be checked for any serious health issues and get vaccinated, and at some point, she would need to be spayed. Because Myles was teaching and I wasn't working, we agreed that I'd take care of making the appointment and taking her. She'd come in partway through and insisted on napping on Myles' lap. Despite the fact that I was the one who pulled her down out of the tree, she had bonded strongly with Myles. After we convinced her to get down, then cleaned up lunch together, however, awkwardness settled between us. What were we supposed to do next?

"I can go home whenever," I said, glancing down. "I don't want to interrupt any plans you have."

"You want to leave?" he asked, bending to pick up Treble, who'd been waiting, sitting near his feet and looking up at him.

"No. I don't want to leave. I just don't want to disrupt anything you have going on. I know all of this was unexpected."

He looked over at me, studying me like he'd been doing a lot. "I have to go help my parents for an hour or two this afternoon, but that's all, really. And I need to go grocery shopping, but I can do that tomorrow." He swallowed. "You can come with me to my parents' house if you want. They want to meet you, anyway. You don't have to help or anything, but you can come with me."

I tried to slow my breathing, but the idea of meeting his parents made me exceptionally nervous. I'd heard him talking to them on the phone when we were in college and knew that he'd talked to them about me back then. But I'd disappeared from his life... several times now. And every time I did hurt him. What did his parents think about me now?

"I don't know," I murmured.

He didn't say anything, and when I looked up, he was watching me, his hands occupied with holding Treble and rubbing under her chin.

"You're even more timid now," he said quietly. "Did something happen?"

I looked down again. "No," I said, my voice weak; I was having trouble talking around my nerves. "I'm just... your parents must hate me, Myles. For what I've done to you. And I don't blame them, I just don't know if I should meet them."

"They don't hate you, Nina. They understand our history, and they don't hold anything against you. They wish things had happened differently, but they don't blame you for that. They really do want to meet you. You wouldn't believe how much shit they gave me when I told them you'd spent the weekend here and I didn't take you over to meet them. But that's not what I'm talking about. You've been extra timid and indecisive since I first got to the park. And you were last week at Bar Vivian."

My heart pounded into my throat, and I swallowed over the lump there, willing my eyes to clear. "I'm really nervous, Myles," I said softly. "*Really* nervous. I promised you that you would never see me again because that's what you wanted, and then I saw you by accident. I don't want to break my promise to you—I don't want to push myself on you when that's not really what you want. But at the same time, being around you is what *I* want." I wanted to add that, after all this time, I could now be with him as more than friends because I was now single, but again my fear of saying something related in any way to Landon when Myles had laid that down as a limit kept me from doing so. My eyes flicked up to his. He was staring at me intently. "My needs and wants have intruded on yours a lot in the past, and I don't want to do that to you anymore. But I can't read you as easily as I could before, so I don't really know what *you* want. And it's making it hard for me to figure out what to say or do." I looked down again, crossing my arms over my chest, wincing as I did.

Myles' hands came into view of where I was staring at the floor, and he set a rather unwilling Treble on the ground before standing up. I kept my eyes on the floor, my heartbeat erratic as I waited for some sort of reply. A few seconds later, that reply came in the form of a bear hug—Myles had me completely enveloped in his arms, held snug against his chest. I wrapped my arms around him and held as tightly as I could. My scratches burned in protest, but I didn't care.

Seconds ticked by and neither of us loosened our hold. The longer we stood that way, the more my tension melted away, and the more emotional I felt. My first few tears slipped out just as Myles sniffled loudly, and he somehow squeezed me tighter. I never wanted him to let go. Eventually, though, he had to.

He sniffled again, swiping under his eyes. "Friends?"

That word gave me a strange mix of emotions. On the one hand, that meant he didn't want me to go away and stay out of his life. On the other hand, I'd hoped he still cared about me the way he did before and that maybe one day we could have a relationship. What I'd put him through must have destroyed the last of his feelings for me beyond friendship, however. That must have been what he meant when he said whatever I had to say about Landon wouldn't matter or change anything. That hurt, but I was glad he was going to stay in my life. I gave a watery smile.

"Friends."

TWENTY-FOUR

"Hey, My—oh my goodness!" Myles' mother exclaimed, exchanging a look with Myles before her eyes flicked back to me with excitement. "Nina! It's so nice to meet you." She pulled me into a warm hug.

"Mom," Myles said with a chuckle, "this is Nina. Nina, this is my mom."

"Nice to meet you, Mrs. Edwards," I said, still in her hug.

"Oh, call me Sarah, honey."

Myles looked nothing like his mom, who was only an inch or two taller than me, petite-framed, and had thick, straight, jet-black hair mixed with silver. She wore jeans and a light gray twinset, and her blue eyes sparkled. That sparkle—that's what Myles got from her, I decided. And that wide grin.

"You finally brought Nina?" a man's voice boomed from another room. A moment later, a man a little taller and broader than Myles appeared, reddish-brown hair sprinkled in the copious gray, and soft, kind brown eyes. His mouth was pulled in, reminding me of when Myles was trying not to laugh. The two of them looked so much alike aside from the gray hair that it was almost uncanny.

I smiled.

"Dad, Nina. Nina, my dad."

"Nice to meet you, Mr. Edwards."

He humphed as he pulled me into a hug just like his wife had. "I've got enough reminders that I'm getting old without someone calling me Mr. Edwards. Call me Marv."

With introductions done, Sarah linked her arm through mine and asked me question after question about everything from where I'd grown up to what hair products I used. It turned out her hair was curly when she was young but went straight while she was pregnant with Myles, and the curl never came back. She reached up several times while we talked and twisted a curl of mine between her fingers; it was obvious she missed her curly hair.

"Sarah!" Marv interjected a while later. "You won't believe this! Myles—tell her."

Myles chuckled, giving me a wink before looking at his mom. "I got a kitten."

Her eyes widened and she dropped my arm in shock. "You got a what?"

"Told you that you wouldn't believe it," Marv laughed.

Myles was full-on grinning now. "A kitten. Fluffy, whiskers, claws. You know, like a cat, but a baby one."

She slapped him playfully on the arm. "I know what a kitten is, Myles." She narrowed her eyes. "Are you joking?"

He shook his head. "No. Ask Nina if you don't believe me."

"It's true," I laughed.

"I can't believe it," Sarah said. Then she turned to me. "Myles never wanted a pet when he was growing up. Ever. He was too interested in playing instruments and didn't want to spend time taking care of an animal. When he went to other peoples' houses, he was completely uninterested in their cats or dogs."

"That's so funny," I said, giggling as I glanced at Myles. "I would never have guessed that with the way he is with Treble."

"Trouble? You named your cat Trouble, Myles?" Sarah asked.

Myles laughed. "No. Although she is a little bundle of trouble. I named her Treble, like Treble clef, but it sounds like trouble because she's also trouble."

I couldn't help snorting just as I had the first time he explained the name, and then when Myles caught my eye, we both burst out laughing at his terrible pun name. His parents stood by, grinning, their eyes moving back and forth between us.

"Well, we have to go meet this Treble," his mom said a minute later. "Let's go."

"Later, Mom—you said you needed help with some things."

She waved her hand in the air. "Yes, changing the air filters—"

"I can do those myself," Marv grumbled.

"Yes, and you can fall off the ladder again, too. Myles will do it. We need help with the air filters, changing the battery in the smoke detector in the hallway, and cleaning the windows—I can't get them to pull in so I can clean the outsides, and you know if your father so much as looks at them, he'll break them. But all of that can wait—I want to meet this so-called kitten you have."

"After, Mom. I want to make sure I get this done for you."

"I'll help, too," I chimed in. "And we'll be done before you know it."

"No, no, no. You can't clean here! You're a guest."

"She's a guest because she doesn't live here?" Myles asked, a mischievous twinkle in his eyes.

"That's right," Sarah replied.

"Well, I don't live here either—doesn't that make me a guest? So, I don't have to do chores here, either?"

His mom swatted him playfully on the arm again, laughing, and Myles wrapped an arm around her shoulders.

"Just kidding, Mom," he said, then kissed her cheek. "I don't mind." He turned to me. "I won't be long." And with a smile, he left the living room we'd ended up in.

"I'll grab the ladder," Marv called, heading the other direction.

"Would you like something to drink, honey?" Sarah asked. "We've got water, juice, wine, bourbon, of course, for Myles, tea? What would you like? I think I'm going to have a glass of wine. This is an occasion to celebrate."

I smiled. "What's the occasion?"

"Meeting you, of course! We've wanted to for years. So, what would you like? Want a glass of wine with me? It's from a wonderful local vineyard Myles took us to last summer. You like red?"

My cheeks were hot and ached from smiling, but I couldn't help it. His mom was so cute and warm and welcoming. "Sure."

"Okay, back in a jiffy," she said, scooting quickly from the room.

While I was alone, I wandered around the room, looking at the family photos that were displayed *everywhere*—on tables and covering the walls. It was like going back in time and watching Myles grow up. He'd told me they barely made ends meet when he was little, and I could see that in the photos—the tattered furniture and faded and worn clothes and shoes. But what struck me the most was the love that was plain as day in every one of their faces, especially when the photo captured them looking at one another. One in particular drew my attention. In the photo, Myles looked to be a preteen—maybe eleven or so—standing in front of his parents with a proud grin on his face, holding a saxophone. Behind him, Sarah was obviously caught mid-laugh as she looked at the camera, her eyes sparkling the way Myles' did sometimes, and Marv was gazing at her with complete and utter adoration. It made my heart skip because it was the way I'd seen Myles look at me so many times before.

"I love that one, too," Sarah said from behind me.

I jumped and turned, laughing at myself.

"Didn't mean to startle you, honey." She held out a glass of wine. "Here you go."

She took a sip of hers and I did the same. While I still preferred bourbon, the wine was pretty good. After another sip, she told me about the different photos, what was going on in their lives at the time, good and bad, and the occasion for the photo. It was clear to me they'd weathered difficulties together as a family and stayed strong rather than being torn apart. It reminded me so much of my own family that I had a sudden wave of grief over no longer having them, and tears spilled from the corners of my eyes.

"Oh, goodness," I breathed out when Sarah looked up and her brows drew in. "I'm sorry. I wasn't expecting that." I controlled my outbreath, staring at the ceiling and trying to get control over my sadness.

"What is it, honey?" she asked with a voice full of kindness, resting a hand on my shoulder.

"It's just... you guys..." My voice cracked and I was now full-out crying. "You remind me so much of my parents."

Her head bobbed up and down, as gently as everything else she was doing. "It's okay to miss them."

"I do," I cried. "I miss them so much."

With that same gentleness, she pulled me into a hug, and I sobbed into her shoulder as I clung to her like I would with my own mom. It felt so good to be held the way my mom used to hold me, and it made it that much harder to rein my emotions back in. She set down her wine glass, pulled mine from my fingers and set that one down, too, then rubbed a relaxing hand up and down my back as I cried, my body shaking, all the pain from their deaths washing over me again.

Eventually, I pulled back, wiping my face, and Sarah produced a tissue seemingly out of thin air. I took it and blew my nose.

"Thank you," I said, my voice still thick and my nose stuffy. "And I'm sorry for crying all over you."

She rubbed my shoulder with a hand. "Oh, honey, it's okay. I know it's hard to lose your parents. The grief never really leaves you." She gave me a watery smile. "I lost mine before Myles was born, and sometimes it hurts as much as it did then. You can come cry on me anytime, okay?"

Her eyes held me with that same level of intensity Myles had— another thing he got from her, I noted—and I knew she meant every word.

"Okay. Thank you."

"Of course, honey." She handed my wine glass back to me, then gave me one more pat on the shoulder before turning. "Come look at these."

I followed her over to a shelf where she pulled out a small album. The cover said "Edwards Family Vacation" and the inside cover was dated for three years earlier.

"Myles took us out to California for a month a few years ago. Have you ever been?" she asked, looking up at me.

I shook my head. "No, I haven't."

Just then, Myles and his dad reappeared. Marv came over and looked over his wife's shoulder, and Myles carried a microfiber cloth and a spray bottle to one of the four windows.

"You'll love this," she said. "You like trees and nature. We saw the redwoods. You would not believe how big those trees are! It's incredible—it defies reality, I swear. It doesn't seem like it could be real. Here—look at this!"

She pointed to a picture of the three of them standing at the base of a redwood tree, and they took up less than half of the diameter.

"Wow," I breathed, my finger moving over the photo. "That tree is amazing."

"They *all* are," she said. "They're all that big. And you just stand there and look up, and they're so tall it's hard to see the tops— sometimes you can't. Then you think about how long they've been there to grow that big and it's just... it makes you feel small, you know?"

I nodded, smiling. I knew exactly what she meant. That's how I felt when I was sitting in a forest and watching the wildlife interact, realizing how tiny a part of the planet humans really are.

"Myles, honey?" she called, flipping the page in the album.

"Yeah, Mom?"

I glanced over and he was finishing the second window. Two more to go.

"Nina has never been to California. She'd love it there—you should take her this summer."

"Oh, he doesn't—" I started.

"Okay, Mom," Myles said over me. "Wanna go, Nina?"

My heart raced, and I forgot how to breathe at the prospect of taking a trip with Myles.

"Nina?" he asked again.

I sucked in a breath. "I mean... of course, but you don't have to take me. I could go myself."

"Oh, but Myles is such a great tour guide. He does all this research before so he knows all the best places to go. He's good to travel with."

"Mom's got a point," Myles said, pushing the last window back into place. "I'm a pretty awesome travel companion." He winked.

"Done with the windows, Mom. And the air filters and the smoke detector. You sure you don't have anything else for me?"

"No, honey. Thank you."

"Of course, Mom," he called as he left the room. He returned a minute or two later without the cloth or spray bottle. "Ready to go meet Treble, then?" He came to a stop next to us, but his smile faltered when his eye caught mine.

"Sure am," she said. "Just let me take our glasses to the kitchen."

When she left for the kitchen, Myles lowered his voice. "Your eyes are red. Why were you crying?"

"I was looking at all your family pictures and just missed my parents, that's all." I huffed out a breath with a headshake because just saying those words made me tear up again.

His eyes searched mine for a minute, then he hugged me. "I'm sorry, Nina. If I could bring them back for you, I would."

"I know. It's okay. It just hits me sometimes."

He sighed, then released me when his mom called out that she was ready. Myles, his dad—who'd been unobtrusively standing on the other side of the room watching us—and I headed for the front door.

Myles' parents and I all stayed for dinner, which ended up being pizza: pepperoni and black olives for Myles and me, and veggie for them. After dinner, we were all still sitting at the table, and Myles went into the kitchen to refill drinks. When he walked back out, he had not only my water, but also a bourbon for me.

"Oh, Myles, get her a glass of wine instead of that awful stuff."

Myles snickered and I smiled. "It's not awful, Mom, and Nina likes it. It's what she prefers."

"Oh! I'm so sorry—I just assumed you wanted wine at my house!"

"It's fine," I replied. "And the wine was wonderful."

"You really like bourbon?"

"I do. Myles actually introduced me to it the night we met, and it's been my favorite ever since."

"Well, how about that," she mused.

As Myles sat back down, Treble came meowing into the dining room, beelining for Myles. He picked her up, mumbling something into her fur before giving her a kiss and crossing his arm over his chest for her. Instead, though, she burrowed into his neck, tucking her face behind his beard, so he held her there.

Sarah shook her head with an expression of wonder. "I just still can't believe it," she said. "You know, most of his life, Myles was really just indifferent to animals."

My eyes darted to Myles and he shrugged with a small smile.

"What changed?" I asked him.

"You," he said after a moment, holding my gaze.

"Me?" I asked, laughing.

He shrugged. "It's hard for me not to get caught up when you're passionate about something, Nina. Your love for all things living rubbed off on me."

I blushed.

He grinned.

I bit my bottom lip.

"Well," Marv said, pushing back in his chair. "I think it's about time for us to get home, Sarah."

My blush spread, and Myles smirked before looking toward his parents.

"There's no rush, guys."

"Oh, I know," Sarah replied, now on her feet. "But it's getting late."

"It's only six thirty," Myles said with a laugh.

"Late enough," Sarah said. "We have things to get back to."

"Like what?" Myles asked. "The Travel Channel?"

"Maybe. Besides, we don't want to be in your and Nina's hair for the evening."

"Mom," he said, his voice more serious. "Nina and I are just friends. *Friends.* You're not getting in anyone's hair. You guys are welcome to hang out with us."

"No, no, it's okay, honey," she brushed him off. She stepped over and kissed the top of his head. "Thank you for your help today."

"You're welcome," he said, giving her hand a squeeze. "Love you, Mom."

"Love you, too, honey."

"Love you, Dad," he said, standing to give his dad a hug.

"Love you, too."

Sarah held her arms out and I stood, returning her hug.

"It was so nice to meet you guys today," I said, pulling back.

She held onto my elbows. "It was lovely to meet you, too, Nina, after hearing so much about you. I hope to see you around more. And I'm here if you want to talk about anything."

I tried hard not to tear up again. "Thank you."

"Of course, honey."

I turned and gave Marv a hug, too. "Nice to meet you, Nina," he said.

Then they were gone. I slid back into my dining chair and just watched the door they'd exited through for a minute.

"So, what did you think of them?" Myles asked.

I turned to him and grinned. "I love them, Myles. They're wonderful."

"I know." He grinned back. "They think the same thing about you, by the way."

"What? How could you know that?"

"They told me when you went to the bathroom earlier."

"Really?" I asked. I was unexpectedly anxious for him to tell me it was true. I really did like his parents a lot, and I realized right then just how much I wanted them to like me back.

"Really. They adored you."

Sitting there with Myles, Treble purring in his arms, after spending the afternoon with his parents—two delightful, kind people who reminded me so much of my own parents—I felt whole in a way I hadn't in a long time, and I became emotional again.

"This has been such an amazing day, Myles. Thank you."

TWENTY-FIVE

My phone rang while I was driving back to Bathlin with Treble after picking her up from being spayed. Just like the day I'd taken her for her first vet appointment, Myles was anxious and calling between classes to check on her.

"She's fine," I said as soon as I answered, smiling and shaking my head. "She's just sleepy, but otherwise her normal self."

He let out a loud sigh. "Okay, good. And no issues picking her up or anything?"

"Nope. None. Though I'm not sure what issues you thought I might run into—I didn't have any the last time I was here with her or when I dropped her off this morning."

"I don't know," he said, his voice muffled. He was probably dragging his hand over his face. "Okay, I have to go, but I wanted to check in. You sure you don't mind hanging out until I get home?"

"Not at all," I replied. "I have studying to do anyway."

"Okay. Thanks, Nina. I appreciate it."

"Anytime. I'll see you later."

The line disconnected and I sighed contentedly, glancing over to check on Treble, but she was sound asleep in her carrier still.

In the three weeks since Myles had come to the park unexpectedly and we'd found Treble in the woods, we'd settled into a routine of sorts together. We chatted daily, sometimes via text, and sometimes over the phone. Then he came on Saturday and Sunday mornings to walk with me in Midtown Park. We talked about Treble and his parents and his students, but carefully avoided talking about the past. Since it had been mentioned the weekend we found Treble, we hadn't brought up the trip to California, either.

Things were strange between us, one moment easy and relaxed like it used to be, then awkward the next in which neither of us seemed to know what to say or do. I kept telling myself that would go away in time, that this new version of friendship between us would take some practice, but I wasn't so sure. Either way, I'd take that awkwardness any day over not having Myles in my life at all.

I got Treble settled into her favorite bed and set it in the living room with me before getting comfortable with my textbook and a spiral notebook for taking notes; the first certificate program had commenced the week before. After two hours, I was stiff and cross-eyed, even using my new reading glasses. I took them off, stood, and stretched. Fishing a ponytail holder from my purse, I flipped my head and gathered my hair, tying it into some semblance of a bun on the top of my head. I got a glass of water, telling myself as I eyed Myles' bourbon that I could have some as a reward after getting through the next chapter. Myles should be home by then anyway, so I could drive home and have a drink once I got there. With my full glass of water, I returned to the living room and hunkered back down after giving some love to a very groggy Treble who quickly fell back asleep.

I was two pages from the end of the next chapter when I heard Myles pull in. I rushed to finish, but I wasn't fast enough, and he walked in while I still had a page and a half left.

"How's Treble?"

"She's good," I replied, my eyes still on my textbook. "I'll be done in just a minute."

"Take your time," he said, dropping to his knees next to Treble. "How're you feeling, sweetie?" he murmured, his voice low and rumbly like it always was when he talked to her. No wonder she liked him so much—I also loved that voice of his. "Huh? Are you hurting? Just sleepy?"

"You know," I mused, still trying to get through the last page of my text. "It will never cease to amaze me that this big, strong man melts into a pile of mush with a teensy weensy little kitten."

He laughed, the sound rumbling through his chest.

My head snapped to the side, and I stared at him with wide eyes. "That's it!" I shouted. "I've got it!"

"Got what?"

"I'm going to bring Treble into class. When your students see you talking to her?" I laughed.

"Still won't embarrass me," he said. "Besides, if you do that," he continued, now talking to me like he talked to Treble, "then I'll talk to you just like this. And you'll be more embarrassed than I ever will."

Damn it. I laughed again. "I give up."

He sat back, a hand still stroking Treble's back as he looked up. "Not for the purpose of helping you, but I *may* have a way for you to accomplish this goal of embarrassing me. *Maybe.*"

I held up a finger and rushed through the last paragraph in my book, then closed it and tossed it on the coffee table along with my notebook, pen, and glasses. "Okay, I'm all ears, not to mention curious why you'd tell me something that would embarrass you."

"Not *would*, but *might*. And I don't really have a choice. I lost another bet with the class."

"Oh no—this should be good."

"Have you heard of TikTok?"

"Social media, right? I've never been on it, but I've heard of it, I think."

"I just learned about it recently when I made this bet. And apparently I've been living under a rock, which means you have, too."

"Say your students."

"And my coworkers—I asked them about it, and they couldn't believe I hadn't heard of it. They said everyone's on TikTok."

"Ha. Not everyone."

He chuckled. "Not us, anyway. Well, it's all videos, and there are these things called TikTok challenges where someone or more than one person does something, and then other people record themselves trying to replicate those challenges."

"Okay..."

"Well, as part of the bet, I now have to record trying to complete five of these challenges, but I have to pick from the ones my kids picked out."

"What kinds of challenges?"

"These are mostly physical, but not like lift something heavy. This is more like put a glass of water on your forehead, then lie down and pick the glass up with your knees and set it down behind your head using your knees without spilling it."

"Oh, shit," I laughed. "I can't wait to record this for you. Because you know I'm not going anywhere until I record them, right? I mean, as your friend, I insist on being here to help you."

"You're full of shit," he laughed. "And you can help me figure out how the hell to get the phone to record without someone behind it, but you're going to be a part of these."

My brow dropped. "What?"

He pulled his mouth in, his eyes sparkling. "Most of the challenges they gave me to choose from—as in all but two—require two people."

"Annnnnd that would be why you were willing to tell me about a way you might get embarrassed... because I have to be a part of it."

He nodded.

I groaned.

He smirked.

And then we were both laughing.

"Okay, fine, show me what we have to choose from."

As I scooted off the sofa to sit next to him on the floor, he said, "I like the glasses, by the way."

I groaned. "They're reading glasses. I have effing reading glasses, Myles. I did not think I was that old."

"They don't make you look old, Nina."

"How do they make me look?"

He stared at me for a second, then looked down. "Here's the first one," he said without answering my question, holding up his phone so we could both see it.

For the next twenty minutes, we watched eleven different challenges. When it got to the twelfth and final one, Myles lowered his phone. "The twelfth one isn't an option."

"Why?" I asked, trying not to smile. If he was determined it wasn't an option, it was likely because it would be embarrassing, which meant I was likely to insist on it.

"It just isn't," he said.

"Show me."

He sighed and stood. I jumped to my feet next to him.

"Let me see it," I said, reaching over and plucking his phone from his hands.

"What the hell?" he said, grabbing out for it, but I was faster and flipped around out of his reach, already working on his lock screen.

"You don't know my password," he said, stopping his efforts to get his phone back.

I finished typing it in and the screen unlocked. I held it up. "Oh, really?"

"How do you know my password?" he exclaimed with a chuckle, lunging for his phone again.

"C minor is your favorite key—it was easy." I ducked under his arm and away from his reach again. "Since I figured that out, I should be allowed to watch this last video."

"You're obnoxious, you know that?"

I laughed.

"Fine. Watch it. These kids think they're funny."

Now that he wasn't trying to get his phone back, I reopened his app and found the last video. As soon as it began to play and the tag at the top explained the challenge, I understood. The challenge was to kiss your best friend. My cheeks burned, and when I glanced over at Myles, he'd sat back down and was petting Treble again, steadfastly ignoring me. I should have closed it, but I didn't. It was already playing, and it pulled me in. Most of them were sweet and cute to watch, the initial shock, and then the reciprocation. A few of them then had messages that it led to a serious relationship between them. In many of them, the person doing the initial kissing had a note that they'd been secretly in love with their best friend for some period of time. When my eyes filled, I closed out of the video and forced a few even breaths.

"Okay, what do you want to start with?" I asked, trying to bring back the playfulness from earlier.

"Well, I think the easiest one is where I'm on all fours, then lift my arms behind my back."

"I'll do it with you."

I got the phone set up and clicked to start recording before rushing over to get on all fours next to Myles. "Hands behind your back," I said before pulling my arms together behind me, engaging my abs. To my left, Myles had tipped forward, nearly, but not quite, hitting the ground. I burst out laughing.

"You work out and have ripped abs, and you almost fell?" I cackled.

He snorted, reaching over and turning off the video. "That was harder than I expected."

"Obviously," I retorted.

He narrowed his eyes. "Okay, the next one will be the levitation."

I groaned. I was likely to fail on that one. "How much do you weigh again?"

He grinned. "Come on, it's my choice and that's what I choose."

I got situated in a reverse tabletop position, and Myles positioned himself over my legs after restarting the camera. I was already laughing before any of his weight rested on my thighs. "This is not going to end well."

My legs sagged as he sat, and he chuckled. "Don't drop me."

"No promises," I grunted out. "Hurry the hell up, Myles."

Chuckling some more, he hooked one foot under my armpit, then the other. My legs were really sagging, but I was still up.

"Arms up, Nina! Arms up!"

One arm lifted, then immediately flew back down and I burst into laughter. "I can't!"

"Just do it, just lift them up."

"I'm trying," I laughed. I lifted both hands and we went crashing to the ground.

We laid there laughing too hard to get back up for several minutes. Every time we tried to, we caught each other's eyes and just began laughing all over again. Eventually, we restarted the video and tried again. It took four attempts, but we ultimately managed to hold it for about three seconds before collapsing, and we were very proud of those three seconds.

The next three challenges passed in similar fashion, taking many failed attempts before we managed to get it. By the time we were done, we were tired, had aching sides from laughing, and it was dinnertime. Myles poured us each a glass of bourbon and ordered pizza. After coaxing Treble to eat and take her medicine, and getting her resettled comfortably into her fluffy bed, Myles turned on The Dovelyn Trio and plopped down onto the sofa so close our thighs were touching.

My breath caught and Myles turned. His eyes fluttered between mine and my lips, then he sucked in a breath and jerked away, his head in his hands. All I could think about was the best friends challenge I'd watched. What would happen if I kissed him? We'd agreed on friendship, and he'd reiterated that repeatedly with his parents, but I knew he wanted to kiss me right then... at least I was fairly certain. But I didn't want to lose our friendship if I was wrong. My stomach flipped over, and my heart skipped what felt like every other beat.

TWENTY-SIX

Leaning forward, I tugged on Myles' wrist to move his hand from his face. He turned, his brow creased in question as he faced me. I inhaled until my lungs were full, moistened my lips, then pressed my mouth to his. For a long, excruciating second or two, nothing happened. Then, just as I was about to pull away, he kissed me in return. Just as suddenly, he stopped and sat back, turning to face away from me. His chest was rising and falling rapidly—as rapidly as mine.

"Myles—"

"You've got a boyfriend, Nina," he said, turning to face me again, his eyes glassy this time.

I shook my head, grasping his hand between both of mine. "No, Myles. I tried to tell you. I broke up with Landon months ago. About a week after I gave you the letter."

His eyes searched my face. "You did?"

I raised my chin, then lowered it in a slow nod.

There was a tense moment in which neither of us moved, though it felt we were getting closer. And then we were kissing again. His hands framed my face and held me to him as he kissed me, telling me the story of his feelings for me with kisses that were hard and soft and fast and slow, hands that moved between my face and circling my lower back, pulling me into him as I climbed over to sit straddled on his lap.

"Oh, god," he hummed out, pressing our foreheads together, then kissing my lips with hard, chaste kisses, again and again, before holding me back just far enough that we could see into each other's eyes, his hands cradling my face again. "Before there's a chance for anything else to happen, for anything else to get between us... I love you, Nina. Fuck, I love you. I fell in love with you listening to you talk about how rosebushes didn't deserve to have Solo cups on their branches the first time I ever saw you. You were unlike anyone I'd ever met. I never told you because I was scared it would change something. I knew you cared about me, but I didn't know if you cared about *me* like I cared about *you*, and you were so independent—I didn't want to scare you away by telling you how strong my feelings were so quickly. But I loved the hell out of you then, and I love the hell out of you now, Nina. Fuck friendship—I want so much more than that with you."

"Myles," I said with my exhale, my eyes flooded with emotion again. "It was the same for me. I think I loved you by the time we made it to the door of Nina's that night. But I'd never met someone like you, either, and I didn't want to make assumptions and push you away. You kept calling me your friend, so I did the same. And those feelings never went away. Ever. I loved you the whole time I was dating Landon, and I wanted nothing more than to leave him for you, but I was too scared because I didn't know if I could handle everything you make me feel, and I didn't know if you wanted more of a relationship than we'd had before, and I knew *I* did. Then and now. I love you, Myles."

"Jesus, I love you, too, Nina."

The story his mouth told next was one of nearly desperate desire, and I matched every stroke of his tongue and touch of his hands with my own. By the time he pulled off my shirt and I was yanking at his, I felt like I might just combust. My bra-clad torso pressed against his, bare and muscled, and I wanted to know what it would feel like to have more of our bodies touching.

Feeling desire was so different; it was something I had only felt with Myles and, for years after the rape, thought I'd never feel again.

But it was a good different—it was agonizingly sweet, and I felt simultaneously desperate to do something more and to draw it out as long as possible. I pushed back and stood, unbuttoning my jeans.

Myles watched, his eyes dark and intense, his chest heaving. I wanted to bottle it up.

"I like this look on you," I said, half-teasing, stopping before unzipping. "Maybe I'll just stay over here and watch you watching me as you wait."

He narrowed his eyes at me, smirking, and scooted forward on the sofa until he was sitting on the edge. Then, without his eyes leaving mine, he stood, intentionally slow. I watched him, my head moving from looking down to looking up, and something about that made my body shiver.

"One thing before this goes any further," he said. "Do you feel cornered or pressured right now, Nina? Or are you doing this because you want to?"

I let out a small huff, then the corners of my mouth turned up slightly. "The only time I've ever felt pressured by you was when you pushed me to break up with Landon."

"So this is what you want right now?"

I chuckled lightly. "This is definitely what I want right now."

"It's okay if that changes—you just have to tell me."

"I will."

A heartbeat passed.

Two.

Three.

His hand hooked into the front of my jeans and he yanked me into him, immediately meeting my mouth with his. One hand flattened against my back, the other slipping into the back of my jeans, grabbing my ass and holding me against him. His erection pressed between my legs in the most delicious way, and I moaned into his mouth. He groaned in return, pressing me against him harder.

My hands slipped between us, and I unbuttoned his pants, then unzipped them, my fingers brushing against his hardness as I went. We peeled the remainder of our clothing off each other, then I pushed him backward until he was sitting on the sofa again. When I lifted a leg onto the sofa outside his, he grabbed my hips and pulled until my other leg was on the sofa and I was straddling him. He kissed me, his hands caressing my flesh but without rushing me to move any faster. Little by little, I lowered myself down over him and gasped, his fingers digging into my hips harder the further down I went, until all of him was inside me.

I wasn't sure why he was so still, but I was grateful because I needed a minute to take in everything I felt right then. The first time anyone had been inside me, I was violently raped. And every time after had been something I was waiting on to end at best, and hurt as much as that first time at worst. I was often not fully present when it was happening, my mind carrying me elsewhere in well-crafted dissociation.

But this didn't hurt—not even close.

And I wasn't dissociated at all—I was fully present.

That was a lot to take in, from the way my belly fluttered, especially when I tightened and felt Myles even more, to the way his fingers felt on my hips, then traveling up my back. From the way his breath felt spreading across my bare chest, to the blend of lust and love in his eyes. From the way I wanted not only to be where I was, but the way I *wanted* to keep going, the way I didn't want this to end anytime soon. I leaned forward and rested my face into the crook of his neck where he smelled like peppery cloves and vanilla, then left a kiss there. He kissed the top of my head, one hand cradling my face and the other smoothing across the middle of my back, and I felt his heart beating rapidly beneath me. Leaning back, I kissed his lips, then pushed my hands into his chest and shifted around. His hands returned to my hips, grasping them and pulling, then pushing, aiding the movements I was leading.

It felt... exquisite... and soon I was lost in the music and making love to Myles. Every so often, he growled against my neck, and I felt the vibrations down to my toes. Our breathing became more labored, and I sucked gently just below his jaw.

"Holy shit," he breathed, shifting us around, but then we fell off the sofa entirely, landing on our sides.

Giggling, I rolled him onto his back and pushed up with my hands on his chest.

"Whoops," I said, still giggling and breathing heavily.

He lifted a hand and slid it around the back of my neck, pulling me down to him where he kissed me until I was dizzy. With an arm around my waist, he rolled us again until we bumped into the coffee table with him on top. He reached out an arm and shoved the table away from us. The sudden movement caused our bourbon to slosh over the sides, getting not just on the table but some landing on my chest and more dripping down Myles' arm.

I lifted my head at the same time I pulled Myles down and flicked my tongue over his bicep, catching the bourbon trailing down his skin. He closed his eyes, groaning, and tipped his head back. I applied pressure against his back, bringing him closer as I used my mouth to clean the rest of the bourbon off his arm and shoulder.

"My turn," he said when I was done, lowering his head to my clavicle, where some had pooled.

My eyes closed and my head thumped back against the floor. As he'd said... *holy shit*. His mouth sucked sensuously around the same area, then moved down to one breast, then the other, then back up the other side.

"Bourbon and Nina tastes delicious," he rumbled.

"Oh my god," I whispered, his words making my whole body shiver.

"I love you, Nina." His voice vibrated against the curve of my neck before he sucked some of the skin into his mouth, running his teeth over it.

I gasped, my whole body tightening in response. "I love you, too, Myles."

He grasped around my triceps and pushed my arms so they raised up to rest on the ground above my head. Then he ran his hands up my arms until his fingers slid between mine, curling over to hold tight. I curled mine, too, and squeezed harder. He moved out of me slowly, then pushed back in hard, holding, and repeated, a grunt accompanying each thrust forward.

"Oh my god," I uttered again, my body invaded with an almost restless feeling. I started shifting in response to that feeling, and Myles pressed my hands solidly into the carpet and moved a little faster and a little harder. Our bodies were covered with a sheen of sweat and made an obscene slapping sound under the music filling the air that both embarrassed me and turned me on more.

My body began to stiffen, pleasure rippling throughout every limb, originating from between my legs. "Oh, god, Myles!" I shouted, then couldn't even breathe.

He pushed harder and faster still, and then his body stiffened while my legs locked around him. "Fuck, Nina!" he growled into my neck.

After another shudder from us both, his body gradually relaxed, and with his stillness, so did mine. He released a hand and cradled my face, his thumb smoothing along my cheek, back and forth, his harsh breath against my skin, his pounding heart over mine. I ran my palms over his sweaty back, feeling the hard lines and soft dips of muscle, marveling that I was actually there touching him right then.

"So, that's an orgasm," I said with a giggle, biting my lip as my face leapt into flames.

He chuckled, the sound vibrating my chest. "Yeah—one hell of an orgasm."

"Is that why I already want to do it again?" I asked quietly, my cheeks getting hotter. I was teasing, but I was also very serious. That was the first orgasm I'd ever had, and while I felt wrung out, physically and emotionally, I wanted to experience what I just had all over again. "I've never done that before," I added in a small voice.

He raised up on one elbow and brushed my messy hair from my forehead. At least half of it had escaped my bun during our lovemaking session.

"You have sex hair and I love it." He kissed my lips, then looked into my eyes. "Yeah, orgasms feel good and you want more of them. But *this*, between us, was different. It was more than just an orgasm, because we have a connection—we always have. I want to do this, with *you*, again, too."

"I can tell," I teased. I could feel him hardening again inside me as he was talking.

He snorted. "I'm trying to be serious here. I'm trying to tell you that we're really good together because we love each other. And that what we just experienced—it isn't like that with other people. What we have is special, Nina."

"You sure it wasn't just a fluke?" I asked, trying not to laugh.

His mouth pulled in. "I'm sure."

"I mean, it could have been," I added.

"Do you need me to show you it wasn't?" he growled out, lowering his head to kiss just under my chin.

My breath caught and I closed my eyes. "Yes, please."

Later, Myles brought in our now-cold pizza that had been left on the porch when we didn't answer the door—we hadn't even heard it or remembered that we had food coming. As the euphoric buzzing in my body calmed to some extent while we munched on pizza and sipped on bourbon, the skin on my back and butt began to feel tight and uncomfortable. When I mentioned it to Myles after wincing when I moved and my shirt pulled tight, he'd tenderly lifted the back of my shirt and discovered I had some rugburn from the carpet. Now I was lying, naked again, face down on his bed, and he was concentrated on rubbing in antibiotic cream over my entire backside. When he reached my thighs, I giggled.

"I've never had rugburn before. Let alone from sex."

He let out a soft huff. "I wish you didn't. I didn't mean to hurt you."

"You didn't, Myles. We were doing that together. It's not like you were doing something I didn't want. This is nothing like the ways some people have hurt me."

His fingers paused and I could feel his body tense. He resumed a second later without saying anything, but I could still feel the tension. When he was done, he gave me a t-shirt and sweats of his to put on in place of my own clothes so my skin would have a bit more space to breathe. He came out of the bathroom just as I finished pulling on his clothes and stopped in front of me, sliding his hands along my arms and lacing our hands together. It made my heart skip and I grinned.

He smiled tenderly back, then released a hand to run it over his hair. His eyes darted away, then he turned, and we walked back to the living room, still hand-in-hand. I wasn't sure what was going on and just waited for him to tell me. Once we were situated on the sofa, his arm around me and holding me into his side, my head resting on his chest, he spoke.

"You said this was nothing like the way 'some people' have hurt you. There were more?"

I shifted restlessly. "I don't know if we should talk about this, Myles."

His palm smoothed up my arm, then squeezed my shoulder as he kissed the top of my head. "I want to know, Nina. I want to understand."

I sat up and took a hefty swallow of bourbon. This was about to get very uncomfortable. "I told you in the letter that I drank a lot and slept with a lot of guys for a while," I said, staring straight ahead through the far wall. "But I didn't really want to. And sex when you don't want it can hurt a lot. Some of the guys were pretty rough, too."

"I'm sorry, Nina."

"It's okay," I said, still staring straight ahead. "It was a long time ago."

"So, Landon wasn't rough like that? He didn't hurt you?"

I sighed, my eyes now scanning aimlessly. "I mean, he was sometimes. Well, not rough exactly, but he did hurt me. He didn't really accept it anytime I said 'no.' Or maybe he thought I didn't mean it. I don't know."

"What did he do?"

The moisture falling down my cheeks surprised me, and I swiped quickly under my eyes. Why was I crying? I wasn't sad about leaving Landon. "I mean... are you sure you want to know this?"

He nodded gravely.

I looked back to the wall and swiped under my eyes again, allowing my body to sink further into Myles'. Feeling him there was like reassurance that what I was about to say would never happen again. It had angered me and upset me before, but now that I'd had a few months of space from Landon, both in time and physical distance, I was having an even stronger reaction to it.

"He..." My breath rushed out, and I laughed a little. "I don't know why I'm crying right now," I snapped, both frustrated and embarrassed for reasons I didn't understand. I sniffled, but before I wiped again under my eyes, Myles did with gentle fingertips. His touch calmed something and my shoulders fell. "If I told him I didn't want to have sex or resisted at all, he would roll me over and pin me face down against the mattress so I couldn't move and tell me he missed me or that he'd done something for me or that he was going away soon or that he'd be quick, then do what he wanted anyway."

I let out a sharp breath. I'd done it—I'd said it. Why it was so hard this time, however, I didn't know. I'd told Leslie before, at least about the last time he'd done it, but this was harder by far.

Myles' body was hardened with tension, reminding me of when we were in the police station years earlier just before he punched one of the officers, but he pulled me onto his lap anyway, wrapping his arms around me. I tucked my head under his chin and curled into a ball, letting the comfort of his arms melt away what I'd just been feeling while telling him about Landon.

"You're safe with me," he said, his quiet, deep voice rumbling under me so I could feel it more than I could hear it. "I promise you're safe. Nothing like that will happen to you again, Nina, I swear."

I let out a heavy sigh and my body relaxed. I believed every word Myles said—I trusted him completely. I knew I was safe when I was with him. I always had been and always would be.

TWENTY-SEVEN

When I woke the next morning, I found Myles in the living room composing again. I rolled my lips under as I watched him and held my coffee, my tummy tightening as I thought about making love with him the previous evening before falling asleep in his arms. It was a like a dream come true—literal dreams I'd had before—to find myself in a relationship of sorts with him after all this time. However we would define this relationship. But it wasn't friendship, that was for sure.

Myles looked up as I sat, noticing me for the first time. His eyes sparkled and a wide grin broke across his features. He looked so happy and excited to see me that I could have purred like the kitten curled up near his feet. I felt so wanted, like I mattered, when he looked at me that way—I always had.

"Good morning," I said, feeling shy and giving him a small smile.

"Good morning, sunshine," he said, wrapping me in his arms and kissing my neck.

I shivered and he did it again. Instantly, my breathing was shallow. He took my coffee cup and set it on the coffee table next to his, then returned his attention to me.

"I've been waiting to kiss you again," he said, his voice husky and a bit gravelly as his mouth met mine.

He tasted of coffee, the smell of which was mixing with the cloves and vanilla of his skin. I could get used to that smell.

The story his mouth told this morning was one of a slow, hot desire, mixed with tenderness. Our hands explored one another with less urgency than the night before, and after pulling off his own shirt, Myles unhurriedly pulled mine off, too. Shifting us so I was lying on my back on the sofa, Myles lowered himself over me, both of us wearing only sweatpants. With another slow, wanting kiss, he pulled away and looked down at my naked torso. Some of the heat in his gaze faded as he shifted his weight to one side. Lifting a hand, he faintly traced his fingertips over the scar on my breast.

I swallowed, feeling vulnerable in a way I hadn't even when I was completely naked. His eyes, now soft with pain, and his fingertips shifted away. He put gentle pressure on my chin to further expose my neck, then skated his fingers over the scar there. I had a bizarre urge to cry, but held it in, swallowing down the unwanted emotion. Myles turned his attention to the very faint scars on my forehead, the tips of his fingers whispering over them. Something about the tenderness of his touch undid my hold on my emotions and tears tumbled from my eyes.

Myles lowered onto his forearms, using his thumbs to wipe my tears from my temples. He kissed me lovingly, gently, our lips barely touching, then rested his forehead to mine. Our noses were against one another and our breaths were mingling. Myles sniffled.

"I'm so sorry, Nina," he whispered, his voice cracking. "I'm so sorry. I wish I could go back in time and protect you. I'd give anything—I'd give my life—to be able to go back and keep you safe."

I cradled his face in return. "You saved me, Myles. Back then, and now, too."

He pressed our lips together. "I promise to keep you safe now. I promise to protect you no matter what. I promise to save you from whatever you need saving from. Always. I swear to you."

I nodded, my tears sliding out faster.

"I love you, Nina."

"I love you, too, Myles."

He kissed the scars on my forehead, then down the side of my face to the scars on my neck before continuing to the scar on my breast. Despite the fact those scars were reminders of the most terrifying and horrific experience of my life, what he was doing sent desire slamming through my body. I shifted as it hit and felt Myles hardening—I wasn't the only one affected right then. Something about sharing that vulnerability about a moment in time that profoundly scarred us both was driving the two of us to wanting to connect physically as well.

Myles slid his arms up behind my shoulders to cradle the back of my head and our kisses became more intense, our bodies rocking together. My fingertips curled, digging into his back, and he groaned, his hips pressing me deeper into the couch cushions.

"Myles," I breathed out between kisses.

"Nina," he replied, his voice as breathy as mine.

The doorbell rang and we both froze, turning to face the front door. Myles' body shifted to block mine protectively from view of the foyer, and then after several tense seconds, a chuckle vibrated from somewhere far down in his chest. He kissed my forehead, then looked at me with mock horror.

"We've been caught making out by my parents."

I gaped at him. "Your parents are here?"

He kissed my forehead again, now grinning, then covered my ears and shouted out that he'd be there in a minute. "Yes, my parents," he said to me. "I forgot we were having brunch today."

My head dropped back against the sofa cushion. "Oh my god, Myles—I don't have clean clothes to wear!"

"You can wear what you've got on—they won't care."

I was wearing his sweatpants and it was his t-shirt on the floor; they may have been clean, but they didn't exactly fit. I groaned. "And what are they going to think about me? I spent the night here last night and now I'm wearing your clothes. And—oh god—you gave me a hickey last night!" I clapped a hand over my neck.

He sat us up, then stood, pulling me to my feet in front of him, sliding an arm around my waist and drawing my body into his after we pulled our shirts back on. He nuzzled into my neck where the hickey was. "They're going to think we're two adults who can have sex if we want to."

"Oh, god," I laughed, covering my face.

"And they'll be happy about it, I assure you," he added, pulling my hands away from my face and kissing me, one hand against my cheek. "Come on, they're waiting." He gave me a quick peck on the nose, then grabbed my hand and led us toward the front door.

"Good morning," he said as he swung open the door, his grin so wide it was practically splitting his face in half.

I, on the other hand, was blushing so furiously it felt like I was holding my face in a campfire, and I had no idea where to look.

"Good mor...ning, honey," his mother said, having paused when the door opened wide enough for her to see me. Her eyes quickly scanned over me, stopping briefly on my hickey before drifting to mine and Myles' linked hands, and at last settling on my face. She was grinning as widely as Myles was. "Good morning, Nina."

His father chuckled and Sarah reached over and gave him a playful smack on the chest. "Manners, Marv. Say hello."

"Hello, Nina. Hello, Myles," he said, still chuckling as they walked through the door, both of them giving us brief hugs.

I wanted the floor to swallow me up. I was mortified by seeing his parents this way. Myles, though, just looked as content as could be, not even remotely bothered by the unexpected appearance of his parents, who obviously knew what we'd been up to.

Once the door was closed, Myles said, "So, I forgot about brunch this morning."

"Obviously," his father snickered. Sarah swatted him again, and he pulled his mouth in, trying not to laugh. Sarah did the same.

"Honey," his mom said, "we can come back later, or we can just do this another time if you want. We didn't mean to interrupt—we didn't realize you had company."

"Nope, totally fine," Myles said, releasing my hand and sliding his arm around my waist, pulling me into his side and kissing my temple. "Nina and I haven't eaten yet anyway. I just need a few minutes to figure out what to make."

"Why don't you let me cook," Sarah said, already heading toward the kitchen. "I'll whip something up. You guys have coffee yet? I can start some."

"We've got some, thanks, Mom," Myles replied, steering us toward the living room, his dad leading the way.

"Told you," he whispered into my ear. "They don't care."

"You were right," I whispered back. "Even so, I'm still embarrassed. I'm a mess."

"Whatever you want to call it, you're beautiful, Nina."

I blushed again and looked down, my stomach flipping over. Myles kissed my cheek.

"What are you and Mom up to today?" he asked his dad as we entered the living room.

His dad sat in a chair and Myles led us to the sofa, where he kept his arm around me as we sat. He had barely stopped touching me since the evening before, and to my surprise, I really liked it. For years since the rape, I didn't like being touched most of the time—not for any reason. But Myles touching me, I liked... a hell of a lot.

I listened to Myles and his dad talk about the errands Marv and Sarah needed to run and what he was hoping to finish working on. Marv turned to me.

"I started whittling when Myles retired us a couple of years ago."

"Retired you?" I asked, my eyes shifting between Myles and his dad.

Marv beamed with pride, his eyes misting. "Yup, Myles bought us the house and gave us a retirement portfolio to live off."

I turned to Myles. "You did?"

He shrugged. "Yeah. I told you I was going to figure out how to do it and that's why Marcus was teaching me to trade. I didn't just use that money for the music programs in the schools—I worked my ass off to make enough to buy them a house and give them enough money that they don't have to work anymore. They've worked hard enough in their lives." He tipped his head in the direction of the kitchen. "Mom always wanted to travel." He tipped his chin toward his dad. "And Dad was always interested in doing things with wood. Now they can do those things."

I leaned forward and gave him a hard kiss on the cheek, my heart swelling. "You're incredible, you know that?"

"You were doing the same damn thing for your own parents, Nina," he brushed me off.

"Hey, Nina, I've got a question for you," Marv said. His voice was enough to give away that he was up to something before I even looked over and saw that same face Myles made when he was trying not to laugh.

Myles chuckled.

The corners of my mouth twitched. "Okay."

"Why are elevator jokes so good?" Marv asked.

I shook my head. "I don't know."

Marv chortled and Myles was grinning, clearly anticipating something.

"They work on so many levels," Marv replied, barely getting the words out before he was guffawing with laughter. Myles' rich laugh also reverberated throughout the room. I bit my cheeks, trying unsuccessfully not to laugh.

"I've got another," he said. "Why did the tomato blush?"

I shrugged. "I have no idea."

"Because it saw the salad dressing."

By now, Marv was bent over in laughter, and Myles wasn't far behind.

"Well," I said, between chuckles. "I see where you get it from, Myles."

Sarah interrupted Marv's bad joke streak somewhere around fifteen to tell us that brunch was ready. My cheeks and sides ached, and I could only imagine Myles and Marv felt the same way. We rose, and Myles told his dad some of the latest jokes he'd told his classes the past week as we walked to the dining room. They were both cracking up as they sat down, and Sarah rolled her eyes.

"Those two can tell the most awful jokes for hours, Nina—*hours*—and still be laughing. It makes me crazy. Can you believe that Marv sat there telling me jokes when I was in *labor*? In the hospital, having contractions, and he's telling jokes." She rolled her eyes again and pursed her lips, looking at Marv.

He glanced up while he was laughing, and I saw the moment his eyes landed on her because something changed. It was subtle—he continued laughing and trading jokes with Myles, but something around his eyes and his mouth softened or something. He was madly in love with his wife, there was no doubt about it. And when I glanced at her, the same thing was happening. The only other couple I'd ever seen with so much love between them even after decades of marriage was my parents.

Out of the blue, I teared up as I looked back and forth between Myles' parents, and I turned to the side, hoping no one had noticed. A moment later, Sarah ran her hand back and forth across my shoulders a few times before sitting down and giving me a warm smile. She'd noticed. I smiled back in gratitude.

"Okay, you two, knock it off for brunch, will you?" she said, giving them each a stern look.

They laughed a bit more, but stopped telling jokes for a while. We ate frittata Sarah had somehow whipped together, conversation revolving around the food and Sarah and Marv's plans for the day.

"I have an announcement," Myles said as everyone was finishing up.

I looked over, as curious as his parents about what this announcement might be.

"Mom, I have something very serious to tell you," he said, his voice filled with laughter.

Sarah rolled her eyes, but she was smiling.

"This might shock you, so make sure you stay seated."

"Oh, for god's sake, Myles," she said. "What obnoxious thing is about to come out of your mouth? Remember that we're sitting at the table right now and keep it civilized, please."

He leaned forward dramatically, grinning during his long pause, his eyes darting to me several times. "I have a girlfriend."

I almost spit out the water I was drinking, Marv laughed with Myles, and his mother rolled her eyes again, swatting at her son.

"Well, no shit, honey," she said, laughing. "I can see that."

"I wasn't sure if we were being too subtle or not," he chuckled.

I snorted, and he pulled me in for a kiss.

"Subtlety has never been your strong suit, my dear," Sarah said.

Somehow, over the next few minutes, the kitchen was cleaned up and Myles and I were going to play a duet for his parents. We ended up playing several before his parents left to run their errands. After they walked out, Myles thoroughly kissed me up against the back of the front door, then grabbed my hand, pulling me toward the living room.

"I have something to show you."

I followed to the piano, where he told me to sit down, then shuffled through the mess of music stacked on a shelf. Before I came over next, I was going to buy some magazine file holders and get all his sheet music and books organized. He returned, placing some sheet music on the music stand.

"I got this quite a while ago, but I was nervous about telling you because I thought you were still dating Landon."

"Speaking of dating," I cut in. "Did you mean what you said at brunch?"

"What? When I called you my girlfriend?"

"Yes," I breathed out, feeling embarrassed for asking a question like that. It felt so juvenile. But with our history of skirting around what to call our relationship, I felt compelled to clarify.

"Nina, in all seriousness, yes. I was messing with my mom at lunch because she's lamented that I haven't had an actual girlfriend since high school and has given me some shit for it in the past. But I was serious. And I meant what I said last night about wanting so much more than friendship. You seemed to agree, so I just made an assumption that meant I could call you my girlfriend now."

"You can," I replied. "I just wanted to make sure I understood and didn't embarrass myself by calling you my boyfriend when I shouldn't."

He gave me a quick kiss. "I am, and you not only can, but I want you to. I like the way it sounds when you say that."

"Say what? That you're my boyfriend?"

He grinned, his eyes darkening. "Yeah, that." His eyes fell to my mouth, but then Treble let out a sleepy meow, ambling toward us. Myles looked down and bent, lifting her and placing her on his lap. She turned in a few circles, then settled, purring.

I turned from watching him interact with the kitten to see the sheet music he'd set out was for "Bring Me to Life" by Evanescence.

"I've practiced it already, but I thought we could practice together. I can also leave you be if you need to practice alone first. I'm sure Treble wouldn't mind some undivided attention, huh, sweetie?"

"I should go home soon, boyfriend," I said. I was snuggled on Myles' chest while he ran his fingers up and down my bare back. After practicing the Evanescence song for a while, we'd made love again, this time in his bed.

"Do you have to, girlfriend?" he grumbled lazily.

I smiled against his skin, then laid a kiss there. "Yeah, I need to shower and get some clean clothes on, and I'd rather not sit in bumper-to-bumper traffic."

"My clothes were clean."

"Yeah... and could fit two of me. I'd like some clean clothes that *fit*."

He let out a long breath, his body relaxed. "Will you come back? Or better yet, can I just go home with you? We could bring Treble with us."

"I can come back."

"I don't mind going to *you*, you know. You always come here. I'd actually like to see your place, you know?"

"No. That's not a good idea."

"Why not?"

"It's not my place, Myles—it's Landon's."

His body tensed, his hand stopped moving, and then he sat up, leaning back against his headboard. I did the same, clutching the blankets over my chest.

"Nina... you told me that you broke up with him months ago."

"I did."

"But you're still living with him?" he burst out, incredulous.

"I mean... technically, yes, I guess. He's been gone the whole time, though—he's traveling for months at a time now as opposed to weeks—and I'm going to move out. He's just letting me stay until I find my own place."

"And you haven't yet? You haven't mentioned anything about looking for a place to live, Nina. I could have been helping you."

"I know. That's because I'm waiting to hear back about the programs I applied to. I don't know which one I'll be doing yet, and they're nowhere near each other."

Myles stared at me, his brows drawn in confusion. "They're far enough apart for it to make a difference in where you live?"

I nodded, looking down at where I was twisting my fingers together. Myles crossed his arms over his chest.

"They're all in different states, Myles. None of them are local."

He continued to stare at me, rubbing a hand over his jaw. "You're moving out of state? Is that what you're saying?"

"I thought you realized that," I said, my voice trailing off.

He turned from facing me to studying the wall.

"Myles—"

"I need a minute, Nina."

I pulled his blankets tighter around me, desperately wishing I wasn't naked right then. When I scanned the room, I saw one of his t-shirts within reach and snagged it, pulling it on over my head. Then I used the ponytail holder on my wrist to hold my hair twisted into a bun on the top of my head. I was still anxious, but those small changes had helped.

As suddenly as he'd turned away, Myles turned back to me. "I have every intention of this thing between us lasting, Nina. You moving away scares the hell out of me, but if you're willing to make it work, I know I am, too. And my life is here, so I don't want to leave, but if I had to, I'd walk away from all of it for you."

I stared at him in wonder. "God, no, Myles—I don't want you to walk away from anything. We'll figure it out. If we've loved each other as long as we have with complete separation for almost all of that time, then I'm sure we can make this work."

"Okay. We're on the same page with that." He swallowed and his body became visibly rigid. "However, you living with Landon is *not* okay."

"I'm not living with him, really—he isn't even there. It was nice of him to let me stay as long as I need, so I'm not moving only to move again in a few months. And it's really convenient for therapy, and the internet is lightning fast, which is good for the classes I'm taking."

"I hear you, Nina, but I have a major problem with you living there with a man who forced you to have sex—who raped you, Nina."

"I'm not," I said, my face burning. I didn't agree with his choice of words—as much as I hated what Landon did, it was nothing like that guy with a knife in the alley—but I didn't want to add to this argument. "I'm living alone right now."

"You're not, Nina, because he can come back any time he wants, and then he'd be there with you. And he's your *ex*, for fuck's sake! Not to mention that I just don't trust him. Not after what he's done to you, and because I know he doesn't do anything out of kindness—everything is calculated to achieve some payoff. There's a reason he's letting you stay there. I guarantee it, Nina."

"I don't think so, Myles, but even if you're right, it doesn't matter. I've broken up with him and I'm moving out this summer—mid-August at the latest."

"I don't want you there another day, let alone the next few months!"

I sucked in a breath, surprised by him raising his voice. He scrubbed a hand over his face, then turned to me, a hand cradling mine. His eyes were glassy, and his thumb moved rapidly over my cheek.

"I can't tell you what to do, Nina. I know that. But I'm *asking* you to think about what I said. Think about how you'd feel if I was the one living with my ex-girlfriend right now, even if she hadn't sexually assaulted me. *I* can't stand the thought—it makes me feel sick. The thought of you with him always did, but it's even worse with what I know now. You can live here, with me, until you leave for school. I'm hoping this is where you'd be staying during your breaks from school, anyway. Treble would love your company, and I'd love being able to see you every day. There's no reason *not* to just move in with me until you get a place wherever school is."

I rolled his words around in my mind. "That's a serious kind of offer to make."

"Nina... I'm *serious* about you, and about us."

I bobbed my head slowly, liking the idea now that it was sinking in. "Okay... I'll move in for the summer."

TWENTY-EIGHT

After Myles and I came to an agreement that I would move in with him soon, I drove home, excitement bubbling up in my chest. I hadn't contemplated living with Myles—this relationship between us was in its infancy—but I loved the idea. It was so sudden and fast, the change between us, but at the same time, the feelings had always been there. How we labeled our relationship had changed, but the way we cared about each other hadn't. And falling for each other years ago had been fast, too, but that had lasted. This could, too... it would.

I waited until I was in the apartment to call Landon so I wouldn't be distracted behind the wheel. Pacing, my heart jumping around wildly in my chest, I dialed.

"Hi, Nina, darling," he answered.

I winced—why was he still calling me darling? Myles would be furious. "Hi, Landon. How is everything?"

"Fine, fine, darling. How are you?"

"I'm well," I replied honestly. "I just wanted to let you know that I'm going to be moving out this week. I'll leave my key in the drawer of the foyer table when I go."

There was a brief silence. "Nina, darling, you can't go yet. I was going to call you and tell you that people are coming to do some renovating. They should be starting next week, and they need someone home while they're working."

"Renovations?" I asked, my feet coming to a halt. Since when was he doing renovations? What needed to be renovated in this place?

"Yes, darling. I'd been thinking for a while about making some changes, but it was never convenient. It occurred to me that while you're not working would be the perfect time."

"But, Landon, I'm moving out. I just told you that I'm moving out. And I told you months ago that I *would be* moving out."

"I know, darling, but I told you there was no rush. There's no reason you need to leave, everything there is already paid for. And you might as well be there since I'm never home—at least someone is actually living there. I'm happy to help you."

"But, Landon—"

"Please, darling. I need *your* help."

His words gave me pause. He'd never told me he needed anything from me, and he'd never, to my knowledge, *ever* asked someone for help. This was a big deal for him. All the changes with me must have been making an impact. And I didn't want to shut him down when he was actually asking for help with something. And I owed it to him after he helped me by letting me stay as long as I had after we were no longer dating. I continued pacing, already dreading the conversation with Myles when I told him I wasn't leaving.

"Okay. How long will they be here?"

"I don't know, darling. Six weeks, maybe?"

"Six weeks?"

"I'm not sure, darling. I didn't ask, and they didn't say. But I can find out if you need to know."

"No, that's fine," I sighed. However long it was, I'd stay for it, so it didn't really matter how many weeks it ended up being as long as it didn't run past mid-August, though I couldn't imagine enough work to be done in the condo that it would take months to complete. "But as soon as they're done, I'm moving out."

"Of course, darling, I understand. Thank you for staying."

When I arrived back at Myles' house, there was a feeling of dread in the pit of my stomach. I didn't want to tell him that I wasn't moving in with him. He wasn't going to take the news well, I knew. And while I felt obligated to help Landon out after what he was doing for me, Myles wouldn't agree.

Myles answered the door by swinging it wide and immediately wrapping his arms around me and lifting me off my feet as he kissed me.

"I love you," he said. Kicking the door closed, he pressed my back against it and kissed down the side of my neck. I was quickly forgetting what I needed to talk to him about, distracted by the hormones that raged through my body in response to his touch and his obvious desire for me.

"I love being able to kiss you whenever I want," he said between kisses in a low, rumbly voice. "I love being able to touch you whenever I want. I love being able to tell you I love you whenever I want."

"I love it, too." It was true; it gave me a thrill and caught me by surprise the way he was with me since I'd told him I wasn't dating Landon anymore. It was much like the way he was years earlier, except more of it. And now he kept telling me how he felt about me.

His kisses slowed, and then we were just compressed tightly together against his door, our hearts beating against each other, the sound of our breaths in each other's ears.

"This is the best, Nina," he murmured.

"What is, Myles?" I murmured back, feeling the exact same way.

"You and me," he replied. "It doesn't get better than this—having you in my arms and knowing you love me and that I get to love you back. And having nothing to keep us apart anymore. This is literally the happiest I've ever been, sunshine."

"I've always liked it when you call me sunshine," I whispered.

He kissed my cheek, then I could feel him smiling against the same spot. "Okay, sunshine."

Myles had prepared dinner—one-pan steak, potato wedges, and carrots—while I was away, and the timer indicated it was ready moments after I'd arrived. We peeled ourselves apart at his front door and walked to the kitchen, holding hands. I couldn't stop grinning or get rid of the blush on my cheeks. Myles was also beaming and couldn't keep his eyes off me. I felt like a young college student all over again and giggled. Myles smirked, his eyes dark and bright at the same time.

With dinner out of the oven and plated up, and a newly-awake Treble fed, we sat at Myles' dining table to eat. Our seats were across from each other, but Myles had hooked his feet around mine under the table, which for some reason struck me as the most adorable thing and I had an urge to fling my arms around him.

"So," Myles said after his first bite of steak, "how much stuff do you have? Could we get you moved tomorrow?"

My stomach dropped and I set my fork down without eating the bite on it. "Actually—"

"Nina, don't," he cut me off, his face having hardened. But he said nothing else, just staring at me intently.

"I spoke to Landon and he's having some renovations done on the condo, and someone has to be there the whole time they're working, and—"

"You've got to be fucking kidding me," Myles muttered.

"It's not forever, it's just going to be a few weeks or so, then I'll be leaving."

"It's *his* condo, *his* problem, Nina. Not yours."

"I know, but he needs help—he can't be there all day for weeks with his job. And I can since I'm not working."

"But it's *his* condo—not yours. You're not dating anymore, you're not related, there's no reason for you to be the one there."

"I know that, Myles, but he helped me out and I'm going to do this to help *him* out. And I can leave after."

"Is that what he told you? That you have to help him because he's helping you?"

I started to shake my head, but stopped abruptly. He hadn't said it that way, but had that been what he meant?

"Nina, he's manipulating you. He told you that you have to help him because he helped you. I told you there was a reason he was doing that."

"No, Myles, he didn't tell me that. He told me he needed my help. And I feel I owe it to him because of what he's doing for me."

Myles eyed me for a minute, his jaw clenched. "You don't owe him anything, Nina. You don't even owe *me* anything. You shouldn't be guilt-tripped into doing things. He's just trying to control you."

I sighed. "You keep trying to make him into this awful person, Myles, and he's not. He's obsessed with his job, yes. He's oblivious to what really matters in life, yes. He's been pushy about sex, yes. I'll even give you that he's a little bit misogynistic. But he's not a bad person. He's not cold and calculating and evil. He's not manipulating me. He asked me for a favor, and I agreed to do it because *I* feel obligated to."

"The only person who's oblivious right now is *you*, Nina."

I stared at him, my eyes flooding with tears. Myles stared back, his face hard. I couldn't sit there any longer and stood, carrying my plate of mostly untouched food to the kitchen. After putting my leftovers away and washing my dish, I walked back into the dining room where Myles was sitting with his head in his hands.

"Maybe I should go," I said quietly.

His head jerked up, his cheeks damp. He no longer looked angry; he looked devastated, and it sucked the air from my lungs.

"Myles?"

"Please don't," he whispered, pushing to his feet. "Don't leave me again, Nina."

He pulled me into his arms and held me smashed against his chest, his whole body tense and shaking. Whatever was happening inside him right then was intensely painful, and it ripped me apart to see him that way. I cradled his head, wanting to take away what he was feeling. We stood that way for a long time.

Wiping his face, he eventually stepped back. He studied me, taking a noisy breath and releasing it. "I'm so scared something's going to happen to you, Nina. That he's going to hurt you again. I feel like I need to protect you, except that I can't when you won't let me. But how would I live with knowing I could have kept you safe this time if I don't? I hate that I didn't protect you before. I knew you walking alone could be dangerous and I could have fought you on it, and if I had, you never would have been raped then. And if you

hadn't, you wouldn't have gone through everything you have since, either. You wouldn't have dated a guy who never really cared about you, who raped you, who's manipulating you now. I don't want to let you down like that again, Nina. I *can't*."

I wrapped my arms around his neck as his made their way around my waist, and we held each other close again.

"None of that is your fault," I said. "It never was. It wasn't your job to protect me then, and it isn't now. You've never let me down, Myles. Never."

"I'm so sorry, Nina," he cried into my neck.

I stroked his hair and let him cry. He'd been holding in that guilt for what someone else had done to me for years, and he needed to get it out. I could understand now why he was so touchy about Landon—he saw him as the same as the guy in the alley, and it was triggering for him. It was why he'd yelled at me, why, despite never having been remotely controlling, he was demanding I move out immediately.

"I'm safe, Myles. I'm safe now. Because of you."

TWENTY-NINE

It was strange waking with Myles Monday morning, knowing he'd be leaving for work. I'd planned to go back home Sunday night, but when he'd asked me to stay with his lips and hands on my skin, I'd readily agreed.

"I wish I could stay here with you," he said as he shoveled down breakfast while I sipped coffee.

"I know," I yawned. We'd been up way too late the night before. "But you have kids counting on their super awesome music teacher to be there for them."

He smiled a little shyly. "I'm trying to be that for them. They need someone like that in their lives."

"I think you're doing it, Myles. It was obvious to me those kids adore you."

"Hm." He swallowed the last of his coffee and put his dishes into the dishwasher. "You'll stay until I get home? And have dinner with me before you go?" he asked, slipping his arms around my shoulders and kissing the top of my head.

I nodded. "Yup."

"Okay, good." He bent and touched his lips to mine. Then he did it again and again. "Mm. I have to go now." He kissed me again. "By the way, the key under the mat?"

"Yeah?"

"Keep it. It's yours."

I blushed and bit my lip for a moment before letting my grin free. "Okay."

With one more kiss, Myles was gone. I yawned, pouring myself another cup of coffee, then spent the next few hours studying, attending livestream classes, and practicing the Evanescence piece for a break. A while after lunch, I deemed myself studied out for the day and went out to get some magazine file holders so I could, at long last, organize the mess of music he had scattered all over the house.

I was still organizing, my hair piled on my head, a bit sweaty, very dusty, and extremely tired when Myles got home that evening.

"What are you doing?" he asked, laughing as he walked into the living room, Treble already in his arms. She'd jumped up from where she was napping next to me the second the front door opened, already more spry after her surgery several days earlier.

The normal mess was magnified as I was going through music and making piles. I'd already been through the exercise once when I decided to organize by type of music as opposed to composer like I originally had it, then decided to do a hybrid, so classical composers would be organized by composer and arrangements of contemporary music would be grouped by type of music and then alphabetized by song title.

I blew upward to dislodge a few locks of hair that had escaped my bun some time before, but they stuck to my sweaty forehead, so I used my hand to shove them off my skin. "Cleaning up your mess of music."

He snorted, crossing his arms as he leaned against the wall. "Looks more like making an even bigger mess to me. Now I'll never find anything."

I narrowed my eyes. "I don't know how the hell you ever found anything before. It was a disaster, Myles! And I know this looks bad, but I promise you that you'll be thanking me the next time you need to find something."

"Maybe. Depends on whether or not what you're doing makes any sense. You organized it by tempo, right?" He quirked an eyebrow, his mouth pulled toward the center.

My eyes were now slits. "Tempo? Are you serious? Or are you kidding? Because this is already the third time I've organized everything today. Don't tell me I need to start over."

He laughed. "You've organized it three times?"

"Well, two and a half. I'm not done with the third time yet. That's what I'm doing now."

He walked over and bent, kissing my cheek. "Sunshine, whatever you choose to do will be just fine."

"Do you really want it by tempo? Because it would be a pain in the ass, but I'll do it if that's what would make the most sense to you since it's your music, not mine."

He chuckled. "No. That would be annoying as hell. I was just kidding." He eyed me. "You okay? I was more expecting you to tell me to go to hell or something with the tempo comment."

I sighed, giving him a tired smile. "Yeah. I'm just exhausted. And aggravated with myself that I didn't think to organize the way I am now to begin with."

He lowered himself to the floor behind where I was sitting cross-legged and began rubbing my shoulders. I closed my eyes and my head melted down until my chin was on my chest. "That feels amazing," I said with a moan. I hadn't realized until his hands were on me how stiff I was from spending hours sitting on the floor without moving around. "How was your day?"

"It was great," he said. I could hear the smile in his voice. "The kids accepted the challenge videos, but they did voice their disappointment that I didn't do any that could make a mess, like the water on your head challenge. However, they were placated because you were doing them with me. They asked again about you coming in to do a slaps tournament, and I promised I'd talk to you about it this evening. I was thinking maybe the last week of school?"

I moaned again. "Sure. Whatever you want as long as you don't stop what you're doing."

He let out a soft laugh. "I'll keep in mind that I can get anything I want from you as long as I'm giving you a back rub." His hands moved down from my shoulders, loosening muscles around my spine. "Gary—he's one of the PE teachers—gave me a flyer today from a piano bar in Midtown. They're doing like an open-mic kind of thing in a couple of weeks. He suggested I sign up to perform, and I was thinking about it."

"Oh you absolutely should, Myles. And then afterward, I can walk over to you and give you a kiss and break the hearts of every woman in the joint." I giggled.

He kissed the back of my neck with a soft chuckle. "Actually, I was thinking you should do it with me."

"Not my kind of thing."

"I know you don't like to perform, but I don't mean by yourself. I was thinking we could play a duet."

I shook my head. "Nope. Besides, you can play way better than the duets we do together. I'll hold you back because I can't match your skill."

"It's not holding me back if it's what I want to do, Nina."

"Even so. I promise I'll be there to watch and support you, but that's about it. Nothing that involves me getting up in front of a crowd." His hands were now on my lower back and I felt like I was melting. "God, that feels good. I think I need these more often."

"I'll tell you what, sunshine," he said, his magic hands moving slower and deeper to emphasize his words. "I'll give you backrubs on demand for the next two months if you do this with me."

I groaned. "Why do you want me to perform with you so bad?"

"Just like everything else, I enjoy music more when it's with you."

How the hell could I say no to something like that?

"It's already late," Myles said against the crook of my neck, one hand in my hair and the other around my back at his front door. We'd had dinner and I was about to head home. "Why don't you just stay again tonight, and I promise I'll let you go home tomorrow."

I giggled. "I have to go home—I have therapy in the morning."

"How early?" One hand had snuck under my shirt and was sliding into the waistband of my pants.

"Eleven," I replied, my voice on the breathy side.

"You can drive in after rush hour and still make it on time." He gave a long, nipping kiss to my collarbone.

"You're killing me, Myles," I chuckled, tilting my head back to give him better access anyway. "I need sleep. That's why I was so grouchy all evening."

"You can sleep here."

"If you'd let me sleep, I could."

"I promise to let you sleep. Now will you stay?"

I snorted. "Okay, yes, I'll stay."

"You have to promise, too."

"For you to let me sleep?" I bit my cheeks so I wouldn't laugh.

"No, for *you* to let *me* sleep, you obnoxious, irresistible woman."

"It'll be hard, but I promise," I replied, giggling.

He grabbed the hem of my shirt and started pulling it up over my head.

"What are you doing?" I laughed as he tugged the sleeves over my arms and tossed my shirt on the floor. "You promised to let me sleep."

"And I will," he replied, hooking a hand into the front of my jeans and turning, pulling me along with him toward his bedroom. "But it's not quite bedtime yet."

He kept his promise.

I did *not* keep mine.

THIRTY

I was practically skipping on my way into therapy. I had so much to tell Leslie, and for once, it was basically all good. I couldn't stop thinking about Myles' growl that he loved me so damn much he felt like he was losing his mind that morning when he left for work or the way his hands had been touching me not long before that. It was like living inside a really, *really* good dream. Everything was rosy and looking up.

"Good morning!" I called out cheerily as soon as I saw Leslie at the doorway to the waiting room for me.

She smiled and tipped her head toward her office, so I rose and followed her, humming a few bars from "To a Wild Rose," which I'd been playing before leaving Myles' house that morning. I was trying to decide whether we would play that one, "Immortal," or "Bring Me to Life" for the piano open mic night; Myles had told me I could decide which piece we'd play, and those were my three favorites.

"So, how's the past week been? What's been happening?" Leslie asked.

I sighed, content and grinning. "I can't believe it's only been a week! So much has happened and it feels like it's been so much longer than that."

Leslie smiled, then I gave her a rundown of everything that had happened in the last seven days since I'd seen her, focusing on the change in mine and Myles' relationship and everything since.

"That's quite a lot of change," she observed. "In a very short period of time. How are you feeling about it all?"

I laughed. "I'm loving life right now."

She smiled. "Okay. Is that all?"

My mind flickered to the fight with Myles over Landon, which I'd skipped over while telling Leslie about the last few days, focusing on all the good things that had happened. My smile faltered a bit and I glanced at Leslie, who was just waiting patiently.

"No," I replied at length. "Myles and I fought—twice—over me still living with Landon."

She nodded with no indication of surprise, but didn't say anything.

"Myles wants me to move out immediately. He wants me to move in with him since I don't want to get a place until I know which school I'm going to."

"And what do *you* want to do?"

"I…" my voice trailed off as I was about to say I wanted that, too. I did. I really did. But it was also so soon and made me anxious. I explained this the best I could to Leslie.

"Did you explain your feelings to Myles?"

"No. We were too busy arguing about Landon. And I ended up agreeing to move in—I mean, I'm more excited than anything else about it—but then Landon told me he's having some renovations done in the condo soon and needs me to stay for a while until they're done. That's actually why Myles and I fought the second time, because I was going to tell Landon I was leaving, and I did, but then he needed some help."

"And why *are* you helping him?"

I sighed. That was a *great* question. "He needs my help."

"Okay. But you can still say no."

Her words hit me hard, like something slamming into my chest. I could still say no. Just because he needed something didn't mean I couldn't say no. I didn't have to do what he wanted. Our entire relationship—the part in which we actually interacted—was predicated on me doing things he needed or thought he needed. Getting his coffee, making and serving him breakfast because he couldn't miss any of the news. Making sure his dry cleaning was picked up and delivered in time for him to always have clean suits for traveling. Ensuring I was home for maintenance calls because he always had something more pressing. Rearranging my schedule to attend his business events because he needed to have a date for them for his image.

And having sex because he missed me and had "needs."

My eyes were darting all around the room, flitting so fast I couldn't make sense of anything they were seeing. I'd spent years catering to Landon's "needs" without a thought for my own. I'd always felt obligated to do the things he wanted from me, like they were my side of a transaction. Just like his pressure made me feel like I could never say no to sex, I'd always felt pressured to do the other things. And before that, I'd slept with countless men because they wanted it and applied pressure to get it. No matter what I wanted, I always complied.

At work, every time someone asked me for help, I gave it. Every time someone asked me to take on another project, another responsibility, I accepted it, even knowing it would mean less and less sleep. Knowing I didn't have the time for it, I still accepted.

But all along, I could have said no... to *all* of it.

My body was now restless, and I couldn't sit still. I stood and paced back and forth across the small office, aware Leslie's eyes followed me but unable to actually hold her gaze. I couldn't make anything in my body cooperate right then—it had taken on a mind of its own. My thoughts were racing so fast I couldn't hold onto any of them. My heart was pounding in my chest.

"I can always say no," I mumbled. Then my head jerked up and I stared at Leslie, suddenly very still, my eyes rapidly filling. "I've always been able to say no. And I haven't because I was afraid of what would happen if I did."

"You can," she said softly.

How much of my life had been driven by fear of what would happen if I said no, all because of one event? It had taken less than ten minutes for that stranger to derail my life, to take my self-confidence and completely extinguish it, to make me perpetually afraid of denying other people something they wanted. I wasn't sure if I was more angry or devastated as the entirety of the impact on my life became clear. In a flash, I saw myself as I was back then, before that night, and could see how my life might have played out. Myles and I would have stayed together, I was sure of it. We'd have gotten married after I finished college, and I'd have become a trail guide like I always wanted in the mountains where I'd grown up. I'd maybe have even had a baby, and my parents would have gotten to know their grandchild. Because I wouldn't have been basically estranged from them—I would have been taking care of them instead like I'd always wanted to—my parents wouldn't have died from carbon monoxide poisoning; I would have made sure they were living in a better, safer home, even if that had meant they lived with Myles and me.

I'd always been able to say no... but I hadn't, and I didn't know if I could anymore.

And now I had no idea who I was.

Or who I could have become.

Everything looked different when I walked out of therapy. Colors were dulled and sounds were grating. Rather than the blue of the sky and fluffiness of the clouds that I'd admired on my way in, all I noticed now was the dirt and trash on the sidewalks, the graffiti on signs and post office drop boxes. The elated, hopeful feeling that had buoyed me had deflated, leaving me heavy and full of grief.

After therapy, I usually went to Midtown Park to walk as part of my post-therapy self-care routine, but the thought of getting myself there felt overwhelming. In lieu of my normal routine, I went home and changed into pajamas. I sat on the sofa and stared at the wall, trying to sort through everything in my mind.

I was still staring at the wall hours later when my phone started ringing. I startled, realizing I'd been in the same spot for a long time and that I didn't know where I'd left my phone. Part of me just wanted to ignore it—I didn't feel like talking—but I forced myself to my feet and shuffled around, following the sound until I found it. I lifted it just as my voicemail picked up—I'd missed a call from Myles.

My eyes stared blankly at the screen as I tried to make myself call him back, but I just put my phone back down and slid down the wall to the floor. I didn't know who this person was, and Myles didn't need that, didn't need to be worried when he had students counting on him.

Who was I really? Who would I have been without that night? That night didn't just change the trajectory of my own life, but indirectly led to the death of my parents. My parents were dead because of me. And they weren't the only ones. There was also an unborn child because of me.

I sobbed into my knees, barely hearing the phone when it rang again sometime later. All of these things that had happened in my life after I was raped in the alley... they didn't have to happen. All those men... I ran to the bathroom and threw up, and then I got into the shower and cried some more with the water beating down on my back. I wanted to go back in time and change things. I wanted to tell myself that I had a choice, that I could say no, that I could always say no. That I didn't have to let them do things to me that I didn't want.

When I got out of the shower, I glanced at my phone, at the missed calls and waiting voicemails and text messages, and felt unequal to the task of even opening them up. It would require effort to read and to listen and to respond—effort I wasn't capable of right then. I left it where it was, flipping it to silent, and climbed into bed.

An hour or so later, the intercom in the condo buzzed loudly, scaring the hell out of me. I nearly rolled out of bed when I jumped, and it felt like I was having a heart attack. Once I realized what it was, I slowed my breathing and ignored it—it had to have been someone buzzing the wrong condo. But then it happened again. Reluctantly, I dragged myself out of bed. If I didn't respond, whoever it was would keep buzzing, and it was a jarring sound I didn't want to hear again.

"Hello?" I croaked out, my throat froggy after crying so much. Then I pushed the button to allow the person on the other end to speak.

"Nina—it's me. Let me in."

I stared at the intercom box. "Myles? What are you doing here?"

"Let me in, Nina. Please."

I pushed the button to let him into the building and unlocked the front door. Then I shuffled back to bed with a small hope that doing so would keep me from facing him in my state. Several minutes later, I heard the door open and Myles' voice calling my name.

"I'm here," I replied, hoping I was loud enough for him to hear. I hugged my pillow tight, burying my face behind it with my back to the doorway.

"Nina—what the hell is going on?" Myles rushed out as he burst into the room in a flurry of energy and tension. He sat on the bed, which I felt move under his weight. "Nina?"

I shook my head and a sob rose up my throat. I tried to hold it down, but when his hand rested on my back, it broke free.

"Oh, Jesus—what happened?" he asked, his voice changing into a different kind of worry and pain, his fingers gentle as they pulled my hair over my shoulder, as they tenderly touched my skin. "What happened, Nina?" He slipped an arm under my shoulders and another under my knees and lifted, rolling me toward him and then holding me curled into a ball on his lap as he pulled the pillow out of my arms and set it on the bed next to us. I was folded into his arms, and he was kissing my forehead every few seconds.

Myles' warmth intensified how much everything hurt and I cried harder, curling tighter into a ball. As much as I wanted to tell him what was wrong... I couldn't. I couldn't speak at all. He ran a soothing hand from the crown of my head down the length of my back, over and over and over, rocking me until my crying slowed. Then he touched a soft kiss to the top of my head and set me down. I watched, feeling lifeless, as he packed a duffel bag with my clothes before flinging the bag over his shoulder.

"Come on," he whispered, reaching a hand toward me.

I pushed to my feet, clinging to him like a lifeline.

The drive to Myles' house the night before hadn't been silent, even if it was without conversation. He'd played a collection of music that made me feel more, and while that meant every hurt inside intensified, it was exactly what I needed. It was like the music understood how I felt, and that made me feel somewhat less alone and hopeless.

The next morning, however, brought no change. I hadn't slept well, woken repeatedly by disturbing dreams comprised of a mixture of past reality and fiction. As Myles got ready for work, I lay on my side, watching, and could see the tiredness and worry around his eyes, in the tight set of his jaw, and the way his mouth was drawn into a thin line. He didn't even seem to notice that Treble was rubbing against his ankles for attention.

"I'm so sorry for doing this to you, Myles," I said, my voice barely above a whisper. I didn't have the energy for more than that.

He looked over from where he was buttoning his shirt. He pushed the last two buttons in, then sat down on the bed next to me. He brushed some hair back from my face and left a long, lingering kiss on my cheekbone. "You aren't doing anything to me, Nina."

I stared into space. I heard him but I wasn't sure I believed it. I could clearly see the link between myself and the pain I was witnessing in him, just as I could see the link between myself and my parents' deaths.

He kissed my cheekbone again, his hand smoothing along my back. "I'm doing lessons after school today, so I won't be home until late. I'll call to check in, but if you need me, you can call me and just tell the office it's an emergency, okay? You can also call Mom. I'll put her number in your phone."

"I'll be fine," I said, my voice hollow.

"If you think you can, you should go for a hike today. And play some music on the piano. It'll help."

"I can't," I said quietly. "I have classes today."

"It's okay if you miss a class. How many classes did I miss to see you? And I'm doing alright." He gave me a lopsided smile.

I tried to reciprocate.

I failed.

His lips turned down at the corners.

"I wish you'd talk to me," he said.

I nodded and swallowed. "I will. I just can't right now."

"I understand." This time he kissed my temple, then pressed a soft kiss to my lips. "I love you, sunshine."

"I love you, too," I said, my voice cracking.

He wiped the tears from my face with his thumb, then rested his forehead against mine. "I have to go. I'm sorry."

"It's okay," I said, sniffling and trying to make the tears go back to wherever they were before he told me he loved me. "Go. I don't want to make you late."

With a final kiss to my forehead, he left.

THIRTY-ONE

I hadn't moved out of bed when I heard the knocking at the door. I ignored it. But then I heard Sarah's voice from somewhere *inside* the house.

"Nina, honey?" she called, her voice projecting but somehow still soft.

I'm gonna kill Myles for sending his mother over. Because falling apart in front of *him* wasn't bad enough. And this wasn't my typical falling apart—I felt so disconnected from reality, like I almost wasn't even real. At the same time, I felt a sense of severe internal panic.

And I was lost.

So lost.

I couldn't see a way out.

Sarah appeared in the doorway, and I rolled my face into my pillow to hide it. Maybe if I didn't move, she'd think I was dead, and she'd just go away.

That didn't work; she climbed onto the bed and stretched out on her side in front of me. Her hand rested on my shoulder a moment, then ran slowly up and down my arm as she tucked her other arm under her head like a pillow. I swallowed, ashamed, but my eyes still darted to hers every split second.

"Do you want to talk about it, honey?"

I twisted my head side-to-side. "I just don't know anything anymore. I don't know—" I hiccupped, and a wail spilled out. I pulled up my knees and squeezed myself into a ball in an attempt to alleviate the pain in my chest. I couldn't even articulate why I was in so much pain right then, why I couldn't talk without crying the way I was. But articulate it or not, it was happening. I was unraveling at the seams, but more like someone was violently ripping those seams apart—this was no gentle undoing.

A warm, soft body that smelled like vanilla and a hint of cinnamon enveloped me, and it was so much like having my mom again that I cried harder, then reached out and clung to her. Time seemed to exist separate from reality as I cried until I was wrung out—nothing more than a dried-out shell—and finally dozed off.

When I woke, it was late afternoon; I'd slept through my classes, but I didn't care right then. I wouldn't have absorbed any of the information anyway, even if I had been online for them. I'd spend extra time studying the next couple of days to make up for it. As I sighed and forced myself out of bed, a heavenly scent reached me— one I hadn't smelled since the last time I'd gone home, the summer after I met Myles. The summer after the incident that changed everything. It was oatmeal raisin walnut cookies—my favorite. My mom used to make them whenever I was upset when I was growing up. We'd sit snuggled and watch a movie, eating the fresh-baked cookies together with a glass of milk.

My eyes were filling again, but I walked through the house, my arms wrapped tightly around myself, to find Sarah in the kitchen, moving cookies from a baking sheet onto a wire cooling rack. She looked up when I walked in, smiling warmly, her eyes betraying worry. It must have been a look all moms learned because it was the same look *my* mom would give me in times like this. I found myself giving her a small smile in return and watched hers pull a little wider, the corners of her eyes crinkling.

"Oatmeal raisin walnut, right? That's what Myles told me was your favorite."

I gave a short nod. "Yeah. My mom used to make them for me. With milk."

"You want some milk? I was gonna make hot tea, but I can pour you some milk instead."

I tried to pull the corners of my mouth up. "No. Hot tea sounds nice."

"Okay, honey, go get comfortable wherever you want, and I'll find you with a plate of cookies and some tea here in a minute."

"Okay. Thank you."

"Of course, honey. That's what moms are for."

We sat together on the sofa and watched episode after episode of *Grace & Frankie*, Sarah's favorite television show. I'd never even heard of it, but the more of it we watched, the more I liked it. Once I'd gotten my fill of cookies and tea, I tucked my feet under me and laid my head on the back of the sofa. Sarah reached over an arm around me and tugged lightly. I gratefully leaned until I was lying down, my head in her lap, and we continued to watch while she absently fingered my curls. She made lots of sounds with her reactions, from laughter to sucking in breaths at surprises or painful moments to moaning at embarrassments. Each one was warm and vibrating and soothing.

She paused before starting the next episode sometime in early evening. "It's a late night for Myles. What would you like for dinner? I can make you something or have Marv run out for something. What do you want, honey?"

My eyes searched aimlessly in front of me. "I don't know. I'm not hungry."

She tugged lightly on a curl. "What did your mom used to do for you?"

"Mom made cookies. That was her thing. Dad always gave me canned chicken noodle soup. Sick or had a bad day, didn't matter—chicken noodle soup. Sprained my ankle? Chicken noodle soup." I chuckled. "When I got my period, he was the only one home and he wasn't sure what to do about my cramps, so he gave me gave Tylenol... and made me chicken noodle soup." By the last word, Sarah and I were both cackling. My dad's deer-in-the-headlights look, how unprepared he was for the situation, was a memory I'd forgotten about.

"He sounds just wonderful."

"He was," I smiled, remembering my dad.

She reached over and grabbed her phone from a side table and called Marv, asking him to go get some chicken noodle soup and some bread to go with it and bring it over for dinner. After she was done with her call, she asked, "Ready?" while holding out the remote.

I sighed. It was the closest to relaxed and not hopeless I'd felt since I'd left my therapist's office. "Thank you. I'm not sure why you're doing all this for me, but thank you."

She was quiet for a while, then sighed. "Honey, if I was gone, I'd want someone to care for Myles for me."

I nodded—I understood. And for some reason, that made me want to talk to her the way I wished I could talk to my mom... the way I would if she were still alive. The way I wished I had when she was.

"I imagine Myles told you about what happened when I was at MU... I mean, he must have, he said he was in therapy for it."

"Mm-hm," she said, her fingers still playing with the ends of my hair. The sensation was very relaxing.

"I never told my parents. I was ashamed. I never told anyone after Myles and I talked to the police after leaving the hospital. I felt so stupid and like it was my fault it happened. If I hadn't been so independent, so determined I could handle anything, it wouldn't have happened. Or maybe I would have fought back and won if I hadn't had a few beers earlier in the night. All those things the police said—the things that made Myles punch one of them—they stuck with me, so I couldn't tell my parents.

"I walked away from Myles because I was trying to cope with everything by not feeling it—it was too much to feel. But I couldn't keep from feeling when I was with him. I always felt everything with him. And it got to be too much."

I continued, telling her everything—about the abortion, about the heavy drinking and how that destroyed my relationship with my parents, even about all the guys after because I became paralyzed and couldn't tell them no. I didn't hold anything back, and through it all, she didn't falter or make any disgusted or shocked sounds at anything I said. She just... listened and took it all in.

So I kept going; I told her all about Landon and about running into Myles and why I'd walked away from him, why I'd sought him out after and why I'd walked away again. I told her about my job and why I'd chosen it and how I lost it. Next, I told her what happened at therapy the day before, the realizations I had.

"I don't know... who I am, who I should have been. I don't know how to live with realizing that what happened killed my parents, that *my reaction* killed them, because if our relationship hadn't been ruined, they wouldn't have been living in that house anymore. I loved them so much, but I caused their deaths, and then they died thinking I hated them."

Sarah let out a long sigh. She dropped my curls and smoothed her hand up and down my arm, giving a little squeeze here and there.

"Something you'll learn one day if you become a parent is that your love for your children is unconditional. It doesn't matter what they do, you still love them. Even if it saddens you or makes you angrier than you've ever been in your life, you still love them with your whole heart. I know your parents loved you, Nina. They loved you until their last breath. And they weren't angry with you. They knew something was wrong. I promise you that. And I promise you they knew you didn't hate them. No matter what you said or how you acted after what happened, they knew. We know our kids often better than they know themselves. And we know when what they're doing is a reaction to something that has happened to them. They never believed you hated them, Nina.

"And you didn't kill them, either. Carbon monoxide did. And it wasn't your fault it happened. There are as many ways our lives can play out as we can imagine, and only one does. But just because it didn't play out another way doesn't mean it's your fault. You had one of the most horrible, violating, destructive things that can happen to someone happen to you, and there's no right way to react to something like that, honey. You were doing the best you could at the time. You can't do more than that."

"I was trying, but I was also failing. If they hadn't died... what would they have thought of me for having an abortion? Without even talking to them?"

"Nina, honey. You were struggling to take care of *yourself* after that. Do you think you'd have been able to take care of a baby? Even if you were giving it up for adoption, do you think you'd have been able to take care of that baby while it was growing inside you?"

I shook my head miserably. I knew I wouldn't have been able to.

"Something like this is never an easy decision. But you were doing the best you could. If you couldn't take care of yourself, you wouldn't have been giving a baby a healthy start in this world."

I sat in the silence that followed, staring through the coffee table, digesting her words, wanting to believe them.

"I know your mom was a lovely woman, Nina, because *you* are a lovely woman. So, I know she'd want you to know that none of this has been your fault. And she'd want you to know that you're strong enough to keep going. Who you once were isn't who you're going to be anymore, and that's okay. We're all constantly changing—or we should be, anyway. The world leaves its impression on us, and it becomes part of who we are, the good experiences and the bad. And that's how it should be. We don't have to know who we're going to be; we just need to be true to listening to our hearts tell us who we are now. You are a rape survivor, Nina. That wasn't always part of who you are, but it is now. And that may mean there are things you've lost, but you now have an opportunity to find new things to be part of who you are, things you might not have found otherwise."

I wiped under my eyes and sniffled, then let out a sigh of my own, my body relaxing. Her words had been a balm to my broken pieces inside, and now they were slightly less sharp.

I woke drowsily to hushed voices around me; I'd fallen asleep on the sofa after eating chicken noodle soup with Myles' parents, still watching episodes of *Grace and Frankie*. Being awake, sleepy, and hearing the soft murmur of voices of people who didn't know I was aware reminded me of when I was in tenth grade.

I'd had a crush on a boy at school and told a girl I'd thought was my friend, and she'd told not only the boy, but the whole school about it, fabricating some of what I'd said to make it a better secret to tell. I'd gone into school to find people watching me while talking behind their hands and laughing. Then, the boy had come up to me at lunch and told me I'd never get a boyfriend because I wasn't pretty enough for one, I was too weird, no one liked me, and he couldn't believe I had the nerve to even have a crush on him. I'd walked out of school and run until I reached the woods where I spent most of my time. I'd sat, crying, in the environment where I felt most at home, which was also the reason everyone thought I was weird, until my parents found me there hours later, worried.

We'd gone home, and my mom had made cookies while my dad made chicken noodle soup, and we'd watched movies until I fell asleep on the sofa, my head in my mom's lap and my feet in my dad's. I'd woken to them talking in hushed tones, my mom playing with my hair, my dad absently rubbing my feet. I'd wanted to die after the embarrassment at school, but in that moment, I'd felt loved and like I would be okay. Rather than feeling like there was something wrong with me, I felt it was okay to be me even if people didn't like it. It was a moment that strengthened my bond with my parents and theirs with me, in spite of being driven by pain and heartache.

And now I had that same feeling. I couldn't understand the murmurs between the voices around me—one of them Myles'—but I didn't need to. There was warmth and love inside my chest again, and while I was completely wiped out, I felt I was also cleared out and ready to begin refilling again.

As I listened to their hum of voices, I realized my head was resting on Sarah's lap, Myles was sitting near my feet, and Marv was in one of the chairs to the sides of the sofa. I focused and was able to make out their conversation: they were talking about Myles' day teaching. I wanted to stay there like that all night, listening to them, but I had to yawn. As I did, I sat up, feeling sluggish.

"Hey there, sunshine," Myles said with a soft smile, pulling me into his arms and giving me a gentle kiss.

I mirrored his smile. "You look tired."

"I am," he replied with a yawn, lifting an arm to stretch. "Ready for bed?"

I looked in turn at Marv and Sarah, who were both smiling affectionately at us. "Yeah. I'm exhausted still."

"Of course you are, honey," Sarah said, stretching herself and standing.

Everyone else stood as well and we all made our way to the front door. Marv pulled me into a bear hug.

"Get some rest, Nina," he said gruffly. "You need it."

"I will," I replied, turning to Sarah. We hugged each other tightly. I felt like a bond connected us and hoped that feeling was mutual. "Thank you so much," I said, my voice muffled by her shoulder.

"Nothing to thank me for," she replied, then dropped a kiss to my forehead. "They love you," she said warmly. "And so do we. You're family now, too, honey."

I pulled her close again, trying not to cry for the millionth time. I didn't know how to articulate how much her presence had meant to me, how badly I had needed exactly that, although I hadn't realized it until she was there.

"I'll check in with you tomorrow," she said, stepping back. "But you can call me anytime. Don't you hesitate to call if you need *anything*."

"I won't," I replied. And I meant it.

After we'd locked the door behind them, Myles and I made our way to the bedroom. I was still in my pajamas, so I brushed my teeth, then crawled into bed while Myles finished getting changed and brushing his own teeth. When he climbed in, he scooted up behind me and cradled my body with his, his arms wrapped tight around me.

He kissed the back of my head. "I was worried about you today."

"I was okay, thanks to your mom. I was mad at you for sending her over here at first, but now I'm glad you did."

"I didn't, Nina. I'd talked to her yesterday when I couldn't reach you, before I went looking for you at Landon's, and updated her this morning on my way in to work, but I never asked her to come over here. She did that herself because she was worried about you, too."

I let that sink in before responding. "Your mom is amazing, Myles. Both of your parents are, but your mom... she's special."

"I know. I'm really lucky."

"She helped me so much," I said, starting to cry again. This time, the tears weren't all sad exactly, but more bittersweet. "It was like having my mom back for a while. And my dad."

"She said you talked to her about everything."

I nodded. "I did. I can't believe she's still okay with me dating you after some of the things I told her, but I told her everything. Once I started, I couldn't stop."

I went on to explain to him what I'd told his mom earlier about what had happened during therapy the day before and how it had impacted me. Myles kept me wrapped tight in his arms, pressing kisses against the back of my head every so often as he listened.

"I think I'll be okay," I said after a pause. "I didn't, but your mom helped me realize I can be." I swallowed. "I'm really sorry I scared you, Myles. I didn't mean to. I just... I literally couldn't talk to you, couldn't even answer my phone. I don't know how to explain it, just that I couldn't do it."

"It's okay, Nina. I understand."

"I'm sorry. I know you were upset, and because of my history, you probably thought the worst, and I didn't mean to put you through that."

"I did think the worst, and I was devastated, but decided I wasn't going to let you go without a fight this time like I have before. I understand what happened and why, though, and I'm not upset with you, Nina. How could I be?"

I sighed. "It might happen again."

"Yeah. It might. Then again, it might not."

"And if it does, it's going to hurt you again."

He didn't respond.

"Are you sure that's something you want to risk?"

"What do you mean?"

"I'm a mess right now, Myles. And it might not be the last time I'm this big of a mess. It's a lot to ask of someone to accept that. I put you through a lot, and your mom and dad. Are you sure you want to sign up for possible recurrences of what you went through in the last two days?"

"Nina, you didn't put me through anything. And we all are messes sometimes. That doesn't matter. I still love you, and I always will. My parents still love you, and days like today will never change that. When you love someone, Nina, that means loving *all* of them. And I sure as hell love you—every last part of you, every last thing about you."

THIRTY-TWO

Myles and I had found a new routine with me having to spend so much time at the condo, though we'd be finding another new one in a little less than a month when he was done working for the summer. I didn't get to spend as much time outside as I wanted, but I was getting up really early to make sure I got in a nice long walk in the park before the contractors arrived. I still didn't really understand what they were working on. They were there for hours and hours every day, but so far it looked like they'd only replaced some trim pieces, painted a few walls, and replaced two toilets, and there was a line of missing drywall in some of the walls like they were updating some wiring or something. I didn't understand what "renovations" they were doing, but it was Landon's condo—not mine—so I didn't ask.

I'd gotten into an argument with Landon the first week they were there. Myles had picked me up right after the contractors left Friday evening, and we drove to the nature preserve he'd told me about months earlier to spend the weekend in celebration of getting accepted into all of the graduate programs I'd applied to. But I'd gotten a call early Saturday morning from Landon that the contractors were waiting at the door to get in. I'd had no idea he'd expected me to stay inside the condo on the weekend as well. He reminded me that I'd agreed to help him out, but I held my ground that I would not spend all weekend in the condo, too. It had taken most of the day after that argument for things to settle between Myles and me; he'd been furious about all of it—Landon's expectations, that he was calling me, that I was still living there at all, everything. Eventually, though, we'd gotten back to our rhythm together.

The next time I'd spoken to Landon, he'd asked me to attend a charity function with him the following week. He'd be back in town just for one night so he could attend the function on Friday evening. I'd agreed, but then remembered a few minutes later that it was the same day that Myles and I were doing the open mic piano performance together. In fact, we were going to be playing several pieces, it turned out—each performer was. We knew what order we'd be playing, but not the exact time that would correspond to, and I was afraid of being late if I went to the function with Landon. I'd felt bad for having to tell him no right after I'd agreed, and he hadn't been too happy about it either, especially when I told him it was because I was going to be performing music live in a piano bar. I hadn't told him it would be with Myles because I was trying to avoid any more tension than necessary, but he was upset with me anyway.

Now, it was the night of the big performance. Myles and I had been practicing for a month, ever since he brought the flyer home, but I was extremely nervous. I'd never done something like this before. The closest had been piano recitals when I was growing up, but those were for a small group of familiar faces. This was going to be a bar full of strangers, and strangers could be incredibly critical. I also really didn't want to mess something up and embarrass Myles.

I'd gone shopping with his mom for a dress to wear, unsure what would be appropriate for something like this. I knew what to wear to a business meeting, to a charity function, or to a company picnic or holiday party. I knew what to wear to hike in any type of weather conditions during any time of year, anywhere in the US. But I was clueless what you should wear to perform in a classy piano bar—this one was nothing like the hole-in-the-wall Nina's I was familiar with in college.

By the time we'd gotten back from the shopping trip, I felt more equipped for the performance, a little excited about surprising Myles with my dress, and even closer to his mom. She'd even told me that she thought of me as a daughter and hoped that was okay with me.

It was *more* than okay with me.

Out of the shower, I carefully scrunched the excess water out of my hair, avoiding rubbing it, which would cause it to frizz. After drying off, moisturizing my face, and quickly rubbing in some lotion everywhere else, I used my fingers to comb through my curl cream before scrunching in a light gel. Lastly, I diffused my hair—it was the first I'd used a hair dryer in a while, but my hair took hours to dry naturally and I didn't have hours left... in fact, I was meeting Myles at the bar in a little over one hour.

With my hair dry, I pulled on the new bra and panties I'd gotten specifically to wear under my new dress. The dress itself was a medium Aegean blue chiffon, sleeveless with a low v in the front and back, a satin sash across the empire waist, and a full skirt that fell a few inches above my knees and rose like a cloud when I twirled. To finish the outfit, I had matching chunky-heeled, strappy, lace-up sandals. I'd never worn a dress or shoes like what I donned for the night, but I loved it. It was more me than the gowns and stilettos I wore to functions with Landon; it was fun and flirty and a little sexy and also comfortable and sensible.

Breathe, Nina. In and out.

I repeated those words to myself over and over in the cab on the way to the bar to meet Myles, but the closer I got, the harder it was to do. I was so nervous I was tempted to back out. *I can't do this. What was I thinking? I don't want to abandon Myles, but he can perform just fine without me—better even. I'll stay to support him, obviously, but I know he'll let me back out of performing if I just—*

The cab stopped, and through the window I saw Myles outside the front door, chatting with someone. He looked handsome in dark gray dress pants, a white button down with the sleeves rolled up to just below his elbows, the top couple of buttons undone.

Not just handsome, but sexy.

I sucked in a breath, now feeling a fluttering in my chest for other reasons. *No. I can do this. He wants us to do this together, and so do I.*

He turned as I stepped out of the cab, and time stopped. He froze, whatever he was saying forgotten, his eyes darkening as he took me in from head to toe, a brilliant smile stretching across his face. And then he was walking toward me. It felt surreal, like something out of a movie, as we reached each other and embraced and Myles kissed me soundly.

"You look incredible," he said into my ear before we broke our hug. His eyes traveled over me again as he stepped back. "Better than incredible. Holy shit, Nina," he laughed, running a hand over his hair then slipping an arm around my waist and pulling me into him, kissing me again. "I've never seen you like this before."

I giggled, blushing. "That's because I've never worn something like this before. Wearing this for you is a first." My eyes darted down. "You look really good, too. I love that you roll up your sleeves like that."

"Yeah?" he asked, chuckling as we walked back toward the man he'd been talking to, who was waiting and watching us with an amused expression on his face. He was wearing jeans and a plaid button-up and looked to be a few years older than Myles.

I shrugged. "I don't know what it is, but I do. I always have."

He grinned at me and I leaned up, whispering into his ear. "Everything I'm wearing matches, by the way."

His brows drew in for a second, then his eyes widened as he understood. My blush deepened and his eyes darkened. He bent and placed a sensual kiss below my ear and I shivered, grinning as widely as he was.

Myles stopped in front of the man when we reached him. "Gary, this is my girlfriend, Nina. Nina, this is Gary, a PE teacher at the school and the one I told you gave me the flyer for this."

Gary held out a hand, smiling. "Nice to meet you, Nina."

I blushed again and returned his handshake. "Nice to meet you, too, Gary."

"We've all been dying to meet this mysterious girlfriend Myles has."

I laughed. "I'm not sure what you mean by mysterious, but this is me." I shrugged.

We made our way inside and toward Myles' parents. There was another twenty minutes before the first performer would start, and in that time, I met so many people my head spun. There were friends of Myles' that had come in from out of town, other teachers, and a handful of students with their parents. Myles said hello to all of them, keeping me by his side with our fingers intertwined or an arm around my waist for all of it. By the time we sat with his parents, I was tired, a little overwhelmed, and my nerves about performing were hidden behind nerves from meeting so many people in Myles' life and hoping I made a good impression.

"You look gorgeous, honey," Myles' mom whispered into my ear, patting my back.

Her compliment meant as much as Myles' had. "Thank you," I murmured in reply.

Myles and I sipped on a bourbon, allowing only one before performing, as we watched and listened to the first three performers. They were good, and everyone appeared to enjoy listening to them, though Myles was better. Not with me, but on his own he was. It made me feel a streak of pride that he was so talented, and I grinned over at him. He caught me and raised an eyebrow in question. I leaned over to kiss his cheek.

It was time. We were the next to last performers, and we were going to do four different pieces—one classic and three contemporary. I rose to my feet as if in a dream when Myles grabbed my hand and tugged. It was suddenly very hard to breathe in there. He slid an arm around my waist and walked us to the stage, and we smiled at the previous performer who was leaving the area. I took a choppy breath in.

"I don't know if I can do this, Myles," I whispered urgently as we sat on the piano bench. "I'm terrified right now."

His arm returned to my waist and pulled me sideways into him while the manager on duty was introducing us over a microphone. "Just imagine we're at home practicing together. Pretend no one else is around."

I nodded, my breath stuttering out.

He kissed my temple. "You've got this, sunshine. I'm right here with you. And you're right here with me. And together we can do anything." He gave my temple another kiss, lingering this time, and after a moment, I felt some of the tension slide away. "Just us," he whispered one last time, then pulled his arm from me to set up his hands on the piano.

Shaking, I did the same. He slid ever so slightly on the bench so we went from just touching to being lightly smushed together. The contact helped. Closing my eyes, I let out a slow breath and we began to play. As Myles suggested, I imagined it was just us in his living room and soon relaxed into the music. At first, I'd been a bit jerky and disjointed, but I was playing smoothly with him by the time we finished the first piece—the classical piece. As Myles changed out the music, there was applause from the bar, but I carefully averted my eyes so the sight of all the people wouldn't set off my nerves again—the applause was bad enough.

During the last song—"Bring Me to Life"—Myles and I were definitely in our duet groove. Something magical happened when we played the piano together; we became extensions of one another. We didn't play strictly according to the cues in the music for slowing down or speeding up or getting softer or louder, but rather according to the emotion the music brought out in us, and playing that way always put us in sync with one another. I rarely felt as connected to Myles as I did when we were playing emotional pieces of music together.

We swayed and moved to the music, and a few tears gathered on my cheeks. In my mind, I was singing the lyrics to Myles. The last notes played, our hands lingered on the keys for a breath of silence before the eruption of thunderous applause. We turned to each other. He'd been as moved by playing that last piece together as I had been, and I reached up to wipe the tears off his cheeks just as he did the same to me. Our hands still framing each other's faces, he pulled me to him and we kissed. He kissed me in that way that told a story, and I was lost in it until the realization the applause was tapering off to be replaced by whistles and cheers made it through.

I laughed and bit my lip as Myles pressed our foreheads together, his thumbs moving over my cheeks.

"I love you, Nina," he said, shifting to press his lips to mine for a slow, chaste kiss. "God, I love you."

"I love you, too, Myles."

He pulled back and grinned. "Damn right you do."

The crowd called for more, and Myles looked at me, questioning with a shrug.

"Not a duet," I responded. "I'm not comfortable playing anything else. But you should play something."

The manager stepped over and asked if we'd mind playing again, and Myles agreed that he would. The manager then spoke into the microphone and told the crowd that Myles would play one more piece. When I moved to stand to head over to sit with the audience, Myles hooked my waist.

"Stay here," he said. "With me."

I lowered back down and rested a palm between his shoulder blades as he played an excerpt from Sarajevo Requiem, one of the most intensely moving pieces of music I'd ever heard, both because of the music and the story that went along with it. It was also Myles' favorite, and that love and connection he had to it came through in heartbreakingly emotional playing.

If the applause was thunderous before, it was nothing compared to now. Myles smiled affectionately, wiping his face, then we stood and stepped from the stage to allow the next performer to get settled. Once we'd cleared the stage and reached a small open pocket of space in the crowd, Myles tugged my hand, pulling me into him, my arms around his neck and his around my waist. He squeezed me so tightly that, even in my heels, I was barely on my toes anymore.

He kissed the curve of my neck. "Thank you for doing that with me," he said against my skin.

I ruffled the back of his hair and sighed contentedly. I hadn't wanted to, and I'd been terrified when we first sat down, but it had been a really cool, empowering experience nonetheless. And seeing Myles in his element up in front of a crowd of people had been awe-inspiring.

"You are such a talented, incredible man, Myles. I'm happy you wanted me to be a part of this with you."

He growled into my neck, then lifted his head to look into my eyes. "You're about fucking perfect, Nina—you know that?"

"Only 'about'?" I asked, quirking a brow, trying not to laugh.

He snorted and my laughter slipped out. He grasped my head between his hands and kissed me hard on the lips. Then did it again and again. "I don't want to stop kissing you," he said between kisses. "Ever."

I giggled. "Then don't."

His mouth was telling me another story when our hands got involved, pulling and pushing and squeezing and touching. Myles growled again, then chuckled, out of breath. "Come on, let's go sit with my parents for this last performance before we do something indecent in here and embarrass them."

My face flamed as he slid his hand across my hips, and we turned to head toward the table we shared with his parents, then stopped short. The blood drained from my face and my heart skipped.

"W-what are you doing here?" the words came tumbling out.

Myles' body was stiff and tense next to me.

"You told me you were performing, darling," Landon said. "You *didn't* tell me it was *with* someone, however. I came straight from the charity dinner to see you."

He was indeed still wearing a tux, looking out of place in the bar.

"But... but *why*?" I asked. I didn't understand why he would be there. We weren't dating, and even when we were, he'd never supported me for something if I hadn't specifically asked him to, and not even then sometimes.

"You told me you like this kind of thing, and I'm trying to do those things you like."

"But why, Landon? I don't..." I held out my hands, at a loss for words.

Myles' hand tightened on my hip, and I glanced at him. His jaw was clenched so hard I was sure it was hurting. It was taking everything in him to stand there and not say or do anything to Landon.

"I care, Nina. I told you that. I'm trying to show you that."

"She's not yours to care about anymore," Myles growled out, his voice low but somehow still clear.

Landon narrowed his eyes but otherwise ignored Myles entirely, like he had been—acting like he wasn't even there.

"Myles, please, don't," I implored in a voice only he could hear. Turning to Landon, I said, "Well, thank you. But you didn't need to do that. I know you hate music, and I didn't ask you to come here."

"That was part of the point, darling."

Myles' hand twitched and I squeezed it with mine to keep him from letting go and doing something that would make a scene.

"Like I said, thank you, Landon. We have to go."

"It was good to see you, Nina," Landon replied. "It's been too long. You look nice, darling."

His eyes drifted down from mine, and I almost jerked my arms over my chest to keep him from looking at me the way he was. Instead, I pushed against Myles to make him move; I could feel the violence building in him like it had that night at the police station.

"You, too, Landon," I said, moving us away from him.

Myles barely took his eyes off Landon until Landon walked out the door and left. By the time we'd made it back to the table and I'd seen Landon leave, I was shaking. That confrontation had been seriously nerve-wracking.

"When the hell did you tell him you'd be here? And why, Nina?" Myles asked, speaking directly into my ear so I could hear him over the music that now filled the air.

"The other day. He called and asked me to go to this charity fundraiser with him, and I told him I couldn't because I was going to be performing here."

Myles scrubbed a hand over his face. "I told you he's not going to just leave you alone, Nina. I told you he was keeping you there for a reason."

"He was just trying to be supportive, Myles. I didn't ask him to or want him to, but give him a break. I dumped all this stuff on him, and then I broke up with him, and he's trying to do the right thing, that's all."

"That's *not* what he's doing, Nina. And now he's there, in the apartment—you didn't tell me he'd be home tonight."

"I didn't think it mattered," I said. "I wasn't going to the charity thing with him, and I'm going home with you for the weekend anyway."

"And if you weren't?" His eyes bored into me.

"I wouldn't be staying there no matter what."

Myles sat back in his chair, his jaw tightening. His mom eyed me questioningly and I mouthed, "Landon." Her mouth pulled into a taut line.

I sighed, reaching over and slipping my fingers between Myles'. Just a couple more weeks, hopefully, then I'd be out of the condo for good, and I doubted once I was gone I'd ever hear from Landon again. Then Myles could stop worrying so much about him. I lifted his hand and kissed the back of it. His eyes found me from where they'd been staring in the general direction of the stage.

"I love you," I said, moving my mouth slowly. I knew he wouldn't be able to hear me, but he'd know what I'd said.

His face softened, the hard lines melting away as he held my gaze. "I love you," his lips replied.

"I love you more."

He shook his head, his eyes serious and intense. "I love you most."

THIRTY-THREE

It took a few days after the open mic performance, but things settled back to normal between Myles and me after the unexpected encounter with Landon. The contractors were now removing bits of drywall all over the condo, and I wondered again if Landon was getting a new alarm system or something, but, again, I didn't ask—it wasn't my condo.

Today, however, I'd had to ask the contractors to leave early because I wasn't going to be there all day. It was a Thursday in mid-June and the last day of classes for Myles. Which meant I was going in for his last two classes to have a slaps tournament with the students. I'd changed my clothes three times, trying to find an outfit that was both appropriate and relatable for the kids, while also being attractive since I was going to see Myles. Not that he cared what I wore—it wouldn't really make any difference to him—but *I* did. I wanted to feel like I looked good when I saw him. It was time to leave, though, so even if I changed my mind, it was too late; I walked out the door in jeans and a sleeveless Evanescence shirt Myles had given me a few weeks earlier.

I arrived right on time, walking into Myles' classroom during a class change. Like the first time I'd ever been there, he was erasing the board when I arrived, and I smiled. Nearly half a year had passed since then, and so much had changed in that time. Myles finished with the board and dusted his hands together after setting the eraser down, turning. That wide grin he seemed to reserve just for me broke across his face, and I felt like a light turned on inside me.

"Hey, sunshine," he said as I neared.

"Hey, Myles," I replied.

He clasped my arms and pulled me in for a quick kiss on my cheek. "You can sit at my desk for now. I have to hand back a test and collect a few more instruments that haven't been returned yet before we can do the fun stuff."

The room filled with kids, and then a bell rang. I watched Myles as he did exactly what he'd said he was going to do, all while the students were mostly staring in my direction, distracted by my presence. Once he was finished, Myles introduced me to the class.

"Okay, class. As promised, we have a guest today who's going to whoop your butts in slaps. This is Miss Covington."

A girl's hand shot up in the air.

"Yes, Shavona?"

"Isn't she your girlfriend? That's what Dwayne said."

I snorted and Myles laughed, his eyes twinkling when he glanced over at me before looking back to the girl who'd asked the question.

"Yes, Dwayne is correct. Miss Covington is my girlfriend. Any other questions? You all remember what order we agreed to go in so there won't be any arguing over who goes before who? Right?"

There were head nods and sporadic "Yes, Mr. E" responses, and everyone got into place. I spent the next forty minutes slapping middle schoolers' hands, watching skeptical expressions shift into surprise and amusement. They all thought they would beat me, and not one kid did. Myles was tickled and the class was giddy with shock about it. All-in-all, it was a lot more fun than I'd expected to have, and the second class was the same. My favorite part of all of it, though, was watching the kids say goodbye to Myles. Both of these classes were eighth graders, and they'd be moving to high school the following year. Some of the kids lined up to give fist bumps or crazy involved handshakes, a few even gave him hugs. It was obvious he'd made a big difference in these children's lives, and they adored him for it. I was as teary-eyed as Myles by the time the last kid had left the room.

"Well, Miss Covington, shall we?" Myles asked, casting a last glance around the empty room.

"Yes, Mr. E, we shall," I replied, giggling.

He slipped his fingers between mine, and we walked through the door and down the hall toward the exit. I marveled, as I sometimes did, at the normalcy of it all. At how natural it was to just hold hands anywhere we went, to greet each other with a kiss. To think about Myles as my boyfriend, to say we loved each other. It had been a few months now, and it was easy to just take that all for granted, but there were moments when I remembered what so many years of my life had been like without him, and I felt an intense rush of gratitude.

"I love you, Myles," I said, glancing sideways up at him as we neared the exit.

He looked down at me with a lopsided grin, his eyes sparkling. He appeared to be having an internal debate. "I love you, too, Nina," he finally replied.

"Took you a while," I teased.

He chuckled. "I was trying to decide if I was going to respond seriously or not."

"What would you have said if you'd decided not to?"

He eyed me, his mouth pulled in. "I love you leagues."

I stared at him; I didn't get it. "Leagues?"

He burst out laughing as he held the door open for me to pass through in front of him. "Yes. The unit of measure that is equal to three miles."

"Oh my god, Myles," I groaned. "That's such a bad joke."

He continued to laugh, pleased with himself. "I've been wanting to do that for so long. I have to tell Dad about that one."

I giggled. "Your poor mom."

"Are you kidding? She's got Dad and me—she's one lucky lady."

"I think we should work on humility."

"Oh, I agree, Nina—your ego is out of control."

I snorted again and bumped my shoulder into him.

He chuckled. "So, what do you get when you cross an elephant and a rhino?"

I groaned. "I don't know. What?"

"Ell-if-I-know."

I tried to hold it in but burst out laughing anyway. "Myles, that's terrible!"

He laughed. "Isn't it? I overheard one of my students telling that joke this morning. It was torture not to laugh so I could explain to this fifth-grader that he couldn't curse in my class."

"I bet it was. I'm impressed you pulled it off."

"Me, too," he chuckled. Shaking his head, he let out a loud sigh, then leaned down and gave me a peck on the cheek. "I can't wait to get you somewhere other than school so I can kiss the hell out of you like I've been wanting to do for the last three days."

I blushed and bit my lip. I'd been wanting the exact same thing after three days of not seeing each other. It had felt like torture, but Myles had had something going on every evening that week because of the end of the school year.

"So, what are we doing this evening?" I asked when we reached his car.

"Wanna pack something for dinner and go for a hike?" he asked as we climbed in.

I looked down at my clothes. "Yes, but all my hiking clothes are back at the condo."

"We'll go by and grab them," he said, a hint of tension in his voice.

I sighed, anxious about it but agreeing.

When we reached Landon's building, Myles parked, and rather than waiting in the car for me, he climbed out when I did.

"I won't be long," I said, uncomfortable with Myles coming upstairs. Everything to do with Landon set him on edge. It was bad enough we were there, but him going inside was likely to create tension for the rest of the day.

He wove our fingers together and kissed me. "I know, but I want to come up with you. I miss you."

"Okay," I breathed out. When we reached the entrance, I typed in my code to get into the building.

"Did you just type in my birthday?" Myles asked, his eyebrows raised.

I blushed. "Yes. It's my passcode for just about everything."

He smiled, looking satisfied with himself, and I rolled my eyes. "But I'll need to change it if it goes to your head."

He immediately affected a scowl and I laughed. He leaned down and kissed me again, his lips lingering on mine. Everything inside me tightened and my blood pumped harder through my veins. I heard the shift in Myles' breathing and knew he'd felt it, too. We pulled apart, but his thumb caressed my hand, making it harder and harder to breathe, and I was impatient for the elevator to arrive.

Once it did, I stepped in and pushed the button for the top floor. Before the doors had slid completely closed, Myles' body held mine against the wall of the elevator. Our hands couldn't decide which parts of each other to touch and tried to touch them all as we kissed feverishly.

"Myles," I sighed out on an exhale.

The elevator door slid open on our floor, and we stumbled out, still kissing, until we reached the door to Landon's condo and Myles pressed me into it.

"Nina," he said, lowering his head to my neck, his hands lacing with mine and sliding them up over my head against the door. His mouth told one of its stories against my skin, one filled with desire. "Open the door," he breathed, releasing my hands.

Disoriented, I bit my lip and turned, typing in the same passcode I used to get into the building and pushing the door open. Myles followed, and less than a second later, we were making out against the door again, only from the inside. In the recesses of my mind, I remembered we were in Landon's condo and shouldn't be doing what we were there, but the thought flitted away as quickly as it had come. I reached down and grabbed the hem of my shirt, pulling it over my head. My hands were still trapped in the material when Myles growled against my skin, his mouth on my breast, and I forgot what I was doing, my eyes falling closed.

Myles kissed upward while my chest heaved, then used a hand to turn my chin and hold it to give him better access to my neck. A small moan escaped me, and I shifted my hips against him. Remembering my shirt when I went to touch him and couldn't, I pulled it the rest of the way off, then tossed it, going to work on unbuttoning *his* shirt. His fingers unbuttoned and unzipped my jeans, pushing them and my panties down my legs until I stepped out of them. By the time he was done, I was unbuttoning his pants. Before I had a chance to push them down his legs, however, he grabbed my hips and lifted me. Holding me up against the door with one hand, he released himself with the other, and I slid down over him, locking my legs around his hips with a loud gasp.

"Shit, Nina," he growled into my neck.

With his hands on my forearms, he held them against the door over my head, my body stretching up from my hips as he moved in and out of me.

"Oh, god, Myles," I whimpered. "Oh, god."

My body tightened before too long, and I shouted out, but he didn't slow, grunting with effort. Having my body pulled taut the way it was with him holding my arms intensified the orgasm that ripped through me and continued all the way through his.

Myles dropped his head to my chest, panting hard, releasing my arms. I wove my fingers into his hair, my own breathing needing to settle.

"Good lord, Myles," I exhaled. "That was…" I trailed off, at a loss for words. "Just holy shit intense."

His laugh rumbled against my chest. "That's an understatement, sunshine." He placed a long, soft kiss on my lips. "I love you so much, Nina."

Once we'd cleaned up, I changed for hiking.

"Pack a bag," Myles rumbled, slipping his arms around me from behind and kissing the curve of my neck. "I'm planning to talk you into staying with me tonight."

I grinned. "That won't be hard since I already want to."

With my bag packed and our hands linked, we headed to the front door again. Now, instead of noticing the picture of Landon and me on the foyer table that I'd flipped down months earlier, reminding me of the relationship I'd had with Landon, all I could see was Myles and me having sex against the door. I smiled and stole a sideways glance at Myles. He waggled an eyebrow and gave a sucking kiss to my neck that made my body clench. I giggled.

"No, Myles, we're leaving."

He shrugged, his mouth pulled in. "I didn't say anything."

"You didn't have to," I laughed.

He tugged sharply, pulling me into him, and kissed me hard. "I can't help that you're irresistible."

"Irresistible, huh?" I said, raising my eyebrows. "I might be able to use this to my advantage."

He chuckled, placing another kiss to my lips, then let me go and opened the front door. "I hope you do, sunshine."

THIRTY-FOUR

During Myles' last week at work, since the teachers all worked a few weeks after the last day of classes, I was in North Carolina looking for housing; I'd decided to attend the forestry program at Foreman University there, but I didn't want to sign a lease without seeing the apartment first. I technically could have driven there since it was only a little over six hours away, but I'd flown and rented a car there because that meant a lot less travel time. I also would have waited and done it with Myles, but this was the week that the contractors were all taking a vacation, so it was the only week I could go without inconveniencing Landon.

I was a bundle of nerves as I left the car rental lot and headed toward my hotel to get checked in. I was excited about this new chapter in my life, about the opportunities ahead once I finished this degree. But I was anxious about being in a town by myself where I knew no one, about being so far away from Myles for extended periods of time, and about somehow ending up in the wrong place at the wrong time again. I made an effort to focus on the excited feelings in place of the others as I drove. Even so, my stomach was in knots by the time I had my key and headed up to my room.

After unpacking for the week, I took a shower to wash off all the travel before initiating a video call with Myles. After twenty minutes on the phone with him, laughing at more ridiculous jokes he'd found that he couldn't wait to use with his students the following year, my stomach settled, and I realized I was starving.

I ordered room service and we continued to talk for hours, keeping the call connected as we ate dinner together, and then as Myles played a few pieces on the piano for me, ending with certain parts of the piece he'd been composing for months. He was getting close to finishing, he said, but was still working on a few areas. It was the first time he'd played any of his new piece for me, and I was intrigued. It was very different from what I'd expected.

"It was a bit jarring and unexpected when you shifted into the minor key section. It took me by surprise," I said, assuming that was an area he was still working on. "As did the later transition back to a major key. It was like the minor section was a separate piece of music entirely and ended up in there almost by accident."

"Mm-hm," he replied, sounding pleased. "That's intentional. The minor section is called an interlude. I've never encountered one done quite this way, but it's what it is. An interlude is a break or shift in the music, but it's temporary, kind of like an interruption. Like a detour if you were driving home and decided to take a route that added on a few miles. That detour would be your interlude."

I remembered what an interlude was from when I took piano lessons and hadn't needed that explanation, but Myles slipped into teaching mode often when he was talking about music. I was sure he'd explained interludes to his class at some point the way he'd just done so with me.

"You already knew that, didn't you?"

I nodded, smiling.

"Sorry," he said, his cheeks turning pink.

"Don't be—it's cute."

"Hm," he replied, then sighed. "Something's missing," he said, looking back toward his music and flipping through the loose pages. "It's supposed to be sudden and jarring when it shifts, it should be evoking a strong emotional response in you, but..." His words trailed off and he bent closer to his sheets of music.

I watched from where he'd perched his phone as he got up and searched for a pencil, returning and writing and erasing furiously, hitting a few keys on the piano from time to time. Inspiration had arrived while he was speaking, and he'd completely forgotten I was there. It had happened many times when I was there with him in person, and I always enjoyed it, watching him so focused and intent and lost in his creation. It was a beautiful thing to see someone so inspired and passionate, and it filled something inside me that it was Myles I was privileged enough to watch doing something that fulfilled him. Something that he was so talented at and put so much effort into sharing with the world.

"That's it," he mumbled, rubbing a hand over his jaw, the scratching of his skin against his beard loud. "That's what was missing." His eyes scanned over the pages, a grin overtaking his face, his eyes wide and bright. "That's it!" he shouted.

I chuckled to myself, watching as he began making changes to several pages. I turned off the lights in my hotel room and snuggled down into my blankets, resting my head on my pillow. I propped my phone in front of me and sighed contentedly. I couldn't think of a better way to fall asleep than watching Myles in his element. It was almost exactly like times I'd been there with him and fallen asleep on the sofa while he was furiously composing or practicing.

"Good night, Myles," I said softly, not wanting to disturb him. "I love you."

The first thing on the agenda for the next day was to visit campus and get oriented. I'd looked at the layout of the buildings on a map, but they were rarely to scale, and I preferred to see things myself anyway. Once I did, I'd get a feel for the surrounding neighborhoods and pick which apartments to visit over the next few days. I definitely wanted to be within walking distance—preferably a *short* walking distance that didn't involve dark streets or alleyways.

I'd picked this school because the program seemed to be the best of the three, but it was also the one I'd secretly wanted to attend anyway just because of its location. While all were in close proximity to state or federally protected forests, this was the only one nestled into a mountain range, which meant plenty of hiking for me.

While technically a city, Carolinatown felt more like a sprawling town, somewhat reminiscent of the one I'd grown up in. The longer

I meandered around, creating my own map of the area in my mind, the more at home I felt, and the more convinced I was that I'd picked the right school to attend. And by the time I made it back to my hotel that evening, I'd narrowed down my living options to three complexes, all within three-quarters of a mile from campus.

"The one I'm most interested in, though, is Avalon," I told Myles as I yawned and climbed into bed. "It's south-facing and it's on a hill, so it has unobstructed views of the mountains. It's beautiful."

"Sounds like it. Send me some pictures when you go."

"I will," I yawned again.

"Are you coming home early, then? Since you'll be done tomorrow?"

"I thought about it, but no. I might not be able to see all of them tomorrow. And I can use the extra time here to check out some of the trails."

"Okay," he sighed, smiling into the phone. "That sounds like a good plan. Though selfishly I hope you change your mind and come home early. I miss you."

I returned his gentle smile. "I miss you, too. I don't know what we're going to do in August when I move out here and we go a lot longer than a few days without seeing each other."

As soon as I'd said the words, my conversation with Landon flashed through my mind—the one where I learned he took care of his "needs" with other women when we were apart. That had hurt, but it was nothing compared to the thought of *Myles* doing that same thing—*that* made me feel positively sick.

"What's wrong, sunshine?" Myles' voice cut through, pulling me back to our conversation. His brow was creased. "We'll miss each other, but we'll be fine."

I nodded, gazing past the phone into nothingness as my eyes glassed over. I couldn't get rid of the thought of Myles with another woman while I was away, despite the fact I knew it was something he'd never do. At least, I didn't think it was.

"So, we're gonna have to be rockstars at communicating with each other to make the long-distance thing work. Let's practice now. Nina, I can see that you're upset about something. I can't hold you right now—listening is all I can do. Please talk to me about it?"

I sighed. My eyes shifted back to Myles' image on the screen, then looked away again. "When I move, we sometimes won't see each other for a month or longer."

I paused.

He waited.

"What about intimacy?" I asked quietly.

"You mean sex?"

I gave a small nod. "Yeah."

"Well, I've always been curious about phone sex. I've never done it before."

A soft snort of surprise escaped me.

"And we have video on our phones, too, so we can see each other, so like video sex. Although audio only would be pretty hot, I think. I love the way your voice gets raspy when you're turned on."

I laughed, some tears spilling over, and I swiped them away, refocusing on the screen. "I was being serious, Myles."

"So was I," he chuckled. "And now I can't wait to try it with you."

I laughed again, gazing fondly at his face on the screen.

He smiled, his eyes searching my face over the video feed. "I mean all of that, but I know that wasn't what you were asking. What's got you worried, Nina?"

"I'm..." I faltered, then tried again. "I'm not okay with you meeting your needs elsewhere while I'm out of town, Myles."

His eyebrows fell toward each other and his forehead crinkled. "You think I'm going to cheat on you? That I'm going to sleep with other women when you're away? Really?"

"No," I replied, tears falling faster than I could wipe them. "I mean..." I looked at the hurt on his face. "No."

"I would never do something like that, Nina. *Ever*. I am, and will always be, one hundred percent faithful to you. Hell, I don't even notice other women. Why would you think I would do something like that?"

I stared away from the screen, wishing Myles was with me so I could curl into a ball in his arms and burrow into his neck and let the feel of his arms and smell of his skin soothe me.

"Nina, talk to me. Please."

So I did—I told him what had happened when I told Landon about him and what Landon told me about having other women when he was traveling.

"What a fucking bastard," Myles gritted out between clenched teeth. "As if he wasn't enough of a son-of-a-bitch already." He sighed loudly, dragging his hand over his face. "Nina. I will never touch another woman as long as I have you. I don't even want to. I don't care if we didn't see each other for the entire eighteen months you'll be living there—the thought of another woman wouldn't even cross my mind." His eyes flitted over the screen. "And just to be very clear, I expect the same thing from you."

My breath huffed out in surprise. "Good god, Myles. I couldn't even think about being with someone else. That's ridiculous. Why would you even—"

"I don't think you would," he cut me off. "But I wanted you to feel that because that's how I feel about the idea of doing something like that to you. There's only you, Nina. There'll only ever be you."

THIRTY-FIVE

It was Friday morning. I had to get checked out of my hotel room, then was going to leave my suitcase with the front desk while I scoped out another trail before heading to the airport. My phone was already ringing, though, and much earlier than normal; Myles usually called and we talked while he was driving to work. Today, however, he was calling before either of us normally woke.

"Myles?" I answered sleepily, on the tail end of a yawn.

"You can't go with Landon tonight, Nina," Myles burst out.

That evening I was accompanying Landon to a big company event like the one when they'd announced the merger. They'd be announcing big promotions, state of the business, including the merger, and the outlook for the next year. I'd already given Landon my word that I'd go with him months earlier. He'd reminded me of that, claiming he couldn't find another plus one so close to the date. I'd agreed with the understanding that it would be the last event I attended with him. Myles had not accepted that news easily, but had eventually let it go when I promised it would be the last time I did something like that for Landon.

"Myles... we've already talked about this. I'm going—I promised Landon. But I will leave as soon as I can, and I'm not spending the night there with him." I rubbed my eyes and yawned again, still trying to wake up.

"Nina, I'm serious. You can't go with him, and you can't keep living there any longer. You have to move out this weekend. He's a bastard, Nina, and I don't trust him."

I sighed. "I know you don't. But he's not the bad guy you think he is."

"Nina. He *raped* you. He slept with other women while you were dating. He's a chauvinistic pig and a misogynist. He was at Marcus' for poker last night and he's a disgusting human being."

"Myles, please stop saying things like that." I wanted to ask him what Landon said or did to elicit such a strong reaction, but I couldn't bring myself to do it. I didn't want to know.

"It's all true! I don't understand why you keep defending the asshole."

"Because he's not as bad as you think he is! I dated him for over three years, Myles—I would know if I'd dated someone as awful as you keep making him out to be."

"It has nothing to do with your judgement—it doesn't mean anything bad about you that he's a jerk. But he *is*, Nina."

But it *did* reflect on my judgement, and I couldn't have been that wrong about Landon. "He isn't, Myles," I said wearily.

"If you'd been there last night, you wouldn't be arguing with me right now. If you'd seen the look in his eyes and heard the things he said... you need to trust me. He's going to do something."

"I *do* trust you. But I'm still going tonight. I gave Landon my word and I'm not going to break it."

"What about your promise to *me*, Nina? Our promise to each other to be in this relationship? You're going on a *date* with your *ex*, Nina—your ex who thinks you aren't really going anywhere, who thinks you *belong* to him like you're a piece of property to be owned, just another asset in his portfolio."

My eyes scanned the wall aimlessly as Myles' words sank in. There was a dueling dichotomy in my thoughts. On the one hand, I could see everything Myles was saying and even believed it. But on the other, I couldn't believe Landon was really that bad. And Myles kept saying he did these awful things to me, but had he really? Yes, he slept with other women while he was traveling, but he'd thought I was sleeping with other men, too. He'd genuinely not understood why that thought was upsetting to me. We'd never had an exclusivity conversation—that was on me for not communicating my expectations, I supposed.

And rape? *Rape?* I'd been raped before, had a knife held against my neck and chest. Landon had never done anything remotely close to that. *But he did push me and do what he wanted even when I told him no repeatedly. Isn't that rape?* I shook my head. There was no questioning that he pressured me into sex. But no way it was rape— I couldn't have been dating someone who raped me. *Except that I did keep dating someone who would hold me down and have sex with me when I said no or resisted.* I shook my head again and banished that thought. Myles' hatred of Landon was starting to get to me.

We argued for a while longer, then I told Myles I had to go so I could shower, and he needed to do the same so he could get to work. I felt very unsettled about our relationship after we ended the call, like I wasn't sure if we'd all but broken up. It almost felt that way. But I couldn't stomach that thought any more than the one about Landon being a rapist, and I pushed it away. Myles and I had been through too much to get where we were for a bad argument to destroy us. I'd see him after the Lorman event, and we'd figure things out— we had all weekend together to do so.

It was a relief when I walked into the condo to find it empty; I didn't want to see Landon any earlier than necessary. I was mentally exhausted after spending all day second-guessing myself in light of how the call with Myles had gone. With a big sigh, I shut the door behind me and glanced around after punching in the alarm code. I still wasn't entirely sure what the contractors were working on. As I inspected the foyer, I decided it must have been the alarm system— there appeared to be new devices for sensing the door opening. I hadn't noticed them before, but the drywall had already been fixed in the foyer, so they must have been there for a while. With a shrug and another sigh, I headed to my bedroom to get cleaned up and dressed for the event.

When I walked in my closet, I startled, looking around me and calling out for Landon, but no one answered. I was alone. But hanging in the front of my closet was a new dress. It was mulberry-colored satin with delicate straps, an open back crisscrossed with those same delicate straps, material that draped almost scandalously low in front, and a full floor-length skirt. Attached to the hanger was a note:

A new dress for you, darling. Please wear it this evening.

I fingered the note—it was actually in Landon's handwriting. Since when did he write his own notes? It wasn't the first time he'd had a dress picked and delivered for me, but the note was always in the hand of the personal shopper. But this was Landon's own handwriting. At least, I was fairly certain it was... I'd only seen his handwriting a handful of times over the years since he had people who did just about everything for him.

The dress was gorgeous and slinky and sexy, and my first thought was that I couldn't wait for Myles to see it. But then I remembered that it wasn't for Myles—it was for Landon. I'd been planning to wear one of the myriad other formal gowns I owned from doing so many of these events over the years—one that was quite a bit more modest than this one. Anything with cleavage drew Landon's eye, and my stomach lurched at the thought of spending an evening with him staring at my chest.

On the other hand, I'd agreed to do this for him, and whenever he'd had a dress delivered in the past, there was a reason—typically he'd coordinated his bowtie and cummerbund with the color, and wearing something else would clash. I could wear black, though, couldn't I? I flipped through my closet, sure I had a modest black evening gown, but I didn't find one. The only modest gowns I had were in colors that would clash horribly with mulberry. With a sigh, I resigned myself to wearing the revealing new gown and hopped in the shower.

Once I was clean, I debated how to do my hair. In the past, I'd straighten it before pulling it into some sort of an updo—either a twist or a bun—since they were classier and what Landon preferred for these events. However, I hadn't straightened my hair in months, and I didn't really want to. The heat was damaging, and my hair, after a haircut and staying away from the blow dryer, was the healthiest it had been in years. I decided to compromise, and after using the diffuser on low heat to help my curls dry more quickly, I carefully pinned them up, strategically leaving a few down.

After packing a suitcase for spending the weeks that Landon would be home with Myles, it was time to go. I left my suitcase by the bedroom door—I'd come back to grab it after I left the event—and got a cab. One more event, and possibly the last time I'd ever see Landon. I felt relief, quickly followed by a stab of guilt—Landon didn't really deserve for me to be so happy to be rid of him.

When I arrived, my eyes scanned the hotel lobby for Myles. Marcus had wanted him to come because he had a big announcement of his own to make related to the merger, but Myles had already been hesitant about attending because I'd be there with Landon, and that was before whatever had happened at poker the night before. If he showed up tonight, who knew what might happen. The anger in his voice that morning had been reminiscent of the anger he'd had at the police station years before.

A ripple of anxiety flowed through me. I really didn't like how things had ended with him that morning. I should have called him before coming to the event. I'd thought about it when I was in the cab, but I hadn't wanted to get into another argument and start crying, so I hadn't. The thing was... he hadn't called *me*, either. And that was very unsettling. It wasn't like Myles.

But that was something I'd have to figure out later—Landon was approaching me.

"Hello, darling," he said, stepping up and grasping my elbow as his eyes scanned over me. "That dress works very well for you."

"Hi, Landon," I replied, trying to rid myself of the coldness I felt toward him. Right then, I was angry at him for the disharmony between Myles and me—I blamed him. I tried to shrug it off and noticed that he was in fact wearing a mulberry-colored bow tie and cummerbund, as I'd suspected. My aggravation softened a little. It was likely planned by his PR team or something based on the theme for the evening. "You look nice, too," I replied as an olive branch. And he did—Landon had classic good looks and he wore a tux well. I preferred Myles' rolled sleeves and tattooed arms, however, and he definitely looked more dapper with a bow tie than Landon did.

We headed toward the ballroom where the event was taking place, in a constant state of nodding, smiling, and greeting people he knew as we went. When we made it inside the doors, my eyes scanned again, but there were too many people—I'd never find Myles, if he was even there.

Usually, Landon would situate me at our table with the wives of the other executives, then make his rounds before everyone was to be seated for the presentations and speakers, but tonight, he kept me with him. "You remember Nina?" he said what felt like a thousand times. He never called me his girlfriend, but the way he smiled at me, his hand resting on my waist when I was shaking hands, projected a different picture, I knew. I wanted him to stop. I wanted the whole evening to just stop, and I wanted to leave. But I couldn't leave because I'd promised him I'd stay as long as he needed me to, and I wasn't going to break my promise. And I couldn't tell him to stop touching me because it was too crowded—there was no way to have a discreet conversation with him, and it would embarrass him professionally if I were to do it within hearing of other people. It was aggravating I needed to have the conversation at all—we weren't dating anymore and hadn't been in months. He'd even seen me with Myles at the piano open mic—he knew I was dating someone else. And yet, the way he was acting was the same as he always had at these events.

More affectionate, actually.

Finally, it was time for people to sit, and when we did, Landon draped his arm over the back of my chair and grasped my shoulder. I sat forward like I would if I were engaged with what was happening on the stage, but it was to get him to stop touching me. He released my shoulder, but then rested his hand against my bare back. Feeling him touching me was all I could think about. I wanted to peel him off my skin and fling his hand back at him, and it took all my concentration not to make a scene by doing so. I didn't want him touching me, but I was also angry—I felt manipulated because he knew I couldn't do something about it there. It felt calculated and planned.

But when I glanced over at Landon and he was intently focused on the presentation up front, I had another stab of guilt—perhaps I was being unfair. He probably didn't even notice he was doing it. I mean, this was how he'd acted for three years, and for him, the months since I'd broken up with him had been status quo traveling on the road. This was the first we'd really been around each other since then. Myles was just getting into my head about Landon being manipulative. It didn't mean I liked the way he was toward me, but I was less angry with him for it. Either way, I couldn't wait until I could leave.

I barely heard any of the presentation because I couldn't focus on anything other than the movement of Landon's fingertips on my back, huffing out a sigh of relief when he moved his hand to clap.

He rose beside me, bending over to speak into my ear. "Don't go yet—I have to speak for a bit, but there's more to the evening."

I dropped my chin in agreement—I understood. The main part of the evening needed to be over before I could leave without it looking bad.

"Thanks, darling," he said, then kissed the side of my head.

I froze, stunned, staring at him as he walked away. All the feelings of anger I'd had a little while earlier came flooding back. I felt a bizarre urge to wipe my hair clean of his kiss. If he tried that again, I didn't care what point in the evening it was, I would walk out. Immediately.

I glanced around me as he walked toward the stage, nodding and smiling at different people as he went. And then I spotted him: Myles. He was five tables over, sitting next to Marcus, who was now standing and heading toward the stage with Landon. Myles was staring at Landon with unconcealed disgust. My heart rate shot through the roof and it felt like it would beat right through my ribcage and out of my chest. This was a nightmare.

Not much longer, Nina, I reminded myself.

Time passed sluggishly and quickly at the same time, and my thoughts were scattered as my anxiety continued to ramp up, leaving me shaky and a little dizzy. That shakiness and dizziness doubled, at least, when one of the women at the table with me leaned over and used her hand to tap at the table in front of me.

"Nina," she hissed. "Go up front." I stared at her blankly, and she rolled her eyes. "Landon asked you to join him up front," she hissed again.

I stood, and she pasted on the smile she normally wore, rejoining the clapping around the room. Why the hell had Landon asked me to join him up front? I felt like I was in one of those dreams when you are called on to give an answer in front of the classroom, but you don't know what the question is. I wasn't sure what to do because I had no idea why I was walking toward the stage. Landon had never called me up to the stage before; he'd never even said my name while up there. I had nothing to do with his success, and I didn't particularly even care about it—I never had.

I wanted to turn around and leave, but my feet continued to carry me to the front of the room as was expected. Everyone's eyes were watching me approach, but only one set mattered to me. Myles was watching me with a startling intensity and an expression I couldn't read. His disgust from earlier was completely masked now, and not knowing what he was thinking was even worse than when I could see he wanted to hit Landon. My heart was barely more than fluttering in my chest, and if I'd been near a microphone, everyone would have heard my breath coming and going in a rapid pant, like Treble's when she was scared the day we found her in the woods.

The night is almost over. It has to be almost over—at least for me. He can't expect me to stay after this.

My eyes remained trained on Myles as I climbed the stairs to the stage and walked toward Landon. Whatever was going through Myles' mind was intensifying the closer I grew to Landon, if his expression was any indication. As I reached Landon, he grasped my elbow and shifted us so my back was to Myles, and I wondered briefly if that had been intentional or not before deciding it didn't matter. I forced a smile as I looked up at Landon, my eyes questioning him, looking for some kind of explanation for why I was up there. He smiled back and looked out toward the attendees. My eyes followed and I immediately quailed. I'd been terrified in the piano bar, which was a fraction of the size of this ballroom. There were possibly a thousand people gathered—maybe more. I stood staring out, not breathing, frozen. There were so many people looking at me right then... it was like a bad dream.

I was vaguely aware that Landon's hand slid from grasping my elbow to my hand, but my eyes were glued on the crowd. Landon was now speaking into a microphone, but I couldn't focus enough to understand anything he was saying, then heard nothing but the whooshing of blood in my ears. My eyes were teary from the anxiety of standing there, and all I could think about was when I'd be allowed to walk away... if I even could. I wasn't sure any part of my body would cooperate right then.

There was a sharp tug on my hand, and my eyes lethargically shifted from the crowd to see Landon down on a knee in front of me. What was he doing there? My head cocked to the side slightly as I tried to make sense of what I was seeing, but it was hard to make sense of anything right then with so many people watching me. He stood and leaned in, kissing my cheek and doing something with my hand as I stiffly looked back to the crowd. I felt like a deer in headlights.

"She's got a bit of stage fright," Landon was saying when sound finally started reaching me, with a good-natured chuckle I'd never heard from him outside of these events, "but she said yes!"

The crowd erupted, people rising to their feet clapping and whistling, and I didn't understand. They were looking at me and at Landon, but why? I turned back to Landon, and he stepped up and grasped my shoulders, his eyes falling to my chest before he kissed at the corner of my mouth. I drew back and he turned and raised our clasped hands to the crowd, placing his other hand on my lower back as he walked us toward the far end of the stage, opposite where I'd seen Myles sitting. My eyes fell when we reached the steps, and when they did, I caught sight of my left hand, which Landon was holding out. I'd thought he was trying to keep me from falling since my legs didn't want to work, but I realized it had been designed to give everyone a great view of the comically large engagement ring on my finger.

Everything clicked into place, and I craned my head around to find Myles, but he wasn't there anymore. I scanned frantically and found him just as he was barreling out of the room. I was still shaky, but I jerked away from Landon. Myles had been right—way more right than I'd thought possible.

Ignoring whatever Landon was saying, as well as the eyes that still followed me, I rushed toward the exit I'd just seen Myles going through. When I reached the doorway, I looked left and right but didn't see him anywhere. I called out his name, but there was no response. I turned, heading toward the hotel entrance, but never saw him. Bursting onto the street, my head flipped one direction, then the other to no avail. Wherever he'd gone, he'd done so quickly.

I needed to call him, but I didn't have my phone. I turned, rushing back into the ballroom, ignoring every person who spoke to me, and grabbed my purse. Myles' line was ringing by the time I made it back to the hallway. It rang and rang and went to voicemail. I hung up and dialed again. And again, and again, and again. On the seventh or eighth time I dialed, it went straight to voicemail. He'd turned his phone off.

I felt panicked and had no idea what to do because I didn't know where he'd gone. Standing on the street outside the hotel, I called his mom out of desperation, hoping he'd called her. But it was clear, once I could speak through my hiccupping cries, that she'd heard nothing from Myles. She promised to call me if she did or if he showed up at home. I stood, turning in slow circles after we hung up, scanning the streets in hopes Myles would somehow appear, but of course he didn't. Eventually, I gave up on him appearing out of nowhere and decided it was time to move out of the condo. Immediately. I just needed to find Myles first.

THIRTY-SIX

I knew as soon as I pulled onto his street that Myles wasn't home; while he always had a spot for me in his garage, he preferred to park in the driveway. I opened the garage just to make sure, but as I expected, he wasn't there. Using the key he'd given me, I went in, but being inside made me uncomfortable after what had just happened. I picked up Treble, who ran to the front door looking for Myles, and petted her as I walked to the kitchen and checked on her food and water. She hopped out of my arms and meowed around my feet, looking up at me.

"I know," I said softly, pulling off the hideous ring I'd just realized was still on my hand and dropping it into my purse. "I want him to come home, too. I also miss him, sweetie."

I bent and rubbed under her chin some more, then sighed. I wasn't sure what to do. I hadn't even gone inside the condo to get my suitcase when I went for my car because I was frantic to find Myles. Now I was in his house, he wasn't there, and I was still in the gown I'd been wearing and not sure where to go. I swiped the tears from my cheeks and let out a sigh. I needed to think and then figure out how to fix this. It was my fault this had happened—Myles had warned me, had begged me to not trust Landon, and I'd refused to listen to him. He'd been right thought; Landon had planned everything. Just like with sex, he was trying to pressure me into doing what he wanted.

I felt stupid.

And angry.

So angry.

At Landon, *and* at myself.

With a final pet to Treble, I left and walked down the street to Myles' parents' house. It was unlikely they'd heard anything without letting me know, but since I was there, I figured I should check. I rang the doorbell and waited, fidgeting and teary. A minute later, Marv answered the door.

"Nina, hi," he said, surprised. He stepped back, opening the door. "Come on in. Sarah's in the living room."

I swiped under my eyes. "Thank you."

He gave my shoulder a pat and shut the front door. I made my way through the house to the living room. Sarah jumped up from the sofa and engulfed me in a hug when she saw me. I broke down and cried into her arms for several minutes. When the tears finally slowed, I stepped back, wiping my face again.

"I'm so stupid," I muttered. "I should have listened to Myles, but I didn't, and now I messed everything up and I can't find him. He's not home and he's still got his phone off. I don't know what to do."

Sarah sat and patted the sofa next to her. "Have a seat, honey." Then she called for Marv to make some tea and bring in a box of tissues.

"Thank you," I whispered, accepting the tissues from Marv when he brought them, then blowing my nose. When I was finished, I dug into my purse and pulled out the god-awful ring.

Sarah tipped her head toward me. "What's that?"

I held it up for her to see, and in mentally replaying what Landon had done, I felt a surge of anger and flung it across the room.

"It's Landon's." Now that I was more calm and coherent than I had been earlier, I again went through what had transpired so Sarah would have an understanding of how the evening had unfolded.

Her brows knit in worry as she listened, grasping my trembling hands in hers.

"Myles... he thinks I agreed to marry Landon. Because I was in shock and confused and terrified and frozen and didn't realize what was happening, and then he was gone after Landon told the room I'd said yes. I didn't say yes! I would never say yes. I don't want anything to do with him. I was just trying to keep my promise to him. I had no idea... and after Myles and I argued this morning about it and didn't talk at all afterward. Myles thinks... oh, god, he thinks I'm leaving him for Landon, that I'm choosing Landon over him."

I cried into my hands as Sarah rubbed a hand over my back in a gentle caress. "Nina, honey, he doesn't. I mean, he might for a little while, but when he stops to think about it, he'll know you aren't. He *knows* you. He *knows* that you'd never do that to him. It just might take him a little time to realize that."

"Even if he does... I've hurt him, Sarah. Again. I've hurt him so much because I didn't listen to him. Because I didn't believe him about Landon's motivations and intentions." I hadn't thought it was possible I was *that* wrong about someone, but I had been.

"Yeah. He *is* hurting right now, wherever he is, because he loves you. And he's also hurting *you* right now by turning away from you like he is."

The same thing I'd done to him several times before. I sucked in a breath. "I deserve it," I whispered, wringing my hands together.

"No one deserves to be hurt, honey," she replied, her words slowed like she wanted to make sure each one had a chance to sink in before she spoke the next.

I nodded absently, but I wasn't sure I believed her. I certainly felt like I deserved it right then. I understood in a way I never had before how much turning away from him must have hurt him because of how much it was hurting me that he was doing it this time. I stood up, restless. I couldn't sit still anymore. I needed to do something. I needed to find Myles.

"Where are you going, honey?" Sarah asked.

I shrugged, my eyes staring through the floor. "I don't know. But somewhere. I have to find him. I can't wait in his house—it just doesn't feel right when I know he wouldn't want me there."

"You're going home?"

"Oh, god, no," I rushed out. "Landon's home. I can't be there when he is. I'll get all my stuff out of there tomorrow, but I can't sleep there when he's there. I think I'm going to check all the bars I know Myles likes and hope he's in one of them. I have to find him."

"If he doesn't want to be found—"

"I have to, Sarah. I have to. I have to find him and tell him it's not true, that I don't want Landon, that the only person I'd ever marry is him. I have to tell him I'm sorry and find a way to fix things. I have to."

She stood and walked to the other side of the room. I turned toward the front door.

"Hang on, honey," she called. A moment later, she joined me at the door and held her hand out. "Take this."

I looked down and felt a wave of rage and anguish at the sight of the ring Landon had bought for me on her palm. "I don't want it. I don't even want to touch it ever again."

"I know, honey, but you might want to give it back to him."

Actually, I did. I wanted to walk up and throw the damn thing in his face. I lifted it from her hand and dropped it in my purse.

"Keep me posted, honey, okay? And be careful. It'll be getting late soon. You can always come back and stay with us."

I sniffled. "Okay. I'll probably just get a hotel close to the condo so I can go over in the morning to get my stuff packed up."

"The offer's on the table if you change your mind." She gave me a tight hug. "It'll work out. I promise."

With a final nod, I left. I drove back to the city and parked in the garage for the condo, but then set out to search for Myles. Two and a half hours later, I still hadn't found him and no longer felt hopeful I would or that I'd be able to repair anything if I did. I also had missed calls from Landon—the most I'd ever received from him—and each one just made me angrier. After the fifth one, I decided I couldn't consider sleep until I'd confronted him and headed to the condo.

I found Landon, still in his tux, watching the news when I walked in. Business as usual, of course. I was furious he'd pulled the proposal bullshit to begin with, but then seeing how unaffected he was by not being able to reach me after I ran out on him just made me even angrier. I stood at the edge of the living room, in my gown, my fists balled, fuming and unable to even find words.

Landon glanced over. "Well, hello, darling. So good of you to finally come home."

"This isn't my home," I gritted out.

"It certainly is when you're wearing my ring," he replied calmly, muting the television.

"Your ring?" I fished it out of my purse and threw it as hard as I could at him. "You can have that back. I don't want it and I never will."

"Nina, darling," he said, fumbling for the ring, then rubbing his temple. "I don't understand what's gotten into you."

"What's gotten into me is that bullshit you pulled tonight, Landon!"

"What bullshit?" he asked, standing up, his jaw clenched. He was angry now—a kind of angry I'd never seen before. "*You*"—he pointed at me as he stepped closer—"changed everything out of the blue. After almost four years together, you changed the rules. You suddenly like and want different things. My life was upended because of you changing the rules. But I listened because I care about you and about this relationship between us. I gave you the things you wanted. I took you to listen to music because you said that's what you liked. I listened to you talk about your feelings and the past, even though it meant disrupting my job, because that's what you wanted to do. I'm putting a sound system in the condo for you because you mentioned you liked listening to music when I was away. I gave you space in the bedroom, and I let go of the affair you were having with that *music teacher* as long as you agreed not to see him again."

He stopped in front of me, glaring. All my anger was now hiding beneath fear. It was the first time Landon had towered over me the way he was right then, and it was really intimidating.

"An affair, Nina. You weren't just having sex. Your words were that you had feelings for him. But I let it go. Then you told me you wanted to move out, and I let you stay here indefinitely. You don't pay for anything, you don't have to worry about anything. And yet you tell me you can't do one thing for me when I needed you to come to the charity event with me because you were doing something else?

That stung, Nina. But again, I accepted it, and I even went to watch you to show you that I cared even though it was interfering with what I needed from you. But what did I find when I got there? That you weren't alone. That you were with *him*, Nina. You told me you weren't leaving me for him, and you'd promised me before that that you'd never speak to him again. I didn't realize your promises were so short-lived."

He stepped forward into me and I backed up; I continued to back up until my back ran into a wall. Landon didn't stop until there was only an inch or two at most between us. His eyes were cold and threatening.

"You were making out with him right there in the bar—in public. The same man you promised you'd never talk to again. And you essentially dismissed me after allowing your lover to speak to me the way he did. I didn't think you could sink any lower than that, but you proved me wrong." He paused for an inhale and exhale, which was strangely unnerving. "I upgraded the security system and now have a camera on each side of the front door. And what did I see? Hm? Tell me, Nina. What did I see on those cameras?"

The blood drained from my face, and I smashed myself harder into the wall behind me.

"I told you before that having sex wasn't something I was going to be upset about—we spend a lot of time apart. But I never dreamed you'd do it inside our home, Nina. And with *him*, no less. I go to review the security footage, and there you are, having sex with him in the foyer."

My stomach lurched. He'd *watched* us having sex?

"*Knowing* that you have sex with others is one thing; I don't need to know anything else about it or think about it. But *seeing* it? It stirred up a jealousy I didn't know I had in me. You're *mine*. But maybe there's a silver lining here, because it made me realize maybe I wasn't doing enough for you. You seem to like his overt expressions of his feelings and affection, so I planned out this proposal—it doesn't get much more overt than what I did for you tonight. I professed my undying love and asked you to marry me in a room full of fifteen hundred people, and gave you a twenty-three-million-dollar ring. That wasn't a smart financial decision, Nina, and I did it anyway *for you*. But you disappeared on me and didn't even have the decency to answer my calls."

He grabbed my wrists and glared into my eyes for a while. "You are ungrateful," he finally said. "I've turned my ordered life upside down for you, and you have no appreciation for that." He stared at me again as I struggled to remember how to breathe. "But I think I have the solution. I watched the recording of you two in the foyer over and over and learned something. You must be bored with our sex life—it isn't all that interesting, after all—and boredom in the bedroom has been the source of many failed relationships like ours." He lifted my hands and pinned my arms over my head. "It looks like you enjoy roughness and being restrained. So we can try that."

"Landon," I ground out, my voice quieter than I'd have liked. "Let me go."

"But, darling, you haven't even given me a chance to show you what I can do."

I tried to push him off, but like when he pinned me face down on the mattress, I wasn't strong enough. "I don't have to give you anything, Landon. And I don't want to. I don't like being restrained, and I don't—"

I was cut off when he forced his mouth against mine, and I jerked my head sideways. He shifted so both of my wrists were clamped against the wall in one of his hands and used his other to grasp my chin and hold my head still.

"Stop it, Landon!" I screamed out.

He crushed my body between his and the wall, and the nauseous feeling worsened as I tried not to succumb to the freeze of panic. I struggled against him as he kissed me again, holding me so I couldn't turn away.

"I've never had sex when I was this angry before," he said. "This will be a first."

"No, it won't," I said through clenched jaw. "Because I am *not* having sex with you, Landon. I. Said. No!"

"You don't mean that, darling—you never do."

There was a rush of sound, a flash of something behind Landon.

"Hey, asshole," Myles shouted, pulling at Landon's shoulder. I had no idea *how* he was there in that moment, but I was relieved. "She fucking said no!"

He punched Landon in the face. Not once. Not twice. But three times before Landon stumbled back with his arms blocking his face.

My arms crossed over the front of my body as I watched in shock. Myles followed Landon as he backed up, knocked his arms down, then hit him again. And again. Landon finally swung out himself, but he wasn't even a threat to Myles, who kept hitting him until he fell to the floor. Myles stood over him, breathing hard, glaring.

"Don't get back up," he warned. "Don't even move, or I'll *really* beat the shit out of you."

Landon glowered at Myles but didn't make any moves to get back to his feet. I looked between the two of them, trying to make myself smaller as faintness and chills set in from the shock. It had all happened so fast, and none of it had been expected.

Myles turned to me and took a hasty step in my direction. I drew back, inhaling sharply. He stopped, his brow deeply creased.

"Are you okay, Nina?" he asked, not stepping any closer.

I stared at him for a minute, not even blinking. I heard the words, but I couldn't find the connection between my brain and my mouth.

"Nina?" he asked again, his voice gentled. He raised his hands in front of him and took a tentative step forward. "Are you okay?"

My head was shaking yes, but then it moved from side to side half a second later of its own volition, and my eyes flooded. I was shaking now that my body was realizing the immediate danger had passed, and my knees no longer supported me. I slid down the wall to the floor.

Myles shot a glance toward Landon, who was watching us but hadn't moved, then stepped cautiously over to me, squatting down in front of me. His hands framed my face. "Nina. Look at me."

I raised my eyes from scanning everywhere and nowhere to rest on his. He looked like Myles—a very upset, worried, hurt Myles.

"Did he hurt you?"

I stared back at him. *Did he hurt me? Did* who *hurt me?* It took a moment, but then I realized he was asking about Landon. I shook my head.

"No. Not really," I whispered.

He looked back over his shoulder toward Landon, his face twisting with rage. "Are you sure?"

"I'm sure."

His gaze returned to me, and he reached down and grasped my hands, standing and coaxing me to my feet as he did. "Let's get out of here," he said, shooting another glare at Landon.

My head bobbed up and down. "Yes, please," I agreed tearily.

Myles' eyes flicked to mine, full of pain, but he didn't say anything. He led us to the front door, and I thought for a fleeting second about the suitcase I already had packed, but I didn't want to be in the condo for even an instant longer than I had to, so I followed him through the door instead of turning back to get it.

THIRTY-SEVEN

Outside Landon's building, Myles turned to face me, his hands in the pockets of his tux pants. He watched me, myriad emotions crossing his face in rapid succession. Finally, I couldn't take it anymore and looked away. I still wanted to fix what had happened at the event, but I was having trouble organizing my thoughts and finding words in my current state. I stared down the darkened street, my arms wrapped tightly around myself. Right then, I wished I had a place of my own to call home.

"You can stay with me tonight," Myles eventually said. He sounded like that was the last thing he wanted. "I know you need someplace to go."

"I'll get a hotel," I said, my voice thin. "There are tons of them not far from here."

I looked up and he continued to study me. I didn't know what he was looking for, and I had nothing to give in that moment. I knew there was a lot I needed to say, but words were evading me right then, my mind blank. I turned to head toward the parking garage to get my car.

"Nina," he called out when I was about twenty feet away. I stopped and turned, but he didn't say anything else. He was standing in the same spot and ran his hand over his hair. After a long stretch of silence, I turned and walked away.

I barely slept after spending close to an hour talking through everything with Sarah. I'd texted her to tell her that I'd seen Myles and he was okay and was probably heading home, and she'd called me right after. We'd talked until Myles showed up at their house, at which point we'd said hasty goodbyes.

Rolling over, bleary-eyed, I looked at the clock. I still had a few hours before checkout time. I wasn't sure what I was going to do, where I was going to go. I had signed a lease for an apartment in Carolinatown, but it didn't start for another six weeks. It would be expensive, but maybe I could find some furnished, short-term housing—I didn't have any furniture. All I had were some personal items and clothes that I needed to get from Landon's. I decided I should book the room I was in for the next few nights until I could find somewhere else to go, then I needed to get some boxes or bags or something for my stuff and get it the hell out of where it was.

I did a mental inventory of what I had there and realized I'd be leaving most of my clothes—I had no use for business wear anymore. As for all the dresses, with the exception of the one I'd worn for performing at the piano bar and two others I'd gotten for going out with Myles, they had all been purchased for and worn to events with Landon—I never wanted to see anything that had to do with him ever again. I wanted to get my stuff that I wanted to keep and pretend I'd never met him.

My hand reached over and found my phone on the nightstand when it buzzed. I glanced at the screen, hoping it was from Myles, but it wasn't—it was from his mom.

> What time are you getting your stuff from Landon's?

> I don't know. I need to buy boxes or trash bags first. Maybe an hour or so I'll go over to start packing.

> Where are you? Marv will pick you up and go with you. He'll bring boxes, too.

He doesn't have to do that. I'm sure I'll
be fine. After what Myles did to him, I
doubt Landon will come near me.

Of course he doesn't have to—that's not
why he's doing it, honey. And he insists
he's going and will camp out at the
entrance to Landon's waiting if you don't
tell him when to pick you up.

I stared at my phone, my fingers hovering over the keys, but I didn't know what to say unless I told her I was about to start crying again, but for different reasons this time. Instead, I told her what hotel I was in.

When Marv arrived to pick me up an hour later, my nerves were all over the place again. I was anxious about being with Myles' dad. Anxious about what he thought of me. Despite what I'd texted to Sarah, I was scared of seeing Landon again after what he'd done the night before. I wished I could just never go back inside that condo, but I had to this last time.

There was a tense silence in Marv's SUV as he navigated the streets toward Landon's condo. I looked over periodically, trying to read him. He seemed disgruntled? Angry, maybe? I wasn't sure. His brow was sitting low over his eyes, and his mouth was pulled into a tight line, but I hadn't seen his face like that before, so I wasn't sure what it meant. If it were Myles, it would mean he was upset and worried. But his dad? I didn't know.

He cleared his throat when we were about halfway to our destination. "Sarah would have come with me to be here for you, but someone had to make sure Myles stayed put until this was done. He doesn't need to be running around hitting this asshole again, and with his frame of mind this morning, that's exactly what he'd end up doing. If it needs to be done, I'll handle it."

I stared at Marv. Had he really just said he'd hit Landon himself? I scrubbed my hands up and down my face. I was running on empty, both physically and emotionally; I was sure I hadn't heard that right.

First, it just seemed bizarre. Second, why would Marv do that? I got along with him and liked him a lot, but I didn't have that same closeness with him that I had with his wife. And I was a source of constant pain for his son—I didn't even understand why he was there unless Sarah had told him to be.

"It's okay. I'm fine. You didn't have to come—I can do this by myself."

Marv turned to me, his face drawn in like I'd just said something crazy. "The hell you will, Nina. That man could hurt you again. You think I'll let you walk in there where he is *alone*?" He shook his head. "I'm gonna make sure he doesn't come anywhere near you, so you can do what you need to do and know you're safe. If he so much as tries, he'll regret it."

I turned to face out the passenger window, hoping Marv hadn't noticed that I was in tears. He sounded much like I imagined my dad would have if he were there. After a minute, Marv reached over and squeezed my hand. He held on for another thirty seconds or so, gave it another squeeze, then returned his hand to the wheel.

He hadn't needed to say a word—I'd understood his message.

He cared about me.

After Marv parked in my spot in the garage, we walked together toward the building, a stack of boxes under one of his arms; he'd brought some from home so I wouldn't have to buy any. My hand trembled when I punched in the code to get into the building, and it trembled when I pushed the elevator buttons. When we got to Landon's front door, however, I wasn't just trembling, I was shaking, and I felt sick. My fingers hit the wrong buttons when typing in the code as a result.

Marv rested a hand on my shoulder, that same disgruntled look on his face. "I'm right here, Nina. I'm not going anywhere."

I nodded quickly, blowing out a long breath, trying to settle myself. It worked enough for me to get the code typed in, though barely. The door swung open, and Marv kept a hand on my shoulder as we walked over the threshold. I was hardly moving forward and wouldn't have been at all if it hadn't been for him.

"Landon," I called out loudly, so he'd hear me over the news I could hear coming from the living room. "I'm here to get my stuff."

I'd texted while waiting for Marv to pick me up, but he'd never responded. He didn't this time either.

I was afraid of what would happen if anyone was startled, so I headed toward the living room with Marv right behind me. At the edge of the room, I stopped. Landon looked over and I sucked in a breath. His face was swollen, his lip busted, blue and purple bruises everywhere. His eyes narrowed and he stood.

"You can sit right back down," Marv said before I found my voice again. His voice was calm and full of disgust, with no trace of his normal humor. "We'll be gone as soon as Nina has packed what she needs. In the meantime, you'll stay where you are. If you even try to come near her, I'll finish what my son started. Do you understand?"

Landon's eyes were slits, but he gave a nod.

"Good," Marv said, then turned his attention to me, his tone gentle. "Okay, Nina, let's go pack."

He followed me to the bedroom and assembled the boxes, then leaned against the wall in the hallway while I rushed through, packing up the clothes and personal items I was keeping. It wasn't all that much—it only filled a handful of boxes. Marv ferried them to the front door as I finished packing them, and in no more than an hour, I was done.

"That's it," I said, my eyes darting around to make sure I hadn't forgotten anything.

"Anything anywhere else? Living room? Kitchen? Any of this art yours?"

"Good god no, I hate the art on the walls. And no, nowhere else. Everything else belongs to Landon."

We exited the hallway, and as we approached the front door, Marv told me to hold tight and ambled off toward the living room.

"We're leaving now," I heard Marv's voice carrying from the other room, "and if you know what's good for you, this'll be the last time Nina ever sees you. Because if you ever go near her again for any reason, if you so much as try to talk to her again, I will break every single bone in your body. Do you understand?"

Marv reappeared in the front hall, and I walked out of Landon's condo for the last time, with what felt like a small army of protection at my back. When we got back to the truck, I was shaky again, and nauseous with relief. Marv insisted on carrying all the boxes inside the hotel while I had some water, and I agreed because I wasn't sure I could carry them right then.

"So, Sarah told me to bring you home with me," Marv said after setting down the last box. "She said you shouldn't be alone right now, and I agree."

I gave him a watery smile. "Thank you. You're both so..." I couldn't find the words, and the tears almost spilled over as I tried. I stared at the ceiling, unblinking and breathing slowly, before looking at him again. "I appreciate it. But I'll be fine. I've been here before and I was fine then—I will be this time, too."

"Seems to me that you haven't been as fine as you thought you were. So, makes sense to me you won't be any more fine this time, either. Come back to the house with me so we can take care of you, at least for today. Everyone needs family sometimes, Nina—let us be yours."

My eyes filled right back up while he was speaking, and as soon as I opened my mouth, they spilled over. I covered my face with my hands, frustrated I couldn't keep my emotions in check, and a very large body wrapped me in its arms. Marv patted my back gently, and I cried harder, soaking his shirt by the time I could even catch my breath. He'd never hugged me like that before, and it felt like my dad was there. Eventually, I stepped back, wiping my face with the hem of my shirt.

"Okay."

THIRTY-EIGHT

The aroma of freshly baked oatmeal walnut raisin cookies wafted through the front door of Myles' parents' house when Marv opened it. "Mm, that smells good," he said, stepping aside for me to follow him, then closing the door behind me. "She's probably in the kitchen if you want to go find her. She'll want to see you right away."

I headed toward their kitchen, and sure enough, Sarah was in there wiping down the counters, a cooling rack overflowing with cookies. She looked up and smiled at me. Tossing the dish cloth into the sink and wiping her hands on her apron, she wrapped me in her arms, holding tight. Her soothing vanilla and cinnamon scent engulfed me as I clung to her and cried again, pouring out everything left from what had happened in the last twenty-four hours.

We spent the next while eating cookies before I took a nap in their guest bedroom; I'd followed Marv to their house in my car, and I was going to drive back to the hotel, but Sarah had insisted I stay a while longer. I was too tired to argue. After a long rest, I woke in the mid-afternoon. Sarah made me a bowl of chicken noodle soup, then we watched *Grace & Frankie* together while Marv whittled. I wondered about Myles, ultimately deciding it was better not to ask. But I got my answer anyway when he showed up before dinner.

I was frozen, my heart in my throat, as he walked into the living room. My eyes scanned over all of him, noting the circles under his eyes and the swelling and bruising to his hands. It felt like my chest was being deliberately, methodically torn apart because I wanted so badly to run to him and bury myself in his arms, to kiss the hands he'd damaged protecting me, but I couldn't... he didn't want the same thing. As the silence stretched out, I began to feel more and more out of place. This was *his* domain—*his* parents' house. It was where he'd want to be at a time like this, and that should come before me wanting to be there because, as much as I loved them, they weren't my parents.

"I-I'll go," I stuttered out, pushing shakily to my feet. "Thank you for... everything," I said to Sarah and Marv.

"Nonsense, honey—you don't need to go anywhere. We haven't even had dinner yet. You said you'd stay for dinner."

"I know," I replied in a voice barely above a whisper, my eyes on Myles. "But... I should go."

"Nina, honey—"

"Mom," Myles cut her off. "She wants to leave, let her leave. It's what she's good at."

His words might as well have been a hit to my gut, pushing all the air from my lungs. My eyes filled with tears, and I turned and rushed from the room.

"Myles!" I heard Sarah chastise. "That was cruel and uncalled for."

"It's true, Mom!" he shouted back.

"You're in the wrong, son," his father's voice chimed in.

"And you owe her an apology," were the last words I heard as I walked out the front door.

I jumped into my car before realizing I'd walked out without my purse. My grief morphed into anger at my own stupidity, and I banged my forehead onto my steering wheel at the mess everything had become. I did it again and again. I'd been wrong about Landon and botched everything with Myles because of it. I'd found a family, but it was someone else's. Everything had fallen apart.

My forehead hit the steering wheel again, and then my door flew open.

"Stop doing that," Myles said. "And where are you going?"

I stared blankly at the instrument panel in front of where my forehead was sitting against the steering wheel. "My hotel," I said, my voice barely above a whisper. I didn't have the energy for much more than that.

"Why did you agree to marry him?"

I sucked in a breath. "I didn't."

"I was there, Nina. I saw the whole thing."

I sighed. "He lied. I didn't even hear him ask. I was panicking about the crowd. When I realized, I left. I tried to find you."

"Then why did I find you in his condo?"

I shrugged. "I'm an idiot. I was pissed off and wanted to confront him and throw that god-awful ring back in his face."

There was a long silence.

Then Myles gritted out, "Get out of the car, Nina."

I turned to face Myles and rested my temple down on the steering wheel, my forehead tight and aching.

He clenched his jaw as he stared at my face, then turned away. "Get out of the car, Nina," he repeated, stepping back and keeping a hand on the car door.

"Why, Myles?" I asked, my voice watery and wavering. "You hate me."

"I'm furious, Nina!" he shouted, his hand tightening on the car door. "I begged you to believe me about him, but you didn't, and because of that he almost raped you again! Jesus Christ, Nina! All I can think about is hearing you screaming 'no' at him while I had to wait for the elevator doors to open, then finding him pinning you against the wall like that, about to... Fuck!"

He turned and paced along the side of my car. Tears trekked over the bridge of my nose as I watched, my head still on my steering wheel.

"It was happening all over again," he said a minute later, still pacing. "Except that this time you'd chosen the guy who was doing it to you."

"I didn't," I said softly. "I know what it looked like, but I didn't."

"You don't get it—I was seeing it happen all over again, Nina!"

My tears came faster. "I do. Because I was there—I'm the one it was happening *to*."

He stopped in his tracks and turned to me, his face collapsing. "I'm sorry, Nina. Of course you do, I shouldn't have said that."

I turned, placing my forehead back on the steering wheel. The tenderness from hitting it had set in, and I winced and pulled back for a second before resting it back down. It hurt—a lot.

"I didn't choose Landon," I said. "I got angrier and angrier the longer I was at the event because he was acting like he did when we were dating, but I didn't want to make a scene and embarrass him. When he called me up to the stage, I panicked. I hadn't even heard him call me at first because I was watching you and wishing I'd listened to you and fuming because Landon had kissed the side of my head. When I got up there and saw all those people looking at me, I was so petrified I didn't see or hear anything Landon was doing. I had no idea until I was almost off the stage. Even then, it took a minute for me to process what had happened. As soon as everything sank in, I looked for you. I saw you leaving, and I ran after you, but I was too late."

I swallowed, letting out a slow, shaky breath. "I'm sorry, Myles. I really am. I should have listened to you, and I didn't. But it wasn't because I wanted anything to do with Landon. I just want you to know that. I know I hurt you, even if I didn't mean to, and that it's far from the first time, and that you hate me. I understand—"

"Nina!" Myles interrupted, his voice loud and strained. "Get out of the damn car. Now. *Please.*"

I honestly wasn't sure if I could stand, but I also knew I needed to get my purse from inside if I was going to be able to drive back to the hotel anyway, so I stepped out onto my feet and stood up. I kept my eyes trained on the ground with my arms wrapped around myself and took a few steps, jumping when Myles shut the door.

He stepped in front of me and said, "Look at me."

When I did, his eyes were cloudy and glassy, and he was clearly in anguish.

"I was so confused and angry when he proposed to you and said that you'd said yes. Instantly, nothing in life made sense anymore. I needed to figure it out, find a way to make what I'd seen make sense. I couldn't. But I couldn't accept it either. That's why I went to

Landon's. I was hoping I wouldn't find you there because, if I did, that would mean that my nightmare was actually reality."

He scrubbed a hand over his face.

"I needed some space to think last night after what I walked in on, to try to sort everything out. I never was able to, not really, but I decided I wasn't giving up—not yet, not that easily. I've never really fought for you before, Nina, but fuck if I'm not going to fight for you this time. But you keep trying to just turn your back on me, and I can't force you to stay."

"I wasn't turning my back," I whispered through the tears. "I realized you would want your parents right now and I was intruding on that. They're *your* parents—not *mine*. And it was obvious you don't want me here."

"I *do* want you here, damn it," he said just below a shout, smacking his hand against the side of the car. "I've always wanted you here! You're the one who always wants to leave."

I shook my head. "That's not what I want, Myles." I sniffled loudly, struggling to talk through the increasing intensity of my crying. "I don't want to leave. It's the last thing I want. All I really want is you, but I made you hate me because—"

His hands framed my face and he cut me off with a hard kiss. "I don't hate you, Nina. I *love* you. I love you so fucking much the thought of living without you again feels worse than dying." He kissed me again, then wrapped his arms tight around me, crying into my hair as I cried into his trembling chest. Every so often, he dropped a kiss to my head. I wasn't sure how long that went on before we were no longer crying, but neither of us moved. I never wanted to move again.

Myles pulled his arms from me, framing my face again, his thumbs smoothing rapidly over my cheeks as he searched my eyes. I lifted my hands and grasped his wrists.

"This—us—is that still what you want?" he asked, his voice gravelly.

I squeezed his wrists and hoped he could see the truth in my eyes. I wanted to fight for him, too. "Without a doubt. I love you, Myles."

This time when he kissed me, his mouth was telling me another story, this one of pain and devastation and desperation, and I welcomed all of it. Everything that was part of our story together.

"God damn, I love you, Nina," he growled against my lips, his hands still cradling my face.

I nodded against him in agreement.

His forehead pushed painfully against mine before he spoke, but I didn't pull away; I wanted to be there. "I'm sorry for what I said earlier. Inside."

"It's okay," I murmured.

He gave a sharp headshake. "No, it's not. I was upset and I lashed out. I wanted to hurt you when I said that about you leaving. But when I did, I just felt like shit, because I didn't really want to hurt you, I just wanted you to stay." He cleared his throat. "Next time, I'll just ask you to stay."

"Okay. And I'll ask if you want me to leave instead of assuming you do."

"That answer will always be no. I'll never want you to leave."

"And I'll never want to go."

Myles ended up driving me back to my hotel to get my things, which were unpacked by nightfall in his house. We'd had dinner with his parents, my thoughts so scattered that I was distracted through the whole thing and couldn't recall a single topic of conversation. I was falling over tired by the time we walked back to Myles' house after dinner, although I also didn't want to go to sleep yet. After the last week, I wanted to find that sense of normalcy Myles and I had before I'd left to scope out housing in Carolinatown.

Apparently, Myles had the same idea, and we ended up in the living room, the lights dim, The Dovelyn Trio in the background and a glass of bourbon in hand. I burrowed into his chest, and his arm wrapped snug around me, Treble purring on the back of the sofa next to Myles' shoulder. As I settled, my body relaxed, letting go of so much tension I'd been holding onto; it felt like I was melting over his body. He inhaled deeply and let it out, and with it, his body softened under mine. He kissed my forehead and I winced.

He sighed. "Please don't do that anymore." He brushed his lips gently over my newly bruised skin.

I shook my head. "I won't. Or at least I'll try really hard not to."

"Okay," he said, kissing the top of my head this time.

We sat for a while, listening to the music together, me with my eyes closed and focusing on the feelings of safety created by the skimming of Myles' fingertips along my shoulder and arm.

"I was so scared," I whispered, suddenly feeling the need to talk about what happened with Landon. "I went over there, angry, and it never crossed my mind I might be in danger by doing that. I threw his ring at him and said something about the bullshit he'd pulled, and when I said that, something in him changed. I'd never seen him angry the way he was. He backed me up against the wall while he was talking. He wasn't yelling, but the way he was speaking, as if he was barely controlled, was even scarier than if he had been, I think."

Myles' body tensed.

"I'm sorry," I said. "You don't want to hear all this. I didn't think about what that would feel like for you."

He squeezed my arm and kissed the top of my head again. "I want you to talk to me, sunshine. I want to hear it if you want to tell me. I promise."

I shuddered. "He installed video cameras and didn't tell me," I continued. "He said on either side of the front door, but maybe other places, too—I wouldn't be surprised. He watched us have sex, Myles."

I could feel a tremble begin as his body became more rigid.

"He said he studied it so he'd know what I liked, and he learned I wanted to be restrained."

"Jesus Christ," he rushed out on an exhale, his arm tightening around me.

I nodded. "Yeah. And I was shouting at him, telling him I wasn't going to have sex with him, that I was saying no, that it wasn't what I wanted, but it was like he heard nothing. I tried to get away from him, but I couldn't. He was too strong. I don't want to think about what would have happened if you hadn't shown up. You stopped him before he could hurt me. Any more than making my wrists sore, anyway."

"Thank fuck I got there in time this time."

"You did," I said, pressing myself further into him, trying to eradicate the memory of Landon from the night before. "But you saved me the first time, too, Myles. You saved me from anything worse, and you saved me by being my rock afterward. And this time you stopped him from doing *anything*. Thank you for being there."

"I'll always be there, Nina. As long as you'll let me, I'll be there."

THIRTY-NINE

In many ways, it felt much further away in time, but it had been a few weeks since the close call with Landon. Of course, there were moments it came rushing back, or the memory visited me in the middle of the night, as well as the memories of the guy with a knife in the alley. But between therapy with Leslie, Myles being Myles—in other words, perfectly supportive—and his parents, who felt more and more like my own parents every day, I was learning how to lean into it when those moments arrived instead of running from the unwanted feelings that were dredged up.

Like most days, Myles had spent the morning composing, then we'd gone out hiking. I was getting stronger, and Myles and I now matched pace on the trails. I was sure I'd be dusting him again by my first break from classes in the fall and told him as much. He'd smirked and told me he'd hold me to that.

I couldn't wait.

Today we were heading over to the Bathlin animal shelter on the way home to find a companion for Treble. Myles had been considering it for weeks, and with my move at the end of the summer nearing, we decided it was time. That way, Treble would have a playmate when Myles was teaching again in the fall and I was gone for graduate school.

I squeezed his hand as we walked into the shelter, remembering the last time we'd been there after finding Treble in the woods. The day things began to change for us. He squeezed back, shooting me a knowing look, and I leaned into him, holding his arm with my other hand. He kissed the top of my head.

"I love you, too," he said.

I smiled. That was *exactly* what I'd been thinking. But he was getting better and better at knowing that, just as I was recognizing when those words were parading through his mind as well. Not that I needed to, because he said them aloud often.

Phoebe was behind the counter again and asked after Treble. We gave her an update, laughing with her about the trials of having a kitten in the house. While she wasn't nearly as young as we'd initially thought because of her size, Treble *was* still a kitten and was starting to live up to her name, from unrolling toilet paper to walking off with Myles' cleaning cloths for his instruments to tackling our ankles when we walked past where she was hiding under a piece of furniture.

We were led through the entrance into the kennel area to the cats—specifically the cats not likely to be adopted before they'd be put down. My heart immediately felt like it was splitting in half, hearing the meows and barks, smelling the urine and feces and cleaning products. It was *loud* because the kennels were full to bursting, and I wished I could take them all home with me. Of course, they all deserved a home where they could have more attention than I'd be able to give if I had that many pets, but it would still have been better than this kennel, and for some... death.

I shivered and Myles leaned over and kissed my temple, pulling me into his side as we walked. "I know," he commiserated. I hadn't even said anything, but he knew exactly what I was thinking and feeling right then. "I wish we could, too."

We spent a long time talking to all the cats, petting them through the grates, reading about them, trying to decide on the right companion for Treble.

"I think this is the one," Myles said. He'd been petting the same all-black cat for a while now. "He or she reminds me of her."

And indeed, this cat rubbed against Myles' hand the same way Treble did, rolling its head into his palm like it was trying to do a headstand there. I looked at the tag on the kennel door. It was a male. "He," I said.

We had Phoebe pull him out, and he immediately took to Myles the way Treble had after we'd gotten her cleaned up. He also liked pushing his head behind Myles' beard and rubbing his face along his neck like he was giving him a hug. Myles' eyes glowed the way they did when he was interacting with Treble—he was in love with the small cat already.

"He's a little over two years old, spayed, up to date on shots. We named him Shadow when we found him. He's a real sweetheart," Phoebe said.

"I'd say," Myles chuckled. He looked at me, his mouth pulled in at the very corners. "I'm going to rename him."

"Oh?" I raised an eyebrow.

He nodded. "Maker."

I deadpanned at him. "You're kidding."

"Nope." He grinned. "Perfect fit for Treble, don't you think?"

"So, it'd be Treble and Maker?" Phoebe asked.

Myles chuckled again and I shook my head at him.

"Yes," I said. "Myles thinks he's funny."

"I *am* funny," he said. "Isn't that right, Maker?"

With Maker in tow, we continued along the kennels toward the exit, passing the rest of the cats and heading through the section with dogs. My feet slowed as I reached out and let them sniff me, taking a moment to give attention to each one. In the next to last kennel was a very, very large mastiff. He was sitting near the back of the kennel, and his tail started thumping against the concrete when I looked in. His head lowered a fraction, then raised, and he let out a small whine, but he didn't rush to the front of the kennel like the other dogs had. He was watching me, but was turned sideways against the back wall.

"Hey there, sweetie," I cooed, squatting down, my fingers hanging on the grate.

His tail thumped harder, and he whined again, made to stand, then sat back down.

"It's okay," I continued. "You can come say hello."

"Hank has been up for adoption for a few months," Phoebe said from behind me. I turned to look at her. "He's five years old and was in rough shape when we first saw him about a year ago. He was badly abused and needed surgery and a lot of stitches. If he'll come over, you'll see the scars on him."

"Oh, god," I whispered, my attention returning to the dog. "Hi, Hank," I said. He trembled a little, but then his tail was going again. "Was Hank his name before?" I asked without turning around.

"Yes," Phoebe said. "That's what was on his collar."

I sighed, tilting my head as I observed him, my heart cracking apart in my chest. He was *so scared*. It was easy to see he wanted to be excited but was afraid.

"Oh, sweetie," I said just above a whisper, sliding my hand through the grate and holding it down.

"You might want to be careful," Phoebe said. "Scared animals can be unpredictable. That's why he hasn't been adopted yet."

"He's not going to hurt me," I murmured.

"Nina, maybe you shouldn't do that," Myles said, a slight edge in his voice.

"He's not going to hurt me," I repeated. I couldn't explain it, but I just knew he wouldn't. "You wanna say hello?" I asked Hank.

Finally, he stopped his stand-sit-whine dance and tiptoed over, his head pulled into his shoulders. His tail was wagging, but he was still whining and obviously scared.

"He never comes over," Phoebe said.

I remained focused on Hank. He approached cautiously, stopping several feet away and stretching out as far as he could go to sniff my hand. I could feel the tension in Myles and Phoebe behind me, but I ignored it. I knew Hank wasn't going to do anything. And he didn't, other than sniff for a while before licking the back of my hand, letting out another small whine. His tongue was larger than my hand; his head was the size of my chest. He was even more enormous close up than he'd appeared to be when huddled in the back of the kennel. After licking me, he slid his nose under my fingers, nudging my hand up over his head. Slowly and with care, I petted him, my eyes taking in the various scars on his face, neck, and shoulders.

"You've been through hell, haven't you, boy?" Just as every time I spoke, his tail whumped more vigorously, and he let out a whine. "I think you need a new name, don't you? How about Handsome? Hm? Do you like Handsome? Because you are one handsome boy, aren't you?"

Within a moment or two, his entire body weight was leaning heavily against the grate as I petted him the best I could through it. He continually turned to lick my hand and shifted to get closer to me.

"You're in love with him, aren't you?" Myles asked after a while.

I responded without looking at him. "Yeah."

And I was. I could feel and understand his fear so well. And everyone was afraid of him for it, but he just needed some love—lots of love. And I could tell he had lots of it to give in return. It was like he was telling me that, and I felt connected to him.

"Can we take him out?" I asked.

Phoebe hesitated, but then agreed. He was put on a leash, which made him cower, and walked outside to a large, fenced area behind the building. His back came up almost to my waist as we walked. I lowered to my knees in front of him and unhooked the leash. He licked my face, then rubbed his head against me. The force of him was so strong and unexpected, I toppled backward, laughing. He followed and licked my face, his tail wagging, with that same whine.

"He's the size of a small horse," Myles laughed.

"A hundred and fourteen pounds," Phoebe said. "He's a lot of dog."

"He's just the right amount of dog," I said.

"So, how does adoption work for the dogs?" Myles asked Phoebe.

I smiled, my heart warming, that he already knew that I wanted to bring this wonderful creature home with us and that he was okay with it. Just rolling with it like he did with everything.

"You're gonna need a bigger car, you know," Myles laughed as we coaxed Handsome out of his SUV after stopping at the pet store on the way home. We'd barely fit our two new animals and new supplies in his large SUV, and I had a small sedan.

"Yeah," I laughed. "You can help me find something before I leave."

We introduced Maker and Handsome to Treble. Within an hour or two, it was apparent what the hierarchy in the house was: Treble, then Maker, and finally Handsome. Myles and I both sat on the floor, leaning back against the couch, interacting with the animals who all seemed to want our company and attention at the same time. Handsome was okay with Myles but preferred me, and he eventually settled onto the floor with his head in my lap, his tail thumping loudly against the rug while Treble and Maker tumbled and played and vied for Myles' attention.

Watching Myles messing with the cats, keeping them riled up and playful, laughing at their antics, it was so hard to believe he'd at one point not cared for animals. He looked like he'd been a cat person his whole life, and the cats adored him in return.

"You know," I said, sipping my bourbon, thinking out loud, "you would be such a wonderful father."

He looked over at me with a lopsided grin after snatching a toy mouse from Maker and tossing it away so the two cats tumbled over each other to get it. "I want to be."

My heart skipped. I was sure he did. He loved kids. And at one point, I had wanted them, too. But I hadn't in years, and I still wasn't sure it was something I could do. I stared into my glass, thinking about what I'd done seven years ago.

"Don't you want children, too, Nina?" he asked gently. "You used to."

I took a sip of bourbon, using the time it was rolling around on my tongue before swallowing to try to unravel my thoughts. "I did. But that was before I had an abortion." My voice was small and quiet. I still felt so much shame about what happened.

Myles scooted over until we were touching and slipped an arm around my shoulders, tugging me into him! He kissed the top of my head. "Why did that make you change your mind?"

Good question. Why *had* it made me change my mind? I'd never stopped to think about that before.

"I mean... how could I ever have a child after what I did?"

"What do you mean?" he asked, his tone still gentle.

My eyes darted around, and I inhaled deeply, smelling bourbon and Myles and, now, dog. I scratched lightly behind Handsome's ears, and he sighed, his head getting heavier on my lap. "I was pregnant and decided not to be—not to have a baby. How can I forgive myself for that? How could I ever deserve to have a child after that?"

"You think having an abortion means you don't deserve to have children?"

"How is it fair, if I do?"

Myles was quiet for a while, kissing my head from time to time. It was such a jumbled mess in my mind.

"Did you deserve to be forced to have a baby that was the product of rape?" he finally asked.

I shook my head. "No. I didn't."

"But since you didn't have that baby, you think you don't deserve to have any other children?"

It made absolutely no sense, but he'd said it. Tears welled in my eyes, and I took and released a shuddering breath. "If I could go back, I wouldn't do anything differently. I would still have an abortion. I don't think abortions are morally wrong or anything. But at the same time, I feel like I *did* do something wrong. And like I have no right to have a child when before—when I had the opportunity—I didn't take it. I know it doesn't make any sense."

Myles squeezed my shoulder and kissed the top of my head again, sighing.

"I just wish I could have talked to someone beforehand," I continued, thinking about all my anxiety and questions back then. "Like, if someone could have prepared me for all the different feelings I'd have, if someone had told me I'd have conflicting emotions afterward, maybe I wouldn't feel this way right now. I didn't expect this, you know?"

"How could you?" Myles replied. "I wish I could have been there for you," he added. "There's nothing I could have done, really, no way I could have fixed what you were going through, but I'd have been there to support you and help you in any way I could, in whatever way you needed."

"I know."

My eyes watched my fingers as they smoothed over Handsome's head. His eyes were closed—he was dozing. I smiled, happy to see him relaxed and feeling safe enough to sleep. Swallowing, I turned and rested my head against Myles' shoulder so I was facing him. His eyes rested on me intently; his focus was entirely on me.

"I'm scared," I said, my voice cracking and my tears beginning to slip out. "I'm scared of not deserving to be a mother after what I did."

Myles rested his lips on my forehead, lingering. "There's nothing wrong with what you did, Nina," he said, his voice low and soft. "You absolutely deserve to be a mother if you want to be one." He pulled back and held my gaze. "You'd be an amazing mother, too. You're kind and patient and have a huge heart. You have integrity and passion, and you're fun and so damn caring. If there was a checklist for being the best mother on the planet, you'd tick all those boxes, sunshine."

My mouth twitched, undecided if it wanted to frown or smile, and I buried my face into Myles' neck, huddling into his tight embrace. I could feel his heartbeat and smell his skin and hear his breathing, and it settled the chaos of emotions in my chest. I didn't necessarily see what he did, but I knew he wouldn't have said it if he didn't see it. And I trusted Myles to guide me through this minefield of emotion surrounding the thought of motherhood.

"I want to be a mother," I whispered, feeling the strength of it as my words came out. I wanted to be to someone or *someones* what my mother had been to me, what Myles' mother was to him. "I'm scared—really scared—but I want to be a parent. With *you*. If you want to parent with me."

His arms snugged me in closer and he left another kiss on my forehead. "There's no other way I would want to parent than with you." Another kiss. "I love you, Nina."

I felt his words even more than I heard them. I felt them throughout my body, in the way he listened and talked to me, in the way he knew me and accepted me. In the way he played music for me and with me and took me hiking because he knew how much I loved it. I felt them in the way he made me peanut butter, banana, and honey sandwiches despite not liking them himself because he knew how much *I* liked them.

"I love you, too, Myles. Always you."

FORTY

Myles had something up his sleeve, though I had no idea what. He'd instructed me to dress for a date, but wouldn't tell me where we were going, and his parents were coming along. And while the four of us had done things together over the last month, he'd never called it a date when we did that. I tried to get more information from Sarah, but she either didn't know or was really good at keeping a secret. Not that I was disappointed—as hard as I was trying to get some answers, I loved the anticipation of Myles having a surprise for me. The whole idea of him planning something, and the act of trying to guess and seeing him grin and shake his head every time I guessed wrong, was maybe better than any surprise could be.

I decided to wear the dress I'd worn for our piano open mic night—because Myles really, *really* loved that dress—and wore my matching lingerie underneath. Of course, I told him that while we waited for his parents outside the restaurant so I could see his eyes flash and grow dark, knowing he couldn't do anything about it.

"Tease," he hissed out, his mouth pulling in as he tried not to laugh.

I batted my eyelashes. "That's what you get for keeping whatever you have planned a secret."

"Well, maybe we'll skip that so I can take you to bed instead," he growled.

My heart skipped and I squeezed my legs together. "Tempting," I replied honestly on an exhale.

"You're killing me, sunshine," he laughed, placing a sensual kiss to my neck.

I was reconsidering his threat to take me to bed instead of my surprise. It was becoming more enticing by the second. Perhaps teasing him had been a bad idea. I turned to him, and we stared into each other's eyes for a moment, our breaths bathing each other's faces. I could taste my want for him and his for me. He lifted a hand and whispered his fingertips over my cheek.

"I'm so in love with you," he said, his voice quiet and serious.

My breath caught. "And I with you."

"That's the greatest thing in the world, being loved by you."

"Shit, Myles," I laughed softly, trying to keep the sudden tears in my eyes from spilling over. "Warn me before you say romantic stuff like that."

He snorted and smirked. "Hell no. Catching you off-guard is half the fun." His smirk fell and he kissed me, telling me another story, this one of intense love and desire.

"Alright, kids," Marv's voice cut in. "Let's go in."

I pulled back, biting my lip as I blushed, embarrassed.

"We'll be right behind you," Myles said, slipping a hand around the back of my neck and pulling me into him for another kiss, separating our mouths reluctantly when he was done several minutes later. I was thoroughly disoriented *and* turned on when he laced our fingers together and we headed inside to have dinner with his parents.

Teasing him had definitely backfired... in the best way.

After dinner, the four of us set out on foot, Marv almost as affectionate with Sarah as Myles was with me. I always loved seeing that and kept stealing glances at them, grinning. Myles squeezed my shoulder after another glance.

"Why do you keep looking at my parents?" he laughed.

I shrugged, feeling my face heat a bit. "They're cute. I want that to be *us* in thirty-five years."

Myles' grin split his face, and he bent over to place a hard kiss on my cheek, but he didn't say anything. He and his dad exchanged a look, and I narrowed my eyes.

"You know, it's uncanny how similar you two are sometimes," I said. "You both get the same mischievous look when you've got a secret, and you look so much alike, down to your beards." The biggest difference was that Myles' didn't have the amount of gray his father's had.

Marv rubbed a hand over his beard. "I didn't used to have facial hair, but then it grew on me." On the last word, he and Myles both burst out laughing. Sarah and I looked at each other and rolled our eyes, but we were both smiling, too.

"Hey, Nina," Marv said, his mouth pulled in already. "Did you know Myles used to be able to play the piano by ear?"

"He still can," I said at the same time Myles said, "I still can."

Marv snickered but held the rest of the laugh in. "No you can't— now you have to use your hands."

Again, Myles and Marv laughed, and I even let a few giggles escape. Sarah was laughing, but batted playfully at Marv.

"Wait, tell her the one you said when I was making pasta yesterday," she said.

Marv chuckled.

"I was making pasta," Sarah said to Myles and me, leaning her head forward so we could see her around Marv as we walked. "The pot had just begun boiling, and I was about to dump in the pasta, and Marv walked over all serious-like and looked down at the pot of water and let out a sigh. Then he said—tell them what you said."

Marv's mouth twitched, his eyes dancing. "Rest in peace, boiling water; you will be mist."

Sarah was laughing before he was finished and swatted at him again. By the time we reached our destination a few blocks later, my sides and cheeks ached from laughing as Myles and his dad exchanged terrible jokes. We walked into Bar Vivian, which I'd suspected might be where we were going once we were a block away, and headed for the only empty table there. It was also the best table in the bar because it had unobstructed views of the stage area. On it was a paper tent with "Reserved: Edwards" on it. I scrunched my eyebrows and gave Myles side-eye, but he just winked at me. He'd pulled some kind of strings because Bar Vivian didn't do reservations of any kind.

Like... *ever*.

Anticipation fluttered in my chest. What was he going to do? Whatever it was, I could tell he was getting nervous as we sat and ordered a round of drinks, his hand running over his hair from time to time, and an intensity invading his gaze which never left me. Seeing him like that only ramped up my impatience and eagerness to find out what he was planning. Myles didn't easily get nervous or self-conscious—at least not for much more than a second or two—so it had to be something significant.

I looked away, focused on the stage for the first time since we'd arrived, and my heart skipped. I glanced back toward Myles.

"Is that the Dovelyn Trio?" I practically shouted, bouncing in my seat.

He grinned. "It sure is."

"Oh my god," I exclaimed, clapping my hands together and shimmying.

Like Myles, I adored the Dovelyn Trio, not to mention that I'd discovered the band with him, and I had spent so many nights snuggled up with him, listening to their music, that I couldn't separate their songs from intense feelings of safety and love for Myles. I flung my arms around his neck, and he grasped my waist with his hands, kissing me back.

"This is awesome, Myles," I said when I pulled back, then gave him another peck on the lips. "I had no idea they were playing tonight. I can't believe we're going to hear them live! This is the best surprise ever."

I bounced again and Myles chuckled, squeezing my sides. When I turned my back to him to face the stage again, he slipped an arm all the way around my middle and pulled me back against him. Lifting my hair back out of the way, he kissed the curve of my neck.

"Love you," he said against my skin.

I tilted my head back, my eyes closing. I loved the feel of his lips and his facial hair on my neck that way. "Love you, too."

Before long, the Dovelyn Trio was playing, and I was lost in the music, sipping bourbon with Myles and his parents. They went through six or seven songs, then Myles leaned forward and kissed my cheek from behind, rising to his feet. I turned back to the stage, figuring he had to use the bathroom, but then he walked in front of our table.

Not just in front of our table, but up to the stage.

My head tipped to the side as I watched, trying to figure out what I was seeing. When I turned to look at Sarah, she just grinned and looked toward the stage. Turning back around, I saw Myles shaking hands with the band members and thought I might pass out. How was he getting to meet them? That was beyond cool; I hoped I would get to meet them, too.

And then—*holy shit*—Myles sat next to their pianist on the piano bench.

One of the band members spoke into a microphone. "We have a guest pianist tonight, Myles Edwards, as we play an original piece he composed." He handed the microphone to Myles.

Myles locked his bright, shining eyes with mine. He took in a breath that held a slight stutter. "Nina, my sunshine, I wrote this for you. It's our story—past, present, and future. I call it 'The End of Interludes.' I love you."

My face flushed furiously, and I practically bit through my lip as I grinned idiotically at him. I felt like a lovesick groupie and wanted to scream out that I loved him, too. Before I had time for what I was seeing to sink in, the band—plus my talented boyfriend—was playing. I recognized the opening bars immediately—it was the piece Myles had spent months composing. I'd only ever heard the beginning or bits and pieces since he'd finished it, and I was excited to hear how the piece came together as a whole.

It began cheerful and pleasant in a major key, though not particularly remarkable in any way I could discern, and carried on this way until rapidly escalating into a euphoria. It was playful and exciting and fast and loud and sounded like the audible equivalent of watching fireworks. It was spectacular, almost like each instrument was inciting the others to a near frenzy, but a beautiful one. Perfect, even, every note in flawless harmony. There was a crescendo, but before reaching the peak, it stopped, the violin sounding as if the violinist had never played before with a streak of discordant sound, followed by complete silence for several measures. Then, gradually, each instrument began to play again, the music this time in a minor key, but with an avalanche of jarring accidentals. The emotion the interlude evoked was in stark contrast to the elation of the first section; it felt depressing. My chest ached listening to it, and I teared up and felt the urge to sob. And just when I couldn't stand it anymore, it changed.

While slightly more pleasant, the change was still part of this interlude, for that's what this dark section must have been after the magnificence of the beginning. Now it mostly adhered to the key, but it was melancholic, like the third week in a row of a steady rain. It dragged on for so long, I began to wonder if this was in fact an interlude or if he'd just completely changed the mood of the piece. But then there was a spark and the same fireworks crescendo as at the beginning before falling into another melancholic interlude with a jarring few measures of accidentals. This interlude was shorter, followed by another fireworks crescendo that came so close to a finale that I was sitting up in my seat, hanging on the notes in the air, waiting for it. But, again, it was interrupted by abrupt accidentals and another dark interlude.

This interlude lasted longer than the previous one, but for less time than the first one. It was no less heart-wrenching, but I felt it was almost less melancholic as it progressed. Rather than an abrupt shift this time, the interlude transitioned slowly into an ecstatic blending of sound that made your heart pump with anticipation. This was finally going to be it... except it wasn't. Suddenly there were accidentals and melancholy and elation happening all at once, the differing instruments at war with one another, in grave argument, and an explosion was imminent.

It hit—a harsh dissonance followed by silence.

Slow and quiet, Myles began to play, the tentativeness becoming more sure with each measure until the other pianist joined in. One by one, the other instruments merged. This was again a combination of melancholy and elation and accidentals, but it was different. They were no longer at war with one another—it was more like an ebb and flow. It went on and on, the differing sounds and keys supporting one another as one would lead to be replaced by another. It didn't have the perfect and ecstatic quality of the beginning of the piece, but this was more. It was deeper and more emotional. I wanted to embrace the music that surrounded me, to hug it close. It felt more familiar, more comforting, and I swayed as I listened with my eyes closed, tears streaming down my cheeks, all the way through the last, lingering note.

The bar erupted into applause, and all four of the musicians on the stage wiped at their cheeks. Evidently, I was not the only one moved by the piece. Myles exchanged handshakes with the band members, who all patted him on the back as well, and headed toward me with a soft, determined smile. I stood and moved toward him, and we met just in front of the stage, wrapping our arms around each other. He hugged me tight, lifting me to my toes, then cradled my face with one hand and kissed the hell out of me.

"I love you, Myles," I said when we broke to catch our breaths.

"You love me enough to get married?" he asked.

"Is that your way of asking me to marry you?" I asked with a small giggle.

"Is that your way of saying yes?" he countered.

"Well, that depends on what you're asking." I bit my lip.

"I am indeed asking you to marry me, woman," he chuckled.

"Ah," I said, giggling. "Glad you clarified."

"So? If that's the question... were you saying yes?"

"In that case... I certainly was."

He pulled out a ring and slipped it onto my finger. It was simple—plain some would say—with a small single diamond nestled into the center of five delicate white gold petals to form a flower. It was both gorgeous and unassuming, fitting on my hand as if it had always been there.

It was perfect—exactly what I'd have chosen myself.

We kissed again for a long time before I remembered we were standing in front of everyone, putting on a show, and I pulled back, embarrassed. I'd completely forgotten.

"Forget about all those people," Myles said, holding my forehead to his. "They don't matter."

"It's a lot of people," I whispered. "And they're watching us."

"So, I guess a big wedding isn't something you'd be interested in?" he chuckled.

I shook my head. "Good god, no. As tiny as possible."

He pulled back just enough to look into my eyes, his thumbs smoothing over my cheeks. "Just my parents and a handful of friends kind of tiny?"

I nodded.

"Or elope to Vegas kind of tiny?"

My heart skipped. "You're serious?"

"Completely."

I sucked in a breath.

He kissed my cheek. "Be my wife, Nina, and take me as your husband."

"When?" I asked, butterflies in my chest.

"Right now, if that's what you want, too."

FORTY-ONE

We came close to flying to Vegas right then and there, but we didn't. Instead, we planned the smallest of ceremonies to take place where it all began: in Marksburg. A week later, we were walking hand-in-hand into a cabin near the trailhead to Kelm's Peak, the hike we'd done together not long before I was raped at knifepoint. The next day, we would have a tiny ceremony at one of the more local trails we used to visit often together when we were in college, with his parents and a college friend of his who was ordained to officiate weddings. Then, the day after that, we'd be flying to California for a week, leaving us two weeks at home as a married couple before I'd be leaving for grad school.

"You sure Handsome and the cats will be okay?" I asked, thinking about our pets. They were all being watched by a pet sitter until Myles' parents returned from the wedding, and then they would be staying with his parents while we were traveling, but I was anxious about leaving them alone.

Especially Handsome. I didn't want him to feel abandoned. And he was so attached to me... I was worried he'd grieve while I was gone. He'd come out of his shell so much in the few short weeks we'd had him, but only when I was with him. He was still really timid when I wasn't. And he was glued to my side when I was home, following me around the house, sleeping by my feet. Myles was actually excited he was so attached to me and would be going to grad school with me—he said Handsome would keep me safe in his absence. I didn't expect to need protection, but I agreed with Myles... Handsome would definitely protect me if the occasion arose. I'd feel much safer with him by my side.

"They'll all be fine," Myles soothed. It was only the thousandth time I'd asked him that since we'd left home earlier that day. "Handsome will be alright. He'll have Mom and Dad, and you know Mom loves him to death and that he likes her second only to you."

I sighed. "I know. I just worry about him. He's had such a hard life—I don't want to cause any stress for him."

He tugged my hand and kissed me. "I'm so, so in love with you, you know."

I laughed. "How did we go from worry about Handsome to being so in love with me?"

"Your concern over him is sweet, and that gigantic heart of yours is one of my favorite things about you."

I blushed, and we stepped inside the cabin. Myles closed the door behind us, setting our suitcases down as I meandered in, looking around at the adorable interior. I didn't make it far, though, before Myles had looped an arm around me from behind, pulled my hair to the side, and was kissing my neck. My breath rushed out and I closed my eyes, leaning my head to the side to give him easier access. It seemed everything made us want to be physically wrapped up in each other. It was already like that to some extent over the summer—it was amazing what discovering that sex could feel good and that partners could be respectful did to my libido—but it had gotten even more intense since he'd asked me to marry him.

He dotted tiny kisses from below my ear, along my jaw, down my neck, and along my shoulder as he pulled the neck of my shirt aside to expose my skin. I was just about to turn around and start undressing him when he let go with a growling chuckle.

"We don't have time for that, as much as I want to," he said, looking away from me. "I really want to make the summit while we're here."

I blushed and stepped up to him until our bodies were touching. He groaned and faced me, his look heating the skin all over my body.

"What if we were quick?" I asked, kissing his collarbone purposefully.

His chest rumbled with a laugh under my hands. "We don't do quick, sunshine." He groaned again. "But if you keep that up, we're going to end up here all afternoon instead of hiking."

"I maintain that we can do both," I replied against his skin as I inched his shirt up. "Unless you think you can't keep up?"

"Challenge accepted," he growled out.

His hand cupped my neck and pulled me to him for a hard, desire-filled kiss. Our clothes came off in a tornado of material flying through the air. The closest furniture was the table in the eat-in kitchen to our right, and as soon as we were naked, Myles had me on it. I wrapped my arms around his neck, my legs looped around his hips. Leaning forward on one hand, his other snaked up the center of my back to cushion my head from the table, and his face buried into the crook of my neck; his breath burst out violently as he moved with strong, hard strokes in and out of me.

The table wobbled and creaked, and it crossed my mind that we might break it.

My next thought was that I didn't care.

Myles' skin became sweaty under my hands, and mine under his. I dropped my head back, trying to catch my breath, and he kissed under my chin, sucking the skin into his mouth and running it between his teeth. As he did, there was a rhythmic tugging as the movement of his hips made my body shift back and forth. He was grunting in effort with each thrust.

"Oh, god," I moaned, feeling the orgasm building quickly. Next, my breath stopped, my entire body tightening like a drum. "Myles... *Myles*!"

He pushed harder, and just when I thought I might pass out from lack of oxygen, he stiffened, his arm crushing my body against his, and I sucked in a much-needed breath.

"Jesus Christ, Nina," he rushed out almost as a single word on a ragged exhale. "Fuck." He planted chaste kisses all over my neck and face, and I touched my lips to his, my tongue whispering along the seam. His mouth fell open and I felt him twitch inside me. He chuckled, then growled and crushed me to him again. "Goddamn, I love you so much."

I giggled, still a little out of breath. "Was that quick enough?"

His laugh began as a rumble in his chest. "That was definitely a record for us." He glanced toward the clock on the wall. "Five minutes, maybe?" He glanced down between us at my body. I was now sitting up slightly and leaning back on my hands, and he flattened a palm between my breasts, then began smoothing it over my skin.

I moaned faintly. "This—this is where we're gonna get into trouble with time," I murmured. "Because I could let you do this all day long."

"I could definitely explore your body all day long, my soon-to-be-wife."

"But we have a hike, remember, soon-to-be-husband?"

He leaned down and placed a kiss to my chest where his palm had been a moment ago. "Mm-hm." He pressed another kiss there, sighing, and gave me a lopsided smile as he straightened. He let out another sigh, and his features shifted, the look in his eyes intense, that same almost-but-not-quite angry look he always got before saying something that was going to affect me strongly. "If it were any other occasion than our wedding trip, I'd say fuck our plans and worship you until you forgot what it was like to exist when we're not making love."

I sucked in a breath.

His jaw tightened.

I swallowed.

"Stop looking at me like that, Nina," he growled with a laugh, running a hand over his hair. "I'm losing my resolve right now."

I giggled; I loved that I had that effect on him. "Alright Mr. No-self-control, I'll stop so we can go hiking."

He snorted. "I have plenty of self-control. Just not when you're sitting there naked and looking at me like all you want in the world is for me to lose that control."

I sat up and wrapped my arms around his neck, giving him a peck on the nose. "Fair enough. And so you know, at least half of me wants exactly that—for you to lose your control and say fuck our plans."

"Nina," he groaned.

I gave him another peck on his nose, then smirked. "We can go now."

He allowed me to hop down, then grabbed a towel from the kitchen for clean-up. "Why the hell do you get so much pleasure from teasing me?" he grumbled.

I waggled my eyebrows. "You're the one who told me I was sadistic."

He laughed.

"But honestly, it's just fun. And it makes it even more... intense when we do have sex. Besides, if it makes you feel better, teasing you tortures me as much as it does you."

He wrapped an arm around my waist. "That definitely helps." He kissed my cheek. "I love you."

I blushed for some reason. "I love you, too."

A couple of hours later, we reached the summit, together this time, and memories of the last time we'd stood there together rushed over me. When I glanced over at Myles, he had a faraway look in his eyes, and I knew the same was happening to him. He held me from behind as we studied the view, pulling my back against him and resting his chin on my shoulder as he sighed.

"You know," I said, thinking back to the day we'd done that hike before, "that was the most fun I'd ever had hiking when I brought you up here that first time."

"Same," he said. "But it wasn't just fun. I was in awe of you, Nina. We joked about you kicking my ass, but in all seriousness—that was so... I don't even know the word for it. Badass, maybe? I wanted more of that, to see you so strong and free and confident. You were in your element out here, and it was incredible to witness. Not only that, but... damn, you were so strong. You really did kick my ass, Nina—I was working *hard*, and you destroyed me on this hike. It... I wanted more of that. More of *you*."

I blushed.

"That ring you're wearing?"

I nodded, leaning my head back against his shoulder so I could see his face. He gave me a lingering kiss on the lips.

"I got that six weeks after I met you."

"You did?"

"Mm-hm. I took that first chunk of money I'd made trading and went looking for a ring a month after Parker's party. It took me a couple of weeks and almost twenty jewelry stores, but then I found that one, and as soon as I saw it, I knew that was the ring. I bought it, and as stupid as it was—I could have lost the damn thing—I kept it in my pocket all the time, waiting for the right moment. I knew I couldn't do it right away—I didn't want to scare you away when we hadn't known each other that long. Though I was positive that all the time in the world wouldn't change my mind about you. It was just one of those things—I knew it within moments of meeting you. Seconds, really. I told you on the way to Nina's that I was going to marry you one day. I was serious about that."

I laughed, remembering when he'd said that. He was a complete stranger, really, but he was going to be kind to turtles, wasn't scared off when I went off about people littering, and had made me laugh harder than I had in a long time. So instead of scaring me, it gave me a thrill. Within an hour of meeting him, it had felt like we'd known each other our whole lives. "I can't believe you've had it that long."

He nodded. "I have. And I almost proposed to you once. The moment was right and everything. It was right here, almost the exact spot we're standing in now. The words were about to come of out of my mouth when you leaned back and almost fell over the railing."

I rolled my eyes. "I didn't almost fall over the railing."

"Yes, you did, Nina—you didn't even realize it, but it was so close. It scared the living hell out of me. To that point in my life, I'd never been more scared of something." He sighed heavily, then gave a shudder as if he was trying to shake off that memory. "Anyway, the moment was gone after that. It might have returned, except we got company."

"Hm," I said, smiling. "Until those people showed up, I thought we were going to have sex and I was ready."

"Fuck, I wanted to," Myles laughed. "I'd been thinking about having sex with you for weeks. And there you were, all sweaty and topless, and staring at me with that same look you had back in the cabin."

"No shit I was staring at you—you didn't have a damn shirt on, and you were in *really* good shape, Myles."

"*Were?*"

I giggled. "Yeah. You're an old man now."

He stepped out from me leaning on him and pulled his shirt over his head, dropping it on the platform next to us.

I bit my lip and took in his sweaty torso. It was much like before, with that enticing trail of hair that disappeared under the waistband of his shorts. But now he was a bit broader. The edges of muscle were somewhat less defined, but I knew he was actually stronger than he'd ever been. His beard now had a few flecks of gray here and there, and there was a different kind of gravity in his eyes—the result of us going through so much and coming out on the other side together.

"You now is perfect."

He pulled me into his arms and held me tight against his chest, and I wrapped my arms snug around his waist. After a while, he kissed the top of my head.

"Love you, Nina."

"Love you, too, Myles."

He let out a sigh. "I can't believe this is the last day we won't be married. That tomorrow, you'll be my wife and I'll be your husband for the rest of our time on this planet."

"I'm nervous," I confessed. "I'm excited, but I'm also really nervous." I planted my chin on his chest and looked up at him as he looked down at me.

"Why are you, nervous, sunshine?"

"I'm scared of troubled times in the future. I've hurt you a lot because of how I've dealt with pain in my life, and I'm afraid of doing that again."

He kissed my forehead. "We are going to hurt each other again. More than once, most likely. We're going to fuck up and make mistakes. It's part of being human, Nina, part of being in a relationship with someone. You might as well accept that now. It will always happen. But it doesn't have to tear us apart. That's what the music I wrote was all about. We had this story that we started together, and then the unthinkable happened and it created this almost unsurpassable rift between us. When we found each other years later, we tried to go back to the way things were, but we couldn't, leading to this war between the two parts of our shared past: the before, and the after.

"But we've found another way, haven't we? We don't keep either part of the past at bay anymore—we let it all exist. You don't run from things anymore, Nina. You tell me about them instead. You let me hold you when you need to be held and listen when you need someone to listen. You work through things in therapy. We both get triggered from time to time, and we're there for each other when it happens; we don't get mad at each other for it. That pain, that shit from the past that we can never be rid of, we've made space for it in our lives, and we're creating something new and different and beautiful with all of it included. That was the last movement of the piece I wrote, the new way of being, a melding of the two befores as well as the now."

Again, he kissed my forehead, lingering a while before slowly lifting his lips from my skin. "What you're afraid of are the interludes in our story. And they'll always be there because they happened, but we won't go through any more of them. We've embarked on the final, blended movement of our lives together—we've already reached the end of interludes."

ACKNOWLEDGEMENTS

Somehow, I find myself once again facing a blinking cursor on a page to write the acknowledgements for a book I've finished. I honestly don't understand how I've been so lucky to have these beautiful characters tell me their stories so that I can write them down for you to read and perhaps, if I've done my job well, see some part of yourself in and find healing.

Thank you, my readers. I've written before about how writing isn't entirely a solitary endeavor, and it really isn't because there would be no writing without someone willing to turn the pages and read the words that have been written there. It still amazes me that you've chosen to do that with something that I've written and I will always be more grateful than you can know.

Kayli, my editor, my sounding board, my voice of reason, my friend. I absolutely, positively could not do this without you. Our paths were destined to cross so that you could help me make sure the stories I'm telling are received the way I intend them to be. I'm not sure anyone has ever gotten me and what I'm trying to accomplish with my writing the way you do. You keep me level and focused and make sure I don't get distracted by all the noise in the writing world that tries to change what I'm doing to be something less original. Your belief in me and what I'm doing, your ability to see my vision as clearly as I do, is invaluable. I say it all the time, but I want to say it again—you're the absolute freaking best.

Joe, you alone can understand just how much of you and me and us are in the stories I tell, and this one is no exception. We've had many interludes but have somehow always found our way back to the music our souls make together. I love you more and most.

As always, I feel incredibly lucky to have the production team I do who work with me to make sure my books look amazing once they reach a reader's hands. I hit the jackpot with them. Jo, as usual, you rock. And Murphy—you always, somehow I'll never understand, make these covers even more beautiful than I imagine they'll be. When I first saw this one, it brought tears to my eyes and gave me chills. It was *perfect*. I hope you never stop doing what you do.

Lastly, a thank you to The Brooklyn Duo for the inspiration behind the Dovelyn Trio; their beautiful covers of popular songs was the basis for my creation of the Dovelyn Trio, which only differed because of the addition of an oboe.

ABOUT THE AUTHOR

Katherine Turner is an award-winning author and a life-long reader and writer. She grew up in foster care from the age of eight and is passionate about improving the world through literature, empathy, and understanding. In addition to writing books, Katherine blogs about mental health, trauma, and the need for compassion on her website www.kturnerwrites.com. She lives in northern Virginia with her husband and two children.

PLAYLIST

My Immortal by Evanescence

My Heart Is Broken by Evanescence

Bring Me To Life by Evanescence

Woman by Emmit Fenn

Slow Dancing by Adam French

Sweet Sacrifice by Evanescence

Black Sea by Natasha Blume

My Addiction by Adam French

Hold Me Down by Mansionair

Haze by breathe.

Grace by breathe.

Are You All Good? by breathe.

Like You by Evanescence

Fantasy by Black Atlass

Us by Movement

Sound of Silence by The Brooklyn Duo

Shatter Me by Lindsey Stirling (featuring Lzzy Hale)

By Katherine Turner

Fiction

Believing in Never

The End of Interludes

Madly, Deeply, Wildly

<u>Life Imperfect Series</u>

Finding Annie

Willow Wishes

Wildflower Promise

Non-Fiction

resilient: a memoir

moments of extraordinary courage